Who hasn't thought Pride and Prejudice could use more dragons?

Praise for Maria Grace

"This lady does know how to tell a story and how to invent an incredible new world ." **From Pemberley to Milton**

"Maria Grace did a wonderful job spinning a tale that's enjoyable for Austen lovers who do and who don't typically delve into the fantasy genre because she does a great job balancing the dragon world she has created alongside Austen's characters." **Just Jane 1813**

"Grace has quickly become one of my favorite authors of Austen-inspired fiction. Her love of Austen's characters and the Regency era shine through in all of her novels." **Diary of an Eccentric**

"I believe that this is what Maria Grace does best, blend old and new together to create a story that has the framework of Austen and her characters, but contains enough new and exciting content to keep me turning the pages. ... Grace's style is not to be missed." **From the desk of Kimberly Denny-Ryder**

Kellynch: Dragon Persuasion

Maria Grace

White Soup Press

Published by: White Soup Press

Kellynch: Dragon Persuasion
Copyright © 2020 Maria Grace

For information, address
author.MariaGrace@gmail.com

ISBN-13: **978-0-9997984-3-0** (White Soup Press)

Author's Website: RandomBitsofFaascination.com
Email address: Author.MariaGrace@gmail.com

Dedication

For my husband and sons.
You have always believed in me.

1
Chapter

Early June 1814

ANNE GLANCED RIGHT and left down the long hall-
way tiled in black and white marble squares, the
portraits of long forgotten ancestors staring down—
disapproving, for they disapproved of everything—
upon her. Yes! No sign of Father or Elizabeth, only
Mrs. Trent, the sturdy, grizzled housekeeper, trun-
dling the recently delivered post toward the parlor.
Anne hurried to intercept, glancing first at the letters
in Mrs. Trent's hands, then cocking her head. Best
not make a sound lest she be discovered. Father and
Elizabeth were always the most demanding when she
had other plans.

Mrs. Trent nodded and handed her several thick
missives from the bottom of the stack. Excellent!

One, sealed with blue wax—and it was the one she was waiting for! She clasped the letters to her chest and hurried outside in the opposite direction of the parlor. Though Father and Elizabeth rarely cared for any news that might come by way of Anne, still it would be better to read her mail alone, especially when the thickest message bore the Blue Order's seal.

The pale green muslin skirts of her day dress swished against her ankles as she darted out of the kitchen door. Yes, it was a bad habit, using the staff's doorways, and it left her smelling like the kitchen. But was it really so bad to smell a bit like baking bread whilst obtaining her freedom? Cook did not even raise an eyebrow at her comings and goings anymore.

Light, bright, and sunny, everything a summer's day should be! A soft, warm breeze kissed her face with the fragrance of peonies and roses—so thick and lovely she could almost taste them weaving together in the sunshine. Her favorite bench in the garden called her, the filigreed iron one, painted white and placed in the middle of the flowerbeds so that Mama could comfortably watch the antics of the local fairy dragon harem. The tiny dragons frequented the lavishly blooming flower beds, especially on days like this when the sun was warm and brilliant and the wind was calm, allowing the garden air to fill with sweet perfume. Mother had liked this place for excellent reasons.

Anne sat down and set aside the first letter. Given the handwriting on the direction, it was no doubt a demand for payment by the wine merchant. That should have gone to Elizabeth or Father since Anne had no authorization to make such payments. Perhaps Mrs. Trent thought Anne might actually manage to see a remittance was made. She was after all quite the optimist.

Good thing she bore disappointment graciously. Anne cracked the flour and water seal on her other letter lest she forget about it in the almost certain flurry the Blue Order's news would bring.

"What are you doing?" A bright pink fairy dragon, Peony, circled, her wings buzzing low over Anne's head.

"I am reading my letters." She shaded her eyes and peered into the sky. "Where are your friends today? You are not usually alone."

"The others are mad at me. Wren-Catcher caught me in a mating flight yesterday." Peony, the lead female of the harem, warbled a self-satisfied little sound.

Anne blushed—dragons lacked discretion, but it was their way, at least according to Lady Russell, and they ought not be rebuked for it.

Peony landed on the back of the bench and peered at the letters, her head cocked so far it nearly turned upside down. Silly little creature. "Why do you sit there staring at those papers? They do not look good to eat."

"No, one does not eat letters. They bear news of distant friends and acquaintances."

"What sort of news? What a strange way to carry news. That is what fairy dragons do, you know."

"You are the post of the dragon world?" Anne chuckled. This was not the first time they had this conversation, but the shatter-brained little flitter-bit never seemed to remember it.

"If that means we spread important news, yes, that is what we do. Why else would even the grumpiest of major dragons tolerate us in their territory? We have our value as more than a snack you may be certain." Peony looked so proud. She puffed her chest and raised her beaky snout. It would not do to tell her just how reliable fairy dragon carried news was generally considered. "What news have you? I can share it if you like."

"I will need to read it first before I can know. Can you wait that long?" Anne scratched under Peony's chin.

"Be quick about it." She stretched and turned her head to direct Anne's ministrations behind her left ear.

Continuing her scratching, Anne scanned Mrs. Smith's letter. "Well, that was interesting. Who would have expected news of interest to Father in this letter?"

"Do tell, do tell!" Peony hopped and cheeped.

"This one is from a friend. It contains some sad news."

"Sad?" Peony fluttered in a downward spiral until she landed on sandy ground in front of the bench and looked up at Anne. "What is sad to a warm-blood?"

The addlepated little creature probably just wanted to mock her. Fairy dragons could be like that, but it was difficult to resist answering a direct question. "Death and loss are sad. My friend tells me she still feels the consequence of her husband's—mate's— death at harvest time last year. According to her, our cousin, who did business with her husband, lost his mate at the end of winter. And it seems his business is not doing well either. Those are sad things."

"Why do you bother with letters when they only bring you sad things?" Peony cocked her head this way and that as though thinking made her head hurt.

"It is not all sadness. She finds herself in Bath, in a comfortable establishment, with good company. Those are all good things. As is this." Anne held up a thick, as yet unopened missive, her heart beating a little faster. "This is a letter, a very long one, from the Dragon Sage herself, telling me more about you and your kind. I count that as very good news indeed."

Peony flipped her wings. "Why do you need a letter when you can ask us directly? Warm-bloods!" Snorting, she launched herself into the sky and flittered away.

Shatter-brained, definitely shatter-brained.

Anne stood and hugged the letter to her chest.

The Dragon Sage, Lady Elizabeth Darcy, had actually written back to her! No, it should not have been surprising. As Anne understood, it was the Dragon Sage's role to answer such missives as hers. But having only been to the Blue Order once—to be presented and accepted by them shortly after she began to hear dragons—it seemed more likely that they would forget her than try to assist.

At first, they had answered her letters promptly and with some attention to detail. But over time, the letters grew shorter and less addressed toward her questions, taking longer and longer to arrive, until they finally stopped. Lady Russell thought it proof the Blue Order was just a matter of pomp and circumstance, not a serious force to be reckoned with. But a few comments in the last letters Father had received from them—*pro forma* reports that went out regularly to all Dragon Keepers—seemed to suggest there were some serious matters afoot, matters more urgent than the needs of a slumbering dragon. So, perhaps the neglect was not a personal affront, but an oversight from an overworked, overwrought office.

It was still possible that the letter contained a reproach for daring to address the Dragon Sage directly and without invitation, but it was unlikely a missive of that length was required for a simple rebuke.

Lady Russell would want to see the Sage's letter for herself. She had insisted a reply would never come. Best get to Kellynch Cottage before some other "urgent" matter arose.

Anne hurried down the shady, hardwood-lined footpath to the flower garden behind Kellynch Cottage. Lady Russell often enjoyed the afternoon sunshine in the midst of the fragrant, exotic blossoms she raised there. "Lady Russell? Lady Russell?"

The regal—yes that was the word for her when she stood in repose amidst her prize possessions— cockatrix posed under a white wooden arbor lined with white and pink climbing roses in full bloom, standing on one leg—her thinking posture—with her head tucked up under her wing. She could—and should be mistaken for a large blue garden statue by those who did not hear dragons. If seen by those who could hear … oh the secrets that had to be kept.

Anne pressed a hand to her ribs. Best not think about that now. One crisis at a time.

"Anne?" Lady Russell pulled her head from under her wing. Her plumed crest of variegated blue, yellow and green feathers sprung up to its full glory. The feathers resembled peacock feathers, without the distinct "eyes." How many ladies would envy such a headdress to accompany their evening wear?

More to point, how many ladies did, unaware that they were being convinced those feathers were part of a turban worn by a fine lady, not perched on the head of a dragon. Anne pressed her eyes with thumb and forefinger. Even after five years, this was all still very strange.

"I have a letter from the Dragon Sage." Anne waved the still sealed missive in Lady Russell's view.

She snorted and shook her head, head feathers flopping to and fro. "I am sure it is merely to rebuke you for your cheek. I do not see why you bother with that slip of a girl."

"As I understand, she is just a few years younger than myself, hardly a slip of a girl." Or so Father was wont to remind her. "Besides, you were the one who mentioned that it was approaching fifty years that Kellynch had been sleeping, and he should awaken very soon."

"I have known Kellynch longer than she has been alive. I do not see why you needed to consult her, or anyone else on the matter." Lady Russell stepped high and long through the rose beds to stand on the path beside Anne, bringing the sweet scent of roses with her.

"Have you ever dealt with a dragon awakening from hibernation?"

"No, but neither has she. I am certain of it. Besides, I am a dragon. That should count for a very great deal." Lady Russell stomped her long-toed, clawed feet, kicking up dust.

"I am sure it does. But have you not told me that you are as different to Kellynch as I am to a horse?" Anne folded her arms across her chest, tucking the letter under her left arm.

Lady Russell snorted.

"What is more, you have said that your kind do

not hibernate. So how would you know anything about hibernation?"

"But I am a dragon." Lady Russell bobbed her head back and forth, up and down, as though that proved her point.

"One with no experience of hibernating nor being awakened from such a state."

"What can an inexperienced girl contribute to this situation that I cannot? Truly, I should be offended by your lack of faith in me. Have I not been your teacher, your mentor in all dragon matters since the day you first heard dragons?" Lady Russell ruffled her full, fluffy wings, throwing up enough breeze to set the flowers around her to rustling.

"Indeed, you have, and for that I am very grateful. I know you have taught me from your wealth of knowledge everything you thought I ought to know." Anne smiled sweetly and bit her tongue. Best not mention that much of Lady Russell's wisdom frequently contradicted the official lore of the Blue Order, and there was a very great deal that Lady Russell failed to mention at all.

"Since you seem so determined, do read to me what this Sage has to say. But do not be surprised when I tell you how wrong she is." Perhaps Anne should have read the letter in private first and only shared carefully considered parts with Lady Russell. Ah well, too late for such ideas now.

Lady Russell picked her way through the flowerbeds, toward a low, wooden garden bench on the border of the sunshine and shade, her high steps exaggerated by her extremely long legs. She perched on the left side of the bench, sitting like a hen on her nest. Anne held her breath and pressed her lips hard.

Lady Russell did not like being laughed at or told she resembled a character from a panto.

Anne wove her way down the path, sat beside Lady Russell and cracked the seal on the letter.

Dear Miss Elliot,

Let me begin my telling you how glad I was to receive your letter. It truly is my pleasure to assist wherever I can in smoothing relations between Dragon Mates. I have tried to answer as many of your questions as possible, but I am certain the answers will leave you with even more questions. Pray do not hesitate to ask them in your next letter, which I expect, dare I say insist, you will write to me very soon. I look forward to enjoying an active conversation with you. I hope you do not think me too forward to say I am fascinated by the circumstances of Kellynch and consider it my privilege to be invited to assist in these matters.

Gracious! That sounded nothing like the correspondence Anne had previously received from the Order. The Sage almost sounded like a friend!

"So, what does it say?" Lady Russell snorted, ruffling the paper just a bit.

"Lady Elizabeth begins with the usual greetings and salutations; nothing you would wish to hear."

Lady Russell rolled her dark glittering eyes and fluffed her wings. Such a temper she was in!

Anne pointed to several lines near the top of the page. "Here, she addresses the matter directly. She says no Keeper alive in England today has ever assisted with a dragon awakening."

"You see, I told you, she knows nothing." Lady Russell pecked at the paper.

Anne jerked it away just in time to keep it from being torn by Lady Russell's sharp beak. "She says she would come herself to assist us, but—and she does not say it directly, but I infer—that she is in a delicate condition and not able to make such a journey."

"That is a very good thing indeed. I have no desire to have such a person poking her nose into our affairs where it does not belong."

"I understand the need for secrecy and discretion here, but truly, she is the Dragon Sage. How could her visit be of any difficulty to us?"

Lady Russell hissed—she actually hissed!—and whipped her head around to glower directly into Anne's eyes. "What does it matter? You said yourself she is not able to travel, so it is a moot point. Has she anything useful to say?"

Anne edged back, eyes watering from Lady Russell's potent breath. Perhaps she should recommend some mint leaves to chew. "This is encouraging, she says she has searched the annals of dragon lore and found several accounts of slumbering dragons awakening."

"She has, has she? I am so pleased for her."

"You need not sit here and listen." Anne stood and sighed. "You asked me to read it to you, but if it upsets you, then I shall take my letter and return home to read it far more conveniently."

Lady Russell blocked Anne's way. "No, no, I would rather know what sort of advice you are getting and trying to follow. Better that I stop you from doing something foolish before you begin."

Anne clutched her forehead and turned her back. "Such faith you have in me!"

"Anne, my dear. You know I have only the best in mind for you. You must know that. How can you expect me to trust a girl I have never even met to give you good advice?" Lady Russell leaned over Anne's shoulder.

"I suppose the faith the Blue Order places in her might be some indication."

"Enough of your cheek. Just read the letter."

Anne returned to the bench and spread the letter over her lap. "Very well. She says that while there are differences by species, there are some commonalities among them. She says they awaken slowly, by stages and may not be fully awake for several days or even a se'nnight or more."

Lady Russell huffed and sneered—a difficult expression to achieve with a beak. "I am certain she is quite wrong about that. Perhaps Kellynch is of a species this Sage knows little about."

"She also says that dragons wake up cranky—very cranky—and one should be very careful not to provoke a cranky dragon as they might be apt to act without thinking."

Lady Russell muttered under her breath, but it sounded like, "Well at least that is sensible."

"…and hungry. Dragons awaken very hungry. She likens it to hatching hunger—which, by the way, you have never mentioned to me."

"New babies are hungry—what is there special in that?"

"Perhaps the amount such a baby might eat. In any case, the letter says that for a waking dragon like Kellynch, we must be prepared with a daily sheep, perhaps even two, for at least a fortnight."

"I am certain that is utterly excessive. Even so, what problem is that? There is plenty of mutton afoot."

Anne looked into the sky and huffed. "I think the shepherds might find it a bit unusual to find so many sheep going missing at once. At the very least it is something I can prepare for."

Lady Russell pawed at the loamy ground. "Anyone with common sense might have come to the same conclusion. You did not need a sage to tell you that."

"Had I known about hatching hunger, perhaps," Anne muttered under her breath.

The Sage went on to say the hunger would depend on how the dragon had prepared for it before hibernation, something Lady Russell had never mentioned. Probably not the best time to mention it. "This, this is interesting." Anne held the letter a little closer to her face. "She says that once the hunger for food is sated, if the dragon is a hoarding type then the hoarding hunger must be dealt with. You have never spoken to me about hoarding."

"What is there to say? Some dragons like to collect things. Those who do, like it a very great deal."

"Is Kellynch such a dragon?"

"I … I … how would I know?" Lady Russell flapped and stepped back.

"She says I should consult the Blue Order Charter to determine if he is a hoarder and what the provisions of the hoard might be. But I have been searching for it since Mr. Elliot asked about it years ago. I have been able to turn up nothing of the charter, so we have little remedy there. You are his Watcher—why do you not know such a thing about Kellynch?"

"You are impertinent today!" Lady Russell snapped her beak hard.

Anne jumped back. "And you have not taught me all I need to know! Why is it so much of what you have taught me disagrees with the writings of the Blue

Order?"

"Because I am a dragon, and I know better! What could they possibly know?"

"A very great deal of very important things it would seem." Anne bit her tongue hard. Reminding Lady Russell that a great number of the Blue Order members were dragons would only make her lose her temper.

Lady Russell glowered at the letter, her expression shifting as she stared into Anne's eyes.

This was not the first time she had tried to intimidate Anne into silence, but today it would not work.

Finally, she squawked and flapped, pecking at the letter. Anne yanked it away.

"Impertinent, headstrong girl. How dare that ridiculous sage meddle in what she does not understand." Lady Russell took several steps back, a shudder working down from her crest to her tail. "What does she know? Do not bother yourself with that … that woman. Concern yourself with dealing with the matters at hand. That is what is important right now."

"As you say." Anne folded the letter and stood. Lady Russell reached for the letter with her beak, but Anne pulled it away. "No, I will keep it. There are some details about the care Kellynch might require when he awakes that I will need to refer to." Not to mention there were many pages she had not yet read.

Lady Russell grumbled under her breath—a sound very like a growl, but she relented and stalked away.

Very odd behavior for her, but Lady Russell did tend to be temperamental.

2
Chapter

Late June 1814

A FORTNIGHT LATER, Anne pushed back from the
Dragon Sage's letter and the open books littering her
oversized oak writing desk and stood, her wrinkled
muslin skirt swishing across her stiff knees. How had
it got so late? The sunlight barely reached her room
now, leaving the soft green walls dark even though
midday approached, drawing the sun to the other side
of the house.

No, it was not ladylike to stretch and groan, but
what else might be expected after so many hours
hunched over books and letters that her entire world
smelt like books? Besides, if there was no one to
watch, was it really unladylike? Surely all ladies
stretched—might it not be that the impropriety of it

came with being observed in the act?

She pressed her pounding temples hard. Why was she even considering such an irrelevant line of thought right now? There were far more significant considerations to dwell upon.

Dealing with a dragon awakening was far more complex and delicate than Lady Russell had led her to believe. She straightened and restraightened the floral curtains that had hung over her shoulder as she studied.

The Dragon Sage had been very thorough in her research, noting every case of hibernations in the last two hundred years—what an enviable library of records she must have access to! The trouble was that there were not many awakenings, and most of those did not proceed well—not to mention they only had written records to go by, no living eyewitness—human or dragon—to the events remained. In two cases, Keepers had been seriously injured by confused waking dragons. In one, the Keeper had been killed and eaten—though to be fair, that was the oldest recorded case, and little was understood about managing a waking dragon, so perhaps that would not be the best event to cite as typical. She laced her fingers behind her neck and pulled her shoulders back.

But then again, Anne knew little about dragons. Her father knew little about dragons. Though Lady Russell was a dragon, it did not follow that she would know very much about Kellynch's specific kind of dragon—whatever kind that was; another useful piece of information that was supposed to be listed in the missing charter, and unknown to Lady Russell. Even the Sage had been unable to turn up Kellynch's charter in the Blue Order records—she had not given up though, but there was no immediate remedy even there.

In the meantime, the Sage's most recent letter, which had arrived only yesterday, suggested that Anne consult the local minor dragons. It was just possible that there might be one in residence who had been witness to Kellynch's last brief awakening—for he had probably awakened fifty years ago, but it seemed that he was still dissatisfied with the Elliots then and immediately returned to hibernation—who might be cajoled into helping her. The Sage included a list of foodstuffs which might be useful in said cajoling.

Of course! What a very good, even obvious idea. One she should have come up with herself. Or Lady Russell. Or even Father. Why did both of them seem so very determined not to know anything more than they already did?

Why did they prefer ignorance—in so many things? Father cared neither to know about the dragon he was supposed to keep, nor about the finances of the estate he held. Somehow, he simply assumed he could go about and do as he liked and things would all work out around him. Neither tenants, nor tradesmen nor servants would ever be a bother to him. All he had to do was act the part of a baronet, be seen doing so, and all would be well in the world. She flexed her hands in and out of fists.

At least she could identify dragon hearers now, even when they were not wearing the Order's signet. Apparently, the knack was a bit unusual, and many found it uncanny. But Lady Russell said Mama could do the same thing; that had been an important part of their friendship. She hoped that Anne might continue to render that invaluable service to her friend, helping her to stay hidden from prying eyes. Avoiding hiring dragon hearing staff was imperative.

Anne threw her hands into the air and wandered to her oak framed cheval mirror. Her dress was rumpled and hair tousled from running her fingers through it. Her appearance was as bedraggled as she felt. If she did not tidy up before leaving her room, an unpleasant lecture from Father or Elizabeth would be certain. She pulled the pins from her hair and reached for her hairbrush.

Lady Russell's secret did explain some of her reticence. Perhaps Anne needed to find a way to help her present herself to the Blue Order so she would not constantly be so nervous and guarded around company with whom she was unfamiliar. But until Anne herself was better informed, she would have little sway with Lady Russell.

One more reason why it was so important to manage Kellynch's awakening properly. If that went well, that should give her better standing with Lady Russell and the Order. And if it did not—well it was possible that she would not be around to worry about the aftermath. She shook away a tremor in her hands and braided her hair. She would prove herself a competent Dragon Keeper—somehow.

Best begin with the matter of feeding him. It only stood to reason that one would be hungry after sleeping for many years. If she was hungry in the morning after awakening, how much more would a dragon want to break his fast? But how to manage so many sheep from the flocks? Wait, Shelby, the lead sheep dog, was a dragon!

Why had she not thought sooner to enlist his help? It should have been so obvious. Lady Elizabeth's last letter had all but said that—why had she not said it directly? Perhaps because she was polite and thought-ful and wanted to permit Anne the dignity of puzzling something out on her own.

When she behaved like that, after only a very few letters, it was difficult not to think of Lady Elizabeth as a friend. Perhaps it was too forward, but for now, it was comforting.

Anne smoothed her dress and slipped on her bonnet. A visit to Shelby was definitely in order.

The afternoon sun proved a bit warmer than she would have preferred, but that was usually favorable for sighting the small dragons that populated the es-tate. Beyond the harem of fairy dragons, and Jet, the big black cockatrice who made the occasional, cranky, snappy appearance, there were not many of them. But the few that there were had become familiar and even amiable toward her—except for Jet of course, he was uniformly cross and crass toward everyone, human and dragon—and still resentful of her restrictions, limiting him in what and whom he could eat.

Like the rest of the estate, the other little dragons came to her when they had need of anything—sometimes even if it was simply a scratch behind the ears. The little puck Beebalm very much liked a good scratch behind her frill. Once one became accus-tomed to her fangs, Beebalm was quite an attractive creature, even cute. Anne chuckled under her breath—Father would never consider a dragon cute.

The pasture's green carpet spread out before her, fragrant with fresh green smells and a soft breeze, dotted with sheep and lambs. She whistled sharply—another unladylike behavior, or so Elizabeth had scolded, though dragons did not appear to concern themselves with such things. Whistling was, all told, the best way to get Shelby's attention—far more effective than shouting his name.

A growly sort of bark in the distance assured her that Shelby had heard and would be on his way as soon as he was able. He was, after all, working, and she should not expect him to ignore his responsibilities.

A few minutes later, the minor drake trotted toward her, his brown and white splotched hide dusty from the pasture, bits of grass sticking to his short pointed ears and long thick tail. His long claws threw up little clods of soil as he walked. He claimed they allowed him to run very fast and turn sharply when he was chasing down the sheep. They also made him a little dangerous looking.

"Good day to you, Miss." Shelby's voice was thick and rough rather like the local shepherds'. He stopped in front of her and bent his front knees in a dragonish bow.

"Good day to you, Shelby." She crouched near him and extended her hand.

He stretched his neck and presented his ears to her for a vigorous scratch. His tail thumped just like a dog's, but he rumbled deep in his throat in an almost cat-like purr.

"Pray, may I ask your assistance? It is for Kellynch."

He sat on his haunches, his brow furrowing. "I suppose. You know he will be awakenin' soon."

"I have been concerned that might be the case. I

have wondered if you were here the last time he awakened."

"I were just a drakling then, but yes, I was here. Remember it quite clear, too. Not the sort of thing that happens to one every day, you know."

"It is a sight few have seen, and I am told no Dragon Keeper alive today has experienced such a thing. Pray, will you tell what you know of his awakening? Anything you could tell me would be most appreciated."

He bumped his head under her hand—his ears were in need of more scratching. "The signs of a waking dragon are quite clear, if you know what to attend to. He will become restless, turning this way and that in his caverns. You can feel the rumblings in your feet if you pay attention."

The Sage had not mentioned such a sign.

"You probably cannot feel it in that house of yours. His scent will also change. When he sleeps, he smells woolly, like the sheep. But when he awakes, his musk grows stronger, and a bit sharp, like piss. As he gets closer to waking, he will snore loud, like distant thunder."

"Have you seen any of these signs? As I understand it has been close to fifty years since he last awoke, and he should be close to rising."

"I had expected to see and hear more by now, but not so much. It is surprising. Perhaps he has decided to sleep longer, perhaps concerned that his territory is still run by Elliots. I think he has been put out with your family for quite some time." Shelby shrugged and scratched behind his ear. "Still though, I would have expected at least a wee awakening, like when one rolls over at night and goes back to sleep. 'Cept I would think he would take some time to eat a mite and survey his territory."

Anne bit her lip. "The Sage said nothing about hibernating dragons having brief wakings."

"Perhaps it is because he is a wyrm, and wyrms do not normally hibernate. That is usually the province of drakes, ones bigger than myself I mean." Shelby chewed at his back claws, freeing some gravel from between his toes. "You are planning to be there when he awakes, are you not? I imagine he will want to meet you. No Keeper attended his last awakening, not your father, not the older Mr. Sir Elliot. It was not a pretty thing."

"What happened?"

"The usual thing one expects. Large dragons are very cranky beasts, and when they are hungry, they are very cross. He was angry to find his Keeper and heir absent and to be attended only by myself. It fell on me and Uppercross—"

"Uppercross knows him?"

"Of course, he does—they are neighbors, why would he not?"

Anne rubbed her hand over her lips. "I thought large dragons were not amiable with one another—is not that why the Blue Order assigns them particular territories?"

"I suppose that can be true, it might even be the usual way of things. But that does not mean that they all do not get along. Kellynch and Uppercross have been friends a great long time."

"I am all astonishment."

Shelby's tail slapped the ground hard, probably annoyed with her ignorance. "You have not met Uppercross, have you?"

"No, not yet. I fear young Mr. Musgrove was a mite put out with me when he married my sister. Neither of them has offered an introduction, and I did not pursue one."

"You should. You know, the Keepers aren't the only ones who can make you an introduction, don't you? Lady Russell can introduce you."

Well, that would have been helpful to know. It would also have been helpful for her to make the offer on her own.

"Once you have met him you will understand. It is hard to imagine that anyone, man or dragon, that would not get along with him. He is just like the Uppercross family—entirely friendly and agreeable."

"I have never read an account of an agreeable major dragon." Quite the opposite in fact.

"He is a wyvern—of all the big ones, they are the most apt to be agreeable."

"I am glad to know that. So, Uppercross was able to help you with Kellynch's awakening?"

"Indeed, he did. He was able to talk sense into that cross creature and keep him from wreaking havoc on the estate. Truly Miss, an angry dragon, large or small, is something to be avoided." Shelby shuddered, scales rippling from his ears to his tail.

"Indeed. I will seek out Uppercross' advice. Would you be able to help me arrange provisions for Kellynch's waking hunger?"

"I have already been working toward that. There is a small flock set aside for that very purpose. Been persuading the shepherd for a year that he did not have as many sheep as he thought."

"That would explain the discrepancy I found in the books."

"That is part of the reason a Keeper of some form or fashion, even a junior one like yourself, needs to be involved as well, to keep the dragon-deaf unawares, you know." Shelby cocked his head and wagged his tail, just on the edge of impertinence. "You will also want oil for his hide. All that time in the cavern will have left him dry and flaky and very itchy. You might want to procure some good stiff brooms to help with the itch."

The Sage had included a recipe for hide oil in her letter. She would have to prepare that herself. Since none of the staff heard dragons, and there were no household dragons to help with a persuasion, too many questions would arise from having a maid do the task.

"Oh, and one more thing. His hoard—he will be very anxious for his hoard. You need to make certain all is in order with that."

Anne's stomach lurched and her face grew cold. "Hoard? Kellynch is a hoarder?"

"Oh yes, he is most protective of his hoard and insistent that his charter is fulfilled exactly."

"How am I to do that? The charter has been missing for as long as I have known of its existence. I do not even know what he hoards." How could Father mislay something so very important? Not to mention, think nothing of it.

Shelby's forehead furrowed and his head drooped a bit. "That is a problem indeed. Kellynch never let on what his hoard might be nor where it was. Hoarders can be so protective and secretive of all things concerning their hoards. Always demanded that the yearly rations be delivered under cover of dark and the like. The Keeper is supposed to know all that and ensure all is kept safe while the dragon is indisposed. Perhaps Lady Russell might be able to help?"

"I have asked, and she is not aware of anything related to his hoard either." Anne bit her knuckle. Certainly, Father had not been spending money on anything as unconnected to him as a dragon hoard.

"That is a problem then. I am surprised his Watcher would know nothing of it." He wrinkled up his snout and squeezed his eyes half-shut as though thinking hard. "Perhaps Uppercross will know something. I do not think he hoards, but perhaps they might have talked about it?" He pushed his head toward her and leaned against her. Was he trying to comfort her? How dear.

"That is a very good suggestion. I will seek him out as soon as I can."

Sheep bleated in the distance. Shelby made a noise like a "woof". "Must be off, excuse me." He trotted off, his tongue hanging out. Was that a normal dragon behavior or did he do that to help him to affect his illusion as a dog?

Hopefully getting an audience with Uppercross would not be too difficult. At least there was someone who could, hopefully, make her a proper introduction.

Why had Lady Russell not already done so? Anne rubbed her cheeks hard. Probably because then she would have someone else to turn to for dragon advice, someone connected directly to the Blue Order, someone who might disagree with Lady Russell's advice—something Lady Russell did not tolerate well.

Perhaps if Lady Russell would not make the introduction, Anne could find her way to Uppercross House and simply introduce herself. If Uppercross was as agreeable as Shelby said, perhaps he would not be affronted.

An hour later, Anne joined Elizabeth in the parlor. Late day sunlight poured through the windows, leaving the pale-yellow room warm and welcoming, even though Elizabeth only acknowledged her with a raised eyebrow and returned to her ladies' magazine. Anne nodded to her and sat at the dainty, oak and iron scrollwork writing desk behind Lady Russell's favorite overstuffed rust-colored chair near the window overlooking Mother's blooming gardens.

"Who are you writing to, Anne?" Elizabeth asked without looking up from her magazine.

"Mary." Not that it really was any of Elizabeth's business, but it was easier to answer her than it was to argue the matter.

"Better you than me. She never has anything interesting to say. She keeps no company of any worth, nor does the Great House at Uppercross."

Anne shrugged. Elizabeth could not be convinced that individuals of small fortune, with no titles or names of note might be worth the acquaintance. She centered a piece of foolscap on the desk and dipped her pen in the ink.

What had Mary said in her last letter, written in handwriting small, tight, and whiny? Ah yes, that she was so very unwell, and none understood nor cared that it was the case. No one attended her—she had run out of her favorite tea—and visits from the great house were few and when they happened, they were very, very short.

"I do not see why you are writing to her. Mary is always sick, complaining, and cross." Elizabeth looked up briefly and rolled her eyes.

"Do be kind. You know how the children tire her."

"That is what governesses are for. She should just send them off to school and be done with it."

"They are too young. I am sure they will go off with Charles' younger brothers soon."

"Not soon enough if you ask me."

"I always make her feel better when I visit. Perhaps I should." Neither Father nor Elizabeth need know who else she intended to visit whilst there.

"Do what you will. I am sure father will not object. He hardly notices whether you are about or not."

"I am glad you agree." Anne returned to her writing and hid her sigh in a polite cough.

3
Chapter

Late June 1814

TWILIGHT.

The last vestiges of sunlight hung low over the ends of the earth as mild salty air kissed his cheeks. Educated people laughed at the thought the world was flat. But here, in the middle of the open sea, bobbing with the restless waves, and no shore in sight, it looked, it felt, otherwise. There on the western horizon, the sun dipped down to hide its light—maybe to rise again the next day. But then again maybe not. Just because it did so every day before was no guarantee it would do so ever again.

The future was as unfathomable as what might lie beyond the line that divided heaven from earth.

"Mrrrow." A large, black furry head rubbed against

Wentworth's leg.

How did Laconia always know when his thoughts had turned maudlin? The tatzelwurm spring-hopped to the railing, lashing his tail tight around it. Only one other on the ship knew the secret of Laconia's legendary balance as he tiptoed on the ship's rails and rigging surefooted as a mountain goat. The rest simply considered him quite the luckiest ship's cat in the history of the navy.

Since the ship's namesake arrived, their prizes had grown larger and more frequent and their casualty rate diminished. Laconia was to thank on both counts. Small sea dragons proved only too willing to reveal the location of valuable prizes to Laconia for the promise that Laconia's sailors would leave them and their hunting grounds in peace. Only a very little bit of persuasion was necessary to convince superstitious sailors to mind their ship's cat's signals. All told it was almost too easy.

He scratched behind Laconia's tufted ears. What a marvelous sound, that rumbling purr. It did something to one's soul. Almost as healing as that steel-rasp tongue of his. According to the ship's physician, tatzelwurm tongues had special healing properties. Wounds they licked were apt to heal quickly and cleanly. Wentworth's shoulders twitched as he kneaded the scar on his forearm.

That cut could easily have gone septic; the tatzelwurm's ministrations had been a test of Wentworth's mettle—entirely worth enduring to be sure, but a test nonetheless. He chuckled under his breath and moved to Laconia's favorite spot under his chin. Laconia rose up on tiptoes and arched his neck for more.

That episode earned Laconia a near reverence among the sailors—no persuasion necessary. They almost fell over themselves to curry favor with him. Moreover, the crew was profoundly defensive of their lucky charm, and rejected any man who did not revere him appropriately. Though it proved a mite difficult on his ego that the ship's cat was possibly more popular than himself, the crew's unity that came with it was valuable.

One more benefit the little dragon had brought into his life.

"You are trrroubled." Laconia rumbled, looking up at him, great gold eyes gleaming in the moonlight. He pressed his head hard into Wentworth's hand and leaned his furry shoulder and all three stones of his weight into Wentworth's chest.

Laconia's powerful purr reverberated through Wentworth's ribs. "Five years we have been together on the Laconia, my friend."

"I am able to watch stars as well as you. I know how long it has been."

"Of course, you do. You know we are sailing for England now."

Laconia chirruped. "And my directional sense is flawless. Why all the useless words?"

"I suppose I am philosophic right now, and you know philosophy uses a great many useless words."

Laconia snorted; the tip of his tail flicked against the wooden railing. It would not hurt the young dragon to learn a little patience.

"You know I will likely be beached when we anchor in Plymouth. With Napoleon safely in exile, there is far less need for ships on the sea."

"That is what troubles you." Laconia pushed the

side of his face against Wentworth's chin. Long prickly whiskers tickled Wentworth's nose as the edge of one fang scratched his cheek.

"Of course, that troubles a sailor. Poor Benwick—he only just made captain on the Grappler, and now this?"

"To take half pay as a captain instead of a lieutenant, without having hardly done the work for it does not sound like such a bad thing." Laconia licked between the toes of his oversized thumbed paw. Could he make his disdain for Benwick any clearer?

"But what does one do on the land? I have been at sea for so long—where do I even begin?"

"With the Blue Order."

Oversimplifying things as usual. "What would they want with me?"

"Modesty is not always a desirable quality in a warm-blood."

"More than once I have heard you say it would be helpful in a dragon."

"Dragon pride is more difficult than warm-blood pride—you are not apt to eat offending creatures." Laconia licked at a loose scale on his thick black tail. It pulled off and fluttered to the deck, twinkling in the rising moonlight as it fell. "You are well known among the sea dragons. They ask for you by name now. Most of those around the English coast and in the Mediterranean know the Laconia by sight and see your arrival as a boon."

"I will miss the many dragon friends we have made. But what has that to do with anything if I am to be beached?"

"As I understand—and I understand a great many things more than you realize—" Laconia pulled back slightly to look Wentworth square in the eye, "—the Order has no liaison to maritime dragons. Perhaps it is time for one."

"They have done without for what? Five hundred years more or less. Why would they need one now?"

"Times change. Men change. The war with France has changed things, no? The Blue Order must change with the times or the Pendragon Accords will become meaningless, and all that has been accomplished will be for naught. Even if they do not want a Maritime Officer, the Dragon Sage can always use those who can assist in dealing effectively with dragons. None can match your ease with sea-faring dragons."

The Dragon Sage was a woman. Wentworth rubbed the back of his neck. That would be interesting. Taking orders from a woman. The whole notion did not seem to bother dragons, but it would take some getting accustomed to for a military man. "Even if I should work for the Order, what else shall I do? Not even the highest officers of the Order spend all their hours working."

"You need a mate."

The word hit like the pelting, stinging rains of a winter gale.

"Your sister and her mate—"

"My sister is a rare and unique woman. Croft is very lucky to have her."

"I have seen. You would benefit to be in the same way as he."

"I dislike the notion of marriage."

Laconia leaned in a little closer, nose nearly touching Wentworth's. "You are still resentful."

Wentworth grumbled under his breath and stepped back slightly. "I have a very great deal to resent. She rejected me."

"Can she hear dragons?" Laconia stretched out, impossibly long, to press his paws to Wentworth's shoulders.

"I never asked."

"You cannot tell?"

"No, it is not apparent to most warm-bloods. She never mentioned it."

"Did you?"

"No! Without a landed dragon, why would it matter? I did not have you then. I had little to do with the Order. Hearing dragons was hardly something I considered significant in a wife."

"Perhaps you should have. You certainly must now." Laconia's fishy breath curled his nostrils.

"You live here amongst an entire crew who cannot hear dragons—save Rylie of course. And you manage quite well indeed. Does it really matter?"

"Here I am a lucky omen, a ship's cat. I will lose that on land—I am told some there dislike cats, and even more black ones. I must have allies I can trust." Laconia shrank back a little. For all his boldness in his home territory, he still—and probably always would—carried with him a not-quite-timidity, but a caution perhaps?—born of his perilous hatching.

"Do you wish to stay with the ship?" The words barely escaped in a hoarse whisper.

"Do you want me to?" Laconia's head and shoulders drooped.

"Do you wish to stay? I have no desire to compel you against your will."

"You are my Friend, my particular Friend. I do not wish to separate." Laconia's paws inched higher on Wentworth's shoulders, and he leaned his weight into them.

"I am glad to hear that." Wentworth wrapped his left arm across Laconia's shoulders and scratched behind his right ear.

"So, your mate must be able to talk to me. And she must like me."

"Why would someone not like you?"

"It happens. I will not live on land with someone who does not like me."

"I would not ask you to do so."

"Perhaps *she* could hear dragons."

"Who? Anne?" God above, it should not be so hard to say her name now.

"Perhaps that was why she rejected you. She could hear, and you did not tell her you could as well. Their estate has a dragon. It only makes sense that she can hear."

"Perhaps, but I still do not think so."

"You should find out."

"Why? It is nearly eight years since I have seen her—I expect she is married off and has a houseful of children by now."

"And if not?"

"She rejected me. I have no desire to see her."

"If you still resent her, you have feelings for her. You should see her." Laconia jumped off the railing and spring-hopped off, disappearing into the deep night shadows.

Stubborn, stubborn creature.

But perhaps he did have a point. Marriage and a proper home, with the proper woman, not Anne Elliot, might not be so bad a thing.

4
Chapter

Late June 1814

WELL, THAT WAS very interesting.

Anne pushed herself up from her perch on a cool and dusty garden rock amongst the fragrant bee balm and brushed the dirt from her skirt. There was a very great deal of dirt. The heat of the day had just finished banishing the morning's cool freshness, and beads of sweat trickled down the back of her neck.

Bother, the dress would have to be washed to get rid of it all. That did not happen nearly so much before she had started speaking to dragons. In the three days since she had been trying to learn more about Kellynch's hoard from the local estate dragons, it seemed every one of her gowns suffered. The whole Dragon Hearing, Dragon Keeping business was very hard on one's wardrobe.

At least the talk with Beebalm had proved productive, if also rather disappointing at the same time. Matters would be so much easier if the little puck only knew where Kellynch kept his hoard. But then again, it would not be very safe if every minor dragon in the territory knew where it was, would it? The logic was difficult to fault. Anne brushed loose dirt from her hands.

Still though, as the Sage's most recent letter predicted, she had learnt much from the encounter. Lady Elizabeth had suggested Anne discover what the puck hoarded and offer something to add to the hoard. Admittedly, it had sounded a bit pointless, but the Sage was sage for a reason, and truly what harm could there be in bringing Beebalm a bit of honey? Especially during one of those times when Jet had disappeared from the estate, and she was feeling safer to be out of her lair.

The transformation in the little green-brown dragon was almost instantaneous. Her eyes went wide and her color seemed to change from dull to glowing. Who would have expected the creature to all but lose the power of speech as she slavered over the sealed honey pot, licking traces of honey from the seal? How funny she looked, on her back, feet in the air, turning the jar round and round in the sunbeam, admiring it from every angle, just before she disappeared with it underground. A quarter of an hour later, Beebalm returned, still looking dazed, like one who had had too much wine the night before, gracious and grateful for the gift she had been bestowed, and ready to offer whatever information she had—which was unfortunately very little indeed.

It was like the monograph on hoarding said: a hoarding dragon was a bit like an opium-eater. When they got what they craved, they were in ecstasy. A little frightening to watch, truth be told. No need to test the warnings of what would happen if they did not receive their prize.

Troublesome, very troublesome.

Anne wiped her hands on her apron and turned down the garden path, air heavy with the sweetness of blossoms and buzzing with the hum of bees at work. One of a Keeper's duties toward a hoarding dragon—and not all of them were, though no one was exactly sure why—was to supply a yearly offering of a dragon's allotted hoard.

Naturally, the household books made no mention of anything being set aside for Kellynch's hoard during his long slumber. No doubt he would require—and was legally entitled to—a full accounting and payment upon awakening. That was indeed a problem.

What would happen if, when, they could not? Father's debts, it seemed, were substantial now. How could they possibly acquire enough to supply fifty years of any sort of hoarding supply to Kellynch, much less something of the sort to satisfy a major dragon? Kellynch was probably not the sort to be satisfied with buttons. She wrapped her arms around her chest and held her shoulders.

The monograph suggested that Kellynch could turn angry, even violent over that. Moreover, he had recourse against them with the Blue Order. If he registered a complaint, then the Order might begin an investigation into the Dragon Keeping that had—or in this case—had not been going on at Kellynch. Father could—no, he would be found negligent, and at that point, all manner of punitive measures could be taken. They probably would not look favorably upon the junior Keeper either.

Father could even lose his estate. That would probably be the death of him, and maybe even Elizabeth, too.

There must be something she could do—there had to be.

"Anne! Anne!" Lady Russell ran through the garden toward her, with wings held wide, in long, loping strides that closely resembled flight.

Anne jumped aside just before Lady Russell collided with her. "Heavens! What is wrong?"

"I must speak to you right away!"

"I can see that! Are you ill? Is someone hurt?"

"No, no. I am afraid it is much worse than that. Come, we must find a private place to talk." Lady Russell pointed with her beak toward the glassed-in conservatory attached to Kellynch Cottage.

Cottages normally did not have conservatories attached, but Sir Henry had installed that for her decades ago to assist in her cultivation of exotic species. Back then he appeared the doting husband …

Anne's face grew cold as she trotted in a most unladylike fashion behind Lady Russell. The news must be dreadful indeed to induce the cockatrix to run so openly.

Lady Russell shut the door to the small, well-filled conservatory and made sure the door from the house was shut and locked as well. "Cover your ears."

Why should Lady Russell issue such an order? Flanked by bushy citrus trees, Anne obeyed.

Lady Russell flapped her wings and jumped to the

top of a statue in the center of the conservatory—the highest point in the room. She threw back her head and trumpeted such a sound! Anne's ribs vibrated with the noise.

Two red fairy dragons—familiar members of the local harem—fell out of the potted orange trees and three dirty garden wyrms—two adults and a juvenile—popped out of the ground, writhing in pain.

"Out, out, all of you get out!" Lady Russell swept them toward the outside door with her wings, her talons scraping along the stone floor.

Anne opened the door, standing carefully out of the way, and closed it again behind the intruders. The warm, still air suddenly weighed as much as a winter cloak.

"Lock the door. There always seems to be some small dragon about to overhear what one does not want heard." Lady Russell stalked back to a stone bench near the central statue and paced long, thoughtful strides around the marble cherub, low hanging branches and vines catching at the spectacular plumage of her tail. "It is not at all what I expected. Not at all. And it is very bad."

"Pray stop telling me how bad it is, and tell me what it is." Anne sat on the cool seat.

"I have found Kellynch's charter."

"Found the charter? Where? I have searched everywhere!"

"That is part of what is so troubling." Lady Russell stalked to a table she used for potting plants and pried open a drawer to remove a crumpled and dirty set of papers.

"Why do they look so ill-used?" Anne took them and smoothed them over her lap, the blue ink seal of the Order prominent at the top of the page—probably how Lady Russell inferred this was the charter—how well she was actually able to read was still a bit of a mystery. At least she was right—it would be awful to have to tell her she was in error. "Where did you find this?"

"On the ground, in the woods, near Kellynch's lair. Many boot prints nearby. I think someone must have dropped it." She tucked one leg up and hunched into her thinking posture. "But who would have had it when neither you nor your father knew where it was?"

"Shelby told me something of chasing an intruder off recently, but as I understand, that regularly happens during a full moon. The cook often sells scraps and used tea-leaves from the backdoor of the kitchen, and not always to the most savory of company." Anne peered at the stains on the papers and sniffed—gravy? "It smells as though it might have been used to wrap leavings from a meal. Perhaps? Father has never been careful with the document. I can only think he must have allowed it to become mixed in with other papers that found their way to the kitchen."

"I do not like it. Strange people, coming and going. Important papers treated like rubbish." She fluttered her wings and settled them across her back. "Perhaps you should read this all-important charter for yourself. The print is too small for my eyes, you see, but I am quite interested to hear what it says."

Anne's heart pounded hard enough to make reading aloud difficult. She traced the carefully written lines with her fingertip. "Dates … name … dragon …family… officers of the Order witnessing, … defining the territory and duties to it. Here, here it is, hoarding …"

"Well, girl, what does it say?" Lady Russell stomped.

"It says Kellynch is a wyrm—it looks as though it might have specified the kind, but those words are too stained to read—botheration! Apparently, he is permitted to hoard wine." What would a wyrm want with wine?

"Wine? I have never heard such a thing." Lady Russell paced around the fat cherub statue, making little squawking sounds deep in her throat. Did she realize angry hens did that same thing?

"Where would he keep such a hoard? Our wine cellar is hardly full. Where else could he keep it? And how are we to pay the portion on fifty years of hoarding? Father's debt to the wine merchant—actually to all three of the local merchants—is extreme. They are refusing to sell to him at all. Mr. Shepherd has been charged with finding another source of Father's favorite wines now that the household stock is dwindling."

"Debts?" Lady Russell bounded to Anne's side in a frightening leap. "I know nothing of this."

Anne set the charter aside—she would have to finish reading that later. "I am surprised you have not heard of the merchants complaining that he has not paid his bills. The situation is becoming quite serious. It seems the sort of thing the fairy dragons would have overheard."

"No one pays those fluttertufts any mind— shatter-brained little creatures, what could they know?" Lady Russell clapped her beak rapidly—an expression of serious displeasure. "How could he? How could he? Debts are very dangerous for a dragon estate. He ought to know that. Surely you can see that."

"You know Father has never cared much for being a dragon estate." Anne rubbed her temples. And yes, it was alarmingly obvious why debt and dragons were a very dangerous combination.

"While that is true, one would think he might be mindful of the very grave danger a hungry and angry dragon might pose to him and his family."

"I think, and I am only supposing now, that he believes the Pendragon Accords will keep him safe from such an outcome. I gather that is a bad assumption."

"When he has violated those Accords himself, he has little to fall back upon." Lady Russell threw her head back, chittering a little like a fairy dragon. "Things are far worse than you even imagine. It never dawned on me that the Elliots might stoop so low."

"What else has my family done?" Anne squeezed her eyes shut and shook her head.

"Well, to be entirely fair, I cannot be certain that it is your family."

"What has happened?"

"Come, I suppose you should see it for yourself." Lady Russell's head hung down almost to the ground as she headed for the cottage door.

"Where are you taking me?"

"Into the dragon tunnels beneath the estate." Lady Russell strode into the cool and mildly damp kitchen with no cook or maid in sight, straight to the basement door. She pointed to a torch just beside the door. "Light that, you will need it."

Tunnels? What tunnels? There were dragon tunnels under Kellynch?

Anne lit the torch from the kitchen fire and followed Lady Russell down the narrow, uneven basement steps. She had never been in a basement before.

What an odd thing to realize. She had lived above a basement all her life and had never ventured inside it. Father said it was the realm of servants and those beneath her literally and figuratively. Did these tunnels that Lady Russell spoke of extend to the manor as well?

Much cooler, dark and dank, it smelt of stone and dirt, and a vague musk that was usually associated with dragons. "Do garden wyrms come here?"

"Occasionally, I persuade the cook to store bowls of scraps down here for them."

"That is kind of you."

"It is useful to have friends among the minor dragons. One never knows when such help might be needed." Lady Russell picked her way down the stairs.

A chill breeze made the torch waver and sputter as they entered a low tunnel in the far corner of the long basement. Any lower and she would have had to crouch to get through it. Who would put a tunnel here? Claw marks suggested it had been dragon dug.

Of course, it had been. How else would Kellynch traverse the estate without being seen? Such things were written of in *Dragon Estates: The design and establishment thereof to the benefit of both species.* It made sense that Kellynch lands would conform to those descriptions even though no current resident treated it as though it were a dragon estate.

The narrow, winding tunnel, floor and walls rough and uneven, led down and to the right, then left, then right again. The sputtering torch light barely allowed her to see three steps ahead of her. Lady Russell ignored three side tunnels along the way and finally ducked into a short, wide passage on the left.

Anne ducked to follow. Hopefully it would not be very much farther—she could not continue in this half-crouch for very long.

"There." Lady Russell pointed with her wing.

Anne took several more steps, holding the torch in front of her. An oblong room, maybe ten feet wide and twice as long and half again as tall as she opened before her. Thank heavens, she could stand straight again!

Several open crates, a small barrel bound with iron hoops, and a broken bottle littered the floor of the blind chamber. Faint scents filled the air: stone, old straw, wood, iron, and weak notes of wine.

"How did you find this place?"

Lady Russell clawed at the stone floor. "The last page of that charter-document has a diagram on the back—it looked like a map to the dragon tunnels—I thought it worth exploring before dragging you about in all the dark and dirt."

Anne touched the nearby barrel that lay on its side. Empty; it rolled away at her touch. The crates, lids pried off and half full of straw, held nothing of value. "Heavens above! This was the hoard?"

"I cannot imagine it could be anything else. Why would anyone but a dragon, especially one who hoards wine, store wine in such an inaccessible place? From the looks of it, the room used to be full."

Anne gasped and fell back against the rough wall.

"Stealing a dragon's hoard is a high crime, and it carries a heavy penalty."

Anne leaned her head back and breathed heavily, but it did not relieve the weight on her chest. "I cannot imagine it was Father who plundered it. I know we have not drunk any of the vintages on these labels."

"It does not really matter. He is Keeper, and responsible for what happens in the Keep. When Kellynch discovers this, he could easily go into a frenzy of hoarding hunger. It would not be unheard of for him to kill his Keeper—and possibly his Watcher—over such a transgression." She bounced from one foot to the other rapidly.

"But the Accords forbid that. Or I thought they did."

"Not when a crime of this magnitude has been committed."

"There is no money to replace any of this," Anne whispered through her hand.

"No money; there is truly no money … your father's debts are that extreme?" Lady Russell peered close into Anne's face, looking rather fearsome in the flickering torchlight.

"Quite extreme, I fear. I overheard a conversation with Mr. Shepherd—something about the local merchants talking about banding together for a writ of debt."

Lady Russell hunched into her thinking posture again and remained silent for several long minutes. "That is bad … and yet, perhaps, yes. I think it might just be the thing. I think I know how we can use it to buy a bit of time for us to solve the problem."

"I do not understand."

"Retrenching—you and I will devise a plan of retrenching that will remove the family from Kellynch for an extended period. That will allow me some time to work on Kellynch and perhaps avert a tragedy. I will present it to your father and persuade him—"

"As I understand, according to the Blue Order, you are not allowed to persuade a dragon hearer." Anne chewed her fingernail.

"This is an extreme situation, and your father has little desire not to be persuaded. Trust me, it is for the best."

"But if we retrench, will that not place tenants at risk from Kellynch?"

"I do not think so. Kellynch will know he cannot hold them responsible for what has happened. I will enlist Uppercross to help with him as well."

"It would have been nice if you had introduced me to him." Anne muttered under her breath, clutching her waist and rocking back and forth against the cold, stony wall. "It seems the only option then. I suppose we must begin immediately."

Yes, it was a sensible idea, completely sensible, and there was hardly any other choice. But was it not a very difficult thing to be forced from her home because of Father's spendthrift ways and a dragon's madness?

July 1, 1814

Four days later, Anne fought the urge to pace about the parlor like an anxious hen, instead forcing her limbs into quietude upon a dark gold wingchair—Mother's favorite chair in this room—pulled near to Lady Russell and the windows. The sunshine yellow walls tried to remind her to be cheerful, but their admonitions were lost in Lady Russell's murmurings.

"If we can persuade your father to accept all this,"

said Lady Russell, waving her wing over the papers spread on the low table between them, "much may be done. If he will adopt these regulations, in just seven years he will be clear." She settled her wings across her back and leaned against the back of her favorite overstuffed chair. Her bright blue feathers contrasted prettily with the deep rust upholstery.

"But is not our very purpose to have him leave Kellynch entirely and refuse this plan of retrenching?" Anne clutched her forehead and stared at the white peonies waving in the garden just beyond the windows. Peony, Wren-Catcher and two of the blue fairy dragons cavorted above the blossoms. How lovely it would be to have wings and join them after these four days wasted crafting pointless plans of economy to present to Father.

Lady Russell huffed and allowed her head to droop. Her very long neck made it a very dramatic expression, but perhaps she could not actually manage anything less sweeping. "I know, my dear, I know. But persuasion is much easier to achieve when the one being persuaded has some inclination to do as you suggest. He will despise these plans so much, suggesting he quit the house entirely and let it to tenants will be simple."

Anne clutched her forehead. What a sad statement that it was reasonable to expect Father to despise sensible economies. "What will you do when tenants have been found for the estate?"

"Much will depend upon the tenants. If they hear dragons … I will not be able to stay."

"Perhaps not at Kellynch Cottage, but surely you can stay. You must; Kellynch will require his Watcher."

"I am well aware of that. But I have become accustomed to living like a civilized creature, not in some dark, dank cavern." Lady Russell snorted and pawed the seat of the chair.

"Perhaps Shelby might be of some assistance. He might be able to provide you accommodations in one of the outbuildings?"

Lady Russell warbled. "Like a pigeon in a dovecote? I think not, I will find my own way, thank you. You just focus on managing your father."

Apparently, the Elliots were not the only ones at Kellynch with the problem of pride. But still, what was Lady Russell going to do?

"Ah, Lady Russell, how delightful to see you." Elizabeth swept into the parlor; her expression far less welcoming than her words.

Anne stood. Lady Russell rose, shaking out her broad wings and tail into something that very much looked like a train. She strode over to kiss Elizabeth's cheek, equally insincere, and peeked over Elizabeth's shoulder. Feathers ruffled down her back like a shudder.

Mrs. Clay, Mr. Shepherd's daughter, who had recently come back to live with her parents in her widowhood, tittered a greeting from behind Elizabeth.

The woman was simply insipid. It pained Anne to judge anyone so, but there it was, the awful truth. Her looks were average at best, and that was the best part of her personage. Her wit, her interests, even her manners ranked somewhere below her beauty. Father seemed to tolerate, even encourage her attendance upon Elizabeth—why he did so was utterly unfathomable. Unless he simply enjoyed seeing someone fawning upon his daughter. That could be it.

"It is good to see you, Miss Anne." Mr. Shepherd stepped into the room, around Elizabeth and Lady Russell, and bowed from his shoulders.

He wore a fine new blue coat and Mrs. Clay a new gown—a pale sprigged muslin affair that seemed intended to distract from the fact she was both a widow and a mother of two young children. They had come into some sort of money recently, according to Mrs. Trent—who also did not approve of Mrs. Clay, but it was not her place to voice such opinions, except to Anne of course. Everyone voiced their opinions to Anne. Whether Shepherd's sudden increase was an honorable inheritance or, more likely, some sort of business venture which would make the improvement in their circumstances far less acceptable to Father, remained unclear.

Mr. Shephard looked a bit haggard, as though he dreaded presenting Father with some sort of news he would not want to hear. Which was probably exactly the situation—had a writ of debt actually been procured by the merchants?

Father burst through the doorway, impeccably dressed and hair artfully arranged, and stopped two steps in, waiting, his features drawn into lines that usually presaged a fit of pique.

Lady Russell curtsied—a curious feat when accomplished by a very tall bird—no, not bird, cockatrix. "Ah, Sir Walter."

Anne, Elizabeth and Mrs. Clay curtsied, and Mr. Shepherd bowed. That seemed to mollify Father's sensibilities just a mite.

He nodded at Lady Russell and gestured for her to take a seat on the settee next to Elizabeth. If anyone else in the room could actually perceive Lady Russell folding herself to perch upon the hard, sleek cushions, they would laugh. There was a reason she did not like that particular seat.

"You look very serious today, Lady Russell." Father noted, his utter lack of interest in the matter clear in his tone. He took two more steps forward, to center himself in the room and brushed imagined dust from his sleeves.

"I am afraid I am. I am pressed by very weighty concerns." She blinked slowly—heavens how long were her eyelashes?

"It is a matter you would like to discuss?" Father's posture made it clear he asked only because politeness required it.

"I must, I must, but I dread the possibility of upsetting you."

"Then perhaps," Elizabeth cleared her throat, "it ought not be brought up at all."

Anne pressed her lips hard and perched on the settee, at Lady Russell's other side. How easily Elizabeth had adopted Father's favorite strategy for managing the unpleasant.

"I wish that were the case, but solicitous as I am for the Elliot name and reputation, I cannot indulge in such luxury. I am aware of a bit of unpleasant business for your family at the moment, and with Anne's assistance, I have drawn up some plans of retrenchment in the hopes of being useful to you." Lady Russell handed the papers to Father, pinched between the two odd little fingers at the tip of her wing.

Mr. Shepherd's bushy eyebrows shot up like a startled fairy dragon, his wide eyes half-surprised, half-hopeful.

"Retrench? The very notion is absurd. An Elliot does not retrench." Father took a step forward and planted his foot very hard.

"Oh, Father, pray, try to see reason. A person who has contracted debts must pay them. That is the law for peers, the gentry and the common alike. Though a great deal is due to the feelings of a gentleman, like you, there is still more due to the character of an honest man," Anne whispered the last few words, heart pounding almost painfully. Too much rode on these next few moments.

Father glowered at her and scanned the pages. He sniffled and snorted and sneered his way to the last page, striking it with the back of his hand. "This is ridiculous. We cannot possibly live the way that you suggest. A baronet must be seen to be living as a baronet."

Lady Russell clucked her tongue. "Kellynch Hall has a respectability in itself which cannot be affected by these reductions, and the true dignity of Sir Walter Elliot will be very far from lessened in the eyes of sensible people, especially when you are seen acting like a man of principle. Have not very many of our first families done, or ought to have done this very thing?"

"What! Every comfort of life knocked off! Journeys, London, servants, horses, table—contractions and restrictions everywhere! To live no longer with the decencies even of a private gentleman! No, I would sooner quit Kellynch Hall at once, than remain in it on such disgraceful terms." Father slapped the papers and tossed them toward Elizabeth.

She caught them and looked at them only long

enough to read a very few lines. "These restrictions are intolerable. No one could live under such conditions." She tossed them behind her back. They rustled as they hit the floor behind the settee.

Anne ground her teeth until they squeaked. Clearly Elizabeth was unfamiliar with the conditions in which most of their tenants lived. Life without two pairs of carriage horses was perhaps not the privation she thought. No, she must not correct Elizabeth when this was all going exactly as Lady Russell declared it should.

"Quit Kellynch Hall," Mr. Shepherd murmured as though considering the notion for the first time. The man was canny indeed. Allowing Father to believe himself the origin of that particular idea would help ensure its acceptance. Certainly effective, but at the same time uncomfortable at the very least, and dare she say, untrustworthy at most. "Since the idea has been started in the very quarter which ought to dictate such things, I have no scruple in confessing my judgement to be entirely on that side. It does not appear that you, Sir Walter, could or even should materially alter your style of living when residing in a house like Kellynch, which has such a character of hospitality and ancient dignity to support. In another place, though, you might judge to regulate the modes of life in whatever way you might choose to model your household and would surely be looked up to whatever you choose."

And just maybe, incorporate a few of those notions of economy. Or perhaps that was too much to hope for.

Lady Russell ducked her head to hide her sharp glance. She had never liked Mr. Shepherd, but this time, he was doing precisely what she wanted him to, without even a hint of draconic persuasion on her part. She should not discourage that. The strain of the effort showed in the creases beside her eyes.

"But wither shall we go, Papa?" Elizabeth pressed her hand to her heart, blinking rapidly. Was she trying to look coy or did she have dust in her eyes?

"If I may suggest, sir," Mr. Shepherd cleared his throat. "There would seem to be three attractive alternatives. London is of course an agreeable possibility, as is Bath. Alternatively, another house in the neighborhood might allow you to continue in the company you are accustomed to."

"Retrench to a house here!" Elizabeth leapt to her feet, losing a little color in her face. "That is completely unacceptable. People here know how we should live. If we were to appear to do otherwise—"

Father stepped to Elizabeth's side and laid a hand on her shoulder. "I agree wholeheartedly. Elizabeth is right. We cannot possibly stay in this region. The loss of dignity is not to be borne. London has a delightful society, though."

"Indeed, it does, the company indeed is very grand. You would enjoy being in very superior company quite often." Mr. Shepherd clasped his hands behind his back. "But how Bath will suffer without your inclusion in its society."

Wily indeed—Lady Russell might learn a point or two about persuasion from this man.

Was that a good thing?

Father's brow furrowed and smoothed several times as he chewed his lower lip. "You make an excellent point, an excellent one. It would be almost criminal to deny Bath our society."

"Moreover, it is a safer place than London for a gentleman in your situation. In Bath you can be important at comparatively little expense. What is more, it is only fifty miles from Kellynch; a far more comfortable journey than one hundred and thirty miles to London. Lady Russell might even spend part of the winter in Bath as well and would be able to be good company to you there." Mr. Shepherd glanced from Anne to Lady Russell as though to implore her support.

Why would he want Lady Russell away from Kellynch?

She pulled her head back and swallowed something between a growl and a hiss which she covered in a less than dainty cough. "I know you do not prefer Bath, Anne. But it does so seem like the ideal circumstance for your family. I must support the notion."

Anne's chest pinched. Perhaps she had not been as prepared as she thought for this eventuality. There were too many difficult memories of her Mother tied up with Bath for her to pretend to be happy about going there, even if it was the best option they had.

"You have been too little from home, too little seen. Your spirits are not high. A larger society will improve them, you will see. It will be good for you to become more known to those in your sphere." Lady Russell patted her hand with her wingtip. She played her part very well.

"Anne need not go to Bath, at least not immediately. Sister Mary is in want for her company. Would it not be better for her to go to Uppercross? Penelope can accompany me to Bath." Elizabeth stared directly at Anne with a cold smile. "It is not as if you will be wanted in Bath." Elizabeth delivered the words as if they bore no more meaning than suggesting a menu for dinner.

Could words land with the force of an open hand? Elizabeth's typical thoughtlessness was only to be expected. But this was something more, intentional, calculated, venting her spleen in the only safe direction.

"Of course, Elizabeth must not be in want of company. Mrs. Clay must join us." Father gestured toward her. "You would not deny us her company, would you Shepherd?"

"Your invitation is most gracious. How could I object?"

Mrs. Clay clapped her hands softly and sighed, far too much like a schoolgirl to be genuine.

Lady Russell chittered under her breath. She liked Mrs. Clay even less than she liked her father, declaring her conniving and dangerous at best, a clever young woman who understood the art of pleasing a little too well. Widows were hardly to be trusted—or at least so conventional wisdom taught.

Still, Lady Russell clamped her beak shut and swallowed back further objections. No doubt even the evils of Mrs. Clay were less than the evils of a hoard-hungry dragon awakening.

"Then, it is settled, we are for Bath."

"Perhaps we should lift a toast to a very promising decision." Mr. Shepherd nodded at Father. "I have an excellent bottle of wine in my carriage, brought in hopes of celebrating such a good plan. Shall I send for it?"

"Yes, yes, that would be most appropriate." Father rang the bell for Mrs. Trent. "I did not know you to be a connoisseur of wine."

"I hardly give myself that much credit, sir. But it is a taste I have recently begun to cultivate."

"I approve, Shepherd, I approve."

5
Chapter

July 10, 1814

WENTWORTH SETTLED HIMSELF into the seat in the dark corner of the dark pub, pulling his deep brown coat a little closer. How odd and uncomfortable it was, being out of uniform—and without Laconia, who hated places like this. The moonless night made the place even darker.

Dark.

Yes, that was what he felt. Dark.

Cramped, crowded and common; this same pub, currently in Portsmouth, existed in every port town. The name of the place never mattered; the same saucy serving maids, the same watered-down rum, the same greasy grey food stuffs on the same battered pewter plates made one indistinguishable from another.

Though there were advantages to being back on land, there were some things about being at sea one missed. On the ocean, one felt a sense of community with shipmates perpetually at one's elbow. Yes, at times it was dreary indeed, the same faces, sometimes even the same conversations day after day. But the reliableness of it all, that was a good thing, especially at times like this. Times when the need for company to silence the annoying clatter in his head overrode the need for the company to be good or of any quality at all, except loud.

Reeson, a tall, gaunt, but seasoned lieutenant from the Laconia, waved to him from the far side of the room. His blue coat hung off him like something handed down to him from an elder brother, and his unruly hair drooped over his eyes—he would rather shove it out of his way than manage it in any fashion, lazy sot. He approached with swaggering steps, a pint in his hand, waving to the plump serving girl with a stained apron, who followed him, a tankard in each hand. He fell into a chair across the roughhewn table from Wentworth.

If his walk had not given it away, his breath did. Gah! The lad surely had several—no, many—pints already. But as drunks went, Reeson was harmless enough. He waxed nostalgic for home and his girl when fuddled. Rather mawkish really, but it was better than belligerent and looking to have a brush with someone. And Reeson's company was still better than being alone with his own thoughts.

"Cap'n," Reeson motioned the girl to set down the mugs.

She slid one toward Wentworth with a saucy wink. He nodded at her. Not the sort of company he favored, or even wanted right now.

"It's been water bewitched ya' know, but what can ya' 'spect in a place as this?" Reeson rocked side to side as though he had not yet got his land legs back.

Wentworth sipped the tankard. Weak and watery—how many had it taken to get Reeson in that state? He must have been here most of the day. "Much better barley broth to be found on the Laconia." He laughed and lifted the mug.

"Aye, that there was. I tell ya', sir, I'm not sure 'bout being beached, ya' know. Can't be anything good come of it."

"I thought you were going to make up for lost time with your wife."

He swayed a bit faster, bushy brow pulling low over dark eyes. "That were the plan, no. It were."

"And now?"

"I'm worried, Cap'n, I be worried." Reeson parked his elbows on the table and pressed his face into his hands.

"Whatever for."

"I 'eard about Benwick's lass, and I can't get the damn thought outta me 'ead now."

Wentworth nearly dropped his tankard and set it hard on the table. "Benwick's lass? Fanny Harville?"

"That be the name me thinks." Reeson emptied the drink he had brought with him and reached for the next. "I dread to think I could be the next to get such news."

"What news?"

"You 'aven't 'eard?"

"Damn it man, tell me what you know." Wentworth balled his fists under the table. Shaking the man in a public house would probably not get the information out any faster.

"A letter come to Blake from Harville 'imself, and it said Fanny Harville were dead."

"Dead?"

"Said she slipped the wind with a churchyard cough near the last full moon, or were it the one before? I can't 'member, but do it matter when it 'appened, if she won't be there when 'e return?" Reeson dragged his grimy sleeve over his eyes. "Don't know what I'll do if I get such news."

Wentworth rose and shoved his pint toward Reeson. "There is no reason to think you will hear such a thing, too. Chin up, you will see. Have you written to her yet?"

"I can't, I just can't. What if she never writes back?"

"Don't be a fool man. Consider it an order, write to her in the morning, and you will have good news by the end of the week." Wentworth rolled his eyes. He used to have to force Dick Musgrove to write to his family, too. That was not an exercise to be repeated ... what was he, some sort of schoolmaster to force his men to practice their correspondence?

He nodded at Reeson and rushed out into the cool embrace of the darkness. A flickering street lamp across the dusty street from the pub offered him a meager refuge within its circle of pallid light.

Dead? Fanny Harville was dead? She had always been so healthy, so strong. A beautiful girl, vibrant, with a quick wit and ready smile. How could she be dead? He clutched the lamp post, knees weakening.

Who else had died since he had been to sea? Croft and Sophy were well—at least as of the last letter he had received. Edward had written to him recently and claimed to be hale and hearty. Bad news from any family he cared about was not likely.

Edward had said nothing about the families near Monkford, though. He usually did, even though he was in Shropshire now. Why had he not offered some report on the Elliots? He always found it great sport to poke fun at them. With good reason, of course.

Had something happened among them? Had the baronet died and the heir taken over? Had he thrown Anne and her sisters out of their home? Laconia still thought him bitter, but even he was not bitter enough to wish that fate upon them.

A cold wave washed over him. He leaned hard against the lamp post. Was Anne dead? Is that why Edward did not mention her, thinking to spare his feelings?

Wentworth snorted and grumbled under his breath. Edward need not have worried. What did it matter? She was hardly his concern now. If she was dead, why would he dread the news?

He leaned his forehead against the cold iron post. Why indeed, why indeed?

The Elliots, none of them were any concern of his.

But Benwick was. Poor sot had just moved onto the Grappler, his first command. To be beached right after making captain, now this? How could a man have such a run of bad luck? One that he surely did not deserve.

Granted, Benwick was not exactly a popular man. Serious and bookish, he lacked a certain charisma that marked most captains of his acquaintance. Seamen often found him difficult to approach, and Laconia claimed a ready dislike for him, as he did for many of the dragon-deaf. But none of that changed the fact that Benwick was a good man. Faithful, loyal and dependable as the day was long. A man of his word whom one could trust to have one's back. The kind of friend one did not turn away from easily.

The sort of man who would be crushed when he heard the news. He had been persuaded not to marry Fanny before he shipped out in the hopes of returning with sufficient prize money that they could be well settled.

Benwick might never forgive himself for that decision.

A man should not be alone, without his friends, at such a time. And he should hear the bad news from someone who cared for him, not a drunk in a pub.

Tomorrow, he would seek out Blake and confirm Reeson's story. If it was true, then he would go to Portsmouth to find the Grappler himself and deliver the news to Benwick.

Then what? He stared into the night sky, stars looking down on him, demanding answers.

Damn it all. He had been planning to take some time and visit with Harville and his family. Laconia liked the man well enough and had been instrumental in Harville's survival from those horrible bullet wounds. Wentworth shuddered. Grisly, horrible, bloody… one more testament to the Laconia being the luckiest ship in the fleet.

He could not impose himself upon a family that might still be in mourning—when exactly had Fanny passed?— Harville's wife had been very close to Fanny, they all lived together whilst the men were out to sea.

Now where would he go?

He leaned against the lamp post, staring into the

dark, rocking slightly as if with the sway of the sea.

Where indeed? He had been out at sea so long now that few places on land felt like home. Edward would surely welcome him in Shropshire. That was certainly an option. Sophy's last letter suggested she and Croft were looking to let an estate—a nice one. They were planning to enjoy this spell on land whilst it lasted. And he was very welcome to spend some time with them when he was able.

Laconia liked them and their Friend White, although how or even if the hippocampus would adapt to life on land was an interesting question. One that might be worth answering.

Perhaps it was time to do just that. Start fresh in an unknown place. Contact the Blue Order like Laconia and Croft suggested, see about work with them. That would certainly be interesting—dragons always made life very interesting.

Perhaps he might even follow Laconia's advice and look for some reasonably agreeable female to make his wife, settle down and begin his life anew. A woman nothing like Anne, of course. Someone with a strength of will and purpose, who knew her own mind and would not be persuaded away from it. Certainly, there must be a dragon-hearing woman like that somewhere in England.

Sophy might know one. Yes, she would be an excellent person to consult on the matter.

If nothing else, Sophy would probably enjoy the opportunity to renew her acquaintance with Laconia. They were rather fond of one another.

6
Chapter

July 14, 1814

ANNE SLIPPED BEHIND Father—naturally he could not move his chair to make way for her—and edged towards her seat in the morning room. Clouds filtered the sunlight, turning the sky-blue walls a touch grey. Mama's watercolor landscapes all looked as though rain might be in the offing. Not a pleasant refreshing sort of rain, but the dreary sort that left a place muddy and sloppy and chilled. At least the warm scents of coffee and fresh toast cut through some of the heaviness.

Elizabeth's place near Father's was empty. That was some good news. At least there would be no talk of the new dresses she wanted for Bath or how restyling her old dresses simply would not do. A small blessing, but one she should be grateful for. Elizabeth had been to school and understood basic maths. Why was it so difficult to understand that their reduced household expenses from going to Bath meant that they might begin paying off their debts, not allow them to spend even more money on things that were largely unnecessary. It had been a bad idea telling Elizabeth new gowns were an unnecessary extravagance. A very bad idea.

Anne paused at the sideboard to pour herself some coffee. A little cream and sugar would do nicely. "I wrote Mr. Elliot a letter of condolence." And informed him that the estate charter had been found—but Father probably did not need to know that.

"For what?"

"The death of his wife. You said it should be done, you did not want to allow the duty to be neglected as it was for the Dalrymples."

He stiffened and set aside his newspaper and harrumphed. "Shepherd has been going on about how the present turn of events is much in our favor. He seems convinced this peace will be turning all our rich naval officers ashore. 'They will be all wanting a home. There has never been a better time for a choice of tenants, very responsible tenants. Many a noble fortune has been made during the war,' he declares. He has hopes, it seems, for getting us a rich admiral."

Anne set her coffee cup on the table and slipped into her chair. "Forgive me for saying so, but letting Kellynch may be a more complicated process than Mr. Shepherd realizes."

"Any man would be lucky to get Kellynch. It would be a prize indeed to him. But I do not know if I am of a mind to let it at all." Father sneered over his shoulder.

"Surely you cannot mean that, you understand—"

"No, no, I—I need hear no more talk on the necessity of it all. I am resigned to a navy man here." He slapped the table with both palms and huffed a breath through his lips—something Shelby did when he was exasperated with the sheep—or their shepherds. "Shepherd assures me that gentlemen of the navy are well to deal with. They have very liberal notions, and are as likely to make desirable tenants as any set of people one should meet with. He assures me they are so neat and careful in all their ways. Everything in and about the house would be taken such excellent care of! The gardens and shrubberies would be kept in almost as high order as they are now."

Patience, she must have patience. One must remember how difficult this must be on Father's pride. Oh, the Elliot pride. "The navy, I think, who have done so much for us, have at least an equal claim with any other set of men, for all the comforts and all the privileges which any home can give."

"The profession has its utility, but I should be sorry to see any friend of mine belonging to it." He leaned forward on his elbows, eyes narrow. "It is in two points offensive to me. First, as being the means of bringing persons of obscure birth into undue distinction, and raising men to honors which their fathers and grandfathers never dreamt of; and secondly, as it cuts up a man's youth and vigor most horribly; a sailor grows old sooner than any other man. I have observed it all my life."

Naturally those would be his objections. "I suppose it will be good then that you will not have to look much upon him when you have left for Bath."

She cringed; Father rarely reacted well to sarcasm.

"About that. You spoke of going to Uppercross, but I think you must come with us immediately to Bath."

"That is not possible." She restrained the urge to slap her forehead. "I have already written to Mary to tell her of my visit." Leave it to Father to invent new ways to make things more difficult for her.

"Then you must tell her of the change in plans. Elizabeth has declared that setting up the household in Bath is disagreeable to her and is better done by you."

Anne held her breath and counted to ten. That was not enough—to twenty. Better, only a little, but better. "Surely you must see that that is not possible."

"And why not?" Anger tinged his voice. Did he think her being disagreeable for the sport of it?

"Have you forgotten about the additional complications the letting of Kellynch Hall entails?"

"What rubbish are you talking about?"

She clutched her skirt to keep from slapping the table. "I know you do not like to think about it, but that does not change the truth of the matter. Kellynch is a dragon estate and there is a dragon in residence. Both factors which must come into consideration in finding a proper tenant."

"Oh, that." Father waved off the notion. "There is no bother with that. The creature has not been seen or heard from in decades. I am quite sure it has quit the place entirely. It will be of no matter to any tenant, naval man or not."

"No. He has not." She enunciated each word, crisply and clearly, as though speaking to a very young child.

"What do you mean? How do you know?" Father's lip curled back.

"I have seen him."

"And what has he said to you?"

"Nothing. He is not taking calls, yet. He is hibernating."

"Hibernating?" Father snorted and tossed his hand again. "Well then, what is the problem? He has no reason to awaken, and all will remain as it has been."

"No, it will not. I have been in regular communication this last month with the Dragon Sage, and she assures me—"

"She? Oh yes, that office is held by a … a woman." His top lip curled back.

"It has been nearly fifty years since his last awakening. That means Kellynch is close to waking."

"I cannot fathom how a woman contrived to get herself named to such an office. I hear she is not but a common woman to boot. Not a title in her family. I declare the Blue Order sounds just as bad as the navy! It is very irregular you know, and I must now reconsider my affiliation with such a group. What does a woman know about Dragon Keeping?"

"A very great deal it would seem. Shelby, the shepherding drake who has been in residence here quite some time, tells me the same thing."

"It sounds, then, as though the creature has the matter in hand. What more have we to do with it?" Impatience and irritation—a very great deal of it—dripped from his voice.

"A waking dragon is a very dangerous thing. Not one to be left to his own devices. We are obligated to provide for his needs—"

Father jumped to his feet. "Obligated! Obligated

you say. What has that foul beast ever done for us to be due this sort of obligation?"

"The land and your title are due to him. You know that."

"I do not see why we should be saddled with such a burden."

"It is your birthright, sir." Anne stood and matched his posture.

"I have no need to sully my hands with livestock, especially expensive livestock that I never chose to keep."

"A major dragon is not livestock. He is as intelligent a creature as you." Possibly more so.

"If he is of such great interest to you, then you deal with him."

"That is the job of the Dragon Keeper."

"I wash my hands of that nonsense." Father grabbed a glass of water from the table and poured a measure into his palm. He rubbed his hands together and wiped them on his napkin. "If it is so important to you, then you take it on." He flicked water droplets her way.

She blinked hard as cold drops rolled down her cheek. "What are you saying?"

He leaned against the table hard enough to rattle the china and stared straight at her. "If Kellynch needs a Dragon Keeper, then you may have the role, since you have an inexplicable appreciation for all things irksome and beneath the Elliot name."

She lifted her chin, voice very even, "Dragon Keeping is a point of pride, not a degradation."

"On that we shall differ. It is of no matter to me in any case. It is now your problem."

"In that case, you cannot insist that I go to Bath

with you, at least not immediately. I must be in the neighborhood to attend him when he awakes."

"Tenants will not let you stay here. You have no place to go but to help your sister in Bath."

"I will go to Uppercross as planned. It is close enough for me to return to tend Kellynch when I am needed. You can tell Elizabeth that I am required to be here to assist the tenants when they move in. Surely that task would be even less agreeable to her than setting up the household at Bath." Anne crossed her arms over her chest—perhaps that would help contain her thundering heart.

"I do not like that lizard—"

"I understand that to call a dragon a lizard is a very high insult. Perhaps it is not a good habit to get into."

Father huffed with a sneer. "You had best inform the creature it is not to cause the tenants trouble. I will not—"

No point in explaining to him the wrongs done to Kellynch meant the Elliots were in no place to demand anything of the dragon. Definitely not. "I will manage it Father. Think nothing more of it."

He sniffed. "You will join us in Bath. None of this changes what Elizabeth wants from you."

"But it does change what I am able to do for her. When the situation allows, I will attend you in Bath."

Father grumbled under his breath, turned sharply and marched from the morning room.

Anne's eyes burned and her hands trembled. This was too much, far too much. Lady Russell, she would know what to do—perhaps she might persuade Father and Elizabeth they did not need her so much in Bath—at least she would be sympathetic which almost as good. She ran upstairs for her bonnet and dashed to Kellynch Cottage.

The morning air hung damp and cool about her, with just the hint of threatening weather on the horizon—by no means certain, but just a lingering possibility that would most likely conspire to be as inconvenient as possible. A bit like Father managed to be. Grey clouds covered most of the sky, hampering the sun and matching her mood.

Just where the path to the cottage crossed the main road to the manor, Mr. Shepherd's mud-splashed black gig drawn by a sturdy grey dappled horse pulled alongside her. He was dusty from travel and his worn portfolio lay on the floor near his feet.

"Miss Anne," He bowed from his shoulder. "Is there somewhere to which I might offer you a ride?"

"I am on my way to Kellynch Cottage." Gracious, she did sound far more breathless than she would have liked.

"I am on my way to the manor. It would be no trouble to pass by the cottage on my way." He climbed down and helped her into the gig.

"Thank you." She arranged her skirts out of his way as he climbed back up and took the reins. "Are you on your way to see Father?"

He cocked his head, eyebrows lowering. "Is there something I should know?"

That was his way of not asking what sort of mood Father was in and if calling upon him now was a bad idea.

It was.

"I have heard from a naval man, an Admiral Croft, who is interested in letting Kellynch. I had thought to show Sir Walter the Admiral's letter of inquiry." He did not look at her as he flicked the reins and urged the horse to walk on.

She clutched the side of the gig as it lurched and lunged through a deep rut in the road. "I fear that now may not be the best time to bring such news."

Mr. Shepherd frowned five different ways before setting his face into a neutral expression. "I see. What do you recommend?"

"You might give me the papers. I can give them to him at a time when he might be the most receptive."

He nodded slowly. "Perhaps you might glance over them as well and, if it is not asking too much, alert me if you see anything which Sir Walter might consider objectionable? I might be able to deal with issues and make amendments without troubling him—or would it be too much of an imposition?"

Croft—Croft, the name was familiar. It seemed there were Crofts on the lists of Blue Order families. If she could discern whether they were likely to hear dragons— "I would be happy to offer my assistance however I may, sir."

Was that a sigh of relief? He stopped the gig at the front door of the cottage and rummaged in his portfolio. "Here are the documents. Feel free to examine them, and if you see any issues with them, send me word. I will work to correct them to Sir Walter's satisfaction." He handed her a thick folio and helped her down.

She examined the papers as she made her way to the front door. The brass knocker was shaped like a dragon—a drake with a long tail and a large ball held between its front paws.

Lady Russell's housekeeper let her in and led her to the parlor where Lady Russell perched in the sun with a large tambour frame holding her latest embroidery project. It was still a wonder how she could use her nimble toes and beak and never misplace a stitch on her complicated work.

"Anne?" Lady Russell peered over the embroidery frame. "You look quite a fright! Pray sit down."

Anne hurried to an overstuffed chair upholstered with pale yellow roses on a light green field, near the peach velvet pouf where Lady Russell perched. The room was small, half the size of Kellynch's parlor, overlooking the garden, the walls painted in dark greens with pale orange and gold upholstery. The effect was exotic, yet somehow soothing. A large bowl of yellow lilies on the round oak tea table in the center of the room perfumed the air.

She collapsed into the rose covered chair as the details of her encounter with Father poured out.

"Your father said what?"

"He said I was to be the Dragon Keeper to Kellynch. I know I should not be so distraught over it, but I cannot help but think Kellynch would have been disturbed to hear it. I am sure it means nothing, though. We both know Father is apt to assign tasks he does not like to me. Where there is some distinction to be had in it, he will readily proclaim the dignity his again." She held her face in her hands, rubbing the heels of her hands into her eyes.

"This is far more serious than you realize." Lady Russell chittered and clucked her tongue.

"What do you mean?" The words barely escaped her tight throat.

"Dragon Keeping is not a household chore that one may simply assign to another."

"I have been doing those duties such as they are, since you first introduced me, as it were, to Kellynch.

Besides I have been the junior Keeper, that should make all this a moot point, no?" Anne peeked over her fingers.

"Doing the duties is not the same thing as having the position. And being a junior Keeper is hardly the same has having the actual position. Allowing a daughter to plan an afternoon tea does not make her mistress of the manor, does it?" Lady Russell covered her face with her wing and shook her head hard. "For a Dragon Keeper to relinquish his duties …"

"Father was just talking, there is nothing official—"

"I am afraid you are wrong. Every dragon knows, if a Dragon Keeper renounces his duties to another, washing his or her hands of it as you described him doing, and it is witnessed by a dragon—"

"Then there is no issue." Thank heavens all would be well. Anne leaned back and heaved a heavy breath. "The conversation took place in the morning room, and there were no other dragons about. So, you can cease your worry. Whatever you fear has taken place has not."

"Oh, Anne. I wish it were that simple. Dragons are never simple. You must remember that we are always complicated, difficult, and inconvenient. Always." She preened her wing. "If just one dragon overheard what was said, you can be certain that the entire estate will know about it in a matter of days. Have you forgotten about the fairy dragons? They are always about and hear everything. That is part of the reason they are so often eaten! Once the conversation is known, every dragon will be looking to you to be the Keeper."

All relief fell away into a little puddle around her chair, and Anne's voice thinned. "Why does that matter so much? Have I not been tending to what has needed to be done?"

"In an unofficial capacity. That is far different from having the official title thrust upon you. Foolish, foolish man. We will just have to hope against hope that you were not overheard and all might remain the same. I will make some inquires just to be certain."

"I thought no one really paid attention to what fairy dragons said."

"News that interesting will surely be attended to. But we shall sort that out when, and if, it comes." She drew a deep breath and let her feathers settle along her back. "I will call for some tea. You look as though you could use some refreshment."

"Perhaps it would be best to wait. There is more."

Lady Russell's head came up sharply, her neck stretching to its full length. "There is more?"

"Mr. Shepherd has arranged for tenants to let Kellynch." She opened the folio and scanned the topmost page.

Lady Russell's beak clacked rapidly, but she said nothing.

"A man by the name of Admiral Croft. He is a rear admiral of the White. He was in the Trafalgar action, and has been in the East Indies since; he was stationed there." She traced down the page with her finger. "He seems quite the gentleman in all his notions and manners and wishes not to make the smallest difficulty about terms. It seems he only wants a comfortable home for his wife—without children I might add—and to get into it as soon as possible and is ready to pay for the convenience." Anne swallowed hard, "He also notes in a very vague and abstract sort of way that he is aware of how 'special' a property

Kellynch is and that he is quite prepared and honored to be able to take residence in a place so reminiscent of his family's holdings."

"You think this Croft is known to the Blue Order?" The question ended in a sort of shriek.

"I recall reading the name in the Blue Order rolls. I think it safe to assume at least the Admiral and possibly his wife are hearers."

Lady Russell jumped up—nearly knocking over her tambour—and paced around the room, hissing and chittering.

"We may even have some ties to these people. Mrs. Croft is sister to a gentleman who had the curacy at Monkford a few years back—Mr. Wentworth." Should it be so difficult to even say that name?

"Wentworth? Oh!" Lady Russell jumped back, wings spreading. "That is enough. I do not need to hear more."

"That name is in the rolls as well—did you know? It seems that the Wentworth family has a long and illustrious history of hearing dragons. Were you aware? I have been meaning to ask you for some time. Of course, the current generations were not included in the old edition of the book that Father possesses, however, it is not a great leap of imagination—"

"That is quite enough. I have no desire to discuss this matter any further." Lady Russell turned her back and hop-stepped away. She usually did that when gravely agitated.

"Perhaps not. But maybe, just maybe I do." Anne stood; paper clutched in her hand. Perhaps it was not fair to spring this upon Lady Russell amidst so many other crises, but then again, fairness did not seem to be among Lady Russell's chiefest concerns.

"I still have not resolved the issue about Kellynch's hoard. I do not yet know how we will manage that issue when he awakes. There is something nefarious afoot, I am sure of it, but I am not certain from which quarter it comes. That Shepherd man and his horrid daughter, I do not trust them. Where did their new fortune and taste for wine come from? Do you not find that quite suspect? Especially when you told me that Shepherd produced a bottle of wine matching the labels we found on empty crates in the hoard room."

Unfortunately, Lady Russell had a very good point.

"And Shepherd is not my only concern! Did not that sheep-drake speak to you of intruders on the estate? It is all most peculiar and needs investigation. I shall leave directly and be gone several weeks—there are those I would speak with who might have useful knowledge for me. You are going to Uppercross no? I will see you there when I know more. Pray excuse me." Lady Russell all but ran from the room in long loping strides, wings flapping; an attitude that might have been humorous in another context.

Anne slowly sank back into the welcoming rose covered chair, braced her elbows on the table and allowed her forehead to fall to her hands. She had long suspected, and now she knew. Lady Russell had persuaded her away from Wentworth all those years ago, not for Anne's best interest, but to keep her own secret. She had violated not only the precepts of the Blue Order—which one might argue did not apply to one not a member of the Order—but of Anne's trust. What sort of friend was she? Surely, she could not have used Mama so ill, could she?

Worse still, Anne's single, ready source of information on the strange world that threatened to engulf her had just proved herself at best untrustworthy and perhaps something far worse—unreliable.

Where could she turn now?

Uppercross. Pray there was help to be had there.

7
Chapter

August 15, 1814

ANNE SETTLED BACK into the seat of the Musgrove's carriage as best she could. The leather seats were cracked in places and it smelt a bit musty, especially in the summer's heat. The springs had lost most of their bounce, so the ride was far from the sort of luxury Father demanded. While it might not have been good enough for him, kindness, wherever she might find it, was far too precious to overlook.

A se'nnight ago, dear Mrs. Musgrove had written her a hasty, alarmed note, fearing that she might be conveyed to Uppercross in a farm cart! Insisting that was not to be borne, she herself set the day and time the Musgrove carriage would come for Anne.

How galling that Mrs. Musgrove had been right.

Her hands tightened into knots, crushing the skirts of her drab traveling dress into hard wrinkles. Father had made no provision for her travel to Uppercross, and there was no money to arrange it herself. Only three miles away, she could have walked there, but not dragging her trunks behind her. At least Mrs. Musgrove's attentions allowed her to save face before the Kellynch tenants and servants. The same ones to whom she would represent the Elliot family after its patriarch departed for Bath.

Anne swallowed hard and pressed into the hard squabs. Father was usually so attentive to the appearance of the Elliot family, but she had never crossed him before; never completely and openly refused his demands. Evidently, there was a price to be paid for such rebellion.

Shelby and even little Beebalm had expressed more concerns for her travels than he, even going so far as to say they did not want to see her going away. For all their draconic oddnesses, they were dear little souls. She wrapped her arms around her waist and pressed her feet hard into the floorboards against another jolt from the rutted road. If only her family were more like them.

Gracious! Did she actually think that? Wishing her family were more draconic? No, she did not. What Lady Russell had done was far worse than any of her family's actions or oversights. She drove the heel of her hand against her chest, but it did little to quell the ache.

Far worse.

Best not dwell upon that now.

Uppercross village, a moderate sized village with buildings almost entirely in the old English style, rose up on the horizon. The only superior buildings were the Musgrove's mansion with high walls, great gates and old trees, and the cottage where Mary and Charles lived. Father approved of that sort of distinction between the landowners and the rest.

The cottage enjoyed its own neat garden with climbing roses and a pear tree trained round its casements. A veranda, French windows and other prettiness had been added on the occasion of Mary and Charles' marriage making it compare quite favorably to the Great House only a quarter of a mile away. Naturally, Mary regularly complained of the privations she endured. Every day was a trial of a staircase too narrow, rooms too small, a smoky fireplace, and furniture that showed its age. At one time, Anne had tried to encourage her, both in person and in her letters, to be thankful for her circumstances. After all, she was the only sister to have married.

That conversation did not go well; not at all. Relations with Mary were much pleasanter now that she had ceased to broach that topic—or any other of real substance—ever again.

A worn-looking housekeeper, grizzled and a bit hunched, greeted Anne at the door—a different servant had greeted her last time she visited—and ushered her to the parlor where Mary was lying on the faded sofa. The once elegant furniture had been gradually growing shabby under the influence of four summers and two children—a point Mary oft bemoaned. But the white plastered walls and numerous windows made the room open and bright. Rambling roses blooming near the open windows perfumed the warm breezes cavorting through the chamber, playing amongst the bric-a-brac on the shelves near the fireplace and the blocks and tin soldiers left strewn on the floor.

"So, you are come at last! I began to think I should never see you. I am so ill I can hardly speak. I have not seen a creature the whole morning!" Mary, lying on the couch in a slightly tattered morning gown and mobcap, flung her arm over her eyes and moaned softly. She did tend toward the dramatic.

"I am sorry to find you unwell." Anne hurried to her side. What an enigma was Mary. While well and properly attended to, she had great good humor and excellent spirits. Any indisposition though—real or imagined—sunk her completely. Having inherited a considerable share of the Elliot self-importance left her very prone to fancying herself neglected, ill-used, and indisposed.

"I do not think I ever was so ill in my life as I have been all this morning; very unfit to be left alone, I am sure. Suppose I were to be seized in some dreadful way, and not able to ring the bell!" Mary pushed herself up to sit and look at Anne with exactly the same long-suffering expression she usually wore. Yet, there was something different, but what? Oh, Mary heard dragons now, that was the difference! "So, I see Lady Russell did not come to call with you. I do not think she has been in this house three times this summer."

Anne winced. How nice to know her company was already insufficient for Mary's entertainment. "Lady Russell has been away much of the summer and is traveling even now. How is Charles?"

"Charles is out shooting. He would go, though I told him how ill I was. He said he should not stay out long; but he has never come back, and now it is almost one. I assure you, I have not seen a soul this whole long morning." Mary fell back into her many cushions. One tumbled to the floor, unnoticed for now. Surely Mary would find reason to complain about it soon.

"And how are the little boys?"

"They are so unmanageable that they do me more harm than good, so Jemima has them now. Little Charles does not mind a word I say, and Walter is growing quite as bad."

"Well, you will soon be better now." Anne bit back words of advice and tucked a lap rug snugly over Mary's lap. "You know I always cure you when I come. How are your neighbors at the Great House?"

"I can give you no account of them. I have not seen one of them today, except Mr. Musgrove, who just stopped and spoke through the window, but without even getting off his horse. Though I told him how ill I was, not one of them have been near me. It did not happen to suit the Misses Musgrove, I suppose. Oh! Anne, I am so very unwell! It was quite unkind of you not to come earlier."

Anne forced a smile—an effort far more difficult than it should have been. "My dear Mary, I have really been so busy, have had so much to do, that I could not very conveniently have left Kellynch sooner."

"What can you possibly have to do? Of course, as a wife and mother, I—"

"A great many things, I assure you. I have been making a catalogue of father's books and pictures. I have been several times with the gardener, trying to make him understand which of Elizabeth's plants are for Lady Russell. I have had all my own little concerns to arrange, books and music to divide, going to almost every house in the parish, as a sort of take-leave on behalf of the family." Best leave out all the discussions with Shelby concerning dragon matters at Kellynch.

"I suppose that is something, but I am still quite put out." Mary sat up straight and glowered at Anne. "But that is no reason to be a rude hostess, I suppose." She heaved herself up from the couch and dusted off her skirts.

"Are you certain you are well enough to be about?" Anne stood. Hopefully Mary would not fall into some sort of swoon. Was it wrong to consider not even trying to break her fall if she did? There was, after all, a pillow already on the floor, perhaps she could swoon toward that.

Gracious that was unkind! What had come over her?

Mary shuffled toward a tired flower arrangement on a small round table near the front wall and plucked at it. "I suppose you would not like to call at the Great House before they have been to see you."

"I have not the smallest objection on that account." Actually, the Great House would be a relief and an excellent opportunity to thank Mrs. Musgrove for her thoughtfulness. "I should never think of standing on such ceremony with people I know so well as the Musgroves."

"As you will. I understand though, according to the books Charles has been making me read, I should probably introduce you to Uppercross first."

"When did you begin hearing dragons?"

"Two years ago, when our second son was born. I am told it happens that way sometimes. This sort of thing always happens to me, that is always the way for unfortunates." She glanced over her shoulder, that dissatisfied sort of look in her eye. "I am also told that there is some sort of dragon at Kellynch, too."

"I should like to meet Uppercross. And yes, there are a number of dragons at Kellynch." Best not mention about Lady Russell right now.

"Really, I had no idea." Mary shrugged and shuffled toward the door. "But then again I suppose as the seat of a baronet it should have more than Uppercross."

Another point that was not worth going into.

"Come along. The lair is not far from here, though I assure you I go there as rarely as I possibly can. I do not like to be associated with that dusty, smelly pace. I am quite convinced the creature is a freeloader and takes far more than that his appointed share whenever he can. Loathsome, low animal."

Was there a single Elliot, besides herself, that did not despise dragons? Anne pinched the bridge of her nose.

"We can get the chore over with, and then you might sit a bit at the Great House. I am sure they will welcome you warmly there." Would Mary be happier if Anne were not welcome? Something in her tone suggested she might.

Mary found a shawl to wrap around her shoulders, muttering all the while about how the walk probably would do her little good and might just leave her very ill indeed. That was probably a hint that she expected Anne to entertain her for the remainder of the day. Not unexpected; so much so, that it was hardly even annoying.

They picked their way through cool, thick woods with large overhanging hardwoods reminiscent of those that contained Kellynch's lair, though it smelt distinctly different, mustier with a touch of pepperiness. Did large dragons in general favor the same sort of places? Nothing in the books she had read suggested so, but then again, Blue Order books rarely discussed those sorts of details. Perhaps the Dragon Sage would know.

Or perhaps Mr. Musgrove. He was a Dragon Keeper. It would be nice to converse face to face with another Dragon Keeper. Odd, how in all their discourse through the years they had never talked about the dragons. Should that not have been a major topic of conversation? Did Mr. Musgrove not realize she could hear dragons? If Charles had not told him, how would he have known?

It was not as though Charles still resented her. He had accepted her rejection of his offer on the basis of the dragon estates easily enough, but they had never discussed Dragon Keeping. Would not something so important have come up in conversation? But then again, Father's aversion to dragons could easily have dissuaded such topics.

"There, look just there." Mary pointed into a dark hillside.

The shadows hid it, but there, covered by a curtain of vines, was the rough cave opening, eight, perhaps nine feet high and of similar, though irregular width.

Mary cupped her hands around her mouth and called, "Laird Uppercross, I have brought you company." She turned to Anne. "There, it is done. If he comes, he comes and if he does not, then we may call this disagreeable duty accomplished and be on about our visit to the Great House."

The hillside rumbled, a little like thunder was coming from within—and that smell! Gah! Anne's eyes watered. Kellynch's lair smelt similar, musky and acrid, but not nearly so pungent as this.

Mary blinked rapidly and pulled a handkerchief from her sleeve.

"Approach." A deep rumbling voice echoed from the dark opening.

Mary rolled her eyes, but Anne forced herself to step forward. The Pendragon Accords kept dragons from harming people, except in self-defense. Had Lady Russell's attestation to the power of that treaty not been so persuasive, running would have been the only sensible option.

"Closer." The voice, aside from being loud and powerful, was not actually unfriendly. There was actually a warm, approachable quality to it.

Anne squinted into the dark opening. "Pray, may I see you?"

"Has Mary prepared you?"

"Prepared me? I do not understand."

A huff and thumping sounded very much like a dragon-sized sigh and impatient foot or tail tapping—did dragons sigh? "Of course, she did not. I did ask you to do so, Mary. Have you forgotten?"

Mary pressed her handkerchief to her face. "It is only Anne. I do not see the need for any fuss and bother on her account. She has been to Uppercross so many times."

"But she has not met me. Do you not remember your first sight of me?"

Mary swallowed hard and took half a step back. "I have not the constitution for such things. Even now your smell—"

Anne edged in front of Mary. "While I have only seen him sleeping, I have seen Kellynch. You will not be the first large dragon I have seen."

"That is some improvement. Prepare yourself, though. I am as tall as two men and a small child atop one another. My tail is as long as a tall man and my wings extend as wide as I am tall."

He was a talkative beast, not like the creatures Lady Russell had described. "Tell me of your color."

"Something not quite green and not quite brown, I should think. I could do with a good brushing and oiling I am sure." He grumbled and stomped.

"Yes, yes, I will be sure to take that intelligence to the Great House when we are next there." Mary muttered something disagreeable under her breath.

"And you should know, I am not the venomous variety of wyvern. I am told my fangs are quite notable, but there is no venom there."

Anne gulped. There were venomous wyverns? "You are most gracious to alleviate my concerns."

"I know there are some who worry about such things." He did not seem to approve.

"Well what else can one think when the stench is so thick?" Mary gagged and coughed.

"Now that you have made our introduction, perhaps you would like to return to the cottage?" Anne glanced over her shoulder.

"I am feeling quite drained. That is a good idea." Mary turned and hurried away. She probably did not realize she had never actually made an introduction.

Heavy footfalls shook the ground under her feet. "It is best this way. She does not like me very well, which is a great shame, as I am actually quite likeable." The curtain of vines parted and a huge, square head poked through.

Fangs! Oh, the fangs! He was quite right about

those.

"As I said, I am not venomous, and since you are not a sheep, you have nothing to fear from my fangs." He cocked his head in such a friendly way, it was difficult not to laugh—but Lady Russell had warned her that dragons—especially large ones—did not like to be laughed at.

"Pray excuse my sister—"

"I know, I well know. She has been here for four years now, remember?" His entire body came into view as he shook away the vines trailing over him.

Though he had told her his size, nothing could quite prepare one for the reality of conversing with such a creature. Not even imagining conversations with Kellynch.

"Since I must introduce myself—and I do beg you to forgive the rudeness of it all—" he dipped his head and shoulders in a sort of gentlemanly bow. "I am Uppercross."

His green-brown scales were dusty and seemed a bit dry—no wonder he wanted brushing and oiling. All over he was thick and square, and seemed to be a bit pot-bellied, rather like Mr. Musgrove. Great, gold eyes lit his face, wide and—was it possible?—friendly. Could a face sporting fangs twice the length of her hand perched above a body armed with talons as long and sharp as daggers be friendly?

Oddly enough, it seemed possible.

"And I am Anne Elliot." She curtsied—was that the correct thing to do? How else did one address a major dragon?

"So, you are the new Keeper to Kellynch." He sat back on his haunches with a bit of a thump and a swirling of dust and studied her, turning his enormous head this way and that.

Anne gasped and pressed her hand to her chest. No! Pray not!

"You did not really think such news would stay quiet for very long?"

"I had hoped that it had not gone beyond our parlor."

He snorted, spraying a bit of slimy spittle. A sort of draconic laugh perhaps?

"You are naïve, my dear, quite naïve. A fairy dragon—they have superb hearing by the way—was the first to take note. Then another heard it as you and Lady Russell were discussing the matter. When two fairy dragons agree on having heard a thing, then it is considered done and true."

Anne gasped and searched for something to lean against.

"You do not seem pleased. I cannot imagine why not. I think it is a very good thing indeed." He shoved a large rock toward her.

She sat down just before her knees gave way. "You do not think well of my Father?"

This time he chuckled—there was no mistaking that sound. "Do you think he made a good Dragon Keeper?"

"It is unseemly to criticize one's own father."

"Dragons are hardly seemly creatures." That seemed something she ought to remember. "The Elliots have not historically been among those considered to excel in the art of Dragon Keeping." The tip of Uppercross' tail flicked against the ground.

"I imagine you are putting it gently so as not to overwhelm my delicate sensibilities?"

"It seemed appropriate to try." Did dragons smile?

It seemed Uppercross did.

"You are very gracious to me. I know it is not considered good form to ask a favor so early in an acquaintance, but I fear I have little alternative. Lady Russell has gone off—"

"In a huff?" His rumble sounded somewhat like laughter.

"She was rather annoyed with me, but she said she had some issues to investigate, some suspicions, but no conclusions, not yet. That being the case, I have no one to turn to for advice regarding Kellynch and what I am told is his imminent awakening."

"You have spoken with Shelby, I suppose?"

"He told me you had assisted with Kellynch's last awakening."

"Indeed, I did. It is rather a long story, so be a good Keeper and duck into the lair, there right at the entrance, and fetch that large brush there. The one with the long handle. I could use a good brushing whilst I talk."

"I have never brushed a dragon before. I hardly know what to do." Anne headed toward the lair.

"Excellent. Then I can teach you how to do it properly. Get on now." Uppercross stretched out full length, like a pug stretched out on a cool tile floor, though pugs were not over twenty feet long nose to tail, with a wingspan to match. Gracious there was a great deal of him!

Anne found a stiff broom just inside the cavern and brought it to him.

"Yes, excellent. Now, begin at my spine ridge and brush in the direction of my scales, not against them—that is quite uncomfortable. A few old ones will come loose, no doubt. Gather those up and keep them. I am told they make an excellent skin lotion for ladies. I am sure you will find a formula written down for it somewhere amongst my Keeper's books. Only the eldest son seems able to hear, though, so you must not share the new secret of your beauty with the young ladies of the house." He snorted a bit of a chuckle that raised a cloud of dust.

"About Kellynch?" Anne stood on tip toes to reach his spinal ridge.

"So, yes, where to begin. Perhaps at the beginning. Through the charter as set forth in the Accords, your family was granted the seat at Kellynch and the responsibilities for the dragon of the same name. Now you do understand the lands belong solely to the dragon, not the Keepers, do you not?"

"The finer points of that are still a bit unclear to me."

"That is why dragon estates cannot be sold except by the direct involvement of the Blue Order. That is also why debt is so very dangerous to Dragon Keeps. A dragon will never permit parcels of his land to be sold away."

She grimaced. So Uppercross knew of their trials as well. Of course, he did—no doubt every fairy dragon within miles of the Kellynch estate would have heard the uproar that caused.

"A Keeper is permitted to live on and use the land, but has responsibilities to the dragon. The Keeper—who as you now know, may be a woman—must ensure all the dragon's needs are met. A dragon must have ready access to food—and of their desired type—and the ability to hunt it if hunting is important to that dragon. I myself would rather not bother with such things. Sheep and geese are delivered to my cavern at regular intervals by a shepherding drake like Shelby, employed specifically for the purpose. She persuades the shepherds to ignore the change to the size of the flocks, you see."

"Are there many minor dragons at Uppercross? Mary did not seem to think so." Anne shook a few loose scales off the broom. They clinked softly as they hit the ground.

"There are only a few who are part of my Keep. A few wild ones always roam about. Fairy dragons, just a few; a cockatrice that most think is a hawk, a small, peevish fellow who quite dislikes that you permit Jet on your estate, says he is quite the bully—all of my dragons say the same and are quite pleased when Jet goes off on those long jaunts away he is so fond of; we really do need to have a bit of a chat about him, but in any case—a few garden wyrms who do an excellent job keeping down the vermin in the garden; and a water wyrm, a very small one, in the local pond.

"They keep their distance from men—you might never see them. That is why Mary is unaware of their presence. If a dragon is not hatched in the presence of warm-bloods, then it never really learns to tolerate their presence. Not that your sister would tolerate their presence, but I digress. Major dragons are never permitted to hatch that way though. They are far too dangerous to be allowed wild. But you already know that."

She did, but the reminder was welcome nonetheless.

"Back to Kellynch. The relations between the Elliot family and Kellynch seemed to suffer its first break on the matter of his hoard. Not only must a Keeper see a dragon has sufficient food, but a dragon's hoard must also be supplied. Now, not all of us are hoarders for all our lives. It is something that is done to attract a mate, but after that is accomplished, for most of us, the compulsion goes away and that is, as it were, that. I am proud to say I am not controlled by such things. I have a few baubles I enjoy keeping about. You might laugh, but I actually have a collection of brass candlesticks." He glanced at her over his shoulder.

Anne chuckled. Did he keep his lair lit with them? How would he manage not to knock them over?

"Yes, they are amusing things, but I do not hoard them."

"What is the difference?"

"Hoarding is like a hunger that becomes more and more intense, or so I am told. A dragon must sate that hunger or risk a sort of madness that will induce him to even violate the Accords in order to acquire what he hoards. For those who do not outgrow the hoarding urge, it can be a very terrible, controlling thing. That is why the hoards are carefully spelled out in the Accords both in the nature of the hoard and the amounts that must be provided."

"I do not understand. Little Beebalm in the garden hoards honey—the Order cannot have got involved with her."

"No, minor dragons have no one to provide their hoards for them, so they must supply them themselves. Most inherit a hoard from a predecessor, and it is something fairly easily accessible. Not so with major dragons. In fact, that was one of the problems that the Accords had to resolve. Too many dragons hoarding valuable items that Keepers could not afford."

"I see how that could be a problem." Anne paused

in her brushing, panting and wiping sweat from her brow with her sleeve.

"So much so that only the largest of the firedrakes are permitted to hoard gold or gems or such things. A Keeper could easily be driven to ruin with uncontrolled hoarding. The lesser major dragons must content themselves with other items. The wyvern Longbourn hoards salt."

Salt? Who would have thought? "What happens if a dragon is not provided with his hoard?"

"It depends. An action can be lodged in the Blue Order court and handled through legal channels. A dragon could arrange for a change of Keeper, through legal or less legal means."

Anne cringed.

"But Kellynch did not want to be bothered with any of that when his previous Keeper—or was it the one before that?— did not adequately supply his hoard. He decided to hibernate and wait for a better Keeper to take the estate and call for an accounting at that time. Unfortunately, that did not happen the last time he awoke, so he returned to his hibernation."

"How long has he been sleeping?"

"A dragon of Kellynch's size and kind can hibernate for fifty years at a time. After that, Kellynch must awaken and fully sate his hunger, manage his affairs, and ideally, decide he is ready to rejoin dragon society. This is his second successive hibernation. After he is introduced to you, though, I think he will decide it is time to resolve the issues and return to the social order. That will happen quite soon, I think, though I would have thought there would have been more clear signs of it by now."

"I am most sensitive to the compliment meant toward myself, but I know little about Dragon Keeping and doubt I could make him very happy at all. Things are very complicated, I fear. Lady Russell and I went to his hoard and it is in an awful state. I fear someone before us found and plundered it—"

"Plundered his hoard?" Uppercross nearly knocked her over in his haste to sit upright. "Oh, that is a very bad, a very dangerous thing indeed, far worse than it not being added to."

She backed up until she leaned against the rockface. "I have already looked into what it would take to replenish it just to where it was under my grandfather, and pray believe me when I say it will be quite impossible in the near term."

"Is that why your father has left for Bath? On Lady Russell's recommendation?"

"I thought it a sensible plan."

"After a fashion, I suppose it is, but insufficient to be sure. I suppose she thinks she will be able to work on him and alleviate his wrath." His huge tail thumped hard against the ground.

"She said something of the sort."

"She has no idea. The dear creature is completely out of her depth. As his Watcher, he will hold her responsible for what has happened and is within his right to eat her for her failure."

"Eat her! That is … is … barbaric!" She slid to the ground and wrapped her arms around her knees.

"Dragon justice often is so. She may well know that and not return at all. I would not have that happen, though, she is an interesting sort of bird."

"What is to be done? Is there anything to be done?"

"That is a very good question. I for one do not

want to see that sort of unrest anywhere in England, but most especially so nearby. I suppose there is nothing else to be done for it." He rose, shaking his wings into place. "Pray tell my Keeper I am for London immediately. I will seek advice from the Blue Order and the Dragon Sage on the matter. I shall have to take the tunnels there, that will take me a day and a half at best. The moon is waning now; if I am lucky and there is no moon, I might be able to fly back which I could manage in a single night. Then it will take some time there. I expect I will be gone a week, then. You may tell my Keeper that, so he will not worry. He does not like it if I disappear without telling him such things."

"I will convey your message. Thank you for your help. I am deeply indebted to you."

"Perhaps not nearly so much as we will be indebted to you for becoming his Keeper." Uppercross disappeared into his cavern.

Whatever did he mean by that and why did it sound so ominous?

8
Chapter

August 15, 1814

LACONIA WOUND HIMSELF around Wentworth's feet as he walked the stony street to the Blue Order office in Lyme. People bustled about, with all the accompanying noise that did nothing so much as remind one that he was no longer at sea and the master of his own ship. Sunny, bordering on hot, the salty sea breeze clipped the edge off the heat and left the shadows beside the buildings notably cooler, almost chilly. A number of people stopped and stared at the sight, not so much because he was walking with a tatzelwurm, but rather because they saw Laconia as an enormous cat, weaving in and out through his strides.

Though it looked like a difficult, intricate dance, Laconia had been doing it since he was a wyrmling. It had become more difficult as he had grown into a substantial creature, nearly three stones in weight with height and length to match, but Laconia insisted. While he was well able to protect himself now, the scars of his hatching trauma still plagued him. Laconia never felt very comfortable in unfamiliar places, around unfamiliar people—he rarely got much more than an arm's length away from Wentworth in such situations.

Like most offices of the Blue Order, this one was entirely indistinguishable from the ordinary buildings on either side of it. Far smaller than the great office in London where Wentworth was first presented to and accepted by the Order, this one appeared little different from the first-rate townhouses on either side of it. Four-stories tall, white brick front with black wrought-iron work, balanced, symmetrical windows on either side, with curtains drawn to block the view from the street. Beneath would be several stories of basement levels with connections to the dragon tunnels that passed through all of England.

The corner of his lips turned up. How surprised the other residents would be to learn what was really going on in the house or that the unusual number of large birds of prey perched along the roof were a cockatrice guard company. Frankly, he still was, and he had known about it for years.

Brass door knockers—drake's heads holding large rings—rose from the great blue doors. That was how one could always tell a Blue Order establishment; the doors were this particular shade of blue. Apparently, the color was made especially for the Order. Order members in the colorman's guilds controlled it quite carefully, so it might only be sold for use on Blue Order buildings. Naturally they had the help of a few conveniently placed companion dragons to convince stubborn customers that green was really a most fashionable color.

He twisted the signet ring on his left little finger— now that he was beached, it was appropriate he wore it. Order members liked to be able to identify one another.

Wentworth rapped on the door. A blue liveried butler, tall, serious, and foreboding opened it, stepping slightly to the right to completely fill up the doorway and block the entry.

"Mrrrow." Laconia looked up at him, sniffing the air, tail lashing around Wentworth's ankle.

The man's eyes widened just a bit, but he held his ground until Wentworth lifted his left hand and his ring—perhaps a mite too close to the butler's face.

"Admiral Easterly is expecting us." Wentworth stepped inside, deftly dodging Laconia's tight weaving. He stooped to lift Laconia and carry him the rest of the way. His long body trembled with loud purrs. Poor creature was truly anxious.

The butler shut the door behind them. "Come this way."

They followed him into a large receiving room, facing the mews. Two large windows, sheer white drapes obscuring the view, lined the far wall. It smelt a mite musty, as though the windows had not been open in quite some time. Many places seemed to smell musty these days. Was it just that all buildings smelt that way when one was accustomed to open air? White paper hangings with Order-blue vines or lines or whatever they were called, covered the walls. The occasional pastel fairy dragon peeked around the vines here and there, probably to make it all more interesting, but utterly unrealistic. Had the artist ever seen what the creatures actually looked like? What was wrong with a simple plain color, or even white?

Two tall, oaken bookcases, showcasing books published by the Order, stood proudly flanking the fireplace opposite the windows while a third filled up the wall between the windows. A slightly worn tea table and several similarly serviceable card tables served as focal points for several clusters of lyre-back chairs near the far wall. Couches, covered in something rusty-colored, with dragon-claw-and-ball feet filled up the rest of the space. The whole effect was rather welcoming, and blissfully quiet. The only other occupants were two brown minor drakes wearing Order livery badges, studying a tome at a table near the windows.

"Wait here, please. The Admiral will receive you shortly." The butler bowed and strode out.

Wentworth took Laconia to a small couch bathed in the sunbeam from the window opposite the drakes. He sat and helped Laconia arrange himself on his lap. "Are you well?"

Laconia grumbled, which to most sounded like a growl. But once one heard Laconia truly growl, one never mistook one for the other again. "I am fine."

Wentworth stroked his silky black fur and scratched behind his ears. "I know the place smells very odd, but you will grow used to it."

"That is easy for you to say. You have never had a smell warn you a larger dragon was about to try and make you his breakfast."

"That was quite the interesting morning, was it not? I would have been consumed right along with you. I do quite remember how that feels." Perhaps Croft was right, he should write that adventure as a monograph on the territorial nature of sea drakes and submit it to the Order for publication. It was quite the story.

Laconia pressed his cheek into Wentworth's hand. "But you did not smell it coming." His tail thumped dully against the cushions as he opened his mouth and flicked his forked tongue in the air.

"You are not accustomed to the smells of land. Anything that does not reek of salt air smells wrong to you."

"While I much prefer that smell, I do not like all these concocted scents that warm-bloods wear. They are offensive."

"As is the term warm-blood—when used by a dragon."

"When they do not offend my olfaction—"

"Ahh, Captain Wentworth!" Admiral Easterly strode in. Tall and broad chested, with a shock of prematurely white hair, he seemed confident and easy here. How odd the buff jacket and navy-blue breeches looked on him, but there was no reason to expect him to be in uniform now while he was doing the Order's business, not the Navy's. "I am pleased to see you again." He bowed to Laconia and extended his hand and allowed Laconia to sniff his fingers.

Laconia flicked his tongue against Easterly's hand. Some of the tension left his shoulders and he rubbed his cheek against Easterly's palm.

"You have become quite the legend in the Navy—the luckiest ship's cat you are called. We could have done with a dozen more like you finding prize ships out there."

"Then why assign so many dragon-deaf as captains?"

Wentworth and Easterly chuckled.

"One can only work with what one has. Come back to my office." Easterly led them upstairs to a room that faced the mews.

The office was small by the standards of landed accommodations, but spacious to any ship's captain. Stark white walls, bare as the clean and polished wood floor; their footsteps echoing off both. Tidy and efficient. Shelves near the window held a sextant, a telescope and books on navigation and nautical dragons—oh! There was one he had not read: *Leviathans, Hippocampi, Krakens and Marine Wyrms: The myths and actualities of the large dragons of the near seas, including the West Indies.*

"Might I borrow that?" Wentworth pointed to the volume.

In a single movement, Easterly pulled the book from the shelf, handed it to Wentworth and pointed to a chair near the worn, dark oak desk that occupied the center of the narrow room. "Ever hungry for learning, aren't you! Of course, you can. In fact, I would even recommend it, given what I have to talk with you about. Sit, sit, be comfortable." He pointed to a cushion on his desk still bearing bits of fur and several scales from its most recent occupant—probably another tatzelwurm. "I would like you to be part of the discussion, Laconia."

Laconia chirruped a sound of approval. Coiling his tail to use like a spring, he launched himself to the desktop. He circled the pillow, sniffing it deeply, fanged jaws half-open and eyes a little glazed. What—rather who—had been there before?

"Do not worry, she does not mind sharing this particular perch. Mina is resigned that my office is a public place."

"I did not know you had a Friend once again." Wentworth drew the wooden armchair close to the dragon pillow and sat down.

"She befriended me when her previous Friend died, another old Admiral. She likes sea-faring men, after they have retired. Mina does not like to sail herself." Easterly looked over his shoulder toward the bookcase.

A fluffy grey head peeked out from behind the bookcase. "Meyrrrrow." High and feminine, it was almost as though she spoke with an accent.

"Pray come out and be introduced."

Mina slither-crept into the light and looked up at Easterly. Perhaps only half Laconia's size, she seemed small, though by feline standards she was certainly substantial. Long and lithe, the silver fur of her front, feline half blended seamlessly into gleaming silver scales on her serpentine tail. Stars above, she was a gorgeous creature. Intelligent deep blue eyes stared up at him, searching his character, his worthiness to be an acquaintance—or at least it looked very much that way.

Laconia chirruped at her. She regarded him a moment, eyes growing very large. Her jaw opened slightly; her fangs evident as she breathed deep. "Mrr-roww!" She sprang to the desk near Easterly.

"Mina, may I present Laconia and Wentworth, Friend of Laconia."

Wentworth bowed from his shoulders to Mina and Laconia dipped his head slightly, but not below Mina's. Ah, yes, dominance, it was always dominance with dragons.

She regarded Wentworth a moment longer, then turned to Laconia. She leaned toward him and sniffed rapidly. Laconia mirrored her. He stepped forward to sniff her neck. When she admitted the attention, he slithered closer, drawing his nose down her entire length as she did the same for him, flowing in a large draconic circle on the desktop. The circle stopped, and she ducked under him, rubbing the top of her head against his belly. He purred and pressed down a mite as though to embrace her as she did.

She slithered around to face him. Wide eyed and blinking, was it possible for a tatzelwurm to be drunk? Dragon thunder! Laconia wore the same expression.

"Yourrr visit is welcome." She pressed her cheek to Laconia's.

Laconia licked her face and rubbed his cheek against hers. "Your scent … is right." He purred and sighed and licked his lips.

She purred and hopped on the pillow, curling into a dainty ball with her chin resting coyly on her tail. Laconia followed, curling around her and resting his chin on her shoulder. By Jove, that was an awfully friendly arrangement.

Easterly lifted his eyebrows and shrugged.

"Your message suggested an issue of some urgency." Wentworth tried not to stare at the tatzelwurm knot beside him, but their very loud purring made it difficult.

"Yes, yes indeed." Easterly tugged his jacket straight and sat down. "I am not sorry to hear you have been beached for the foreseeable future. I know that is anathema to many Captains, but truly, we need men like you for the Order."

"Like me?" So many things that could mean, and not all of them complimentary.

"Proven dragon-hearing men who can follow orders, who can manage themselves in a crisis, and make good decisions on their own. Exactly what the Navy has trained you for."

Laconia's ears pricked, and he fixed his eyes on Easterly, wrapping his tail a little tighter around Mina.

"What is happening?"

"Where dragons are concerned, there are always a great many things happening. But, since the revolution in France and most recently the war with Napoleon has affected the continental dragons, times are especially turbulent."

"What has that to do with English dragons?" Wentworth crossed his arms and leaned in, heart beating faster. Damn battle reflexes kicking in.

The tip of Laconia's tail twitched and his forked tongue flicked. He felt it, too.

"Major dragons along the coast, both land and the few marine ones we have relations with, have been on edge watching for signs of invasion. I will tell you privately, it is a good thing that never happened. The Pendragon Accords were never written to consider the ramifications of an invading foreign army from the continent."

"Why not? The Romans—"

Easterly lifted open hands. "Yes, yes, just chalk it up to arrogance. It is a problem that is being addressed in London even now. A joint committee of dragons and Blue Order Officers, including representatives of both the Army and Navy, is attempting to draft new provisions to deal with the matter. But in the meantime, we must soothe ruffled scales as it were, and I need Dragon Mates like you to do it."

"Whose scales are ruffled?" Laconia's tail twitched faster.

"Have you met Cornwall?"

"The Prince Regent or the firedrake?" Prickles started at Wentworth's scalp and raced down every limb.

"Either, both? They are not exactly dissimilar." The admiral snorted. "Of course, I never said such a thing."

"Of course not," Wentworth muttered.

"In any case, we have received a number of complaints from minor dragons of the Cornwall Keep. Cornwall has been unusually restive of late. They fear there is something seriously the matter and, worse still, Cornwall is contemplating handling the matter himself. It is rarely a good idea to permit major dragons to manage affairs on their terms."

"Is that not what the Accords are for?" Blood roared in Wentworth's ears. He fought the urge to spring to his feet.

"It is precisely why there are Keepers assigned to the major dragons, charged with handling issues for the dragons. While I have known a great many hotheaded and stubborn men, I have yet to meet one who rivals the amount of damage an angry dragon can cause."

"Then why is the Prince Regent not managing the matter?"

Easterly glowered.

That had been a stupid question.

"The key issue here is that a particular kind of diplomacy is needed—"

"You think Laconia and I are suited for that?"

Wentworth sneaked a quick glance at Laconia.

"I need a man who has had dealings with nautical dragons, as the matter involves sea hold property."

Now he had to move! Wentworth jumped up and paced the length of the far too short room. "Cornwall is a fire drake—a land dragon. You mean to tell me now that land dragons have sea holdings?"

"That is the heart of the current debate. Here." Easterly plucked a thin red leather-bound volume—a monograph perhaps—off the shelf and handed it to Wentworth as he strode past. *Determining the Boundaries of Major Dragon Holdings: The Implications and Complications of Instinctive Dragon Territorial Determinations Intersecting with Human Traditions and Law.*

Damn, that looked complicated.

"Unfortunately, the legal codes have not been rendered very clearly. In the current situation, I am not even certain Blue Order codes cover the situation."

"And what precisely is the situation." Wentworth fell into his seat with a dull thud.

"Cornwall has laid claim to something off his coast that we are not even sure exists." Easterly pressed his temples hard.

"So, the dragon might be mad?"

"Some have entertained that possibility."

"You want us to go and confront a fire drake—a royal firedrake—who may well be touched in the head—as mad as the king himself?" Wentworth dropped the monograph on the desk.

Mina started; Laconia glared at him.

"In short, yes. And, the Prince Regent might also be very interested in the matter, should the news reach him directly."

"The Prince does not know the nature of the situation?"

"He has not informed us of any problem and the Order has not contacted him regarding the complaints—yet."

"You must be joking? That amounts to keeping secrets from the crown!" Wentworth threw his head back and huffed. "I might be beached, but I am hardly dicked in the nob myself, and I am quite certain Laconia—"

"We have dealt with worse." Laconia lifted his head slightly, glancing from Easterly to Wentworth. "You recall that sea drake who tried to refuse to grant us passage through her territory? She had an entire battalion of sea drakes and marine wyrms ready to do battle for the territory."

"What has that to do with—"

"Or the herd of hippocampi who thought you violated their fishing ground?"

"Again, what has that to do—"

Laconia stood and walked across the desk to look Wentworth in the eye. "What else are you going to do until you find a mate?"

Wentworth's jaw dropped and he sputtered. "Dragon's blood and sea foam!"

"You will mind your language around my mate." Laconia glanced back at Mina and chirruped.

"Your mate?" Wentworth and Easterly said simultaneously.

"Yes." The tatzelwurms hissed.

"You see, finding a mate is not so difficult a matter to resolve." He curled around her again, running his nose along her silky silver fur. "Had you the wherewithal to find your own, you would not be at loose ends right now. You must have a way of keeping yourself occupied until …"

Wentworth slapped his forehead. "How do you intend for us to get to Cornwall?"

9
Chapter

August 16, 1814

THE NEXT MORNING, Anne saw Charles off from the morning room. He was going fishing, or at least he claimed to be. Who really knew what that gentleman might be up to during the day—or so Mary complained. Was it wrong to be glad Mary retreated back to her bed with a sick headache after Charles' departure? Not glad about the headache to be sure, but for the moments of peace and quiet that followed.

The little square morning room boasted ample windows on the north and east sides, making it bright and inviting, in a vaguely chilly sort of way. Mary wanted to paper the white walls with something floral and fashionable, but so far, the desire had not amounted to any action. All told, that was probably for the best. It would be a shame to so alter the most appealing aspect of the space. The round, worn table was too big for the room and if the seats nearest the door were taken, the dance required to reach an open seat was less than elegant. The old, off-level sideboard tucked into the corner between the windows did nothing to improve the situation. On the contrary, Anne sported what would surely become a colorful bruise in the center of her back from trying to dodge around it.

A blue and white platter of cold meat sat in the center of the table—ham perhaps? It was difficult to tell—Mary's cook was new and still had much to learn. The coffee was tepid and the buns dry, day old at least. Anne slathered butter on a bit of crumbly bread and popped it into her mouth before the bun could fall apart entirely. Butter definitely helped.

Best finish quickly, there were so many things yet to be done today. Two houses in the parish should be called upon; she had not taken leave of them yet. And there was a message from Uppercross to deliver to his Keeper. Mr. Shepherd should be consulted regarding the tenants—she pressed her temples. Did they hear dragons? How complicated this could become and only Shelby remained to help—

"Miss Elliot?" A young girl—a scullery maid by the look of her, appeared at the window. "The master, Mr. Musgrove, he said to give you this." She handed Anne a folded note through the open window. "He said to make sure you read it straight away, Miss."

Anne unfolded it. "I shall do so immediately. You may tell him so."

The girl curtsied and hurried away.

Pray come see me in the morning room~CM

Odd, but not inconvenient. She tucked her light blue shawl around her shoulders—the Great House could be chilly and her yellow muslin gown provided little buffer against that—and headed for the Great House.

Louisa and Henrietta—Charles' jovial but dragon-deaf sisters greeted her in the spacious front hall with the warmth of sisters. At just twenty and nineteen, the girls had returned from school at Exeter with all the usual stock of accomplishments, and were now like thousands of other young ladies, living to be fashionable, happy, and merry. Their dress had every advantage, their faces were pretty, their spirits extremely good, their manner pleasant; they were of consequence at home, and favorites abroad. Truly they were the happiest creatures of her acquaintance even without the benefits of elegant and cultivated minds—one of Mary's favorite complaints about them. They each looped an arm in hers and ushered her through the dimly lit, paneled corridor to the morning room.

Twice the size of the cottage's morning room, with a long table, and narrow sideboards, one could move about the space with ease and grace. The southern windows did not provide as much light, but the painted yellow walls made the very most of it. A blue and white bowl of dainty yellow roses in the center of the table offered its perfume beside a rack of toast and two pots of what appeared to be berry jam. Watercolor portraits of the entire family, surely done by Henrietta and Louisa, lined the walls, each painting resembling someone just enough to be recognizable but not flattering. Such doting parents to go to the expense of framing each one!

Charles sat in the middle of the long side of the table, away from the door, a recently emptied plate before him. Charles? Given Mary's mood, it was difficult to blame him, but really, he was better than such subterfuge.

Mr. Musgrove set aside his newspaper and rose from his place near the windows. Everything about him was old-fashioned and comfortable: the cut of his suit, the style of his thinning hair, his rounded belly, even his manners. "Thank you, girls. Your harp awaits you. Run along now. And close the door behind you."

"Oh, Papa!" Henrietta and Louisa giggled and shut the door as they hurried off.

Charles stood and bowed from the shoulders. "Good morning, Anne." Guilt and a boyish pleading for secrecy filled his green eyes.

"Miss Anne! I am pleased to see you. Do sit down. I hope I did not startle you with my note this morning." Mr. Musgrove held out a chair for her near his own. "I was charged with relaying a message to you. I saw Mr. Shepherd whilst in the village this morning. He asked me if I would deliver this to you." He handed her a leather folio tied with a red ribbon.

"Thank you. I was very glad to receive your invitation as I have also been charged to bring a message to you. From Uppercross."

"Uppercross, really? You have already been introduced?" Charles's bushy eyebrows knitted into a solid line above his eyes.

"Mary took me to the lair and introduced me yesterday."

"She did not mention that to me," Charles grumbled somewhat under his breath.

Mr. Musgrove sat down and smoothed the table-cloth in front of him. "If Uppercross did not object, then I suppose I should not either. What was his message?"

Perhaps he should not be upset, but no doubt he was. Mary taking precedence once again. Thankfully, the Musgrove family did not class her with her sister. Anne quickly explained Uppercross's journey and the reasons for it.

"I see, I see. The situation is rather unusual, is it not? But we should not dwell upon it, not when there is a celebration to be made. Do get the sherry, will you Charles?"

"I am afraid I do not understand," Anne said.

"You are too modest. But we have heard quite reliably, have we not? You are the Keeper to Kellynch, now." Mr. Musgrove took the decanter from Charles and poured three crystal glasses. "We shall have a toast."

"I am not sure I understand the to-do. The matter seemed of little note to my father." She took a glass from Charles.

"I trust that you will forgive me for observing that your father has neither been fond of Dragon Keeping nor has he excelled in the business of it, thus Kellynch's hibernation. While a gracious solution to a difficult problem, it has not been without disadvantages, particularly for Uppercross who has managed much of Kellynch's business. But now, you will set it all to rights."

"Set it to rights?" Anne swallowed hard. "I am afraid I do not really know what that means or exactly what a Keeper does day to day. I have attended the concerns of the minor dragons on the estate, but as to

Kellynch—he is still quite a mystery to me."

Such a peculiar look Mr. Musgrove gave her as he set down his glass. "I am all agog."

Charles' lips wrinkled into a disapproving frown that he often used when annoyed with something Elliot related. "Perhaps those books ... shall I get them?"

"Yes, yes, that is a capital idea, a capital one." Mr. Musgrove tapped his fingers along the edge of his jaw. "I cannot say I am surprised, no it is entirely in Sir Walter's character, but it is disappointing that he would not have prepared you more thoroughly."

Charles waddled in, arms laded with heavy leather-bound tomes—eight at least. Mr. Musgrove jumped up, took several from the top of the stack, and set them on the table.

Charles dropped the rest near Anne, rattling the glasses and china on the table. "Here you go. The very books father used to teach me the regular duties associated with major dragons. I am sure they will help you very much indeed. Between what you can find in those books and Uppercross, you will have all you need to know."

"And you may have free reign in the Uppercross library any time you choose. There are several generations of dragon knowledge collected here." Mr. Musgrove patted the pile of books.

None of those titles looked familiar. So very much she did not know! Was it wrong to notice that neither of them offered to teach her anything himself? Probably. "Thank you, I very much appreciate it."

"This one in particular might be of great use right now." Mr. Musgrove freed a thick, dark red volume from the bottom of a stack. *The Non-resident Dragon*

Keeper: The correct manner in which a dragon estate might be occupied by non-Keepers and with special attention to the protocols and ceremonies necessary to respect the dragon territory.

Heavens, that looked very useful—and very intimidating.

A sharp rap at the door sounded. "Mr. Musgrove, are you free for a moment?" That was Mrs. Musgrove.

"Pray excuse me a moment." He shambled off.

Anne ran her fingers along the cover of the book. "Do you really think it will all be so easily made right, Charles?"

"Dragons can seem very complicated at first, I know. They certainly did when I was first learning. I do wish your father had been more attentive to both yours and Mary's educations in that regard. I know you did not come into your hearing until late, but still—ah well, no point in dwelling on that. But really, I have not found Uppercross so taxing. He is rather easy to deal with all told. Unlike my wife who I wish you could persuade not to be always fancying herself ill."

They chatted a few moments more. Anne excused herself and extracted Charles's promise to bring the rest of the books to her room at the cottage in exchange for her promise to keep his secret from Mary. She waved to Henrietta and Louisa as they practiced harp and pianoforte in the drawing room, and slipped out of the front door.

A sunbeam caught her just outside the door and she pressed the heavy tome to her chest. Secrets, so very many secrets. Was this what it meant to be acquainted with dragons? Nothing was what it seemed, and everyone had some sort of secret. Was this the sort of life she wanted to live? Did she even have a choice? She forced her feet to move.

Several songbirds—yes, they were birds, not fairy dragons—twittered from tall hardwoods near the path to the cottage. Was it wrong to be relieved something still remained exactly as it seemed? A gentle warm breeze rattled the branches above and sent a stray leaf falling gently to the red folio atop the darker red book. The message from Mr. Shepherd. How had she forgotten that?

She opened the folio and withdrew a neatly penned message.

How unusual. The tenants, the Crofts, had arrived two days ago, and he was persuaded—how interesting he chose that particular word—to permit them to take possession of Kellynch since the family had already vacated.

How irregular, very irregular. And a little suspicious.

The admiral and his wife are all that is amiable and gracious. I am sure they would take no offense if you, Miss Anne, were to call upon them before their previously agreed upon possession date at Michaelmas.

How was one to take such a suggestion?

By doing as she was asked. After she had time to read her book.

But even that volume would offer her little guidance on how she was to face the Crofts and all that they reminded her of.

August 20, 1814

Several days later, Anne sipped a cup of fragrant tea and nibbled a slice of half burnt toast, alone, at the too-large round breakfast table, quietly celebrating her success at avoiding another bruise from the corner of the sideboard. It helped that she had not been carrying Mr. Musgrove's book into the morning room as she had the last several days. The tome had proven instructional, though overwhelming, and intimidating just as she feared. So many protocols for the letting of the estate, so many particulars of the ceremony—always about dominance—to introduce the tenants (who should have already been approved by the dragon himself) to the dragon.

They should be hearers, but if they were not? Whatever would she do then? It seemed none of the rules pertaining to that possibility had been followed and the problems that could arise out of that …

Mary trundled in, slightly stooped. Complaints about the aches in her back would soon follow, no doubt.

Mary made a bit of a show sitting in her customary place, as though to ensure any who watched would note the quiet way she bore her discomfort. "Dear me, the Crofts are to come to Kellynch soon, are they not? I am glad I did not think of it before. How low it makes me!" She poured herself a cup of tea.

"They have already arrived. I mean to visit them today." Anne murmured—it was generally best to keep such corrections spoken quietly.

Marry blinked at her. "They are due a visit, that is true. It is the only polite and proper thing to do. But what a dreadful task, seeing someone else making themselves at home in a place they have only let." She leaned back in her chair until it creaked and pressed her hand to her stomach. "The very thought gives me quite an ill sensation."

"I am sure it is nothing more than the discomfort of becoming accustomed to something disagreeable." A sip of tea helped Anne swallow back her more distasteful comments.

Mary slapped the table hard enough to rattle the tea cups. "It is disagreeable, most disagreeable. But I am not convinced that it is not something more. I think it must be the odd tasting lamb at Mrs. Musgrove's table last night. Did not I tell you that new curry sauce—it tasted so odd, so unusual. I am certain that is what has done it. I feel very ill indeed."

"Shall I prepare you some mint tea? That always settles your stomach."

"No, no. I am far too ill for that. I am certainly not up for any visiting today. I will go and lie down. I may be there for the rest of the day altogether." Mary rose and trudged away.

Perhaps it was better to face the task without Mary's company—no, definitely it was. Mary knew nothing about what Anne had been reading and would surely have made things more difficult. It was definitely for the best.

Cool, sweet late summer breezes reminded her of how much she enjoyed a walk, particularly an easy one like the mere three miles between Kellynch and Uppercross. The shady footpaths were level and smooth; with little rain the few last weeks, the way was firm and without mud puddles to dodge. Bleating sheep filled the still green fields and pastures as the fragrance of wild flowers and grasses distracted her attention from what could become quite distasteful.

She crossed a particularly narrow stile into one of Kellynch's fields. This stile in particular had a nasty habit of snagging one's skirt if she were not especially careful. That rusty nail really ought to be hammered back into place. She gently lifted her skirt off the nail and turned toward the pasture

Heavens above. What was that? An unfamiliar creature, totally different to anything she had seen before, stared at her. It was as tall as a small horse— no, more like a pony; its front half resembled a fell pony more than any other creature. The face and front of the body were covered with fine silver-white hair, but what should have been a mane was more fin-like. In place of the typical equine feathers near the hooves, there were silvery, iridescent fins. The back half of the creature resembled a very large blue-grey snake, curling into a thick coil so that it seemed to sit upon as it regarded her. The eyes were very large, framed by long eye-lashes, and a blue very similar to the color the Blue Order claimed as its own. How odd, and tranquil and beautiful.

What was it? In some ways, it resembled a tat-zelwurm that appeared to be half-cat and half-snake, or a cockatrice that resembled a mix of falcon and snake. But who had ever heard of a beast resembling horse and a snake?

"I am a hippocampus." The voice had an odd watery quality about it. The creature unfurled its tail and approached her.

She stiffened her back to quell the instinct to run.

"You have never seen one like me, have you?" It stopped and cocked its head.

"I am afraid I have not. Forgive me, I am given to assume you are some sort of dragon. Am I correct?" She clutched the stile, her knees unsteady.

It nodded and smiled—smiled?—showing a sharp row of teeth. It was a predator; most decidedly not horse-like. "Indeed. I am a marine dragon. Few of my kind are apt to come ashore. It is so—dry and coarse and disagreeable."

Her skin prickled and her cheeks grew cold. She stammered over several words before she could speak. "I imagine it is. I am not sure of the proper etiquette; pray may I introduce myself or should I wait until Uppercross might be called upon to do so? I do not know when he will return though, so it could take some time before he is available for the service."

"That seems rather inconvenient. I will take no offense if you introduce yourself." Something about his tone reminded her of Shelby, the shepherding drake, who was always kind and helpful.

Her knees stopped shaking, and she dipped in as much of a curtsy as she could manage while holding the stile. "I am Anne Elliot—"

"Of the family of Kellynch?"

Odd that he would know that. "Indeed. May I ask your name?"

The hippocampus strode—or slithered? Really it was an odd mix of both—a bit closer. "I am White, friend to Admiral Croft who now resides at

Kellynch." He leaned his head forward somewhat like a bow.

"You are Friend to them?" She exhaled slowly. They were Hearers!

"Proudly. They are excellent Friends. They were pleased to learn from the local fairy dragons that you were the new Keeper of Kellynch, though it does seem the sort of thing that should have been discussed when the estate was let."

Anne winced. Lady Russell was right. Those fluttertufts were very talkative. "That is a very new development to which I am still trying to accustom myself. The arrangements for the lease were made before I was named Keeper."

"That explains a great deal." White shook his head and snorted. "You should talk to my Friends, they have many questions for you."

"No doubt. I was on my way to see them. If you will allow me passage through this field …"

His ears pricked, and he cocked his head. "Yes, I do suppose it is right of you to ask me that. I still have not become accustomed to the customs on land. Would it be rude of me to suggest I might convey you there faster than you can walk?"

"You would convey me? I did not know dragons would … ah … stoop to offer such a service."

"It seems a most practical solution, considering the urgency of the matters at hand. I have seen many riding horseback in the country here, and I am said to look like a horse. You have ridden a horse have you not?"

"Indeed, I have, but pray forgive the observation, you are hardly a horse. I am not certain I would know how."

He pawed the ground a bit and moved closer. "If you use the stile as a mounting block, you can perch right there on my shoulders, behind my neck fin. My Lady Friend said my shoulder bones were quite well set, rather resembling a proper saddle. She said my gait was far smoother than any horse she had ridden. I will not let you come to harm."

There was something so soulful in the depths of his blue eyes. "I thank you for your offer." Even if she did not, refusing a helpful dragon did not seem wise.

He shook his head, neck fin flopping to and fro, and made an odd sound halfway between a squeal and nicker.

With the aid of the stile step, she managed to settle herself on his back, and he was off! Without reins or a saddle, it was difficult to know what to do with her hands. True to his word, though, his gait was unnaturally smooth, simply a joy! They quickly arrived at the manor's front door and he dropped to his knees to allow her to slide off his back.

White knocked on the door with his front hoof—apparently it was somehow softer than a horse's hoof, and unshod, of course. White called out another odd sound and a moment later, a man who could only be Admiral Croft opened the door.

He was tall, like Wentworth, and broad in the shoulder, sporting a bit of a belly like most men of middling age. His dark hair was streaked with grey, but his brown eyes sparkled with merriment and good humor. Weather worn and tanned, his skin announced his naval profession, but he was certainly handsome enough to satisfy Father's tastes.

"My dear fellow! You have already made a new friend? I am not certain how I feel about you escorting random young ladies to the house." Admiral Croft balanced his hands on his hips and studied Anne.

"She is not random, pray give me some credit for decorum. She is Anne Elliot, daughter of this house and Keeper to Kellynch."

Admiral Croft's face shifted subtly into something half-surprised and half-welcoming. "Ah, Miss Elliot, I am delighted to make your acquaintance. Your call has been most anticipated. Pray come in. If you wish to join us, White, we shall go to the back room and open the French doors to the garden."

"I will see you in a moment." White bowed and glide-trotted off.

"You have already impressed him, Miss Elliot. He does not often bow to us warm-bloods." Admiral Croft winked and ushered her inside.

The front hall was as it had always been, with gilded paper hangings and several portraits of ancestors above the narrow table that held a tall white and gold vase with a bouquet of fragrant yellow lilies. Though the halls of Kellynch were intimately familiar, somehow, entering them as a guest, they felt strange, even a little cold.

Mrs. Trent made a startled little sound of recognition upon seeing Anne, and hurried off with the admiral's instruction to ready the back parlor and summon Mrs. Croft there.

"What do you think of my Friend, Miss Elliot?" He gestured for her to walk on.

No doubt that question was a test that would determine the future of her relationship with the Crofts.

"He is a remarkable and considerate creature. I have never met one like him before."

"Few have. I confess, I was surprised and not a little pleased that he decided to join us here. We have been Friends for a long time. Sophy and I both would miss his companionship." Somehow it was pleasing to know they were so fond of their Dragon Friend.

"He is uncommonly friendly."

"You think so?" He tapped his chin. "Interesting. I have not heard that description of him before. Most find him a bit stiff and formal. I confess, I was surprised he allowed you to ride him here."

"It was his idea. I would never have asked for such a favor."

"I am sure you are all that is proper. I have no doubt it was a courtesy offered as you are the Keeper here." He clasped his hands behind his back, lips pursed as though deep in thought.

They entered the parlor where Mrs. Croft awaited them. The room felt so different with the French doors open—since Father never allowed them to be open, she had forgotten they were even there—and the breeze off Mother's garden filling the space with perfume. And so bright now! The yellow walls resembled sunshine itself. How much Mother would have loved it this way.

Mrs. Croft, though neither tall nor fat, had a square sort of uprightness and vigor which gave importance to her person. Bright dark eyes, good teeth, and altogether an agreeable face rendered her more handsome than pretty. Her weather-beaten complexion, matched her husband's, probably the consequence of being at sea with him, making her seem older than her real eight-and-thirty years—if she

recalled Wentworth's comments about her age correctly. Her face resembled his greatly—perhaps too
much. And she clearly heard dragons.

"Miss Elliot, you do us a great kindness in calling
upon us today." Mrs. Croft dipped in a pleasing curtsy, her dark green floral calico gown swaying with her
graceful movements. "Pray, be comfortable, refreshments will be brought shortly. I heard you walked all
this way from Uppercross."

"All but the distance I carried her." White stood
just outside the open French doors and poked his
head in. "Might I come in?"

Anne's eyes bulged.

"Just a moment." Admiral Croft dragged a roll of
heavy sailcloth from behind a screen and rolled it out
in front of the door. The Crofts must have brought
that with them—it certainly was not in the household
inventory they had left at Kellynch. "Mustn't damage
the floor or carpet after all."

White entered the room. Father would turn seven
shades of purple if he thought a horse was joining the
conversation in his parlor, much less a dragon.

"Do not fear, I am persuading the housekeeper
that I am not actually in the room, just standing outside—my Friends are ever so fond of gazing at me."
Did White just wink at her?

Admiral Croft guffawed and patted White's neck
with unabashed affection. "He is a fine specimen to
be sure."

"I hope you will forgive us. I assure you, the floors
and furnishings will be well protected when White
comes inside. I had hoped that this being a dragon
estate would ensure you would be understanding of
our Friend." Mrs. Croft bit her lower lip.

Anne sat in Lady Russell's favorite rust colored chair near White and the French doors. How strange to be in her place. "As you may have ascertained by now, my father thinks little of dragons. But I can hardly fault you for wanting your Friend to be welcome, too. I am sure it will be fine." Actually, she was not, but it was the polite thing to say. However, Lady Russell had often taken tea at Kellynch. If one dragon was welcome, then White should be as well. "I do have some concerns though. It seems a bit forward to bring them up now—"

"Where dragons are concerned, everything seems quite forward." Admiral Croft chuckled as he pulled a pair of floral upholstered armchairs near Anne and White. He gestured Mrs. Croft into one and settled into the other.

"I have not been Keeper long enough to know."

"We had heard something to that effect, but it is often difficult to decipher what a fairy dragon is saying." Mrs. Croft glanced through the window toward the garden where the little feather-scaled spies resided. "Especially when they are harried by a rather intimidating cockatrice."

"A large fellow, jet black feathers and scales?"

"You know him?" Mrs. Croft's eyebrows rose.

"He has been warned not to interfere with the local harem. He comes and goes, it seems, and perhaps seeing you here, he believed himself free of my restrictions upon him." Anne peered into the garden, not that Jet was likely to make himself known at such a convenient moment.

"I will be happy to have words with him." White bared his teeth, just enough.

"I do not imagine that you were warned that Shelby, the shepherding drake, has chased intruders off the estate regularly at the full moon either." Anne bit her lip and sighed.

"Nor did the solicitor mention anything about the dragon or Keeper in any of our dealings with him." Admiral Croft crossed his arms over his chest and frowned.

Anne hung her head and sighed. "Father has had little interaction with Kellynch through the years, and it seems he rather carelessly passed the duties to me just before he left for Bath. Our solicitor is not a member of the Order."

"I see, that is rather irregular." He rose and rubbed his hands together. "But what is done, is done I suppose. I imagine you will introduce us to Kellynch properly soon? That formality should have been addressed before we took possession, but we can remedy that now. I've no doubt he will be a reasonable fellow."

Anne cringed. "That is part of the problem I am afraid."

"What do you mean?" White nudged her with his very soft nose.

"Kellynch has been hibernating for quite some time now."

"A hibernating dragon?" Mrs. Croft gasped. "I had no idea things were so bad." She covered her mouth with her hand and gazed at the admiral.

"I am afraid so. I am told he should be awaking very soon. As I understand, it is a rather dangerous time for all involved."

"How is it to be managed?" Admiral Croft paced across the French doors, hands behind his back.

"I have been in contact with the Dragon Sage. Uppercross, the wyvern from the next estate has gone to London to consult with her directly. I expect him back very soon. He has pledged his assistance with the entire matter. It appears he was involved with Kellynch's previous awakening and the two are amiable with one another."

"I see. That is certainly not what I expected in coming here."

Anne grasped the edge of her seat and stared at the floor. "I am sorry you had to learn of the situation this way. I have spent the last several days studying an Order manual on the matter. There are provisions for when an estate must be 'inhabited by non-Keepers'— as it calls the situation—while a Keeper is absent from the estate due to travels, Order responsibilities, hibernations or other factors."

"Really?" Mrs. Croft's jaw dropped.

"What are the protocols?" Admiral Croft returned to his chair and braced his elbows on his knees, full focus on Anne.

"As I understand, the new residents are to refrain from approaching the lair or the woods containing it and await an introduction by the dragon's Keeper. A stand-in for the Keeper must be appointed and approved and provided residence near enough to the estate to tend the dragon's needs. Then, the dragon will have the right to accept or refuse the new residents. I will remain in the neighborhood until Kellynch awakens and these things have been managed." Best not mention that she still had no idea how to manage a waking dragon. It did not seem the kind of thing to discuss upon a first meeting.

"That sounds far simpler than I would have expected." Admiral Croft's lips wrinkled.

"There is a matter of some concern regarding you, White." Anne looked up into his compelling blue eyes. "Minor dragons are not to be brought into residence when the major dragon is not available. A matter of territorial issues as I understand. It could be dangerous for you if Kellynch awakens and finds you here."

White shifted from one foot to the other, pawing the sailcloth. "Kellynch is a wyrm as I understand. They have particularly nasty tempers. Perhaps I should stay elsewhere until he awakens and a proper introduction can be made."

"Where will you go?" Mrs. Croft asked.

"As soon as Uppercross returns, I would be happy to introduce you to him. I would not be surprised if he would welcome you to stay with him a while. He is an excellent fellow who likes stories a great deal. I think he would be very interested to hear tales of the sea."

"My brother, who spent some time in this country, said the same thing of him." Mrs. Croft tapped her finger against her lips. "It was you he had the pleasure of being acquainted with during that time, so I understand."

Anne swallowed hard. Perhaps they did not know the painful history she shared with Wentworth. It would be like him to keep such information to himself. "I did not realize Captain Wentworth was acquainted with Uppercross."

"I believe it was just a brief introduction, not a particularly substantial acquaintance. But we are expecting him here soon. I dare say you will be reacquainted with him soon as he is planning to visit with us." Admiral Croft's tone betrayed no hints of deeper understanding.

Visit? Wentworth!

"Pray excuse me," White nickered. "But I believe we were discussing the safety of myself, which I daresay I find a much more compelling topic than either of your brothers."

Anne blinked several times and shook her head a bit as though it would settle her thoughts. It did not. "Of course, you are correct. I expect Uppercross any day now. Upon his return, I will send a servant with an invitation to Uppercross Cottage. Introductions will be made, and I am certain all will be settled agreeably."

The suggestion was readily agreed to and refreshments brought in by Mrs. Trent. White whispered the entire time about how he was in the garden, calmly watching them while Mrs. Trent blinked and shook her head.

Mrs. Croft poured tea as Admiral Croft launched into some sort of story, but Anne could hardly follow it, her heart thundering almost as loud as her racing thoughts. Was Wentworth, her Wentworth, really due to visit Kellynch very soon?

And what would she do if he was?

10
Chapter

August 25, 1814

A VERY FEW days later, Mr. Musgrove had called upon Kellynch and whilst there, also met Captain
Wentworth who had apparently already arrived to visit the Crofts, without Anne having been informed. Of
course, why should she have been informed that the
man who had once asked to marry her, for whom she
was no longer to have feelings or thoughts, had arrived? In the course of the most agreeable visit (as he
had, with great enthusiasm, told Anne, Mary and
Charles over dinner), a date was fixed upon for the
new denizens of Kellynch to come to Uppercross for
dinner.

That day was today.

Anne paced her small room tucked into the gable
of the cottage. While there was nothing wrong with a

small room, it did limit one's ability to pace. Five steps from the window to the door, with three extra to skirt around the dressing table near the window. Just less than six from the door to the closet door in the corner. The narrow oak four poster bed stopped her from completing the five steps to the next robin's egg blue wall, but she did get to walk extra steps around it, so that was pleasing. Another six steps and she returned to the window, light ivory curtains fluttering in the warm, green-scented summer breeze.

What would it be like meeting Wentworth again? Did he even want to see her again? Did she want to see him?

Bless it all, she did. Deeply, achingly, she did.

She pressed her hand to her chest, but the pressure did little to ease the pain. Surely, he did not wish to renew their acquaintance. Had he wished ever to see her again, he need not have waited until now; he could have done so long ago, when his naval career had given him sufficient prize money for the independence that was necessary to facilitate a marriage. That was the reason she had been persuaded to give for refusing his proposal. Back when she believed everything Lady Russell tried to persuade her of.

He had been angry then—angry at her refusal, angry at her reasons, simply angry at her. Surely his pride was wounded—whose would not be? But her reasons were not utterly untoward. Any sensible person would have agreed. Lady Russell—whatever her true motives might have been—was correct as to the uncertainty of his future and the grim possibilities for Anne, and any children she might have had, should things not have gone as they did.

If Wentworth was half the man she thought he

was, he could understand that. Surely, he must.

Even so, Lady Russell had been wrong, very wrong. Wrong in her predictions for the future and wrong, almost unforgivably so, to persuade Anne of something in Lady Russell's best interest when she claimed to be a friend. Selfish, unkind, unfeeling creature!

Anne pressed her cheek against the window frame—white-painted wood, peeling a bit, smelling a slight bit musty. How different things might have been without Lady Russell's "sound advice."

But now? Now all that was to be done was to live with the consequences. So frightfully many consequences.

How many friendships had Lady Russell's influence ruined? She had not liked Mrs. Smith and often argued against Anne's correspondence with her. But Mrs. Smith heard dragons and Lady Russell did not like Anne's acquaintance with dragon hearers she did not know she could persuade. Anne's throat knotted so tight she could barely breathe.

Merciful heaven! Lady Russell had been intentionally separating her from dragon hearing companionship for at least the eight years since Wentworth, quite possibly more. There would be no more of that, though it would not be pretty convincing Lady Russell of it.

And there was still Wentworth to be considered. She dragged her sleeve across her blurry eyes. It had been eight years—eight years! She should be indifferent to it all by now. It should be so—now she must make it so. Somehow.

A shriek, the kind that walked with death, pierced the walls.

She flew downstairs, nearly tripping on the slightly too short middle step on the way down.

Jemima, nursery maid to Mary's children, sturdy and weather-beaten as a trusty garden gate, stood in the front hall, panting and trembling. Young Charles sagged in her arms like a half empty sack of flour. Mary wrung her hands, hovering nearby. The boy sobbed softly, tossing his head with each cry.

Mary wailed again and grabbed Anne by the shoulders. "Anne, Anne! What shall we do?"

Jemima staggered closer. "He fell, Miss, from the large oak tree. I told him not to climb it. I told him so sternly."

"Take him to the drawing room and lay him on the couch. Send the stable boy for the surgeon." Anne dashed into the parlor ahead of them and laid out a ragged blanket on the shabby couch.

The boy was limp, crying out in pain, his side stained with blood. With Jemima's help, and Mary looking on in—thankfully—silent horror, Anne removed little Charles' torn waistcoat and shirt through his whimpered protests.

Merciful heavens poor child! A long, jagged gash ran down his side, bits of broken crockery protruding from the wound. And his collarbone—there was no mistaking the large bump at the base of his throat—it had been knocked out of place.

"Cook put the old chamber pot under the tree, thinking she would have the girl scrub it later. It was quite foul. I told her it were foolish to leave it there, I did. It belonged with the washing, but it smelt so bad she said …"

Anne swallowed back the acid in the back of her throat. "Mary, go to the kitchen and have cook brew up some strong poppy tea."

"That is a good idea, I am sure I shall need it."

"Not for you! For little Charles. The bone must be reset, but it will go much better if he has had the tea first."

"How would you know?" Mary snorted and tossed her head. "I am his mother, I should know—"

"Do you wish to take over tending him?"

"I shall see to the tea." Mary trundled off.

"Jemima, I need clean water and bandages to clean his wounds. Go quickly now." She scampered off, with a quick nod and a wide-eyed look. That was a familiar look, one that usually meant its bearer was relieved that someone else had taken charge of the situation. A very familiar expression, indeed.

Now was not the time to dwell upon that. No, she should be thankful for the providence of being here to assist her unfortunate nephew.

She knelt beside him. He whimpered, and she smoothed his hair back with her hand. No doubt the collarbone was causing him the most pain now, but that would be set right as soon as he had some poppy tea, and the surgeon arrived to assist her. The deep cut was the bigger problem. His clothes smelt of the chamber pot. The wound would infect and those outcomes were rarely good.

What would Mary do under such strain? It was hard to imagine. But one should not borrow trouble. One thing at a time.

Jemima arrived and Anne cleaned and dressed the wound, the room spinning a little with each bit of shattered crockery she had to free from the boy's side.

"What has happened?" Charles burst through the door, shouting.

Jemima hurried to him and explained.

"What is to be done?" Charles knelt beside Anne, desperation in his eyes, laying his hand on his son's head.

"Mr. Robinson has been sent for. When he comes, the bone can be dealt with, and he shall tell us more. I have sent Mary to have poppy tea made. The boy and his mother will need it."

"Of course, of course. Is there anything else to be done?"

"The Great House should be informed."

"Yes, I shall do that now." He clambered up and rushed out. Charles was a good sort, but not for nursing. Best have him off with something active to do.

The maid led Mr. Robinson in just as Mary arrived with the poppy tea. She immediately poured herself a cup. Mr. Robinson stood beside her, a large brown medical bag in his hand. Squarely built and of unremarkable height, he balanced back and forth on his toes, the heavy mutton chops tinged with grey along his jowls flexing as he worked his tongue along his cheek, surveying the situation.

"You have done well to clean and bandage the wound, Miss Elliot." Mr. Robinson nodded at her, somber to the point of being grave. "Give the boy some tea, and I will address the bone."

Little Charles' eyes drooped quickly under the influence of the tea.

"Mary, perhaps you and Jemima should go find some clean linens to make up the couch for the boy to sleep on tonight."

Mary opened her mouth—to argue no doubt, as that was what she did as though by reflex—but Jemima urged her toward the hall and upstairs.

Mr. Robinson clucked his tongue. "Thank you. It is often best not to have a mother observe such a procedure. If you will assist me and keep the boy still as I maneuver the joint into place." He pointed to little Charles' uninjured side and showed Anne how to place her hands to hold him still.

It would be rude to inform him that she already knew. One of the farmer's children on Kellynch had suffered a similar injury. The family could not afford a surgeon, so it had fallen upon Anne to tend him. Thankfully, her copy of Buchan's *Domestic Medicine* did not fail her, and she was able to set the bone to rights. It had not been a pretty process.

Mr. Robinson hardly seemed more expert than she. Still, it was preferable to manipulating the bone herself. After several minutes of manhandling, the sickening pop of the bone returning to place announced his success. Anne panted hard—retching was not the thing to do now.

"Have you more bandages? The shoulder must be held in place for at least a month so that it might heal strong enough that this will not easily happen again."

Anne produced bandages and helped him wrap the shoulder tightly to the boy's side, then tie the arm up in a sling.

"The arm has every chance of mending well, if …" He glanced at the bandages across the boy's ribs.

"I understand."

"I will leave you with some wash for the wound, and an ointment you may use upon it. Call me when the boy becomes feverish—I fear it will not be long before it all starts. I also have a tonic you may give his mother when she becomes too agitated." He turned to his large bag and handed her a small brown bottle.

"Measure it by drops into her tea. For now, there is little else to be done. Keep him still and quiet, watch and wait. And pray he shall be spared."

"Of course." Anne saw him out.

She closed the heavy plain door behind him and leaned against it. What would she tell Mary? The truth would drive her to hysterics, and Anne would have two invalids to care for. Charles probably already suspected the truth—

"How could you send Mr. Robinson away before he consulted with me?" Mary shrieked, standing on tip toes, Jemima beside her with a bundle of linen.

Charles and a party from the Great House tumbled in on a wind of chaos and confusion.

Henrietta and Louisa plied Anne with a thousand questions, none of which they gave her opportunity to answer. Mrs. Musgrove fussed and cooed over the child, murmuring concerns under her breath. Hopefully Mary and Charles could not hear what she was saying. Though accurate, none of that would improve the general level of agitation.

The child will be quite well, there is nothing to fear.

Deep, soft and soothing—who was that voice? No doubt it was a dragon, but one she had never heard.

There is no need for everyone to be here. He will recover. You should all go to the Great House for dinner as planned. You have guests.

While outlandish, that was the very thing that Anne most wished for. But why was a dragon trying to persuade them of that? And what dragon could it be? Uppercross had not yet returned from London, though a fairy dragon had told her earlier in the day it would be soon. Perhaps he had brought someone with him who was inclined to help her?

Charles leaned over the boy and tutted under his breath. "I say, he is going on so well, and I do so wish to be introduced to Captain Wentworth, that, perhaps, I might just join them for dinner at the Great House."

"You think we should go on and have dinner in spite of this?" Mrs. Musgrove asked.

Yes, you should. There is no need to worry. Do not suspend your pleasure on such a trivial matter.

"It seems little Charles will be quite well, Mother. I think he is right." Henrietta looped her arm in her mother's. "Come, let us go see everything ready." She led her mother out, Louisa close behind.

How odd. Charles heard dragons, he should be able to detect the dragon voice, not succumb to its persuasion. How very odd. But then again, he was subject to Lady Russell's persuasions, so perhaps it was not so odd at all.

Mary elbowed her way past Anne, dabbing her eyes with her handkerchief. "Oh! no, indeed, Charles, I cannot bear to have you go away. Only think if anything should happen?"

"He will be fine. He need only be kept in bed and amused as quietly as possible. What is there for a father to do? My father very much wished me to meet Captain Wentworth, so I ought to go. With your sister being with you, my love, I have no scruple at all to go. I am sure you would not like to leave him yourself, but there is no harm in my going."

Mary turned to Anne with a huff. "This is always my luck. If there is anything disagreeable going on men are always sure to get out of it. Very unfeeling! I am sure, I am more unfit than anybody else to be about the child. My being the mother is the very reason why my feelings should not be tried. I am not at all equal to it. I have not the nerves for the sort of thing."

No, she does not.

The strange rumbly voice was right. "Suppose you were to go, as well as your husband. Leave little Charles to my care. No one can think it wrong while I remain with him."

Mary's brow knit—she must be thinking very hard. "Dear me! that's a very good thought, very good, indeed. You, who have not a mother's feelings, are a great deal the properest person. I shall certainly go; for they want me excessively to be acquainted with Captain Wentworth, and I know you do not mind being left alone. Yes, it is a very good plan indeed."

Charles and Mary retired to their quarters to get ready for dinner. Silence fell heavily upon Anne's shoulders, almost too heavy to bear—the voice was gone, too.

What sort of mischief was about? Anne peeked out the windows. Nothing. Not surprising though, if a dragon, especially a small one, did not want to be seen, it usually was not.

A quarter of an hour later, Charles and Mary, dressed and ornamented for dinner, departed for the Great House, Mary chattering gaily as though nary a thing were amiss.

How could one who heard dragons be so easily persuaded? Lady Russell once said it was a simple thing to persuade someone of something they already wanted to believe. Apparently, it was frighteningly simple.

Anne pulled a faded floral armchair near the sleeping boy and fell into it. Perhaps a little of the peace and silence would seep into her thrumming, tingling nerves.

Let me in. Something pawed at the glass of the window behind the tea table.

Anne dashed to the window. Great glowing gold eyes stared at her through the glass, set wide in the face of a large black cat.

"I said let me in." The cat sat back, revealing a thick, scaly black body behind the feline forepaws.

There was a picture in one of Father's bestiaries that resemble the creature—a tatzelwurm?

"I will not harm the boy. That is in fact why I am here. I want to help." His rumbly-purring voice seemed kind and friendly. "Do you not know of the healing properties of the tatzelwurm?"

Anne frowned and her brows knit—Elizabeth thought that a most unfortunate expression—yes, she had read something to that effect. Yes, the Sage had mentioned it in one of her letters. "Who are you? I cannot allow every dragon that claims to be amiable into my brother's house."

"I suppose that is true and to be expected." He cocked his head and seemed to think. "My name is Laconia. My Friend is Frederick Wentworth. If you are the Miss Elliot I believe you to be, you will know his name and know that he would not send one who wished you ill."

Anne gasped, the lightheadedness she had kept at bay threatening to overcome her. "Wentworth sent you? I did not know he had a Dragon Friend."

"We met in Gibraltar. As I was hatching, I was set upon by a band of *things* that he called apes. He hates them, you know. He rescued me, and we have been friends ever since."

Wentworth detested Gibraltar's apes. There is no way the dragon could know that without knowing Wentworth. Moreover, rescuing one in desperate straits was exactly the sort of thing Wentworth would do.

Anne opened the window. A very large, very black Tatzelwurm spring-hopped inside.

Such a strange way he had of moving. Even though White had a similar shape, he glided smoothly, pushing forward with his tail as his forelegs walked, while this creature seemed to hop on his coiled serpentine tail.

Laconia rubbed himself around her legs, breathing deeply. How soft his glossy fur! "You smell of hippocampus. A familiar one."

"I visited with White not very long ago."

"If he admits you to his acquaintance, then you will do." He rose up on his tail, reaching above her waist and peeked around to look at little Charles. "May I approach the young one?"

Anne gestured toward the couch. "The bone has been set properly. The real concern is the cut on his side. It is likely to infect and turn putrid. His parents do not yet know the extent of the danger."

"Show me the wound." Laconia put his front paw up on the couch and sniffed little Charles head to toe, paying particular attention to his bandaged side. "I was the ship's cat on the Laconia. It was known as the luckiest ship in the fleet. Our sailors often through what killed men on other ships. While our ship's surgeon was good, I was the reason for it. You see, my spit has curative properties. When I lick a wound—whilst it might not be considered a pleasant experience—it will not putrefy. Wentworth heard of the boy's injury—you are well aware of how fairy dragons know everything that happens—and asked me to see if I could be of service."

Anne chewed her lip. The story sounded true. It was the sort of thing Wentworth would do. But if she were wrong, and the tatzelwurm meant mischief—they were not known to be reliable creatures … On the other hand, what harm could he truly do? Though the surgeon did not say it aloud, they both knew that the boy stood little chance of surviving a serious infection. Already sweat beaded on his upper lip, and the glow of a burgeoning fever rose on his cheeks.

"Shall I remove the bandages?" Anne asked.

"It would be helpful. Has he had a draught to make him sleep?"

"Yes, I do not expect him to awaken for hours more."

"Good. I am told my tongue is rather like a rasp, not pleasant on open wounds. I do not wish to cause the young one distress." Laconia sprang up beside little Charles. Gracious, he was nearly as long as the boy was tall! He purred.

The purr was decidedly cat-like, but more; deeper, fuller, rounder, rather like Laconia himself, like a cat but more. The sound seemed to soothe little Charles into a deeper sleep.

Anne untied the bandages. Red skin around the ragged seeping wound already appeared inflamed. She grimaced—pray the dragon could help him.

Laconia sniffed the wound, mouth half-open exposing a mouthful of sharp pointed teeth, framing his forked tongue. "Yes, this is bad. Good that it has not waited too long or it might have been too much even for me. Hold the boy's hand and speak to him whilst

I manage this. Sometimes even with a draught, they can get unsettled."

She wrapped little Charles' hand in hers, and Laconia settled in to lap the wound, starting at the bottom and working his way towards Charles' face. He stirred and whimpered, but with Anne's soft voice in his ear, soon settled, crying out only occasionally as Laconia addressed particularly deep gashes.

How gruesome, even ghoulish, as the creature appeared to lap the boy's blood! But the intelligent purpose in those eyes evidenced the good will he radiated.

"You may reapply the bandages. I think it is clean now. Should you see any signs of infection though, send for me immediately. I will be at Kellynch with Wentworth. I will return and do this again. I think he will recover well." Laconia sat back on his tail and licked his broad thumbed paw and scrubbed his face with it.

"I am in your debt. Is there anything I might do for you?"

"I should like a saucer of cream if you please. That is not something to be easily found at sea." He settled himself across Charles' lap and began to purr. The boy snored softly.

"Certainly." She returned from the kitchen, saucer in hand. "Where shall I place this?"

"On the table is fine." He jumped to the small table beside the couch and lapped, tiny bits of cream splashed and clung to his face. "Very fresh. Most excellent. Now you may tell me why you broke Wentworth's heart. He is such an even tempered warm-blood, except where you are concerned. You are the one thing he will not speak to me of."

"He remembers me?" She forced her jaw not to gape.

"Drives himself to drink every time he does. And I do not like you very well for that." Laconia made a sound between a snort and a snarl then sat back on his haunches—his coiled tail rather—and stared at her. "But you are not what I expected. Why did you refuse him?"

He was still so affected? He must despise her! "In truth, I made a mistake. I allowed myself to be persuaded by … by an argument that made sense, made by someone I once respected. I have never stopped regretting that decision."

"That is good. But have you stopped being easily persuaded?" He sat up very tall and looked her straight in the eyes. There was something very challenging in those gold eyes.

"I hear dragons now—I am a Keeper. I must not be easily persuaded anymore."

"You are not what I thought you would be." Laconia studied her, a little like a cat studying its prey, but there was nothing dangerous in his posture. "Pray, scratch my ears now." He leaned his head toward her and she scratched behind his ears as his purr rumbled through the whole room.

Wentworth might never admit her acquaintance again, but somehow it helped—just a little—to know his Friend did not think ill of her.

August 26, 1814

The next morning, very early, Laconia called upon Anne and Little Charles, before even Cook had begun stirring. Pale rays of sunrise lit the room just enough to see the faded and slightly shabby surroundings, but not enough to drive the evening's chill back. Sleeping in an armchair left her sore, stiff, and as tired as she had been when she fell asleep. She opened the window to admit Laconia and paced several circuits round the room to shake off the morning's nip.

Together, they checked the boy's wounds. Much improved, though Laconia insisted on licking them again to be certain. It might be difficult for him to return again later, when the boy's mother was about—Mary might be able to hear dragons, but convincing her to allow one to lick her child's wounds was probably beyond the bounds of what she would accept.

Laconia repeated the rather gory process. Thankfully, the boy had another cup of tea during the night and did not fully awaken during the ministrations. Anne rebandaged the wounds, which were already looking substantially better than the evening before, and brought Laconia another dish of cream. Though he had not asked for it, he lapped it up, tail flicking happily.

He stopped mid-lap and sat straight up, looking at her, droplets of cream clinging to the fur and whiskers around his mouth. "I nearly forgot. I heard a harem of fairy dragons chattering this morning. Uppercross has returned and would like to speak with you."

"Thank you. I shall go to him directly. Shall I arrange an introduction for you? He really is a delightful, jolly fellow."

Laconia cocked his head and stared at her. "A jolly fellow? I have rarely heard a major dragon described so. Crusty, cranky, and generally ill-tempered is usually how they are depicted—which is easy to understand when the Pendragon Accords dictate that they spend hundreds of years submitting their primal urges to the treaty's rules while they endure the company of lesser, warm-blooded creatures."

"That is not a very flattering depiction of dragon-human relations." She scratched behind Laconia's ears.

"It is better for us minor dragons who are more on an equal footing with you warm-bloods. But our nobility, the major dragons—do you really think even your nobles are equal to the majesty of the dragons they Keep? Your father for example? I have heard he is a dreadful Dragon Keeper." A shudder ran from Laconia's ears down to the tip of his serpentine tail.

"I suppose you are correct. But it is difficult to consider. One does not always like to be reminded of their given place in society."

"I well understand. One does not like being reminded that one is not just predator, but prey as well." He shrugged and returned to his cream.

Anne swallowed, prey? But then again, in some ways, that was quite the way of the human world as well.

Less than an hour later, Laconia accompanied her into the fresh morning air towards the dense Uppercross woods until the path to Kellynch diverged from the one to the dragon lair. Heavy branches overhung the path, rendering it far cooler than the morning air they had left near the house. Green loamy scents and a touch of dragon musk hung in the still, quiet air. So much like the path to the lair at Kellynch. Was it that way all over England?

A tall figure in a blue coat, brown trousers and tall boots trod the path ahead of them, familiar, and yet not. He stopped and turned in their direction.

Wentworth.

Laconia spring-hopped to him, crossing the distance in just a few long bounds. "The boy improves. He will be well."

Wentworth crouched to scratch Laconia under the chin. "That is good news indeed. I pray I have not overstepped by suggesting he attend the boy last night." His dark eyes fixed on her, not quite staring, but examining, studying—and no doubt finding her wanting.

She dropped in a small curtsey. "It was kind of you to consider us so. Laconia's assistance was very welcome."

"She is quite competent and cared for the boy very well without me. I only did what she could not." Laconia looked over his shoulder at her, the tip of his tail flicking slowly.

Wentworth nodded and stood.

"Would you like me to introduce you both to Uppercross? I am on my way to his lair now."

"Thank you, Miss Elliot, but Mr. Musgrove, his Keeper, has already offered to perform the service later today." His voice was all that was polite, formal, and cold.

"I hope very much that you are right, that Uppercross is as agreeable as you say. It would make our time in this county much more agreeable." Laconia's voice had all the warmth Wentworth's lacked. In light of what Laconia had said about being prey, it made sense he would rather have his Friend with him for such an introduction. Sometimes Elizabeth made Anne feel that same way, too.

"Pray excuse us, my sister expects me soon." Wentworth bowed once more and disappeared down the path, Laconia in his shadow.

It was over! Thank heavens, the worst was over! Her hands trembled as she pressed them to her cheeks. She had seen him. They had met. They had been once more in the same space.

Eight years, almost eight years had passed, since all had been given up. How absurd to be resuming the agitations which such an interval had banished into distance and indistinctness!

And yet, with such feelings—the depth, the warmth—eight years may be little more than nothing.

He was hardly altered since that time, and not for the worse. The years which had destroyed her youth and bloom had only given him a more flowing, manly, open look, in no respect lessening his personal advantages. He was the same Frederick Wentworth.

But now, how were his sentiments to be read? Cold and formal, polite and stiff. No trace of any former feeling in his countenance. He had not forgiven her. She had used him ill, deserted and disappointed him; and worse, she had shown a feebleness of character in doing so, which his own decided, confident temper could not endure. She had given him up to oblige another—even if that other had been a persuasive dragon. Each of those thoughts was clear in his expression, his posture, his tone. He had no desire of meeting her again. Her power with him was gone forever.

Cold suffused her limbs, followed by a sort of numbness. Better that than the pain his memory had once elicited. Yes, it was definitely better.

At least for now, when there were other matters which required her attention. Once those were addressed, she could enjoy the luxury of examining her feelings and laying them to rest once more.

Or not.

She turned to the path leading to the lair. Hopefully Uppercross had learnt what to do in light of the damage to Kellynch's hoard. Anne swallowed hard. What Laconia had said about being prey, did that extend to Keepers who displeased their dragon? Every joint in her body threatened to melt. There had to be another way.

The vine-covered hillside appeared through the veil of trees, the musky odor of wyvern permeating the still air. Anne cupped her hands around her mouth and called, "Laird Uppercross, you wished to see me."

The ground beneath her feet rumbled a bit and the vines on the hillside gave way to reveal a familiar square, scaly, toothy face. She held her breath to contain her gasp. Would she ever grow accustomed to those fangs?

"Good morning, Miss Anne." Uppercross bobbed his shoulders in a small bow.

What was there to do but curtsy in return?

"I am glad to see you. One never knows if a fairy dragon will deliver a message."

"Which is of course why you told no less than six

of them as I understand."

"Actually, I spoke with an even dozen."

"And it was Laconia who actually delivered the message." Anne giggled. "How was your trip to London?"

"Long and dusty. I itch. Brush and oil my hide whilst we talk?" He ducked into the cavern and pulled out a pail of oil and a stiff broom. Would it be wrong to tell him he looked a little like a maid about to go to her work? But he did look just like that as he handed them to her.

Birds squawked overhead, the limbs above them rustling loudly. Lady Russell landed in a graceful flurry beside them and settled her wings across her back. "That task should be done by his Keeper."

"Lady Russell?" Anne nearly dropped the broom.

"When did you arrive?" Uppercross lay flat on the ground and fluttered his left wing, a sign of where to begin. He angled his wing to remind her to brush in the direction of his scales. "Brush the dust off me first, then dip the brush in the oil and work it into my scales."

"Just now, I came here directly, and I need you both to pay attention. There are important issues to tend to." Lady Russell held her wings open, suggesting a lady standing akimbo.

"All of which can be accomplished whilst I am brushed." Uppercross snorted.

Anne avoided looking at Lady Russell as she reached across Uppercross' wing. Gracious it was difficult to reach the far edges whilst remaining in a ladylike posture. "Before I forget, there is an urgent matter I must discuss with you. The Crofts have already taken possession of Kellynch—"

"They were not due until Michaelmas!" Lady Russell squawked something that sounded very untoward. Did dragons use invectives?

"And they have Dragon Friends with them. As I understand, it is not safe for them to be on the estate—"

Uppercross' tail thumped. "Shards and shells! No, it is not. Kellynch has never been welcoming to minor dragons in his territory in the first place. He must not wake up to find strange dragons there."

"White is a hippocampus, he is Friend to the Crofts—a very kind fellow whom I think you will like very well. Laconia is a tatzelwurm and is Friend to Mrs. Croft's brother, Captain Wentworth, who is staying with them right now. Have I your permission to introduce them to you?"

"Wentworth is here?" Lady Russell's eyes grew wide.

"Kellynch's Watcher should have thought to introduce the minor dragons who have arrived on the estate." Uppercross glowered at Lady Russell.

She jumped back, flapping.

Anne scrubbed Uppercross' wing with the oily broom, her back turned to Lady Russell. Best not look at her now. "Would you consider allowing White, and perhaps Laconia as well, to remain on Uppercross lands until such time as I am able to make an introduction to Kellynch?"

"I am very fond of company. I have never met a hippocampus. Living at sea, I am sure they have some excellent tales to tell. That would be fitting payment for accommodating them in my lair."

"In your lair?" Anne stopped brushing.

Lady Russell squawked something that sounded

like 'You must not.' Why would she say such a thing?

Perhaps she did not want Laconia—and possibly White—to learn of her true nature and perhaps share it with their Friends. Wentworth had no idea of either her real identity or her role in Anne's refusal. What would happen if he knew?

"Why ever not? It is the most comfortable place for a dragon on the estate, and my guests should be comfortable. I insist."

"Laconia will be very surprised. I invited him to come this morning, but he refused. I think he was afraid your ire would result in him being eaten."

"He is right to think such things." Lady Russell stamped alternate feet. "He does not belong in a dragon lair, his Friend should—"

Uppercross lifted his head and snorted hard enough to ruffle Lady Russell's head feathers. "Nonsense! I insist you set his thinking to rights! Make us an introduction, and let him see I will enjoy his company most heartily."

"I will do so as soon as possible, this afternoon if I can."

Lady Russell bugled—a piercing, tone impossible to ignore. "Have you forgotten there are issues more important here than planning a tea party?"

Uppercross wriggled in the dirt, turning his spine ridge toward Anne. "Indeed, there are. I fear the news is not good."

"What do you mean not good?" Lady Russell paced along his side, approaching Anne.

Anne stepped away, dipped the broom in the oil and walked to Uppercross' other side.

"The opposite of good." Uppercross huffed.

"You watch your tone with me." Lady Russell

made a pecking motion toward him.

He sat up, nearly knocking Anne aside, and glared down at Lady Russell. "You had best watch yours. Need I remind you? You are not a landed dragon and here in England, that gives us precedence."

"Things are different in Australia."

"Which is a penal colony, and perhaps not the best model of civilized behavior." Uppercross somehow had a little laugh in his tone. "Nonetheless, it would behoove you to remember your place, if not here— because I am quite liberal in my attitudes—on Kellynch, where the resident dragon is not."

"Pray forgive me, but I do not understand." Anne set the broom aside and leaned against the hillside.

"I have spoken with the Dragon Sage myself." Uppercross flicked his tail toward Lady Russell making her jump to avoid being knocked over. "She researched the matter of the hoard quite thoroughly, and I fear what she found was not at all in your favor, *Lady* Russell."

Anne looked from one dragon to the other as they glared at each other. What had come over Uppercross?

"As Kellynch's Watcher, you are legally responsible for the condition of his hoard."

Anne gasped and crumpled down to sit on the cool dusty ground.

"But I knew nothing about it." Lady Russell's feather-scales pouffed making her very large and round.

"Be that as it may, it is part of his territory, and that is what you agreed to take responsibility for when he permitted you as part of his Keep. It was your responsibility to find out such things before you agreed to be Watcher."

"That is not fair! How was I to know?"

"You did not think that there would be rules to such things?"

"I had just moved to England with my Sir Henry who took Kellynch Cottage. Besides Kellynch was half-asleep when the agreement was made. He told me nothing. How was I to know?"

"Yes, yes, things are done differently in Australia. I know. But that does not absolve you for the responsibility to have found out before you entered into a contract with him. Sadly, the damage is done. It is your responsibility to find a way to pay back all that has been lost to him."

"How am I to do that? How can I possibly afford to do that?"

"I have no answer, nor did the Dragon Sage." Uppercross leaned close, almost touching his nose to her beak. "She suggested Lady Russell might come to her directly and perhaps the two of you together could work out the matter."

Lady Russell stomped both feet, tearing at the hard ground with her long talons. "I have no need to meet with an upstart young woman who—"

"Who was given the office, had it especially created for her, because of her unparalleled understanding of dragons." Spittle dripped from Uppercross' fang.

"I can do very well on my own, thank you very much. Moreover, I bring news of something far more significant than the issue of the hoard being stolen."

"Where have you been?" Anne asked.

"Here and there. Checking on several theories of my own."

"What have you learned?" The edges of Uppercross' nose curled back. If he had been a man, Lady Russell would have deemed him impertinent.

"This." Lady Russell reached under her wing and pulled out a gold coin.

"Pendragon's Bones!" Uppercross growled and backed away.

"I do not understand."

"That is a gold coin. Something lesser dragons are not permitted to possess, even to touch." His eyes narrowed toward Lady Russell. "Where did you get it? Through legal means?"

"Do you consider finding a thing legal means?"

"Where did you find it?" Uppercross whispered.

"That is the problem." Lady Russell sank into her one-legged thinking posture.

"Pray, be direct with me for I have not your understanding of the matter. Where did you find it, and what does it all mean?" Patience, she needed patience as she paced.

"I found it in the tunnels near the hoard room and the lair."

"I am sure it was not there when we visited the hoard room."

"By my brood mother's bones!" Uppercross trumpeted loud enough to send birds scattering from the trees. "Gold is the most precious hoard, and highly regulated. We cannot possess so much as a single coin, unless it is the hoard we have been provisioned in the Pendragon Accord. Only a few of the fire drakes, the royals, are permitted gold. If there was gold in Kellynch's tunnels, it had to be there illegally."

"But how would it have got there? Kellynch could not have done it."

Lady Russell tucked the coin back under her wing.

"That is a material question. With Kellynch sleeping, someone else must have brought it in, knowing the consequences of it being found. A gold coin is a very precious thing for one to just simply lose, is it not? Someone is trying to lay a crime at Kellynch's feet when he has done nothing wrong."

Uppercross blinked rapidly. "I suppose that makes sense. But who would do such a thing? And why?"

"Surely Sir Walter would not." Lady Russell said.

"No, not Father. I cannot see that he would know the laws so well as to even think of it. Kellynch has been asleep and out of mind for so long, I do not see him being bothered at all by him. But" Anne stood and paced near the lair's entrance. "This sounds a bit ridiculous, but my father's heir, William Elliot. He is set to inherit the estate, and has no more fondness for dragons than my father or his father before him. If he could find a convenient way to rid himself of the obligation, I am sure he would do so. I remember years ago, he came to visit Kellynch, and he made his distaste for major dragons very clear to me. He does not want to be bothered by any responsibilities to them or the Order."

"It does make sense, I grant you. But it is a very extreme thing and for that I think it unlikely." Lady Russell, chittered under her breath. "I had another thought though. I think it could have been accidently left by those who stole the wine. Considering Shepherd's inheritance included a number of gold coins—"

Anne gasped. "How do you know that?"

"I do not like that man at all. I do not trust him. He was among those theories I have been investigating."

"Did you investigate Mr. Elliot as well?"

"As a matter of fact, I did. I know you do not like him, so I did look into his doings. While I cannot say he is entirely untainted, I feel certain—"

"Such intrigue. I do not like it at all. I do not like any of this." Uppercross stood and joined Anne in pacing. "It would be best if Kellynch would simply awaken and deal with this all directly. I will call upon him and see if I can encourage him to awaken. It could take several weeks to arouse him if he is not quite ready. I will inform you as soon as there is anything to tell you. In the meantime, entreat White and Laconia—and you Lady Russell as well—to stay here at Uppercross until the danger of his awakening has passed."

"Thank you, no." Lady Russell flapped her wings. "I do not like a lair, and I should continue my investigations."

"As you will." Uppercross shrugged and trudged into his cavern.

Anne's stomach pinched. Very odd—Lady Russell's behavior, Uppercross's concerns. All of it. That could only mean one thing. It must be very bad indeed.

11
Chapter

August 29, 1814

TWO DAYS LATER, Wentworth obeyed Sophy's summons to join her for nuncheon in the parlor. Sophy was a dear sister to be sure, but there were times that it seemed being married to an admiral made her too apt to think she too could order him about at her whim. On the other hand, being married to a seaman herself, she tolerated the foibles and coarseness that came along with that vocation with good cheer and aplomb—much more than many women were apt to do. So, it was little enough to tolerate a few of her idiosyncrasies as well. At least most of the time.

Kellynch's parlor had not changed since—well, since then. Hardy surprising, considering there was no proper mistress to see to updating and redecorating the place. The walls were still yellow, and the windows and French door still took up all of the longest wall. Lady Elliot's garden, in full bloom, boasted only a few new plants—and of that he could not be entirely certain. Damn it all, even the furniture had not moved since he had made Anne an offer here, in this room.

Why had he agreed to stay at Kellynch at all?

Because he was frugal and the admiral forceful. Damn.

The fragrant victuals Sophy had ordered for nuncheon, now laid out on a side board opposite the windows, were perhaps a bit more hearty than was standard, but for that he could hardly complain. Cold ham and duck, cheeses and fresh, hot bread. The dainty bites that some fashionable tables served proved more irritating than they did restoring. He heaped his plate full and took the stiff, rust colored chair near the floral couch.

Laconia jumped through an open window and settled himself beside Sophy—what would the officious Sir Walter think of his humble "ship's cat" sharing his fine furnishings? Sophy stroked his luxurious fur, only to be rewarded by a dragon-sized purr. Ingratiating creature. For all the years he had spent in the near exclusive company of men, Laconia took an immediate liking to female presence. Odd, how he seemed to like the stroking and doting that tended to go with that.

"You do not approve of me petting your dragon?" Sophy quirked her brow at him. She was handsome as ever, cutting a fine figure in her navy-blue tailored gown, but the years at sea had taken their toll in a weathered complexion and deep creases beside her eyes.

"It matters little what I think. It is for him to decide."

"Rightly said." Laconia flicked his tail slowly.

"I must ask though, where have you been?" He tossed Laconia a sliver of ham that he caught with his long tongue. "You have been notable by your absence. Come to think of it, I have not seen much of White either."

"We are both staying with Laird Uppercross." Laconia licked his shoulder. Even after all these years, it was odd watching a forked tongue perform such a service.

"With the wyvern?" Wentworth asked. "Why ever for? They are not precisely known for their hospitality."

"Apparently there are exceptions to every rule, and Uppercross is exceptional. He is quite fond of stories, especially those of far off places, and happy for our company in exchange for some tall tales every evening."

"How extraordinary." Sophy said. "I would very much like to meet him."

"Why are you staying there?" Wentworth took a long draw from his lemonade. Gah! He should have asked for beer.

"A waking dragon is not a beast to be meddled with. Better that White and I be well out of his way until proper introductions can be made."

"Then the fairy dragon chatter is true? There is a Kellynch dragon, and he is hibernating?"

"And his Keeper is Anne Elliot." Why did Laconia seem to smile upon saying that name?

Yes, he had heard that too, but had dismissed it as one did with most of what fairy dragons said. "Anne is a Dragon Keeper now? Far better I am sure than her arrogant father, but still, it is so strange to consider. Why did you not mention any of this, Sophy? I would have thought a slumbering dragon on the estate a detail worth noting." Wentworth bounced his heel on the carpet. The presence of a hibernating dragon should have been mentioned …

"You used to know Anne, did you not?" Sophy asked.

"Quite well." Laconia looked at him pointedly.

"It is of no matter now. I saw her in passing at Uppercross. She is so wretchedly altered. I hardly know her at all." Wentworth grumbled a sound Laconia ought to recognize as a warning. He had been completely unprepared to meet her, utterly unhappy that he did so unexpectedly. Avoiding her all together would have been far preferable.

"That is untrue." Laconia rose on his forepaws. "It does not take very much to extrapolate that you have not forgiven her. You believe she used you ill, deserted and disappointed you. And worse still, she showed you a feebleness of character which you could not endure. You have never approved of those who seek to oblige others, you think it weakness and timidity."

"Frederick? In what sort of way did you know Miss Elliot?"

"Had I wanted you to know, I would have told you." He slapped the arm of his chair.

Sophy snuffed and frowned. That look—she purposed to get the truth from him. And she probably would, but not today.

"It hardly matters—I am not here to concern myself with the affairs of local dragons. It is my object now to marry as Laconia has been insisting I do. I fully intend to settle as soon as I might be properly tempted. One might say I am ready to fall in love with all the speed which a clear head and quick taste might allow. Either of the Misses Musgrove might do."

Laconia hissed, hackles rising. "Neither of those feather pates hears dragons. I will not have them."

"Surely you cannot mean anything so rash." Sophy stroked the back of Laconia's neck.

"Yet, here I am, Sophia, quite ready to make a foolish match. Anybody between fifteen and thirty may have me for asking. A little beauty, and a few smiles, and a few compliments to the Navy, and I am a lost man. Should not this be enough for a sailor, who has had no society among women to make him nice?" Perhaps she would leave him be.

"You are just trying to be contrary. I know how much you like to provoke an argument just for the sake of the exercise." She shook her head. "I cannot think of this as an advisable way to proceed along this endeavor.

"I have my concerns as well." Admiral Croft swept in like high tide, heading directly for the sideboard. "Do not be in any hurry, you may stay with us as long as you like, provided you make use of the time to make a good decision."

"He may well require some assistance with that." Laconia muttered and laid his head on his paws.

Wentworth leaned back and took several large bites of cold ham and cheese—fresh foods were still quite the pleasant novelty—and chewed very slowly. "That might not be the only reason why I impose upon your hospitality a bit longer."

"What is going on, Wentworth?" the Admiral asked.

"I am on business for the Blue Order."

"I am not surprised they got their talons into you as soon as you were beached." He turned to Laconia and tossed him a piece of cheese. "I imagine you had something to do with this as well?"

Purring loudly, Laconia caught the treat. "I did not instigate it, if that is what you are asking. But I did suggest it was a good idea. The man's rigging was coming loose after taking word to Benwick of his woman's passing."

"But you said you were not concerned in the affairs of local dragons. What errand have they sent you on?" Sophy asked.

"I have been to Cornwall."

"Cornwall?" Croft fell heavily into a floral armchair near the couch. "Can such an errand be anything but serious?"

"I fear the dragon may be losing his mind—or thinking he is Napoleon with the right to take whatever he wants."

Sophy gasped. Laconia leaned into her, purring in a soothing rhythm.

"Like the king?" Croft stroked his chin. "I have never heard of a dragon losing its wits, even in extreme old age. And I thought Cornwall not that old yet."

"That may be so, but the creature is laying claim to some kind of property underwater, just off the coast at Land's End. He claims it is the Merchant Royal, the one that sank in 1641."

"No, you must be joking. That ship is said to have carried tons, many tons, of gold and half a million pieces of silver at least." Croft brushed the idea aside. "But if that is true, the money is—was, and now possibly is—the property of the British government."

"That is not what Cornwall says. He claims that because it is on his territory, it belongs to him and him alone."

"How can he claim it as his territory? Has the Prince Regent weighed in on the matter?"

"According to the dragon, coastal territory includes a particular distance of ocean as well. As to the Prince—" Wentworth shrugged. "Experts in such matters are searching for that information now. As I understand, little regarding marine matters is included in the Accords."

"What are you to do about it?" Sophy asked.

"If the ship is there in the first place, which is far from certain, then it must be ascertained if it actually lies in this zone of contention. Then, if it does, it seems a Blue Order Court must be convened to determine if a land dragon can have marine territory. If the dragon, like a fire drake, is unable to swim, then it cannot reach the territory and if it cannot reach the territory, can it actually hold it?"

Admiral Croft dragged his hand down his face. "And if the dragon does not get the decision he is hoping for?"

"Then a great deal of unpleasantness may ensue; he is a royal dragon after all and they are quite accustomed to getting their way, even more than the average major dragon. As I understand, the Dragon Sage has already been summoned to assist in the matter, but as she is just completing her confinement, travel is still a mite complicated for her." Wentworth swallowed another mouthful of lemonade.

"Damned inconvenient to have a woman in that position." The Admiral took a large bite of buttered bread and jam.

"I suppose so," Sophy looked down at Laconia—avoiding looking at either of them most likely—and scratched under his chin. "But considering that in all these centuries, there has never been a man able to fulfill the task, so the position did not even exist, I hardly think your criticism fair."

Wentworth chuckled. "She does have a point, I suppose. In any case, I was hoping I might approach White for his assistance. My hope is that, with Cornwall's permission of course, I might take a small vessel out off of Land's End, and White might help us ascertain if the vessel is there, and if so, where precisely it is."

"I imagine that bit of information is to be delivered to the Order, not to the dragon himself?"

"It would be altogether safer that way, no? Do you think White will be willing to assist me in the endeavor?"

"If you can pry him loose from Uppercross' company." Sophy winked at Croft.

"I will be happy to reintroduce you to Uppercross, since you were already acquainted once. He does not seem to require a great deal of ceremony." Laconia licked his thumbed paw, chewing a bit at his claws. "Unless you would prefer Miss Anne to do it instead."

"Thank you, no. You will do very well I am sure." Anne Elliot a Dragon Keeper? How was that possible? Surely, she did not hear dragons when he had known her—did she? If she did, she had never made it known—but he did not wear his Blue Order ring then. With no Dragon Friend then why would he?

Cold sweat prickled his upper lip. Could it be? Was

that why she had refused him? She needed a husband who could hear dragons? The room wavered just a bit, no, no, it could not be. Surely, her refusal was just as he understood it to be.

Surely it was.

September 12, 1814

A fortnight later, Wentworth trudged up the steep, shop lined street leading to the Bath's Blue Order office, Laconia trot-hopping beside him, the faint sulfur-mineral scent of the waters lingering in the air. The usual city sounds—carts, horses, shopkeepers, tradesmen and customers—surrounded them, almost, but not quite enough to distract him from his errand. Despite the cool edges on the breeze, sweat trickled down the back of his neck, soaking through his shirt and into the collar of his dark linen coat. Why was so much of Bath uphill? Always uphill. On cobblestone streets.

The yellow-orange Bath stone building adjacent to the Pump Room, that was home to the Bath branch of the Order, was easy to pick out for the platoon of cockatrice on the roof. Odd how something so ostentatious was the very thing that offered the office both secrecy and protection.

White was using the dragon tunnels in order to meet them at the offices. Passing as a horse had its limitations, not the least of which was being seen entering a building other than a stable. There were definite limits on what people could be persuaded to accept.

The Order's signature blue door with a drake's head brass knocker greeted him. Somehow the familiarity was comforting—the only thing right now that was. A blue-liveried footman permitted them to enter—after he presented his Order signet of course.

The tall, lanky footman escorted them to a waiting parlor with a view of the mews at the back of the building. The parlor, easily twice the size of the similar room in the Lyme office, boasted furniture—chairs, tables, perches and cushions—suited for both humans and dragons. Pale green, tall walls—not arsenic green—surrounded them, with many portraits of significant Order members, human on one wall, dragon on the opposite.

A drake on a bench and a cockatrice on a perch conversing near the far windows turned to acknowledge their entry, but then returned to their business. Three snake-like zaltys curled on cushions near the fireplace opposite the window, so deep in conversation with a pair of deep green pucks that they did not even recognize Wentworth and Laconia.

Laconia immediately claimed a high stool with a soft cushion and low rail around half of the seat, placed between two large bookcases, below the portrait of a blue Pa Snake. He curled his serpentine tail around his forepaws, relaxed, but alert. "So many dragons and dragon mates about."

Wentworth pulled a high chair close to Laconia and sat down. "It does seem very busy here." Odd, especially with an air of anticipation lingering about.

The clip-clop of hooves resounded from the far corner of the room. White appeared through a shadowed doorway obscured by more bookcases—an entrance from the tunnel system below the city.

Wentworth beckoned him near. "Is everything all right? I expected you would be here ahead of us."

"Yes, yes, all is well, just a little disordered at the moment." White snorted and shook his head, flapping his neck fin to and fro.

"Disordered? What do you mean?" That was never a good description in connection with anything draconic.

"The tunnels are rather chaotic right now. I have never seen so many dragons gathered in a single place." White's eyes were large and rimmed with white, his nostrils quivered as he breathed hard.

"Dragons gathered? The offices are busy, but not so much as to suggest a gathering."

"Have you not heard? The Dragon Sage is coming to Bath."

Laconia rose on his forepaws and mrrowed.

Was this her response to the issues with Cornwall?

"There are receptions and salons planned, both for the major dragons and we minor dragons as well! I am all astonishment that such a significant officer of the Order would make particular arrangements to see the lesser dragons." White pranced on his forelegs.

Laconia purred. "I have heard talk that she is quite unlike other warm-bloods, more cold-blood than warm-blood."

"That is a strange description for a woman." Wentworth tried not to sneer. She hardly sounded like a pleasant sort.

"I think few would consider it a compliment. But I hear she does. The drakling Pemberley will be with them as well, I am told, as will her fairy dragon Friend. The local fairy dragons are all atwitter that an important warm-blood esteems one of their kind so.

Little twitter-pates."

"Yes, they are." Admiral Easterly strode in, white hair done in some sort of frowsy-blowsy hairstyle. Between the hair and the lack of uniform, he barely looked like himself at all. "The entire office here seems at sixes and sevens trying to prepare for the visit. That is why I have been recalled from the Lyme office. Can you imagine, dragons arriving early to ensure they have a seat at one of her salons?"

Mina, looking particularly sleek and well-brushed, glided in on his heels.

"It is a heady notion to be sure." What sort of person was this Sage? Did she exercise powers of persuasion over dragons as they did over people? No, Wentworth had never heard of such a thing, but might it be possible? Maybe she was even a dragon herself…

"I would declare it all stuff and nonsense except I have been reading that book—*A Commonplace Book of Dragons: A Dragon Friend's Guide to Dragon Companionship*—she wrote and it is quite insightful. I think it may become a new standard among Dragon Mates. There are so very few volumes that give more than cursory treatment to those of us who consort with minor dragons."

Mina hopped up beside Laconia. They twined together, purring loudly. No wonder Laconia had been so anxious to arrive in Bath.

"Shall we to my office then?" Easterly led the way up two flights of stairs, to an office at the end of the corridor, facing the street. As with all the street-facing windows, the curtains were tightly drawn. A transom window, opened slightly, allowed light into the office, which was reflected off strategically placed mirrors.

Though not quite sufficient for reading, it was bright enough to appreciate the half dozen brightly illustrated maps that hung framed on the walls. Several wooden arm chairs and a carved dragon stool clustered near the window, while a large pale wood desk took up the opposite wall. Just enough room was left between that they could enter the room without tripping over one another.

The tatzelwurms curled on the stool, clearly more interested in one another than the matters at hand. There was a reason the species had a reputation for being rather addle-brained, even the most steady and reliable ones, like Laconia. Ah well, he deserved a bit of happiness, might as well enjoy it when he had the opportunity.

White sat beside Wentworth, tail curled beneath him much the way Laconia often sat. They were such very different creatures; it was odd to see them resembling one another in such a way.

"So then, what of Cornwall and the Merchant Royal?" Easterly pushed back his coat tails and sat.

Wentworth gestured at White.

"After some cajoling, Dug Cornwall—"

Wentworth patted White's shoulder. "He is the master of understatement. This dragon deserves a post in His Majesty's diplomatic corps for the way he managed that crotchety old bag of spit and fire."

"Did Cornwall actually spew venom at you?" Easterly raised an eyebrow.

"I can show you the jacket he ruined."

"Bring it in, and I shall see it is replaced." Easterly ground his forehead into the heel of his hand. "Was the entire encounter like that?"

"It changed when I told him that it was my hope

to find the wreck and prove that it was in his territory," White said. "But we have told him nothing of our findings. It is not a wise thing to present a firedrake news he does not want to hear."

"So, the wreck is not in his territory? Or did you not find it at all?"

"Those questions are difficult to answer." White looked at Wentworth.

"Need I ask you for a full explanation?"

Wentworth leaned forward, elbows on his knees. "We found a pod of sea dragons with knowledge of the area. They led us to a site off Land's End—"

"You found a wreck?"

"It is difficult to tell." White whickered and tossed his head.

"How can it be difficult? You either did or you did not."

"Have you ever swum in the ocean?" White tapped the tip of his tail on the bare wood floor.

"No, I do not swim."

"Then I understand your confusion. Let me explain." That was the same tone White had used when dealing with Cornwall. The admiral probably would not have been complimented to know that. "The ocean is not like the land, in many ways. First, the water is constantly moving, this way and that. Imagine walking in a constant strong wind that changed direction one moment to the next."

Easterly's eyebrows rose.

"Ocean water is also rarely clear, more like a constant fog that varies from rather diffuse to nearly opaque. Moreover, the sunlight only penetrates the water to a limited depth. The deeper one dives, the darker it gets, until it is difficult to see at all. I am told at the deepest depths, the darkness is complete."

"I had no idea."

"Then there is the matter of pressure. The weight of the water presses down on one as one dives. The deeper one goes, the more water presses down, until the press is unbearable. Only a very few of us can dive very deeply." One could almost see wire-rimmed glasses perched on White-the-school-master's nose.

"How could I not know this?" Easterly snorted.

"Few warm-bloods do. I searched for the wreck myself, but you can imagine, it is no easy task. Moreover, there are parts of the ocean beyond Land's End that are far deeper than we expected, rather like a deep canyon under the ocean."

"A canyon under water?"

"The sea floor is many things you would not expect. Yes, there are mountains and canyons beneath the sea. And some of those canyons are very deep. Too deep. I could not explore it myself. I did see a bit of debris that resembled a mast protruding from the canyon, but in the murky dark, I could not be sure."

"And where were these interesting bits?" Easterly folded his arms over his chest as though certain he would not like the answer.

"What I found appears to be on the line where the sea dragons say the land is divided from sea."

"Of course, it was. Of course." Easterly threw up his hands. "This will not do. We must find out more. Have you any recommendations?"

"Marine wyrms can dive far more deeply than I or the pod of sea dragons we encountered. As I understand it, they can dive the deepest of any dragon, having the ability to breath like a fish whilst they are below. Their eyes are suited for the dark and their bones stronger than other wyrms. You need a team of marine wyrms to investigate and give you better information than I can supply."

Easterly stared at the ceiling and frowned. "Do you know how many marine wyrms there are attached to English lands?"

Wentworth grimaced. "Surely there must be a coastal dragon or two."

"There is one, Exactly one."

"Who is it?"

"Kellynch."

Wentworth gasped. Surely not! What would a marine wyrm be doing with a landlocked estate?

"As I understand, your brother Croft has recently let that estate. I am sure you are familiar with the problem, then."

"The dragon is hibernating to get away from a long line of atrocious Keepers."

"Precisely. He is soon to awaken, and we need to convince him to assist us in this matter, for the good of the Order. Considering Sir Walter Elliot is the Keeper—"

Wentworth chewed his upper lip. "Not any longer. Sir Walter's second daughter, Miss Anne Elliot, is now Keeper."

"What? That has not been registered with the Order."

"I am hardly surprised." Wentworth pinched his temples with one hand. "But all the local dragons have acknowledged it, so it might as well be properly registered."

"You know this woman?"

Laconia licked Mina's head and flicked his tail. "She is hardly an experienced Dragon Keeper to be sure. But she is kind, compassionate, and capable. She has the makings of a decent Dragon Keeper."

Easterly racked his hair back. "There is only one thing to be done for this. Wentworth, you must find this woman and work with her as Kellynch awakens. The two of you must convince Kellynch to work with us so that we might settle this matter with Cornwall quickly, before any more trouble ensues. We do not need the Prince Regent getting involved."

"Sir, with respect, there must be another—" Wentworth shrank back from Easterly's withering look.

"He does not like Miss Anne." Laconia muttered.

"You do not?" White's tail thumped the floor. "I cannot fathom why. As warm-bloods go, she is quite decent, thoughtful and respectful. What is there not to like about her?"

"There is a history," Laconia said.

"What is that supposed to mean?" White asked.

"Whatever it means, it does not matter. It must be put aside in favor of what the Order requires. However much you might dislike it, Wentworth, it must be done. Consider it an order."

One he dare not disobey, though the possibility had never tempted him so much. "Yes, sir."

Laconia purred. How good of him to be so pleased.

Had he intentionally contrived to have Easterly order Wentworth to do precisely what Laconia wanted? That was probably a bit farfetched. But only a little.

Chapter 12

September 19, 1814

IT WAS A very fine cool September morning, several days after Wentworth returned from his trip—was it Bath Louisa said he had visited? Not that it mattered really. Even if he had news of anyone she cared about there, she would hardly ask him for it, and he would hardly offer to share it otherwise. He had barely spoken to her since he came to the country, and then only words required by simple civility. A man scorned was not a charitable creature. His resentment was deep and intractable, and though the sting of it was difficult to bear, she could hardly argue its justice.

Was it wrong, though, to wish he might be a little more understanding? Perhaps. And even if it were not, it was impractical.

A vaguely chilly breeze ducked around the drab

floral curtains in the morning room, fluttering them against the stark white walls in its attempt to cool the fragrant morning coffee far too soon. The toast on the too-large round table was already cold, so it seemed fitting.

Would it matter to him that she had changed her mind? That back then she had been persuaded in a draconic fashion—not that he was ever likely to know that. Lady Russell would surely not trust him with her secret and she would not return Lady Russell's betrayal in kind.

Probably not.

He was not the type of man to allow for such things. He might have been once, but no longer, given the way that he had looked at her on the few occasions their paths crossed.

Across the breakfast table, Mary sighed. It was not that there was really anything to sigh about, only that Anne was not paying enough attention to her. It was her first salvo in what would be escalating efforts to achieve her goal. Best compose some sort of conversation—

A knock at the door! Excellent.

A moment later, the Misses Musgrove tumbled into the parlor, giggling and laughing, in a way that was all joy and little propriety.

That would surely give Mary a topic of conversation. More likely several.

"We are going to take a long walk." Louisa, rosy-cheeked and a little breathless with her golden-brown curls peeking from under her straw bonnet, tousled by the breeze, looped her arm in Henrietta's.

"But we are sure you will not like to come with us." Henrietta leaned against Louisa, her red cloak pulled back over one slim shoulder.

"Why does everyone suppose me not to be a good walker?" Mary harrumphed, rising slowly. "I should like to join you very much. I am very fond of a long walk."

The Misses Musgrove exchanged aggrieved looks. If Henrietta and Louisa did not want Mary to join them, why did they come by and announce that Mary would not want to go? Did they not yet understand that was precisely the way to convince Mary to do something she would otherwise refuse to do?

"But you were just saying you did not feel well this morning." Anne glanced at the Misses Musgrove who nodded vigorously.

"I am feeling much better now." Mary crossed her arms and tossed her head. "Besides, I am sure time in the fresh air and sunshine will do me very well indeed."

Anne bit her tongue. Had Mary already forgotten how much fresh air and sunshine disagreed with her and were apt to give her quite the headache?

"Will you join us, Miss Anne?" Oh, the pleading look in Louisa's eye.

No doubt, she hoped that Anne would be ready to accompany Mary home when she inevitably declared herself tired and not wanting to go on. That way, the Misses Musgrove could avoid disruption in their plans.

Ah, well, it was pleasing to be useful, whatever the fashion. "I should very much like a walk this morning."

The girls left to wait for them outside, and probably to mutter what a burden was theirs now to bear.

"I cannot imagine why they should suppose I

should not like a long walk," Mary said as she went upstairs. "Everybody is always supposing that I am not a good walker. Yet they ask, though they would not have been pleased if we had refused to join them. When people come in this manner on purpose to ask us, how can one say no?"

A quarter of an hour later, the little party walked briskly through the garden paths, a little barren now that autumn was fast upon them. How disheveled a garden seemed without fragrance. Unlike the gardens at Kellynch that were maintained so something fragrant bloomed there three seasons a year, Uppercross had no such attentive gardening. Only late spring and summer blossoms graced its beds, rendering the approaching autumn sparse and brown and a bit crunchy.

Soon they left the gardens, and the footpath led to a stile that would take them between the hedgerow and the ripening fields, in the direction of Winthrop, the Hayter's home. Was this their purpose in going out today? Henrietta had seemed a little withdrawn towards Charles Hayter since Wentworth had come. Was Louisa trying to rectify that?

That of course begged the question whether it was a favor to Charles Hayter and Henrietta, who had seemed genuinely fond of Charles Hayter, or to merely distract Henrietta from Wentworth. Louisa was a sweet girl, but even sweet girls experienced jealousy … Best not continue along that line of uncharitable thoughts.

"Look! Look there! I see Charles and Captain

Wentworth." Henrietta pointed down the path and squealed softly.

"It cannot be them. They were gone hunting this morning. They cannot be back so soon." Mary refused to look in that direction as though that would make them disappear.

The taller of the men, a fine figure of a man, waved at them. Indeed, it was Wentworth. Anne's throat tightened. She pulled back her shoulders and straightened her spine. He might dislike her, but he would not see her wilting in his presence.

The Misses Musgrove ran toward them. Mary, who never did like to be left out, did likewise. Anne approached the wide space in the path flanked by dense hedgerow at her own pace.

"… that young dog we brought along was definitely not ready for the hunt, so alas we are home early." Wentworth rolled his eyes a bit. Did he not approve of any creature undisciplined?

"We are going for a long walk. Do join us!" Louisa looked up at him, batting her eyes.

"Capital notion, what say you Musgrove?" It seemed as though Wentworth was deliberately avoiding looking at her. Which was just as well as she would not be batting her eyes at him.

She should probably turn back. With Charles now available to entertain Mary, what need was there for her to go along?

"You should go with them."

Anne peered into the hedgerow just behind Wentworth. A furry black face with golden eyes peered back at her. What was Laconia about?

"Go with them. I need to talk to you."

"We can talk at the cottage," she whispered behind

her hand.

"No, the fairy dragons are in the garden gathering nectar from the last of the summer blooms. I do not wish to be overheard. Come walking with us." He stepped out of the bushes and purred.

"Is that your cat, Captain?" Henrietta took a step toward Laconia. "He is a very handsome cat."

Laconia turned his nose up at Henrietta and spring-hopped to Anne. He purred louder and rubbed himself around her ankles.

"He seems to like you very well, Anne." Louisa sounded a little jealous.

"I do not like cats." Mary sniffed and stepped a little closer to Charles.

Wentworth, his chiseled features dark and brooding, stared at Laconia. It seemed as though he wanted to say something, but he did not.

"Let us go on then." Louisa marched ahead, Wentworth on one side, Henrietta on the other.

Charles, albeit reluctantly, took to Mary's side, leaving Anne to walk between the two parties with only Laconia as a companion.

"What glorious weather for the Admiral and my sister! They meant to take a long drive this morning; perhaps we may hail them from some of these hills. They talked of coming into this side of the country. I wonder whereabouts they will upset today. Oh! it does happen very often, I assure you; but my sister makes nothing of it. She would as soon be tossed out as not." He stole a quick glance at Anne.

Surely, he could not mean that. White drew their gig—mostly for the sheer novelty and amusement of it; what an excellent story it would make to share back with his sea dragon friends—and he was far too kind and steady a creature to allow either of them to come to harm. Why would Wentworth taunt her so?

"Ah! You are teasing, I know." Louisa giggled and slipped her hand into the crook of his arm. "But if it were really so, I should do just the same in her place. If I loved a man, as she loves the Admiral, I would always be with him, nothing should ever separate us, and I would rather be overturned by him, than driven safely by anybody else."

"Had you?" He glanced over his shoulder at Anne, again. If he had something to say to her, why did he not just address her directly? This really was unseemly. "I honor you! It is the worst evil to be a yielding and indecisive character. Let those who would be happy be firm."

Anne looked away. Laconia mrrowed, the tip of his tail lashing. It was nice to have a defender.

Wentworth had never been apt to be cruel, but it seemed time—and what she had done—had taken a toll on him. But that did not mean it was not growing tiresome.

They gained the summit of a most considerable hill, the one which parted Uppercross and Winthrop. Winthrop House, without beauty and without dignity—at least according to Father—was stretched before them at the foot of the next hill: an indifferent house, standing low, and hemmed in by the barns and farmyard buildings. Exactly the sort of place that Father declared he would never visit.

"Bless me! Here is Winthrop. I declare I had no idea! Well now, I think we had better turn back; I am excessively tired." Apparently, Mary agreed with Father.

Henrietta shrugged and moved to turn back, but

Charles and Louisa came alongside her, almost as though they were of a single mind.

"No, we are so close, it is only right that we should call upon my Aunt Hayter. Mary you will come with us." Charles beckoned Mary and took Henrietta's arm. "I know she will want to see you as well. It will do you both good to rest a quarter of an hour in her kitchen."

"Oh no, indeed! Walking up that hill again would do me more harm than any sitting down could do me good." Mary squared her shoulders, pulling her shawl tight around them, and tried to look resolute.

"I said you will come with us, and come you shall." Charles glowered that certain look he had when he was absolutely not to be argued with.

Laconia whispered to Louisa and Henrietta. *You want to go, and you want Mary to accompany you.*

Wentworth's brow shot up.

"Pray Mary, we do so like your company, and we know Aunt Hayter does, too. You will be most welcome." Louisa said, though she seemed a little surprised at the words coming out of her mouth.

You want to go. Laconia stared at Mary. *You want to go.*

Mary gave way, and the little party headed down the hill.

Anne and Wentworth stared at each other for a long moment. A sharp wind carrying thin grey clouds along to blot the sun, rattled the hedgerow and set the fields waving. Someone had to break the silence.

Apparently, it would be her. "Mary is good-natured enough in many respects, but she does sometimes provoke the Musgroves excessively with her pride—the Elliot pride, they call it."

"I recall it well." Wentworth muttered through his teeth.

"They would have been happier had you married Charles." Laconia sat back on his tail and looked up at them.

"How did you know?" Anne gasped.

"He offered for you … and you refused him?" Wentworth's eyes widened and his voice softened just a mite. "When did that happen?"

"In the year nine."

"You did not accept him." Wentworth tried to catch her gaze as though to confirm what he had heard. His was not the only offer she had refused.

"Why did you refuse?" Laconia asked.

Blessed draconic directness. Anne tried to force a smile, but something that was likely not a glower was the best she could muster.

"As the only dragon hearing sibling, I had a duty to Kellynch as heir to the Keepership. Charles is heir to Uppercross. Two Keepers—or those who will be Keepers—should not marry."

"So, you expect to marry the heir to Kellynch estate?" The tip of Laconia's tail flicked.

Wentworth wore the oddest expression.

"You told me you had something to discuss. Let us not be distracted." She crouched down and fixed her gaze on Laconia.

He seemed to frown—at least his fangs showed, and he seemed displeased. What was he about? "This concerns you too." He beckoned Wentworth with his broad thumbed paw.

"Me? I have no idea to what you refer."

"You will. It is regarding Kellynch."

"Kellynch?" They said simultaneously.

Wentworth crouched down near them.

"Yes. You should know, Miss Anne, that we have been bidden by the Blue Order, to enlist Kellynch's aid in a most significant matter."

"His aid? Forgive me but I am confused on two matters. First, he is hibernating. How is he to be of assistance to anyone? And in the second place, I am given to understand that I am his Keeper now. Is it incorrect to infer that such requests should go through me?"

Laconia wrinkled his nose at Wentworth. "That is what I told him."

"I know you do not wish to deal with me, and for that I can only express my deepest regrets. But the facts cannot be changed. Any matter involving Kellynch requires that I become involved as well."

Wentworth blinked at her as though staring at someone he hardly knew.

"Over the last day or so, Uppercross heard rumblings that he thought to be the sounds of a dragon awakening. But when he went to Kellynch, the lair was empty."

"Empty? He is gone? That cannot be." Anne sat hard on the dusty ground. "Shelby told me he would be hungry and has arranged a flock of sheep to sate him. Perhaps Shelby has taken him to that field which is out of sight of the rest of the estate? I would have thought Shelby would have told me though."

"Sheep?" Wentworth looked utterly baffled. "What would a marine wyrm want with sheep?"

"A marine wyrm? What are you talking about? Kellynch is a land dragon, a wyrm, but he lives on land. You must be mistaken." How could he make such an error?

"No, he is not. I saw the scales left behind in the lair. There is no doubt," Laconia said. "Kellynch is a marine wyrm. He would want fish, in great quantities upon his awakening, not sheep."

"I had no idea of his true nature! Even the charter did not—no wait, perhaps it did, that part was stained and smudged. It could have named him a marine wyrm. But why would such a dragon have a land-locked holding? The charter mentioned something about a debt owed from one dragon to another—"

"Which dragon?" Wentworth's brows knit.

"That part was partially torn and stained, but it might have said Cornwall."

Laconia arched, fur pouffing, and chittered.

Wentworth exchanged a troubled glance with him, but shook his head when Anne raised her brows at him.

"If he does not want sheep, but seeks fish, where would he go?"

"To the sea—I imagine Lyme the most expedient place. There are dragon tunnels directly between here and Lyme. It was the route Admiral Easterly suggested we use once we obtained Kellynch's consent to help us." Wentworth chewed the inside of his cheek. He did that when deep in thought.

"I am told that a wakening dragon is not in his right mind until his hunger is sated. It sounds as though he could be a grave danger. I must get to him. But how? And if he is out to sea, then what am I to do?"

Laconia stepped his front paws on her knee. "There is little choice, we must find a way to go to Lyme. We can help you find him, even if he is at sea. It is imperative that he acknowledges you as Keeper, and you bring him under proper regulation immediately."

"I fear he is right. The possible consequences of this are unfathomable." Wentworth dragged his hand over his mouth. "Since we are under orders from Admiral Easterly to obtain Kellynch's help, I suppose we are now obligated to assist you in this matter as well. I will find a way to get both of us to Lyme."

"Kellynch's help? In what?"

"It does not matter until we have found him." Laconia glanced over his shoulder at Wentworth, who nodded. "That is our sole focus right now."

"I am not certain how, not yet in any case. But we will help you get this sorted out." He gazed deep into her eyes with that soul touching look of his.

Something different from the resentment and judgement she had seen earlier. A remainder of former sentiment; it was an impulse of pure, though unacknowledged, friendship; it was a proof of his own warm and amiable heart, which she could not contemplate without emotions so compounded of pleasure and pain, that she knew not which prevailed.

September 20, 1814

An invitation for dinner came just after midday the following afternoon, brought by Henrietta who did not even spend a quarter of hour in the parlor with them. Mary, naturally, took offense at what must have been an unintended slight. But that was only to be expected.

Charles and Anne waited in the cramped vestibule

by the front door while Mary finished her very long toilette for dinner, barely managing to avoid knocking into the small half-table holding an oversized vase of wilting hot house flowers.

"We may give Wentworth the credit for our invitations tonight—and perhaps the fact that Charles Hayter has not been invited." Charles murmured as he watched the staircase, likely for signs of Mary.

"I do not understand."

"That is because you are not the matchmaking sort." Charles tipped his head and raised his eyebrows. "I have never seen a pleasanter man in my life than Wentworth. And, from what I have heard he himself say, he has made not less than twenty thousand pounds by the war—a very suitable fortune for either of my sisters. He would be a capital match for either of them."

Anne winced. Though they were pleasant girls, neither were Wentworth's equal in sense or consequence; after all, neither heard dragons.

"But I do worry for Charles Hayter. He and Henrietta have long been fond of one another. We always thought—mind you, it would not be a great match for her—but if Henrietta liked him that would be the thing—and she seemed to like him." Charles cocked his head at the sound of footfalls on the stairs.

"I have always thought Captain Wentworth liked Henrietta best." Mary declared as she reached the bottom step. Her pronouncement had all the Elliot pride of assurance that she was right.

"I have always thought Louisa more suitable." Charles opened the front door and ushered them out.

The four o'clock sun hung just above the trees, the last vestiges of afternoon warmth just barely cloying.

Birds, and a few fairy dragons twittered in the trees along the footpath. Did Mary and Charles even recognize the little dragons were there? Probably not—they were rather inconvenient all told. Did they know about Kellynch's departure? Was word of his unusual awakening already circulating around England and her reputation as a Dragon Keeper deteriorating before she had even truly begun?

"I think having him marry either could be extremely delightful. Upon my word it would. Dear me!" Mary gasped and pressed her hand to her chest. "Just think, if he should rise to any very great honors! If he should ever be made a baronet! 'Lady Wentworth' sounds very well. That would be a noble thing, indeed, for Henrietta! She would take precedence over me then. She would not dislike that. Sir Frederick and Lady Wentworth! It would be but a new creation, however, and I never think much of your new creations." Of course, Mary would focus on that.

"I think Charles Hayter would be very disappointed by such a turn." Charles kept his eyes carefully forward, away from Mary.

"I cannot think him at all a fit match for Henrietta; and considering the alliances which the Musgroves have made, she has no right to throw herself away. I do not think any young woman has a right to make a choice that may be disagreeable and inconvenient to the principal part of her family, and be giving bad connections to those who have not been used to them. Consider, who is Charles Hayter? Nothing but a country curate. A most improper match for a Miss Musgrove of Uppercross."

"Nonsense, Mary. I grant it might not be a grand match for Henrietta, but he has a very fair chance, through his friends the Spicers, of getting a living from the Bishop in the course of a year or two. Moreover, he is the eldest son and will inherit a very pretty property. The estate at Winthrop is not less than two hundred and fifty acres, besides the farm near Taunton, which is some of the best land in the country. A very respectable holding. Henrietta might do worse than marry Charles Hayter. I think if she has him, and Louisa can get Captain Wentworth, I shall be very well satisfied."

Mary walked a little faster to pull just ahead of Charles and glower back at him. "It would be shocking to have Henrietta marry Charles Hayter; a very bad thing for her, and still worse for me. I wish that Captain Wentworth may soon put him quite out of her head. As to Captain Wentworth's liking Louisa as well as Henrietta, it is nonsense to say so. He certainly does like Henrietta a great deal the best. You agree of course, do you not, Anne?"

Mrrrow.

"Pray go on, I have a rock in my shoe, and I must right it." Anne leaned against a small tree along the footpath and waved them on.

Mary did not even glance over her shoulder to check on her, just continued her diatribe against Charles Hayter and in favor of Wentworth.

"Why was she not drowned at birth?" Laconia emerged from the undergrowth, licking his shoulder.

"It is not something human parents are apt to do."

"Perhaps they should. I hardly see she is fit for anything. It seems she cannot even breed sensible offspring. What proper creature falls out of a tree?"

Anne chuckled and scratched under his chin. "I do not suppose you called me out to discuss my sister's offspring."

"No." He wound himself around her ankles. "I like you. You are sensible, not like those twitterpates your sister wishes to force on my Friend."

"I thank you for the compliments, but I do not understand to what end they lead."

"The silly sisters cannot hear me, and I do not like them. Not at all."

"I see why that might upset you." She extended her hand to offer a scratch.

He bumped his hand under her fingers. "Since I must not persuade a dragon hearer—especially of something they do not wish to be persuaded of—I must ask you to convince those two that the sisters are not for him."

"I do not think they will listen to me very well. It has never been their way."

"No one on this Keep—no warm-blood—speaks better sense than you, it is well known. Promise me you shall work on my behalf."

"I will do what I can, but I have not your persuasive powers. Can you not work on Henrietta and Louisa yourself?"

"Wentworth would not approve. He needs a mate. He wants a mate. But I do not like those girls. I do like you." He purred so loud his side vibrated under her hand.

"I am honored."

"His fortune is due to me, you know. How do you think he found so many prize ships? I spoke to the sea dragons on his behalf. There is a reason I was considered the luckiest ship's cat in the fleet."

"You are a great friend to be sure. I am certain he would not abandon you in favor of a mate you do not like."

"The urge for a mate is very strong. He should seek you. You smell right."

What a dear creature, but surely, he did not understand so very much about the complexities of the human heart. "I think him very sensible and steady. Should the worst happen though, please know, that you might always have a home with me. I will ensure that Kellynch accepts you. As a marine wyrm, he might even like to have one in his Keep who understands his home territory."

Laconia looked up at her and purred. "You are truly a good Dragon Friend."

"I am afraid I must get in to dinner before I disrupt the entire party." She gave him a final scratch and hurried to the house.

The maid led her to the drawing room where the rest of the party waited. Louisa and Henrietta sat on the sofa on either side of Wentworth all but fawning over him. No wonder Laconia was distressed.

"Now you are here, Miss Anne, dinner may be served. Come now." Mrs. Musgrove called from the top of the room.

At Uppercross the dining room was a merry place, full of warmth and companionship, if not the most elegant furnishings or refined dishes. Only one mirror above the fireplace reflected the tallow—not wax—candles in pewter, not polished silver, candlesticks on the table. No fancy French dishes or towering jellies filled with fruit graced this table. But the dishes were plentiful, if mundane, and fragrant. And if someone's manners slipped and she scooped with the near side of their soup spoon not the far, or one of the ladies enjoyed a hearty portion of her favorite dish, no one appeared to notice, nor was it brought up in hushed conversation during the days following.

Her father had dined here not infrequently, as was expected for neighbors to do. But he pronounced it a beastly affair, an unfortunate consequence of being the leading family in the neighborhood and therefore having higher standards than their hosts.

She could not agree. No amount of fine food could substitute for pleasing companions and easy manners.

Wentworth's manners were easy, readily answering questions about naval matters: how one lived aboard ship, the food there, the servants, the suitability of the accommodations for ladies.

"With all due respect, ladies, I would never willingly admit any ladies on board a ship of mine, excepting for a ball, or a visit of a few hours. This is from no want of gallantry. It is rather from feeling how impossible it is, with all one's efforts and all one's sacrifices, to make the accommodations on board such as women ought to have. I hate to hear of women on board, or to see them on board. No ship under my command shall ever convey a family of ladies anywhere, if I can help it."

"But has your sister not been often on board with the admiral?" Louisa asked from Wentworth's right side.

"Surely you could not disapprove of that?" Henrietta pressed from the left. "I heard you brought another officer's family to meet him, so you have had ladies aboard your ship."

"I would assist any brother officer's wife that I could, and I would bring anything of Harville's—the officer of whom you speak—from the world's end, if he wanted it. But do not imagine that I did not feel it an evil in itself."

"When you have got a wife, you will sing a different tune, no doubt." Mr. Musgrove chuckled as he poured wine for Anne and Mary.

Wentworth grumbled under his breath.

Mrs. Musgrove looked from Wentworth to her daughters, then Mary and Anne. "There is nothing so bad as a separation. I am quite of that opinion. I know what it is, for Mr. Musgrove always attends the assizes. I am so glad when they are over, and he is safe back again."

Anne glanced at Wentworth but he looked away. Far be it from him to admit perhaps the life of a sailor's wife—one of constant separation—could be difficult. But wait, those creases beside his eyes. Perhaps it was something else. Perhaps.

"Shall we to the drawing room?" Mrs. Musgrove, all smiles and good cheer, placed her napkin on the table beside her empty plate and stood, a benevolent queen surveying her grateful subjects. How bright and truly happy she appeared, as if she genuinely enjoyed the simple graces of hospitality.

Anne sighed and fought back another wave of regret. Yet one more unfavorable comparison between the Elliots and the Musgroves.

She followed the rest of the company out of the room. Mary looked over her shoulder from the front of the group and glowered. Yes, technically Anne should take precedence over most of the company. But among such a gathering of friends and family, was it truly necessary? Being an Elliot did not require she flaunt her rank, did it?

In the cozy, old fashioned drawing room, she took

her place at the pianoforte. Anne had taken the place at the pianoforte so often, Henrietta and Louisa had begun calling it 'Anne's seat.' Tucked in the corner nearest the fireplace, it allowed her to discreetly survey the entire room with its somber family portraits lined along the dark wood paneled walls, and staid, traditional furniture; the cluster of chairs, newly upholstered in a pale striped print, around the worn card table where Charles and his father sat; the matching settees with high wooden backs and thin lumpy cushions, facing each other in the middle of the opposite wall where the Musgrove ladies monopolized Wentworth's attention; and the lonely window seat where Mary sulked in the dimmest part of the room, without conversation or company. Tomorrow she would complain bitterly of the inattentiveness of her hosts.

No one seemed interested in a dance, so Anne began to play something soft and restful, a tune she knew so well it required no thought to play, one that soothed her soul.

"You mentioned your trip to Cornwall, sir." Mrs. Musgrove smoothed her full, old fashioned skirt over her lap. "But you said nothing more of it. Was it a pleasant one?"

"The sea air alone was enough to do a land-locked sailor a world of good." Wentworth glanced toward Anne.

She nearly missed her fingering.

"So, our country air does not suit you?" Charles pulled his chair close to the settees.

Henrietta and Louisa tittered.

Wentworth cocked his head and raised his brows. "When you visit London, do you not find you long for the freshness of the country air?"

"Well said, sir, well said." Charles chuckled and laid his hands over his belly. Soon, his portly stature would match his father's. They were so alike in looks and humor.

"Then you do understand. A sailor always longs for the sea and the companionship of his shipmates."

"So, you say we are not sufficient company for you?" Mary sniffed and wrinkled her nose as if detecting a foul odor as she forced herself to move toward the conversation.

"Not at all." Wentworth's voice turned entirely patronizing and not at all pleasant.

Anne winced. He had used that tone with Mary back at Kellynch those many years ago.

"If you were to experience the sea for yourself, I am sure you would understand." Wentworth fixed his eyes on Anne, a commanding look if ever there was one.

"It would be quite an experience to see the ocean." Hopefully that was what he wanted her to say.

The entire room turned to stare at her as Wentworth walked to the pianoforte. Was it just her imagination, or could she feel the heat from his body as he stood beside her?

"Sounds like an interesting thought. I would like to do that one day." Charles propped his feet on a nearby stool and crossed his ankles.

"What a wonderful thought, Charles!" Louisa clapped. "Why do we not go to visit Lyme?"

"That is a very interesting notion my dear, a very interesting one indeed." Mrs. Musgrove clasped her hands together very tightly. She did not like the idea, but was far too polite to say so in company.

Mr. Musgrove cleared his throat. "Travel can be a

very good thing for young people, I think. There is much to be learned in seeing other places ... and the sea ..." He swallowed hard.

"It was at Gibraltar that you first met our brother, was it not?" Henrietta asked.

Louisa gasped. They generally tried to avoid any mention of Dick, which would invariably turn the conversation maudlin.

Mrs. Musgrove fixed her gaze on Wentworth. "You need not be afraid of mentioning poor Dick before me, for it would be rather a pleasure to hear him talked of by such a good friend."

"Ah! Those were pleasant days when I had the Laconia!" His smile seemed a bit forced. Was it Dick, or was he frustrated that the conversation was not going according to his intentions?

"And I am sure, sir," Mrs. Musgrove said, "it was a lucky day for us, when you were put captain of that ship. We shall never forget what you did. Poor dear fellow! He was grown so steady, and such an excellent correspondent, while he was under your care! It would have been a happy thing, if he had never left you. I assure you, Captain Wentworth, we are very sorry he ever left you."

That expression Wentworth's wore! He had probably been at some pains to get Dick off the Laconia rather than appreciate his presence. Instead of indulging that sentiment though, he sat beside Mrs. Musgrove and spoke about Dick with so much sympathy and natural grace, as showed the kindest consideration for all that was real and unabsurd in the parent's feelings.

Louisa harrumphed not-so-softly. Was she jealous of Wentworth's attentions to her mother? Though

Dick's sisters did not share his parent's grief at his loss, they should be more sensitive to their parent's pain.

Or perhaps it was simply that she did not like her conversation usurped toward another's topics.

Wentworth's cheeks tightened—a tiny look of disapproval he had perfected for use in the Elliot household when he must not speak his feelings about Sir Walter and his eldest daughter. Perhaps Laconia had overestimated Wentworth's fondness for Louisa.

"I do believe that everyone should see the sea at least once in their lives. One cannot understand a sailor lest they have seen the sea." Wentworth kept his tone quite mild.

The skin along the side of her neck prickled. Wentworth's gaze, equal parts warm and commanding, had wandered to her.

"It would be interesting to see what Dick wrote about in his letters," Anne said softly.

Why did so many eyes turn on her when she spoke?

Mr. Musgrove cleared his throat. "I do believe a trip to Lyme might be accommodated."

"Thank you, Papa!" Louisa clapped softly. "As soon as may be possible, tomorrow even—" She turned and clasped Henrietta's hands.

"No, my dear, that is not practical. I think such a trip would be better made in the spring."

Louisa slouched and huffed. "No Papa, we cannot wait until spring. That is entirely unnecessary."

"But the weather must be considered."

"The weather has been very mild, and we have no reason to think that will change in the immediate future. Besides, that is all the more reason for us to go immediately. We can be off early in the morning and back in the same day."

Wentworth pinched his temples with thumb and fingers.

"No, I draw the line at that notion, child." Mr. Musgrove folded his arms over his chest.

"Papa, you cannot withdraw your permission!"

"The effort would be too much on the horses. I must consider them. They cannot go both legs of the journey in a single day. On that I am firm."

"Very well then," Louisa frowned briefly. "I suppose we must stay the night then."

"The night? Where will you stay?"

"I am certain my friend Harville—" Wentworth muttered to his hands.

"You cannot impose on the hospitality of a family we do not even know." Mrs. Musgrove eyes narrowed, and her mouth set in a determined hard line.

"An inn, Mama. I am certain there are inns at Lyme. Are there not, Captain Wentworth?" Louisa batted her eyes at him. When had Louisa become so headstrong and inconsiderate?

Perhaps Wentworth's initial attraction to her had been the appearance of firmness and decisiveness. Somehow, he seemed less pleased now.

"Yes, there are. I know of several respectable establishments. But young ladies should not make such a trip alone." Wentworth peeked at Anne, a hopeful note in his voice.

"How can you say we will be alone in your company. Captain Wentworth?"

"You must have a chaperone, and on this I will not be moved." Mrs. Musgrove glanced at her husband who nodded.

"But Mama, if Henrietta goes, is that not—"

"No, it is not. You need the guidance and protection of someone older and more sensible than yourself. Miss Anne," Mrs. Musgrove reached toward Anne, "I declare, I know no one with more good sense than yourself. Perhaps you would consider making the journey with our girls?"

"That is an excellent notion." Something in Wentworth's tone—was that a note of relief?

"Please, Anne!" Henrietta jumped up and hurried to Anne's side—or was it to be close to Wentworth?

"Yes! That is the perfect solution! Anne, you must go with us!" Louisa beamed. "Then it is settled—"

"Settled? Settled?" Mary cried. She paced along the center of the room. "I do not see how this is settled at all. Why should this be settled? I do not understand why Anne should go. She is nothing to you. I am your sister. Who more fitting to watch over you and protect you than your sister? Truly, who is Anne to you?"

Anne's cheeks burned and she pinched her temples. If only she could hide beneath the piano until this humiliating episode was over!

"Why must I stay at home? I do say, it seems when there is a gay outing to be had I am always the last to be thought of." Mary dabbed her handkerchief to her eyes.

"There, there, Mary dear." Mrs. Musgrove rolled her eyes. "No one intended to leave you out. You have said so many times that you dislike the carriage, we were only thinking of sparing you a half day travel in one."

"I should like to see Lyme." Charles sat up and squared his shoulders. "I do not see why we cannot join the party."

"There you have it," Mary nodded sharply. "With Charles and I, there is no need for Anne to make the journey."

Wentworth cleared his throat and glared at Charles.

"You may have precedence over your unmarried sister," Charles shot a sour look toward his wife, "but that does not mean you should also exclude her. Anne has had little opportunity to travel and if the rest of us are going, then she too should have the opportunity. Will you join us to Lyme, Anne?"

"I think Miss Anne should take in the sea," Wentworth said.

"Then it is decided." Charles brushed his hands together. "We are all for Lyme."

Wentworth looked pleased, but was that only because of the business that had to be accomplished? It seemed that it should be so, but something about his tone suggested more.

13
Chapter

September 21, 1814

ANNE LED THE party from the cottage as they met the rest of the traveling company at the Great House the next morning. Wentworth intended that they would enjoy—or endure according to Laconia—a rather early breakfast and set off punctually after that. He had always been an optimistic man.

He should have consulted with Anne on the matter before setting his expectations. She could have informed him of his folly: Mary would invent concerns and complaints enough to delay them no less than an hour; Mrs. Musgrove would fuss over her daughters' departure and insist on additional items for their comfort which would have to be packed and added to the carriage; Mr. Musgrove would offer—largely unnecessary but kind fatherly—advice to

Charles who was driving the curricle meant to carry himself and Wentworth; and all told, they would not leave much before noon, at best.

Anne was of course correct; they did not depart until nearly two o'clock. Wentworth was not pleased. When the curricle rode close to the carriage, she could just make out Laconia trying to ease his Friend's temper, reminding him that the late afternoon and early evening were the times they would most likely find signs of Kellynch, so perhaps the turn of events might actually be to their advantage. The rest of the party would be tired upon arrival and want to relax at the inn while they could get themselves directly to the seaside undistracted by other frivolities.

Wentworth must have agreed as he took some pains to explain to Charles the serious nature of their visit to Lyme—which of course must be kept from the dragon-deaf Misses Musgrove. Charles suggested that Mary need not know either as she had little taste or patience for dragon business and would likely complicate matters for them if she were too aware of what was really going on. He was, of course, correct.

Anne glanced at Mary, who appeared not to have heard the conversation at all. Perhaps she did not—it was difficult to hear even with Anne's preternatural hearing, and she was concentrating intensely on it. All told, that would be best. Mary did not like to be left out of anything, even those things she was not truly interested in, rather like going to Lyme. She complained and fussed the entire carriage ride there—at least when she could get a in word edgewise between the Misses Musgrove's lively conversation. While there was little substance to their chatter, it was light and pleasant and a welcome distraction from the other issues on her mind.

Matters like meeting Kellynch for the first time—and without Lady Russell to ease the introduction. Father really should be present. It was his final duty as Keeper to introduce her to Kellynch and receive his approval on her new role. Then again, Father probably did not know that, and he certainly did not care.

Which was why Kellynch had been slumbering and they were all in the very great pickle they were in.

The carriage descended the long hill into Lyme and rolled to a stop near an inn, one of the ones that Wentworth suggested was suitable for a party of ladies. A modest structure, three stories high, clad in grey, weathered wood, it bore a faded sign declaring it the "Siren's Song." She peered at the sign a little more closely. In the background there was a small creature that resembled White very closely. Was the innkeeper a member of the Order?

In but a few minutes, Charles and Wentworth secured accommodations and ordered dinner whilst the ladies waited in the carriage.

"What shall we do now?" Louisa exclaimed as Charles handed her down from the carriage to the cobblestone street.

Colorful buildings lined the streets beneath slightly grey skies, each shouting as though trying to attract its share of the conversation on streets that were mostly quiet, even a little barren. Laconia had mentioned the summer months found the place quite lively; he liked it much better this way.

"We are quite off season." Mary glanced about and sniffed. "I do not see any amusement or variety which Lyme as a public place might offer us in early October. Oh, but look there! That carriage, it seems familiar. Anne, pray come."

With Charles' help, Anne stepped out of the coach, a sharp, salty-fishy smelling sea breeze catching her full in the face. Mary would prove difficult enough on her own, no need to provoke her now. "It is just a carriage, like many, I do not see anything distinct about it."

"Look at the gentleman who just came down. I think we know him. That profile, it is very like the Elliot countenance." Mary pointed at a gentleman in a well-tailored dark suit and tall hat, with his back turned toward them who disappeared through the door of a pub.

"From that angle, he could be anyone. I doubt any of our acquaintance would be at Lyme now." And if it was who Mary seemed to think it was, it was far better that they had no dealings with him.

"Of course, because you know everything." Mary's lip curled back, and she tossed her head and turned her back. "As you will. I am quite certain of what I saw."

Anne turned back toward the rest of the company. Charles rolled his eyes. Laconia pressed against her leg and hissed softly.

"Do not be disappointed, Mary, there is plenty to be appreciated here," Henrietta leapt from the carriage into Wentworth's hands. "This principle street seems to hurry directly into the water. We must go to the sea shore immediately, it demands it of us."

Charles shrugged. "What say you Anne? Do you think it a good plan?" There was a knowing look in his eyes.

"It is a good plan indeed," Wentworth said and offered his arms to Louisa and Henrietta. They set off down the street.

"That was rude." Laconia muttered, rubbing himself around her ankles. "He should not snub you so."

She stooped to scratch his ears briefly. "I suppose he knows best how to handle these matters."

"Why? Simply because he is an officer? Or do you think it because he is male? You know the Dragon Sage is female. You are not at a disadvantage with dragons for your sex."

"I appreciate knowing that. But he has been a member of the Blue Order far longer than I have, and he has had far more training in dragon matters than I have, both of which should give him an advantage in the current situation."

"I suppose." Laconia trotted so close beside her, he brushed her ankles. "Have you been to the sea before?"

"No, I have not."

"I am sure you will like it very well."

Halfway down the hill, the view widened and there it was. The sea.

Anne stopped, jaw agape. There was so much of it; continuing until blue disappeared into blue. What was it like where the sky and sea met?

And the sound! Oh, the sound! The winds rushing past her ears, blowing her bonnet, pelisse and hair all frowsy-blowsy. And the waves, their unremitting churning, pounding against the shore, lapping, over and over again, whitecaps running toward them, then away. Did it ever stop?

She covered her ears a moment, a blessed release from the thrumming noise. No one else seemed to feel the ache of the relentless sound. Wentworth glanced back at her, just briefly, and nodded as though he understood. Perhaps it was the price of a more developed preternatural sense of hearing.

What would the sunset over the sea look like? The clouds at dawn? A storm on the horizon? Would that she could linger here and find out.

The wind picked up as they walked toward the Cobb on the west side of town, whipping chill sea spray over them. How curious the smell of the salt air—one could almost taste it. How strange to be able to taste the air.

"This reminds me of being at sea." Laconia kept very close to her. "Be careful that you do not slip. The stones are slicker than you would imagine."

"I see what you mean. It seems you have an advantage with so many toes available to grip these stones."

"Tatzelwurms are considered to be the luckiest of ships' cats because of that. Our balance is exceedingly good." He stopped short. "Bother, must he go there?"

"Where? What do you mean?"

"He is heading for those houses there." Laconia pointed with the tip of his tail. "He needn't bother. I doubt they will be of any help."

"Who?"

"His friend, Harville. He was lieutenant for Wentworth, then made captain himself. Benwick is probably with him too. That will be ruddy inconvenient."

"Why?" Anne crouched to sooth Laconia's fur.

"Benwick is dragon-deaf and terrible dull to boot. He can be of no help in our efforts. Moreover, he will talk you to death if you allow it. You should avoid him."

"Those are very strong words. You do not even talk about Mary that way."

"She is not dragon-deaf."

"The Misses Musgrove then."

"They are silly flitter-bits, rather like human fairy dragons, I think. One gets their fill of them quickly, and then it is done—or at least it should be."

"I still do not understand."

"And now he brings them here to us. I am sure they will be of little use." Laconia growled under his breath and spring-hopped away.

Anne turned to go after him, but her foot slipped and Charles caught her under the arm just before she fell. Mary glowered at her.

"Pay her no mind," Charles said, "She does not like the sea spray and is angry that we went walking when she would rather have sat at the inn."

"Perhaps I should walk back with her?"

"No, no, we should meet Wentworth's friends. It would be most rude to avoid the introduction. Harville, as I understand, is the tall one there. The woman must be his wife, and the short man must be Benwick. Benwick had been first lieutenant of the Laconia. Captain Wentworth calls him an excellent young man and an officer. He had been engaged to Captain Harville's sister, and is now mourning her loss. They had been a year or two waiting for fortune and promotion. Fortune came, his prize-money as lieutenant being great; promotion, too, came at last; but Fanny Harville died the preceding summer while he was at sea. Captain Wentworth believed it impossible for a man to be more attached to a woman than Benwick had been to Fanny Harville, or to be more deeply afflicted under the dreadful loss. It all seems a very sad business."

A dragon-deaf man, in mourning for a lost love would certainly not be very helpful in their urgent quest. Perhaps that was why Laconia objected so much.

The parties met at the Cobb near the ocean, and Wentworth made introductions. Captain Harville was a tall, dark man—who clearly heard dragons—with a sensible, benevolent countenance; a little lame; and in want of health, looking much older than Captain Wentworth. Captain Benwick—as dragon-deaf a man as she had ever seen—looked, and was, the youngest of the three, and, compared with either of them, a little man. He had a pleasing face and a melancholy air, just as he might be expected to have, and drew back from conversation.

Mrs. Harville, a degree less polished than her husband, seemed, however, to have the same good nature and ability to hear dragons. "Pray all of you, do come sit with us awhile. The wind is cold, and I am quite sure the ladies are chilled."

Mary sniffled. "I am quite cold."

"Then it is settled," Harville declared and beckoned them all follow him.

The house was just off the Cobb, narrow, wedged between two far nicer dwellings. Within, the rooms were small, even cramped, but Captain Harville and his wife toured the house with them, explaining how he had supplied many of the deficiencies of lodging-house furniture. Those places were easy to spot by the rare species of wood, the excellency of the workmanship or the presence of something curious and valuable from the distant countries Captain Harville had visited. They made the house a picture of repose and domestic happiness of which Anne had hardly seen the like.

With no small amount of shuffling, a barely sufficient number of seats were procured, nearly half from other rooms and the party sat down in the awkward little parlor. Anne's knees touched Louisa's next to her and nearly bumped into Benwick's on her other side. Wentworth and Harville on the other side of the room had to adjust the small table between them several times to allow them room enough to sit on two bare wooden stools. Mrs. Harville chose to stand behind the settee where Charles, Mary and Henrietta squashed in together. She was probably the most comfortable one in the room.

Louisa leaned toward Anne. "These sailors, I am sure are the best of men. Their friendliness, their brotherliness, their openness, their uprightness. I am sure they have more worth and warmth than any other set of men in England. Only they truly know how to live, and they only deserve to be respected and loved far more than they are."

Thankfully, Captain Harville spared her the need to respond to the melodramatic declaration by launching into a story about their days on the Laconia.

A tiny bird chirruped sweetly in a cage hanging from the ceiling behind her. Anne turned to see that the cage locked from the inside, and it was no bird, but a fairy dragon. She gave the tiny creature a small wink.

"We have not had company in a very long time. Will you be visiting with us long? Have you interesting stories to tell?" The bright yellow fairy dragon twittered.

"It has a pretty song, has it not? I had no idea a canary could produce such a melody until I came to the Harvilles." Captain Benwick gently pushed the cage to set it rocking.

"Totally deaf, that one. But at least he likes my songs." The little fairy dragon pouffed her feather-scales.

Benwick turned to study the creature, peering intently. "I wonder what it sings of. I can just imagine there are words to go to its song."

"What do you think it might sing?"

The fairy dragon wrinkled her beaky nose and snorted.

"I am quite certain it must cry 'I can't get out! I can't get out!' just as Sterne's starling did." Benwick shrugged, though he seemed very certain of what he was saying.

"He is an idiot. Of course, I can get out." The fairy dragon flittered toward the little lock. "You see, it was formed just for me, to allow me to do just that. I have nothing to bemoan. Not a thing. I am warm and dry and well fed. The woman gives me honey. I am entirely content."

"She does not seem too unhappy to me." Anne said. "I think she seems quite happy with her situation. When one is so small, it must be comforting to have one larger to keep one safe."

"I do not see how it could not but lament its captivity. I have tried, you know, on more than one occasion to free it. But the latch is very well fashioned and only Harville knows the secret. 'Disguise thyself as thou wilt, still, Slavery,' said I—'still thou art a bitter draught!'"

Even for a poetry lover, he seemed a bit melodramatic. "You read a great deal of poetry, then, sir? Do you favor *Marmion* or *The Lady of the Lake*?"

Now distracted, he launched into an animated discussion of the two works. But unlike many, he allowed her to comment and even listened to what she said. It was difficult not to immediately like the gentleman on that basis alone, even if his literary analysis was a bit long-winded.

Laconia jumped through an open window and spring-hopped straight toward her.

"So, Laconia has followed you even here, Wentworth?" Harville said. "The damn luckiest cat in the fleet I am sure. How many times did he steer us away from the storms and straight to prize money?"

"Quite often I would say." Wentworth reached for Laconia, but he dodged away and hopped into Anne's lap.

Harville elbowed Wentworth. "Looks like you have a rival for his affections."

"Laconia is quite personable."

"Personable, yes, but I have never known him to snub you."

"Her lap is very comfortable." Laconia leaned into Anne. "And she knows how to scratch."

"I do not like ... cats. They make me sneeze." Mary muttered.

"I like them very well indeed. And I think he is very handsome." Louisa declared, reaching across Anne's lap to pet Laconia.

Laconia's tail lashed hard, though he endured the intrusion patiently. Anne laid a calming hand between Laconia's shoulders.

"It is often best to be introduced to a cat before you begin petting him." Anne nudged Louisa's hand away.

"I have never thought Laconia liked me." Benwick glowered at Laconia with a sideways glance.

"He is right. I do not." Laconia's words had a growling note.

"I am not sure why though. I get on with that bird just fine."

"Because the bird is a fairy dragon, you twitterpated warm-blood and you have no idea what you are talking about."

Henrietta tittered. "It sounds as though he might be answering you."

"And she is just as twitterpated. One of those two fluttertufts would do well enough for the dragon-deaf buffoon. He knows little better nor do they." Laconia hopped off her lap and wove around her ankles. "He..." he jerked his head toward Wentworth, "should pay you better deference as a Dragon Keeper."

Harville's eyes widened, and he turned to Wentworth who nodded.

"He is quite fond of you, Miss Anne!" Louisa sounded a little perplexed.

"I cannot imagine why." Mary muttered.

Laconia turned to her and hissed softly.

"Laconia! That is unnecessary." Wentworth admonished.

"She is horrid."

"Perhaps I might go to the kitchen and find him a tidbit?" Anne looked to Mrs. Harville.

"Of course, that is an excellent notion. What creature is not a bit peevish when hungry?" She beckoned Anne to follow her.

Anne picked up Laconia and held him close. Gracious what a substantial fellow he was!

His tail wrapped nearly all the way around her waist. "I like her."

Mrs. Harville found several fish heads from the makings of dinner. She put them in an old wooden bowl on the floor near the fireplace. "That should do for him."

Anne let Laconia jump from her arms. "Do enjoy the treat now."

Laconia looked over his shoulder. "Do not exaggerate."

Mrs. Harville chuckled. "I know, you prefer cream, but I have none, so you will have to make do. Pray Miss Anne, you will have to excuse, Laconia. As I understand, there has been a longstanding dispute between Benwick and him. You see, Fanny, our sister, could hear dragons, and he cannot stand the thought of a woman who hears being attached to a man who cannot."

"It is a travesty, an abomination." Laconia snarled. "It only leads to all sorts of grief, particularly when the party involved is so resolutely deaf that they cannot be persuaded beyond being convinced that I am a cat."

"You are too hard on the poor fellow. He has some admirable qualities." Wentworth and Harville slipped into the kitchen.

"Shall I serve some refreshments to keep the rest of our company occupied?" Mrs. Harville asked with a knowing cock to her head.

"You are a gem, my dear." Harville winked at her.

A few moments later, she walked out with a tray that Mary would have considered poor at the very best, but no doubt contained the best the Harvilles had to offer.

"You have news?" Laconia rose up high on his tail.

Wentworth nudged Harville with his elbow.

"Nothing concrete yet. But the local cockatrice have reported sightings of a large, unfamiliar dragon near shore, and evidence of extensive feeding." Harville stroked his chin. "That may not be the dragon you are looking for, but we do not usually have unfamiliar dragons spotted in these waters."

"If that is Kellynch, how are we to make contact?" Anne reached behind her to lean against the uneven worktable.

"Dusk is usually a good time to find sea dragons." Laconia's tail and tongue flicked in synchrony.

"Usually that is so, but the chatter is that this one prefers the early morning. If you come to the shore near sunrise tomorrow, where the local cockatrice gather, I am certain any number of them might be of help to you."

Kellynch, was close, so close. Close enough that she dreaded meeting him with every fiber of her being. "That seems to be what we should do." Her voice barely quivered as she spoke.

"Laconia and I can meet with him." Wentworth sought her gaze, his voice low and soft.

"No, it is a Keeper's responsibility. I will not repeat my father's mistakes."

Laconia hopped to the worktable, pressed close to her side and purred.

"We will go with you then. One can never have too much help when an unsettled dragon is involved," Wentworth said.

"I will welcome it." Pray he and the dragon would both find her worthy of the task.

14
Chapter

September 24 1814

WENTWORTH BLINKED HIS eyes in the first rays of morning light. He stretched his long limbs, groaning as he knocked his fists into the wall behind him and his feet into the footboard of the too-short bed. He did not think himself so very tall, but rented rooms always seemed unable to accommodate his frame.

He sat up and scrubbed his face with his hands, knocking his elbow into the bedpost. Blast and ruddy bother. It was not as if these accommodations were that much smaller than he was accustomed to at sea. But at least there he was master over the arrangement of things.

Here, there was too much mismatched furniture jammed into the room in an ill-guided attempt to make it seem more than it was. What was wrong with only placing the necessary items in and leaving out the clutter?

Carefully standing, he stretched again and sucked in the scents of salt air and baking bread. He licked his lips. That was one thing he missed at sea and probably indulged in far too much when ashore: a variety of fresh bread. At least the inn served plenty of that at breakfast.

What was to have been a visit of just a day had now stretched out into its third morning. Such was the hospitality of the Harvilles and the draw of the sea—and the stubbornness of Kellynch. He muttered and grumbled under his breath; there had only been one other dragon in his acquaintance so intractable.

It should have been pleasing to note how much Louisa liked the sea and the company of sailors. It should have been, but with Anne there, it was not. How was it that Anne could say nothing, just be in company with them, and all his attention focused on her? Constantly. Whether he wanted it there or not.

Some part of him would have preferred to like Louisa—simple, sweet, stubborn Louisa—and be done with it all. It would be much easier if Laconia agreed.

He was the one who had insisted Wentworth take a wife. Now he was solidly opposed to the woman he had all but settled on—settled on until Anne reappeared.

Oh, Anne. Bloody hell and damnation, Anne! If only she were still the same spineless, weak-willed woman he had left. It all would have been so easy. But damn it all, she had changed.

How deep did that change run? Was it real or just an affectation for some benefit he could not comprehend?

Laconia had no answers, but he had been determined to find out.

Where was that creature? Probably curled up asleep at the foot of Anne's bed. It was difficult to discern which was more maddening, Laconia's fondness for Anne or his dislike of Louisa. He really needed to harden himself to the idea that Wentworth would choose his own wife—it had been Laconia's idea in the first place that he needed to take a mate—a wife rather.

He shook his head sharply and pulled out his shirt to begin dressing. Perhaps he had been too long in the little dragon's company.

Laconia had already warned him that he would not stay if Wentworth took a wife who did not hear—or frankly, one he did not like. It had been one thing living aboard the ship among the dragon-deaf crew. There he was a good luck charm and treated as such. Cats generally did not get nearly so much respect on land, so he insisted on the need to be properly appreciated by any mate—wife—Wentworth took.

How could he choose between his Friend and a wife? What a strange position to be placed in.

"Mrrow." Laconia jumped on the window sill with a heavy thud and scratched for purchase. It had not been designed to accommodate one of his remarkable size.

"Where have you been? I left the window open for you all night."

"Anne's bed is softer, and she does not snore." Laconia leapt from the window sill to the bed.

"You did not seem to mind all those years you spent shipboard."

Laconia sniffed and licked his shoulder. "I have a choice now. She is soft and smells far better than you."

"That tends to be the way with women."

Laconia's ears stood up and the fur on his neck pouffed. "Do not start that conversation now. That one is no substitute for Anne. She has good sense and is kind."

"Louisa is kind." He edged toward the mirror to tie his cravat.

"And utterly stupid and stubborn. She cannot hear me and treats me like a common rat-catcher. I will not live that way."

"Then perhaps I will inquire of the Blue Order, and we can attend some of their events in Bath together."

"But Anne is here and is perfectly acceptable. And she is a Dragon Keeper." Laconia's voice took on a nearly persuasive edge.

"How is that an advantage?"

"You have always been one to seek to improve yourself. What greater improvement can you obtain within the Order than to become mate to a Keeper and possibly even a Keeper yourself?"

"Anne can never inherit that property. So how does that improve my situation?"

"Once Kellynch meets Anne, he will find he finally has an acceptable Keeper. He will see she is elevated to Mistress of the estate and has a proper husband."

"Superseding the established lines of inheritance? That sounds like the plot of some ridiculous novel. Even if it were possible, I have fortune enough. I do not, I will not marry for profit. Besides, Kellynch has not even met her. There is no guarantee he will like her any better than the other Elliots who have Kept Kellynch. I do not even know how they will be made to meet at this point."

"Soon, possibly even today. Last night I was out talking to the local sea dragons at the Cobb. They have seen Kellynch. He has been gorging himself on local schools of fish. They say he is reaching the end of his hunger and will be turning back for shore very soon. Granted it seems rather early for sating a hunger from a fifty-year hibernation, but the local cockatrice expect him to go to a sea cave they all know of to sleep off his gorging. Apparently, his disposition has been very bad."

"Then it seems we should get out there immediately."

"Anne must come with us. She is the proper Keeper and—"

"Yes, yes, all the rules state the Keeper must be part of this process. I am well aware. I am sure we will find her when we go downstairs. She has always liked an early breakfast."

Laconia followed him through the dim, narrow corridor to the tight stairs leading to the common rooms, weaving between Wentworth's feet as he walked. "You need to keep Benwick away."

"Because you fear he is already forming an attachment to Anne?"

"Because he is a dragon-deaf fool—"

"And you do not wish to see her live with a dragon-deaf man."

"You are jealous."

Damn it all, he was right. "Of what?"

"Of the fact I like Anne."

No, the problem was that despite all pride, he liked

her, too. Damn it all. "Nonsense."

Laconia stopped short and nearly sent Wentworth tumbling down the uneven stairs. "Benwick is a problem because he cannot be persuaded. If Kellynch, in a fit of temper—"

"Kellynch is hardly a fool. He is far too old to dare expose himself that way to the dragon-deaf. Perhaps a wyrmling might, but not a venerable wyrm. You underestimate him." Wentworth stepped over Laconia and continued to the foot of the stairs.

"And you underestimate the scope of the problems—"

"Good morning, Captain Wentworth." Anne appeared at the open stairway door.

Tea and Bath buns sat at the center of the single long table in the middle of the still unpopulated room. A sharp breeze whistled though the windows carrying the distinct taste of rain. Laconia springhopped to her and wove himself around her ankles, purring.

She crouched to pet him. "It is good to see you, my friend."

"Might I sit with you?" Wentworth asked. "Laconia has had word that Kellynch may be nearby, perhaps even in the harbor this morning."

Anne gasped and swallowed hard as she collapsed into the nearest chair. "I suppose then we—I— should go out to find him immediately."

"No, you should not go out on your own." Laconia jumped in her lap and glowered at Wentworth. "We should accompany you and help you speak to him. You have never spoken with him before, and he might be cranky."

"Every major dragon is cranky." Wentworth

snorted.

"Uppercross is not." Such fire in the glare she gave him!

"He is the single exception in all of England, I think. The rest are uniformly grumpy and cross, all the time."

"I am afraid he is right." Laconia turned a small circle in her lap. "It is in our favor, though, that it seems Kellynch is well fed now. That will improve his mood dramatically."

Dainty footfalls sounded on the stairs.

"I am quite convinced that, with very few exceptions, the sea air always does good. There can be no doubt of its having been of the greatest service to Dr. Shirley, after his illness, last spring twelve-month. He declares that coming to Lyme for a month did him more good than all the medicine he took and being by the sea always makes him feel young again. Now, I cannot help thinking it a pity that he does not live entirely by the sea." Henrietta paused at the end of the stairs and surveyed the room.

"I wish," Louisa appeared behind her, rosy-cheeked and smiling, "I wish Lady Russell lived at Uppercross, and were intimate with Dr. Shirley. I have always heard of Lady Russell as a woman of the greatest influence with everybody! I always look upon her as able to persuade a person to anything! She would surely be able to persuade Papa to allow us to visit the seaside quite often."

He had heard that name before—she was some friend of the Elliots, though he had never met her. Anne, though, cringed at the mention of the name. Why? Had there been some sort of falling out? Laconia stared at her intently, brows knitting as though thinking very hard—which was not something one often saw a tatzelwurm do.

"Look there! It is the carriage Mary remarked upon yesterday or perhaps it was the day before! It looks like it is going down to the shore!" Henrietta pointed at the window.

Anne stared, as though thinking as hard as Laconia.

The waiter came into the room.

"Pray," said Captain Wentworth, immediately, "can you tell us the name of the gentleman associated with that particularly grand carriage?"

"Yes, Sir, a Mr. Elliot, a gentleman of large fortune, came in several nights ago from Sidmouth. I 'erd it said he was going on now for Crewkherne, on his way to Bath and London."

"Elliot!" Mary cried from the stairs, Charles just behind her. What was she doing up so early this day? "Bless me! it must be our cousin; it must be our Mr. Elliot, it must, indeed! Charles, Anne, must not it? How very extraordinary! In the very same town with us! Anne, must not it be our Mr. Elliot? My father's next heir? Pray sir," turning to the waiter, "did not you hear, did not his servant say whether he belonged to the Kellynch family?"

"No, ma'am, he did not mention no particular family; but he said his master was a very rich gentleman, and would be a baronet someday."

"There! you see!" cried Mary in an ecstasy, "just as I said! Heir to Sir Walter Elliot! I was sure that would come out, if it was so. Depend upon it, that is a circumstance which his servants take care to publish, wherever he goes. But, Anne, only conceive how extraordinary! I wish I had looked at him more. I wish we had been aware in time, who it was, that he might have been reintroduced to us."

"Oh, I think not." Anne frowned deeply. "Our family has not been on such terms with him for many years now as to make renewing the acquaintance at all desirable."

There was something more to this than she was saying. She knew this man more than her sister seemed to understand.

Mary dashed to the window with Louisa and Henrietta to try and catch sight of Mr. Elliot's carriage.

Anne leaned forward and whispered, "Mr. Elliot has no love for dragons and no desire to be a Keeper. He seems content to allow the matter to fall upon me. An arrangement that has not been worked out to anyone's satisfaction at this time."

Wentworth dragged his hand down his face and stared at her. What was she not telling him? Was she promised or even betrothed to Mr. Elliot? Now was not the time to discuss that matter with her.

"I cannot imagine he knows Kellynch is here. I am probably inventing trouble, but he must not see Kellynch before I …"

Thunder boomed across the sea. Pendragon's bones! It was dragon thunder!

"Kellynch is in the harbor." Laconia jumped from her lap and spring-hopped for the door.

"I think it a very good time for a walk, Miss Anne." Wentworth stood and offered his arm.

"What a lovely idea." Anne moved to his side.

"Yes, yes, do bring us!" Henrietta and Louisa crowded around Wentworth, forcing Anne aside.

"We shall all go." Mary harrumphed and slipped her hand in Charles' arm.

Before Wentworth could protest, Anne reached the door and followed Laconia out into the street.

Wentworth hurried Louisa and Henrietta to catch up. Anne had not got very far when she was stopped by Benwick, Harville and Mrs. Harville just a few yards from the inn's door. How could they all possibly appear—wait, was Harville here to try and occupy the dragon-deaf in their party? Of course, why else might he appear here and now?

"We thought you might like to take a walk about Lyme." Harville looked over his shoulder toward the tall stony Cobb. "But it sounds—and tastes—like it might rain."

"I cannot see a cloud in the sky." Benwick peered in that direction. "There is nothing to worry for. We should take the opportunity as we have it. Is that not what you would say, Miss Elliot?"

Anne stammered something and was ushered along by Benwick toward the Cobb.

If only she had any strength of character and purpose, she would have insisted—what would she have insisted? With Benwick so profoundly dragon-deaf, she had to be very careful. No dragon could help him forget anything she said to him in error. Damn it all! Laconia was quite right!

Wentworth hurried Henrietta and Louisa along to catch up but did not manage the feat until they reached the Cobb. How quiet and deserted it was, perhaps because of the dragon thunder. Benwick began a conversation with Louisa and Henrietta.

Wentworth edged closer to Anne who stood several steps away. She stared into the grey sky, squinting and pointing. "I know that cockatrice, I am sure of it. But why would Jet have followed Kellynch here?"

"Gracious, how the wind has picked up!" Mrs. Harville clutched her bonnet. "I think we had better go down the stairs, where there is more shelter from this breeze."

Harville took her arm and helped her down the steep, slick stone stairs. Benwick moved to Anne's side and offered his arm to do the same.

Thunder—dragon thunder rang out across the harbor. Wentworth peered into the sharp salt breeze. Bloody hell, there was an angry dragon nearby. Very near.

"No, no, pray wait, Anne. You will jump me down, will you not, Captain? The thunder, the weather, it is nothing to me." Louisa pulled him toward the steps, past Anne and Benwick.

"No, not now, Louisa. Now is not the time. The steps are too slick and the stones too hard for your feet. You will hurt yourself."

"I am determined, sir. Did you not say how you admired that in a character? I am determined now, and I will not be dissuaded."

Wentworth ran down the steps. Stupid, stupid girl!

"Pray stop her, Captain Benwick!" Anne cried, pushing him toward Louisa.

"You shall not stop me!" Louisa laughed

Stubborn, foolish girl!

Benwick strode toward her as another clap of dragon thunder echoed over the water.

Henrietta screamed and pointed.

A large head rose from the harbor.

Louisa screamed and lost her footing. Benwick grabbed her arm. They both tumbled over the edge of the Cobb. The sick smack of flesh on stone roiled his stomach. Wentworth ran to them. There was no wound, no blood, no visible bruise; but her eyes were closed, she breathed not, her face was like death. Benwick wore the same expression, his forehead cut on the stones and bleeding.

"She is dead! She is dead!" Henrietta cried and swooned into Harville.

Anne was beside Wentworth, taking Louisa's hands and rubbing them. "She is not dead. Not now. There is hope, she breathes! Fetch a surgeon."

Wentworth sprang to his feet.

"No, send Harville, he knows where to go."

"Yes, yes, I will go." Harville hurried off.

Behind them, Mary cried out and moaned, clutching Charles. Useless woman. Damn it all, where was a ship's surgeon when one needed one?

"What is to be done now?" Wentworth turned to Anne.

"Take them to the inn."

"No, to our house," Mrs. Harville insisted. "It is so much closer."

"To the Harville's then. Surely Charles can manage Louisa. Can you manage Benwick?"

"I will." Wentworth waved Charles to his sister.

Anne scurried off to put Mary and Henrietta in Mrs. Harville's care, then returned. "I will stay here and deal with Kellynch. We—I—cannot risk anyone else being hurt by his unseemly behavior."

"But he—"

"Is my responsibility and my problem. I am the only one here with authority to manage it. I will do just that. Take care of those who have come to harm because of him. Go now." She pushed his shoulder.

Did she realize the danger she was in? There was no predicting Kellynch's state right now. Certainly, he was angry, and he might very well take it out on her, believe it his right to harm her as representative of the family that had failed him. Something in the cast of her jaw and the look in her eye said that she knew. It also said she would not be persuaded against it.

"Stay with her, Laconia. Help her if you can. I shall join you as soon as I am able." Wentworth rose, Benwick draped over his shoulder like a sack of soggy grain.

"Come," Laconia pointed with his front paw. "There is a little cove along the beach. I think he has gone there to meet with you."

"He knows I am here? Why did you not tell me?"

"I only learned just now, from one of the cockatrices that passes for a gull. He screamed a warning as he flew from the dragon thunder."

"I must go." Anne dashed off in the direction Laconia pointed, the tatzelwurm in her wake.

When had such a sensible, determined woman taken the place of the malleable Anne Elliot, and how had he missed the transformation?

15
Chapter

ANNE RAN TOWARD the beach, the awkward, ungainly run of a newly born colt, half boots sliding on the rocks. Carefully, carefully! She must not slip on the slick stones and add another fall to their misfortunes. Who then would there be to tend to Kellynch?

Laconia paused for a moment when they got to the beach, his wide thumbed paws sinking in the wet sand. She paused, panting for breath as he pulled out one foot, then the other, shaking the sand loose. With a swish of his serpentine tail, he set off again, taking the lead toward the water's edge. The soft crunch of the sand clinging to her feet, the sea spray in her face and the unrelenting pounding noise of the waves; so foreign to her existence until now, some sort of strange prelude to the coming encounter?

How far down the beach would they have to go? Would anybody find her should something untoward happen or would she simply be counted lost and forgotten? No, this was not the time for such thoughts.

Sea birds—or might they be dragons; they probably were dragons; she dare not look overhead to check—cawed above as though leading the way toward the cliffs. Yes, yes, they were leading the way.

Her skin prickled as cold droplets of sweat or maybe it was salt water, trickled down her neck. How many dragons were going to be involved in this affair?

Her lungs ached for air; her legs burned. Pray it would not be much farther, this pace was too much!

Laconia stopped, feet digging into the sand. "He is just there, in a cleft in the cliff. The local dragons say there is a cave behind it that he has inhabited, like an inn."

She peered into the cliffside, partially obscured by the waves and spray. There, a sliver of darkness against the lighter rock. Of course, it would be dark and narrow, just like the tunnels at Kellynch. "Is there a dragon innkeeper?"

Laconia made a sound that could only be called a snicker. "It is more like the military choosing to board in a private house. The local minor dragons dare not refuse."

"So, he is a bully?"

"He is a major dragon. Size and power give him the right to take what he wants from those below him. And he has to give what is demanded of him from his superiors. Is that so different from the warm-bloods?"

In short, he was indeed a bully. "Probably not, but we do not eat our inferiors."

"I grant you have an advantage in that. Shall I announce you?"

"I think there is little alternative. I suppose just walking in on him would be a bad idea."

"Yes, it would." Laconia—what did one call a movement that was part walk and part slither?—made his way to the dark sea cave opening.

Dragon thunder roared, echoing off the cliffs. Her heart pounded nearly as loud, making it harder still to breathe. Were those rocks falling into the sea because of it, or was it simply a coincidence? Another peal of thunder drove her to her knees, covering her ears. How could she possibly face a creature that made such a sound?

She cast about—only lonely beach, even the birds—or dragons—overhead had scattered away. There was no one to come to her aid—or her rescue. No one but herself to depend upon.

Was it so very different from how life usually was though?

A large wave splashed over the beach and lapped at her feet. Cold droplets splashed her face, trickling like tears down her cheek—but tears were warm, even hot. No, tears would be for later. First, she would face the dragon.

Gathering her skirts, she followed Laconia's distinct tracks. Did local children think these the tracks of mermaids? Was that why those stories abounded?

Acrid dragon musk mixed with salt air hung heavy near the cliff. So similar to the way Kellynch's lair smelt at home. Laconia's trail disappeared into a split in the cliff face. How could a large dragon have gone inside? It seemed barely large enough for Anne to make her way through.

As she squeezed her way, sometimes pushing through sideways, between the cold wet stones, the sound of lapping water came at her from both sides. There must be an underground passage within. No wonder Kellynch would have liked it.

She stumbled as the tight passage abruptly opened, and she clutched the wall for balance. Blinking furiously, she willed her eyes to quickly adjust to the dim light.

"Who goes there?" The wall rumbled at the deep booming voice.

"She is—" That was Laconia.

"I did not ask you." Water splashed, and it sounded as though Laconia shook and sputtered.

Anne stepped forward and squinted. A large shape appeared out of the gloom, vaguely familiar. "I am Anne Elliot, the new Keeper of Kellynch."

Loud slithering and a cold, ominous presence drew close. A large head, toothy and shaggy hovered near her face, breathing, panting, huffing. Oh, the breath! Rotten fish and pungent acid, with dragon musk. She gulped back bile. Casting up her accounts would not make for a good first impression.

"I do not know you." The words came in an angry clipped staccato.

"We have not been introduced. I understand Laconia came with that intent."

"I do not know him either."

"Lady Russell was to have introduced me."

"Where is she? We have a debt to settle."

"I am pleased to make your acquaintance, Laird Kellynch. I am your new Keeper." Anne curtseyed deep and lowered her head as much as she could without putting her face in the sand. Not a textbook greeting by any stretch, but hopefully it captured the spirit. After all, none could call this a proper meeting in the first place.

She rose, slowly, carefully.

He breathed hard and cold slimy spittle flew into her face. "I did not give my approval for a new Keeper."

"You were hibernating. There was no means by which your approval could be sought."

"Does the baronet still live?"

"He does, but he has made me Keeper." She wiped the spittle from her face with her hand and blinked hard, her vision clearing just a bit.

Kellynch was long—it had been difficult to tell whilst he was asleep just how long he was. Even now, with a great part of him in the water, she could not tell for certain, but he was probably at least fifteen, maybe twenty feet long. And thick. Two large men might barely be able to join hands around him, though his body got thinner towards his tail. Several fins lined his sides, probably of some use for swimming, but of little use on land. Spinal ridges coursed down his back growing smaller towards his tail. His head was somewhat triangular and a bit serpentine, with prominent fangs within a mouth filled with very sharp pointed teeth.

His eyes glistened red in the low light, weaving back and forth before her, mystic and hypnotic.

"Stop that!" Laconia shouted and slapped his tail against the wet sand. "You do not treat a Keeper as prey!"

Anne jumped back.

"I have been wronged, stolen from!" He reared up. Sand slipped as he slithered the rest of the way out of the water. "I have my rights. It is set out in the treaty. She must pay!"

Anne edged back, but it was more reflex than defense. Could she get into the tight cleft in the rocks faster than he could strike? No, no human could move so quickly.

"I have done nothing. I was not Keeper when your hoard was taken. I only learned of it recently. I promise the matter will be rectified."

"The treaty has been violated, making all agreements null and void. Your promise is worthless."

"You are the dragon of Kellynch, and my family is bound to you by treaty and by principle. I will see to it that you are satisfied."

His face rushed toward her. "When? On all counts?"

"I do not know yet. My father has only just retrenched. I have not yet worked out how long it might take to repay … Lady Russell will help me work on him. Are there more issues than that of the hoard?"

Kellynch swung his head, as though searching the cavern. He paused a moment, peering back over his coils, hissed and shook his head, then flung himself back at Anne. "So many wrongs. Not merely my hoard. That is the last of many insults."

No, her knees must not buckle. If she fell before him now, like that, it might trigger his prey instincts—or so the Sage had warned in a recent letter. If she met her demise at his teeth, it would not be as some sort of instinctive snack. "What wrongs, what insults? If I do not know, how can I right the wrongs you have suffered?"

"Nothing I have been promised, since the beginning, has been honored. Nothing. I only want what is due to me." His breath came in hard, angry snuffs.

"I will see you have your wine."

"And the rest? My lair, my food, the personal attentions due me, a proper territory?"

What? Wait, this was nothing like when Beebalm was offered honey. Where was the slavering, the writhing in anticipation, the relief that the aching desire would be met? "Tell me what has been denied, and I assure you, I will make it right. It may take some time, but it will be made right.

Kellynch roared, the sound bouncing off the rocks like knives to Anne's ears. "If I cannot trust dragons, how can I trust you? The debt is due now. I want it now, and if I do not have it now, I will take my payment in other ways. Blood is not unheard of."

"If that is to be the case," she swallowed hard and balled her fists, "and I grant you that it is a possible remedy under the Accords, it is a matter to be decided by the Blue Order. You must go to them and plead your case."

He slapped the water with his tail, dousing Anne and Laconia with an icy cold splash. "I want satisfaction now! No one would fault me. I am in the right."

"No one in the Blue Order, no dragon of the conclave would support you. Capital punishment of a Keeper must follow a certain protocol." Pray he could not see her trembling. The Sage said showing fear before a dragon was to behave like prey.

Something crunched in the soft sand. Laconia wrapped himself around her legs, hissing at Kellynch.

"You think that half-wyrm will defend you? You cannot—"

"Stop. You have no right!" Wentworth's voice boomed behind her.

She jumped and turned, slipping in the sand, and

landing hard near Laconia. Kellynch dove for her but Wentworth cut him off, brandishing a sword.

Where had he got that?

"You will stop now. You have no right." Wentworth flashed the sword in the sliver of light. Was he wearing a large cape as well?

"Who are you to tell me my rights?" The skin behind Kellynch's head swelled.

"I am witness to your own violation of the Pendragon treaty."

"I have not violated—"

"You showed yourself in the harbor, in the daylight, and the dragon-deaf were present." Wentworth flicked his hand, gesturing her and Laconia away.

"I saw that there were cockatrices present to persuade—"

"Then you admit you acted with intention, completely contrary to the treaty."

"They will persuade—"

"No. You were seen by those who are immune to persuasion."

"That is hardly my problem. It is yours. Since you are aware of the problem, you are now under obligation to manage such warm-bloods. Or so the Order demands."

Heavens above, Kellynch knew the provisions of the treaty well.

"Two were injured directly because of your actions. An inquest must be held when the dragon-deaf suffer injury by a dragon's action."

"I am the injured party! My hoard—"

Wentworth lifted a hand to silence Kellynch. "Are you injured, Anne? Can you walk?" He reached for her hand and helped her to her feet.

He caught her gaze and held her with the force of his strong arms. Gracious! That look, had he ever looked at her that way before? Pray that he would again!

"Laconia, see her out of this place. I will finish the discussion with Kellynch."

"She is my Keeper. My issue is with her." Kellynch lunged toward her, but pulled back well before he reached her.

"I was sent by the Blue Order to speak to you directly. I insist that you now deal with me exclusively since you have clearly demonstrated that you cannot properly honor your Keeper."

"I am the one dishonored!" Kellynch's roar dislodged small rocks from the walls above.

Anne covered her head against the painful rain. He waved her toward the narrow passage. Laconia bumped her legs, insisting. She hurried for the exit. The frigid rocks embraced her, tight and cold as death, fighting to keep her within. Only Laconia's insistent nudging and nipping kept her pushing through to the sunlight on the other side.

She collapsed on the wet sand, in the living warmth of a meager sunbeam, choking back sobs.

"Are you hurt?" Laconia rubbed his head against her cheek.

"Is it true what he said? That Kellynch has violated Blue Order law?"

"The Order is very strict toward major dragons. They cannot allow themselves to be seen outside of dragon hearing company. If not using the dragon tunnels, they must travel only under cover of darkness with an entourage of persuasive minor dragons to assist in their cover. Only when there is clear evidence that they are under threat of death is there any acceptable reason for doing as he did." He purred against her chest.

Such a warm and soothing sound, easing her racing heart. "Why did Wentworth bring a sword? Will he fight Kellynch?"

"No, it was not a Dragon Slayer blade. Only the most skilled swordsman could hope to even injure a dragon with that. Kellynch is well aware. That sword is a symbol given by the Order to demonstrate that Wentworth is on orders from them."

"You mentioned that before. What sort of orders?"

"When one deals with major dragons, things can change very quickly. Agents of the Order are trusted to accommodate those changes as necessary. He will see that Kellynch reports to the nearest regional office, at Bath, for a full inquiry into this situation."

"How does one make such a creature do anything?" And why had he not answered her question?

"You need not worry. It will be done." He bumped his head under her chin. "You are cold and shivering. You must return to your friends. They will help you."

"What am I to tell them?"

"The Harvilles surely understand, their fairy dragon will have seen to that. Charles is well aware."

"But Henrietta, how is she to be managed—"

"She is dragon-deaf and stupid as well. The fairy dragon will persuade her and it will be well. No more talk. You need to get warm and dry."

She clambered to her feet, knees weak, feet heavy and followed Laconia toward the Harvilles'. Gracious, the little house was a long way down the coast.

Laconia led her through the still open front door of the Harville's house. Though by the position of the sun, at least several hours had passed since the tragic event, the home seemed in every bit as much of an uproar as it might have been when the injured parties arrived.

The young girl-of-all-work quickly informed her that Louisa was upstairs in Mrs. Harville's own bed, having once opened her eyes, but soon closed them again, without apparent consciousness. The surgeon had already come and gone. He said of both Louisa and Captain Benwick that their heads had received severe contusions, but he had seen greater injuries recovered from. He was concerned with the cut Benwick had suffered though, as it had caused him a great loss of blood. Anne dismissed the girl to her work.

"Shall I look in on that man?" Laconia frowned, fangs exposed, as only a tatzelwurm could manage.

"It would be good of you to do so. Perhaps, if you try to persuade him whilst he is unconscious, it might muddle his memory of the event a bit."

"That is not an entirely ridiculous thought. It is certainly worth trying." Laconia chirruped and spring-trotted upstairs.

A mass of footfalls, some firm, some dainty and tentative, filled the narrow staircase and soon, the front room was full of troubled souls seeking repose in the mismatched assortment of seats. Captain Harville hurried to his liquor cabinet and moved the two stools in front of the empty fairy dragon cage. No doubt it was upstairs trying to help manage the impressions of the dragon-deaf.

Charles acknowledged Anne with a nod and beckoned her to sit near him on the settee. "Henrietta remains with Mrs. Harville and Louisa. I fear the shock of all this will affect her quite badly."

"She must be watched for a brain fever!" Mary flapped her hands as though she did not know what to do with them otherwise. "I am sure it will be a danger to her. I am sure I might be in danger of it myself, for I saw everything just as she did. I heard it all—that sound, like a melon striking—"

"Mary," Anne laid a very firm hand on her shoulder and encouraged her to perch on the settee. "We were all there, too. I am sure it serves no good purpose that we should rehash it all. For there is no changing what happened. We must determine what is to be done now."

Mary harrumphed and glowered at Anne. If there was one thing she did not like, it was being stopped in the midst of her grievances.

Harville passed out glasses: brandy to Charles, wine to Anne and Mary.

"Anne is right." Charles took a large gulp of brandy.

Mary snorted.

"We must consider what is to be done now." Charles pulled his shoulders back and tried to look as though he were in charge. The effect was hardly what he would have hoped for.

"Surely she cannot be moved. I must insist that Louisa stay here with us. It is already arranged, and I will not be moved." Harville tried to sit on a stool near the liquor cabinet, but it seemed he could not rest and settled for leaning his shoulder against the wall.

"That is very good of you, Harville. Very good of you, indeed. I cannot put into words how much we appreciate your hospitality. You must though allow our family to be of use to you whilst Louisa stays with you. Who is to tend Louisa? Someone of her family must be with her in this time. It is a comfort she needs and deserves."

"Mrs. Harville is a very experienced nurse and our nursery maid, too. Between these two, she could want no possible attendance by day or night." Harville glanced toward the narrow staircase.

"Henrietta must go home. And Uppercross must be informed. Her parents—" Anne stood and moved toward the opposite side of the room, mostly to be at some distance from Mary.

"Yes, yes, of course you are right. The news must be conveyed." Charles said.

"But how is it to be broken to them? I will not be the one to tell them." Mary folded her arms over her chest and tossed her head.

"No one has said it should be you." Anne clutched her hands together tightly lest they betray her less than gentle feelings.

"And the time! It is already so late. If we go today, we cannot possibly arrive at a tolerable time. To be traveling so late!" Charles pressed his temples with thumb and forefinger. He never was much more useful in a crisis than Mary.

"All the more reason that someone must resolve on being off for Uppercross instantly," Anne insisted.

The front door swung open and slammed against the wall behind it. "Musgrove, either you or I must go to Uppercross immediately." Wentworth declared, looking directly at Anne.

His expression betrayed little about his conversation with Kellynch. But the fact he was alive and apparently uninjured spoke volumes. And the way he looked at her—what was it? Respect, concern, warmth?

"Of course, you are right." Charles clapped his hands on his thighs. "I am resolved, I must not leave Louisa at such a time. But, as Anne said, Henrietta, she must go, too. She is so young and inexperienced; I am certain that she would be worse than helpless here. Mrs. Harville does not need yet another to care for."

"Then it is settled," Wentworth gestured toward Charles, "that you stay, and that I take your sister home. One should stay to assist Mrs. Harville, though. Mrs. Charles Musgrove will, of course, wish to get back to her children; but if Anne will stay … there is no one so proper, so capable as Anne."

Anne fought the urge to allow her jaw to drop. He meant what he was saying, but why? Surely, she could not stay here. Matters with Kellynch had reached such a state that the Blue Order had to be consulted, and the nearest office was in Bath. She had to get to Bath.

"You will stay, I am sure; you will stay and nurse her?" His tone was not disingenuous, but something in the tilt of his head, the tightness of his eyes—it demanded she comply with his path.

What was he about? Was he trying to usurp her role with Kellynch? It seemed the obvious thing, but he had stood before Kellynch on her behalf and protected her from the dragon bent on wrath. Chided that dragon for failing to honor her properly. If he was the same man here as he was in that moment, then he would not be trying to overthrow her now. "I will be most happy to remain. It is what I have been thinking of and hoping to be allowed to do. A bed on the floor in Louisa's room will be quite sufficient for me. There is no need to put anyone out on my behalf."

Wentworth nodded just a mite.

"Heavens no! No, that will not do at all. I am wretched at the very thought." Mary pressed a hand to her chest, tossing her head back with a truly theatrical flair.

"Nursing is not your province; you have said that often." Anne carefully avoided looking at Mary. "I am not troubled by it."

"The injustice of it!" Mary sprang to her feet and threw up her hands, nearly knocking them into the bookcase behind her. "How can I be expected to go away and Anne remain? Anne is nothing to Louisa. I am her sister. Who better has claim to the right to remain?"

"But Anne is so useful in these matters." Charles muttered to his hands, his cheeks flushing puce. He did not conceal his anger well.

"Am I not to be as useful as Anne? And to go home without Charles, too, without my husband! No, it is too unkind."

"But your children?" Wentworth's plea seemed forced.

"Jemima has them well in hand, I am sure. They are in good care with her. I am sure I would go distracted with them, there at Uppercross, with Charles here, and knowing that Louisa was suffering." Now they were at the truth of the matter.

"Surely you can see the sense. I insist." Charles' voice lowered several octaves.

"No, I cannot. I only see the cruelty."

Charles pinched the bridge of his nose and looked at Wentworth.

Wentworth frowned, but it was hardly a genuine expression. "I suppose it must be so. I shall have a servant gather Anne and Henrietta's things from the inn and ready the curricle. We shall leave as soon as all things are arranged." With a nod at Anne, he excused himself and strode out, purpose in his heavy steps.

An hour later, he returned for them with the curricle. Henrietta had spent most of that hour sniffling and crying and recounting, over and over again, the events as she remembered them. With a little help from Daffodil, the fairy dragon, and Laconia, Henrietta seemed quite convinced that Louisa was startled by the thunder and slipped off the stairs despite Benwick's gallant efforts to catch her that resulted in his own injuries. Mary readily accepted that version of the events, especially with Charles supporting it.

Hopefully when—not if, pray not if!—Louisa and Benwick awakened, their own memories of the events would be so muddled, they would easily agree with the events as Mary told them. And even if not, after such a traumatic blow to their heads, no one would give credence to a story of a dragon sighting from them.

Wentworth handed them both up into the neat little curricle, smelling of leather polish and horse. He insisted Henrietta take the place between Anne and himself. It was a tight fit, with three of them in a seat designed for two, but for a few hours, it would be manageable. Laconia bolted through the door, jumped up, and settled himself around Anne's feet. He would not have fitted had she sat in the middle.

The sun was far past its zenith. They would have to make good time to avoid being on the road after dark. But the sky was clear and the breeze crisp and salty. The weather would be on their side. The horses always seemed to walk better when it was not too hot. And the roads were in good condition, dry, and the old ruts recently repaired. Yes, everything seemed in their favor, if of course one did not consider major dragons.

"I took a moment to procure this from the apothecary for you," Wentworth handed Henrietta a small brown bottle. Laudanum no doubt. "It will sooth your nerves and allow you to sleep on the journey."

"Thank you, but I am sure I am fine." Henrietta's hands trembled, her face pale and eyes red from crying. Her bonnet sat slightly askew and the buttons of her spencer were misaligned.

"No, I think the captain is right. You will be in no state to comfort your parents if you are fatigued by the journey." Anne pressed Henrietta's hands between hers.

"If you are certain—you are always right." Henrietta uncorked the bottle and swallowed the contents. Before they had reached the summit of the first hill outside Lyme, her head lolled onto Anne's shoulder. Wentworth paused the horses and helped arrange Henrietta as comfortably as possible between them.

"With us on either side, I am sure she will not fall out of the curricle." He said, urging the horses into a quick walk. "I hope you approve of the draught.

There are things that must be discussed, and it seemed the most expedient way."

"Ordinarily, I do not think very well of them, but in this case, it seems an appropriate means." She tucked the empty bottle into her reticule. "You made it seem to all the world that you wanted me to stay behind at the Harvilles'."

"Would you be surprised to know I learned from watching you manage your sister in that same way? Set her up to protest what you do not want her to do and demand to do exactly what you want her to do?" He cocked his head and raised his brow.

"I had not realized anyone else might consider the same tactics. You were never given to much patience with her."

"I still am not."

The horses' hooves clopped and the wheels crunched along the road in a soothing rhythm that could easily have taken the place of another conversation. It was not as though Anne was short of points to ponder. And yet, Wentworth said there were things to discuss. Why was he not broaching them?

"So, what of Kellynch?" Her nails drove into her palm as she clenched a fist in her lap.

"The matter is complex."

"That tells me nothing."

"It is too complex for either of us to manage. It must be settled in a Blue Order Court."

"At Bath?"

"At Bath. I took the liberty of ordering his attendance there. I trust they will support my decision when I explain to them what I have seen."

"And what have you seen?" She stared at the sun sinking down into the trees ahead—anything but

Wentworth's eyes.

"You were spectacular."

Her cheeks prickled and burned. "What are you talking about."

"You have never been trained up for this. You have never even been introduced to Kellynch nor seen an angry dragon. And yet you stood up to him. There are not many who could do such a thing."

"It is not such a significant thing. I do not know why you remark upon it. It was what had to be done."

He guffawed and flicked the reins. "It is no ordinary thing. You have shown yourself worthy of being a Keeper in a way that generations of your family have not."

"I hope that is a good thing."

"It is. It should be. I hope it is."

"Why would it not be?"

"If only it were so simple. But it is not. It is complicated, so damned complicated."

"How is it complicated? What is happening?"

"You must get yourself to Bath to be in attendance at the Blue Order and at the Court when they need you."

"You are not going to answer my question."

"No, I am not."

"Why? Should I not know what is going on with the family Dragon?"

"No, not yet, not right now. It is best you do not know. That will protect you."

"From what? Kellynch?"

"You do not need to know right now."

Laconia jumped in her lap. "Trust him, he is right."

He stopped the curricle and took her hands in his

across Henrietta's softly snoring form. Warm and strong through his gloves, they were steady and secure. "Please Anne, permit me, allow me the privilege of protecting you in this."

How strange. He wanted to do something for her. How did one react to that? When was the last time someone had offered such a thing?

Lady Russell had, but it hardly seemed the same.

No, not at all.

"Trust me, Anne. I fear I might not have been worthy of your trust once, but pray now, believe in me."

Laconia purred loudly and bumped their joined hands with his cheek.

"If Laconia trusts you, then I suppose I must as well," she whispered, and he smiled.

16
Chapter

September 24, 1814

WENTWORTH BADE ANNE stay in the carriage with
Henrietta, now awake, alert, and wringing her hands,
whilst he broke the news to the Musgroves. Less than
a quarter of an hour later, Mrs. Musgrove's screams
of shock and agony pierced Anne's ears, even through
the stout stone walls of the house. Without preternatural dragon hearing, Henrietta remained completely
unaware. That was for the best. No daughter could
bear such sounds from her mother with equanimity.

Half an hour after the screaming ceased, Wentworth ushered them into the Great House's chaos,
Laconia close at their heels. He stayed only a few
minutes to see Anne take charge of the situation—
which seemed the only reasonable option, as all the
Musgroves seemed far too distracted by their distress

to make anything resembling sensible decisions.

His parting from her was brief: a reminder to get to Bath as soon as possible; he would go on ahead to manage the situation with Kellynch as best he could and assist her when she arrived. Then he was gone.

She had not felt lonely without him in a very long time. But now, the old emptiness returned, larger, colder, darker than ever before.

Something about the way he spoke those words, though—they were a promise of his help, his support, and perhaps even something more. The way Laconia purred and wove between his feet as he said them suggested the latter. She would have liked to dwell upon that more, but the demands of the Great House kept her fully occupied for the next two days. Given the way every idle thought of Wentworth distracted her thoughts and disquieted her soul, it was probably for the best.

September 28, 1814

Late morning sun warmed Anne's face as she stood outside the front door of the Great House. The earlier flurry of activity had settled and the Musgroves' old coach carrying Mr. and Mrs. Musgrove, Henrietta and Sarah, the old nursery maid who would assist in Louisa's care, trundled down the road toward Lyme, worn springs leaving the carriage bouncing and swaying with each rut in the lane. The quiet coming from the house felt somehow loud and oppressive. Perhaps she had just become accustomed to the chaotic bustle in that very short time. Birds and fairy dragons twittered overhead, the latter complaining that they missed the sweet nectar of the garden flowers.

She glanced at the house, but turned toward the cottage instead. There were a few things left there that she would want in Bath now that matters were settled here. Had Kellynch already arrived there? Surely it could not take a dragon very long to get from Lyme to Bath. Or was he biding his time to arrive on his terms instead of the Blue Order's? She strode into a swath of shade, provided by the same hardwood stand that surrounded the Uppercross dragon lair, and drew her shawl more tightly over her shoulders. Was it truly cold that flitted across her shoulders, or the sense of—what did one call that emotion?

Not fear, no it really was not that. Nor was it dread—what would be would be and in many ways there was little she could do for it. No, it was something worse. Loneliness.

It nipped at her heels, dogging after her, insisting she recognize its presence, call it by name. No wonder Wentworth encouraged Laconia to be with him at all times, and the Crofts made a way for White to be near them. She had grown accustomed to the companion dragons' presence even in just these few weeks. Now without them—and him, though it was difficult to admit even in the privacy of her own heart—everything felt cold and empty.

A quick blue blur in the woods caught her attention. That particular shade could only mean one thing.

"How well you look, Anne." Lady Russell sauntered through the trees toward her, her head feathers bobbing with each long step.

Anne stopped—it would be more polite than continuing on her errand. "Where have you been? You have been gone such a long time and much has happened—"

"What business of anyone is it where I go? The cottage is maintained in my absence; my housekeeper has instructions as does the solicitor." Heavens she was touchy with her clipped staccato tone.

"I was in very great need of your help in Lyme. One might even say desperate for it. Friends should be there for one another at such times."

"Are you suggesting I am some sort of companion dragon? A sort of pet to follow you around at your beck and call?" The final word ended with a hiss.

"Excuse me?" Anne stepped back, hands on her hips, and glared. "You have always declared yourself to be my friend. But perhaps I have expected too much out of that appellation." Not perhaps, definitely.

Lady Russell blinked several times and fluffled her wings across her back. "Yes, yes, of course. Forgive me. Trying to investigate this whole matter and find out what you need has simply been exhausting. So very trying—I should have thought you would be a little more patient with me. I have just been in Bath you know."

"Bath?" Anne's mouth went dry and she swallowed hard. "I had no idea. Did you see Kellynch there?"

"Kellynch? In Bath? No, of course not. Why would he be in Bath?" Lady Russell began walking toward the cottage. "I visited your father and sister at Camden Place."

"How are they?" It was the polite thing to say, but hardly her primary concern.

"I am very sorry to say that Mrs. Clay is still with them."

"I am not surprised, for Elizabeth did engage her for her company. She would be a simpleton indeed if she were to leave a day before Elizabeth's dismissal of her, considering she is there at very little expense to herself."

"Unfortunately, you are right and the article has availed herself of every advantage to be sure, flaunting the new wealth her father has come into." Lady Russell chittered under her breath and flipped up dirt with her talons.

"You do not believe it was a simple inheritance?"

"I have found no reason to trust in that. Her father often visits, and nearly always with an excellent bottle of wine—a vintage that I am sure was part of Kellynch's hoard—to share with your father."

"That does not make him a thief. Kellynch could not possibly be the only holder of that particular wine." The man was canny, too canny to present his employer with goods stolen from his own estate. No, it just did not make sense.

"It does not suggest his innocence either."

"Are you certain there was no sign of Kellynch in Bath?"

"I hardly know." Lady Russell stomped and stopped, flapping her wings for emphasis. "I was not there looking for him. I am far more concerned about your father's affairs."

"Affairs?" The hair on the back of Anne's neck prickled. "You think that there is something between him and Mrs. Clay?"

"I would not go quite that far. Not yet in any case. But they are often in the company of one another, nearly every evening. And too much familiarity between them, I would say is a very bad thing. Furthermore, I have noticed her in the company of Mr. Elliot."

"Mr. Elliot is in Bath? He was in Lyme not very long ago."

"I have been investigating him as well. I know you have been suspicious of him." Lady Russell's brows rose, bobbing her bright blue head feathers just so. Such a self-satisfied expression.

Anne pinched the bridge of her nose. "You say Mr. Elliot has been in the company of Mrs. Clay? Why—what has she to offer him? Why is that significant?"

"She can offer him what any woman can offer a man. She has no shame! But more importantly, I think he is keeping her close for fear of what she may steal from him."

"What can she take from him? She is hardly clever enough to plan some sort of thievery. It seems it was difficult enough for her to plan a wardrobe to take to Bath."

"His birthright If she can induce your father to marry her and she bears him an heir—"

Anne choked back a laugh. "While my father might—enjoy her company—he would certainly never marry her. She has no wealth, no connections, no title. Whatever could persuade him—"

"The promise of an heir. If she falls with child, then he will marry her."

"He would not lower himself to take such a wife."

"She has two sons by her late husband. Your father wants a son. She had proven she can bear them. That will be sufficient for him—should his rendezvous with her bear fruit."

To talk about anyone so—much less her father! Anne shuddered.

"And if you think the household is poorly managed with your father at the helm, what would it be like with Mrs. Clay?"

"What a beastly thought."

"It is imperative that you go to Bath immediately so you can work on this situation."

"He does not listen to me. Would it not be far better for you to simply persuade him of what is good for him, as you have often done?" Those last words had far more of an edge than Anne had intended.

"You are a clever girl. You will think of something."

Anne squeezed her temples. "I do not understand. You have always been so ready to do exactly that."

"Your family needs you in Bath, you must go."

It was not as if Anne did not need to be there in any case. Why was it so hard to simply agree and end this uncomfortable interview? "You will come with me then?"

"No, no, I have already been to Bath, and there is nothing—"

"What ho? Miss Anne?"

Anne jumped and looked over her shoulder. "Mrs. Croft!"

Lady Russell took two long steps backward until she stood in the midst of a patch of thorny vines.

"Miss Anne, it is so good to see you!" Mrs. Croft hurried to them, her grey walking dress dusted with leaves and spots of mud. "Who have you with you? I have never seen a cockatrix of your design before. You are a very fine dragon indeed." She curtsied toward Lady Russell.

Lady Russell squawked and snapped her beak in Mrs. Croft's face.

She jumped back, throwing her open hands in the air. "Pray excuse me, I meant no offense."

"You should learn some manners." Lady Russell hissed and launched into the air, so much like an angry goose that Anne pressed her fist to her mouth to stifle the welling laughter.

"Well, that was an interesting performance." Mrs. Croft peered into the trees as if to try to catch sight of her again.

"I am afraid Lady Russell was not prepared to make your acquaintance." Anne pressed the back of her hand to her mouth.

"That was Lady Russell?" Mrs. Croft's face lost most of its color.

"Yes, she lives in the cottage—"

"I had no idea. This is most unusual. Pray would you come to Kellynch with me? The Admiral would like to hear the news of Lyme and learn more about Lady Russell." Why did she look so troubled? Surely, Lady Russell was not the first rude dragon she had encountered.

A quarter of an hour later, they had gathered in the parlor with Admiral Croft, the French doors open and the sail cloth on the floor to accommodate White. Was it odd that it just seemed the right way of things, to include him in the conversation now? Probably.

Nothing had changed in the room, not the pale-yellow walls, not the sandy colored tile, not the pale oak furnishing upholstered in gold and orange. Yet it hardly seemed the same room her mother had decorated and enjoyed so many years ago. Was it the dragon, the Crofts or both that made the difference?

Admiral Croft pulled a chair close to White and sat beside him, one hand resting on the hippocampus' shoulder, White leaning into him slightly. "Wentworth came by for only the briefest of moments to declare himself on his way to Bath and to expect our assistance to be needed there. He said you would be able to tell us more."

Anne quickly conveyed the news of the accident in Lyme.

White shook his head hard enough that the fins on his spinal ridge swayed and flopped as he made a noise partway between a squeal and a nicker. "All this is very troubling news indeed."

Admiral Croft chewed his bottom lip. "Kellynch has committed a very serious crime indeed, both in being seen and in being the cause of such serious harm to the dragon-deaf."

"What will the Blue Order do?"

"That is an excellent question, for which I do not have a good answer. It is difficult to predict."

White pranced with his front feet. Laconia did something similar when he was troubled. "When major dragons are involved there is a very fine line to be walked in keeping the dragons in order. It is difficult for such powerful creatures to submit themselves to a treaty with warm-bloods. While the letter of the law may be quite harsh, often their judgements reflect a greater leniency. But it has been a very long time since such a thing has happened, and they may choose to make an example of Kellynch. He could lose his lands and be banished."

"Would not his anger have deadly consequences to anyone near?"

"It is possible. But the open ocean, even the continent is a dangerous place for dragons. The Pendragon Accords do not extend there. Major dragons are in fear for their lives. The Netherford dragon in Derbyshire sought asylum here from France. He has made it clear to the conclave that conditions in the continent are unenviable at best. And for sea dragons—pirates, fishing boats, whaling ships—it is not safe there either."

"But we have another serious problem, I fear." Mrs. Croft's voice was strained and her face still a mite pale. "Anne just introduced me to our neighbor, Lady Russell."

Admiral Croft's brow's knit into a single shaggy line above his eyes. "Why did you not invite her in? She will think us abominably rude for not inviting her."

"She flew away before I could."

The admiral's eye's bulged, and his jaw dropped.

White pawed at the floor, neighing.

"It appears that our neighbor is not a Lady at all, but a very rare sort of cockatrix."

"She is from Australia," Anne whispered.

"Dragon's fire!" the admiral jumped to his feet and paced the length of the room and back. "A cockatrix?"

"I do not understand. She has been here many years. Kellynch has even appointed her as Watcher over his estate whilst he sleeps."

"Are you unaware of what Lady Russell is doing?"

"I have no idea what you are talking about."

White step-slithered very close to her and put his head in her lap. "I am so very sorry there has been no one to help you understand."

She laid her hand on his head and stroked his cool smooth cheek. "What am I to understand?"

Admiral Croft drew a long breath to fuel his deep, serious tone. "I know she is your friend, but what she is doing is very wrong. Very, very illegal."

Mrs. Croft approached and rested her hand on Anne's shoulder. "A dragon must never represent itself to be a human unless it is for self-defense, and even then, it is admissible only when done for the shortest time possible under the direst possible circumstances. What your friend has been doing is an inconceivable breach of the Accords."

"I never thought—I had no idea." Anne clutched her hands and pressed them to her mouth. "She is not from here, perhaps she did not know the law."

"Ignorance is no excuse. Oh, this is bad indeed." The admiral huffed out a low breath through pursed lips. "She is only a minor dragon and cannot hope for the sort of leniency that might be extended toward Kellynch."

Mrs. Croft paced between Anne and Admiral Croft. "I think her only chance is to present herself to the court before they send someone after her. She can petition for mercy on the grounds of her ignorance and her assistance toward Kellynch."

"And if they do not grant it?"

"Dragon justice is swift and merciless." White snorted, pulling himself up to full height. "If you want to save your friend, get her to Bath and seek out the Dragon Sage. If there is anyone who will be willing and able to find a way to protect her, it is Lady Elizabeth."

October 2, 1814

Three days later, the long case clock in the front hall of Uppercross Cottage chimed three long, lonely times. Anne lay awake, staring at the fine cracks of the ceiling plaster, lit by the bright moonlight through her window. She sat up and slipped her dressing gown over her shoulders. The nights were growing colder now.

Three days she had been searching for Lady Russell, and three days the stubborn cockatrix remained steadfastly hidden. Perhaps it was for the best. How was she to persuade Lady Russell that she must return to Bath—how was such a creature to be worked on?

And yet, if she did not—Anne shuddered. There could be no good outcome if she did not. The Crofts were now obligated to report Lady Russell to the Blue Order as the criminal she was. Though it was tempting to try and plead with them for mercy, she could not. What right had she to ask them to compromise not only their integrity, but their standing with the Order itself? No, she could not.

No less than five times she had set out to write to Lady Elizabeth for insight, for advice, for comfort, for leniency upon Lady Russell. Five times she never got past the first few lines. This was not something that could be contained in a few words scratched upon foolscap. No, this was one of those situations that had to be dealt with face to face, to acknowledge her culpability in the whole matter.

She should have known—she could have known. It was in the books she had been studying. She had looked it up after Admiral Croft had offered her the reference. He was right, it was there. He did not condemn her, though. Since her circle of Blue Order acquaintance was so small, and those other dragon hearers she knew were under Lady Russell's influence, there was little reason for her to have recognized what would have been obvious to others. If anything, Uppercross had greater blame, knowing full well Lady Russell's transgression and yet choosing to keep her secret.

But even if the Order was understanding, the matter certainly would not reflect well upon her ability to properly Keep Kellynch. And if she could not Keep Kellynch, who would?

Merciful heavens, she was effectively responsible for two wildly law-breaking dragons. Not even the Dragon Sage could find a way to excuse that! She had failed, everyone, in every way possible.

Now all that was left was going through the formalities to face it.

At least not everything was bad news. There was some small comfort in that the Musgroves and the Harvilles had become fast friends. All that civility towards one and all must have created an excellent atmosphere for convalescence. Both Louisa and Benwick were improving steadily, though neither yet might be moved from their surroundings.

Mr. Musgrove had learnt the truth of Louisa's accident first from the Harville's fairy dragon, Daffodil, then from Charles himself. Not surprisingly, he took the news very poorly and expressed certain hard feelings toward Kellynch and the Keeper who should have better managed that dragon. Charles had taken his father aside and explained some of the complexities of the situation to him, upon which he recanted his hard feelings toward Anne, though it was intimated that Sir Walter might not be welcome company in Uppercross until—and perhaps unless—Louisa demonstrated a full recovery.

Pray—for so many reasons—that she did.

The clock chimed seven o'clock. Anne forced her sandy eyes open. She had fallen asleep sitting up, her dressing gown still awkwardly tucked over her shoulders. Everything ached—that was not a good posture for sleep, but at least it meant she had slept. That was something.

In just an hour the carriage would arrive to take her to Bath. How Wentworth had worked on Father to have the family coach transport her, she could neither fathom nor know how to thank him. She could think about that on the drive to Bath. For now, she needed to tuck a few more things in her trunks and find some breakfast.

A quarter of an hour later, Anne sipped a cup of tea in the morning room. A bit tasteless and cold, but none of Mary's servants seemed particularly attentive when the mistress was away from the cottage. But it and the overbaked hot cross buns, slathered generously with butter would tide her through the first half of her journey and that was all she could really hope for this morning.

Rap, rap, rap!

Anne jumped. Lady Russell pecking at the morning room window? She flung open the window. "Good morning! Do you wish to come in?"

"No, I prefer to converse through the open window." Lady Russell thrust her head forward in a manner that felt rather cross.

Anne hurried to the front door and ushered Lady Russell into the morning room. She sat across the round table from Anne, preening her magnificent wings and chittering under her breath.

"I will be leaving for Bath soon. You are coming with me, no?" Anne said softly, sipping her tea as though it was the most ordinary of conversation.

"Good, good. I am glad you have taken my advice." Lady Russell continued to work on a particularly troubling feather-scale.

"I know you heard my question. It is not like you to ignore me this way. Pray give me an answer. The coach is supposed to be here in a quarter of an hour."

Wings fluttered and head feathers flopped one way then another as Lady Russell settled into her chair. "Now what was it you were saying, my dear?"

Anne forced herself not to crush her skirt in her fists. "The coach is coming to take me to Bath. I want you to come with me."

"I am not certain. I have been traveling so much recently. I am quite tired of it all."

"I recall you have mentioned that." Railed on and on about it, in fact. "You never did tell me where you went when you left. Or what it was you were doing whilst Kellynch was awakening, all alone. Leaving me to deal with the matter on my own." Botheration, that was probably not going to be helpful—Lady Russell was so much like Elizabeth at times like this!

Lady Russell grumbled—or was that a low growl?

"I am sure you have a very poor memory. I distinctly remember telling you my plans."

Now was not the moment to call her out as a liar. "I assure you, you did not. Will you tell me again now?"

"I was consulting with someone whom I know regarding Kellynch's situation, how to manage the loss of his hoard. I thought there must surely be some way to mollify him."

"Why did you not tell me sooner? What are we to do?"

Lady Russell tossed her head, setting her head feathers bobbing in her eyes, and sniffed. "I did not tell you sooner because I was unable to come up with anything useful. Everyone was in agreement that the situation was indeed dire, but none offered a speck of useful information ... Except for one."

Something about the way she said it... "And who was that one? Is it someone I know?"

"It might have been."

"Who did you speak to and what did they tell you?" Anne forced the words through her teeth.

"You have become quite rude, you know? I do not approve of the tone you are taking with me at all."

"And I do not approve of the way you are toying with me. If you have nothing further to say to me, then I will take my leave of you now."

Lady Russell spread her wings as though to block the way to the door. "Do not get all in a dither, my dear girl. I am merely hesitant to say because I do not think he is someone you have fond feelings toward."

"Who are you talking about?"

"Mr. William Elliot."

"Mr. Elliot? What were you doing with him? The

last time I parted company with him, you proclaimed a hearty dislike for him and the insult he offered to me, and the danger he posed to you. Then, most recently, you speculated that he was in a dalliance with Mrs. Clay. How does any of this predispose me to think he is a man to whose opinions I need to listen?"

"Yes, yes I do recall that quite well. But I have recently learned a great deal more about him." She clacked her beak rapidly. "Much has changed in the years which have passed since you parted ways with him."

"Tell me." Anne glanced at the long case clock through the morning room door. Time was running out!

"Since the death of his wife, he has seen the error of his ways, repented of the insult he offered to you, and taken upon himself to learn more about Dragon Keeping. He earnestly desires to be an upstanding member of the Blue Order and do credit to the family name when he takes over Kellynch. He even wishes to make amends to you."

Anne harrumphed. "You said he had some sort of insight into our problem with the hoard."

"Yes, yes, it seems he has studied the issue extensively in the Blue Order archives."

"To what ends?"

"It is all rather complicated, and I do not think I can explain it properly. When you are in Bath, you must see fit to speak to him. I insist. You will be in Bath; he will probably call upon you."

"No, I will not." Anne's heart thundered in her ears.

"What do you mean you will not?" Lady Russell flapped and backed up several steps.

She pulled her shoulders back and sat very straight. "We were under no good terms when we last parted company. I can hardly seek him out to speak to him about these matters."

"I told you, he will certainly come to you. You would not choose to be missish if he visits?"

"It is hardly a fitting topic for polite conversation."

"It is your family business."

"Dragon Keeping is not a business, and I have no intention of talking to him of that or of anything at all. I will not see him." Oh, the glare that earned her!

"You would not dare be so rude! He is friendly with your father and sister. I am sure he will be often at Camden Place."

"I will not speak to him—"

"You must!"

"—unless—"

"Unless what?" Lady Russell was all but salivating.

"Unless you come to chaperone our meetings."

"Chaperone? He is your cousin. You hardly need a chaperone."

"I will not speak to him otherwise." Anne folded her arms over her chest and turned her shoulder to Lady Russell. "Will you come to Bath with me or not?"

"Bath, Bath, Bath! Every time we talk you find reasons for me to come to Bath. I do not want to go to Bath." Lady Russell stomped both feet and hissed.

"Very well then, I refuse to talk to Mr. Elliot. There is nothing more to be done for the matter."

"Your duty to Kellynch requires it of you."

"I have no reason to believe that Mr. Elliot knows anything about dragon keeping or hoarding. That is your notion, and as far as I am concerned, it is entirely unproven. I will have nothing to do with him."

"I insist." Lady Russell stomped and fanned her tail, nearly knocking the candlesticks off the sideboard. Good thing the candles were unlit.

"And yet I am unmoved."

"This is most unbecoming, Anne."

"I am protecting myself from an unwanted acquaintance as you taught me."

"Anne!" Lady Russell hissed and growled.

Anne shrugged. "As you wish. You will excuse me. I must be ready for the carriage."

Lady Russell hopped up and down and fluttered her wings, hissed and growled—a fine portrait of a draconic temper tantrum.

Anne stood, curtsied and turned toward the door; her steps bathed in calm dignity.

"Very well then. I shall meet you in Bath and you will talk with Mr. Elliot—yes?"

"With you as chaperone, I will."

17
Chapter

October 5, 1814

LACONIA WOVE AROUND Wentworth's feet as he
strode briskly—all but ran really, uphill—to the Blue
Order offices, beads of sweat trickling down the back
of his neck despite the morning air. Just how many
dragons were gathering in Bath? The air was awash in
their musk. The dragon-deaf population was convinced that the Avon stank for some unknown
reason. It seemed the Dragon Sage had concocted
that persuasion, now perpetuated by every minor
dragon they encountered.

It was clever to be sure, but was such a disruption
of the dragon community wise? Poor Laconia was
half beside himself knowing there were so many
predators so close. The Pendragon Accords could
only do so much to mollify blood-borne instincts.

Why did the Sage warrant such risks?

The plain, four-story yellow-orange Bath stone building was as unremarkable as it had ever been. But the cockatrice guard perched on the roof took notice, dispatching one lieutenant to fly over them, confirming their identities and squawking it back to the captain still on the rooftop. So, they were not just expected, but anticipated.

Blast and botheration! He should have reported in days ago. He would have liked to have reported days ago. But when the dragons were not complicating his life, the weather was. Damned flooded roads, broken wheels and lame horses!

Breathe, Wentworth, breathe! The material thing was that he was here before either cranky lizard—who was worse, Kellynch or Cornwall?—appeared, so the Order would be prepared to receive them both. Hopefully. If not—breathe! Breathe!

A footman showed them directly to Admiral Easterly's office. Light, and a sliver of cool air, poured in through the transom window above the tightly drawn curtains. Spartan as ever—how had he managed to shoehorn a bookcase into the small room behind the desk? Clearly it was necessary, the way the shelves bowed under the neat stack of books and papers.

Easterly, in what looked to be a new blue suit and freshly trimmed hair, rose from behind his desk. "I was beginning to fear something untoward had happened to you. I am pleased to see you."

Laconia jumped up to the pillow on the large desk, tail whipping. Mina, sleek and silver but still shy, slithered out from a large, hay-filled wooden box on the bottom shelf of the bookcase. Was that a nesting box? She jumped onto the desk and rubbed cheeks with Laconia. They twined round one another, sniffing and purring in a tight circle until they knotted themselves together on the desk pillow.

Wentworth scrubbed his hot cheek with the back of his hand. Perhaps they could be just a mite less open in their affections?

Easterly shook his head at the tatzelwurms, flipped his coattails out of his way, and sat behind his desk. "The Dragon Sage has got wind of the situation with Cornwall and has requested a full briefing on the matter as soon as there is news."

Wentworth pulled a small, wooden, lyre-back chair close to the desk and dropped onto it hard enough to make it groan under him. "Has she that much sway that she can demand—"

"Indeed, she does, and with good reason. The woman was introducing her infant to the dragons in the salon—the infant! Apparently, the baby girl can hear even now and has no fear of the dragons. The dragons seem to think it a privilege to be allowed to interact with a warm-blood hatchling as they call her. Unprecedented!"

What kind of woman presented a baby to dragons?

"I should like to meet the creature." Laconia licked his paw and the top of Mina's head. "We are never permitted at human hatchings although you attend ours."

Wentworth rolled his eyes. "I cannot fathom a woman who would permit, much less instigate, such a thing. Her husband—"

"Is a Knight of the Order and appears completely supportive of the entire scheme. It is extraordinary. In any case, I must deliver your report to her."

"I am afraid you will not be very pleased. Nothing

is as it should be."

Easterly dragged his hand down his face. "Go on."

"We have just come back from Cornwall."

"You were able to garner Kellynch's assistance, then? Why did you not write to me of it? Keeping me abreast would be appreciated."

"The entire affair was not according to our plans and changing so rapidly that writing would have been impossible." Wentworth tapped steepled fingertips together. "Kellynch awakened from his slumber without our knowledge."

"How is that possible? Slumbering dragons do not simply awaken quietly." Easterly sat up very straight.

"Precisely. We have no idea how it could have happened, only that it did. Uppercross discovered it, but when he went to investigate, Kellynch had already departed. And that is only the start of it all."

Mina's eyes widened, and the tip of her tail flicked. She licked Laconia's cheek, a mite harder than seemed necessary.

"We found him in Lyme," Wentworth lifted open hands as if to stave off the inevitable reaction. "In the worst possible way."

Easterly blanched. "Surely not."

"We can only suppose he went there to sate his hunger in the fishing grounds. But—and I cannot fathom why—he showed himself at the harbor, in the middle of the day."

"Dragon's bones! Have the local cockatrice and fairy dragons handled the matter?"

"In so far as they are able, but—"

"No, pray do not tell me—" Easterly squeezed his eyes shut and clenched his fists.

"There were two injuries—the dragon-deaf daughter of the Uppercross Keeper and a dragon-deaf sailor, Captain Benwick."

Easterly pounded his desk. "And the Keeper Miss Elliot—"

The tatzelwurms jumped and hissed.

"Was present—she was integral to arranging our presence at Lyme. Although she had never met Kellynch prior to that moment, she sought him out and stood her ground, calling Kellynch to order. Even when he threatened her with death, she stood." Wentworth's heart pounded and his mouth went dry—the look Anne wore at that instant. Had it not been such a dire moment, it would have been magnificent.

"He threated to kill her, his Keeper, at their first meeting?" Easterly lost color in his face. "What sort of dragon is this?"

"He was enraged—between his hunger upon awakening and the disruption of his hoard. He did have cause under the Accords."

"His hoard?" Easterly half-jumped to his feet then forced himself back to his chair. "I have not been made aware."

"As I understand it, Miss Elliot has sought the Sage's advice on the matter. In short, it appears the entire hoard of wine has been stolen."

"Dragon fire!" Easterly slammed his hands on his desk.

Laconia jumped to his feet and bared his fangs. "Mrrrow! You will stop doing that now. My mate is disturbed by it, and so near to clutching, she does not need an inconsiderate Friend."

"Clutching? So soon?" Easterly gasped. He raised open hands as if to push back too much information.

"Pray let us discuss that after Kellynch. So, his hoard has disappeared and he has awakened and left his territory to feed in the ocean? There he confronted his new Keeper—I assume he was not aware of the change either—and in doing so, exposed himself in public?"

"Essentially, yes. I intervened after he threatened Miss Elliot, reminding him of his own serious transgressions—and I did not even mention his failure to perform his duties according to the estate charter. I then ordered him to report to the Order in Bath that he might face the Blue Order Court."

"Then, where is he? With so many dragons in the area, we would know if he were here."

"Apparently, he did not come straight to Bath, but paid a visit to Cornwall first. A cockatrice brought us word, so we hastened there. And before you ask, no, neither I nor White nor Laconia can fathom what drove him there since I was never able to bring him the Order's request for his assistance."

"Dare I ask what you found?"

"By the time we reached Cornwall, the local dragons told us Kellynch had been there, but had already left; they had no idea of his destination. Dug Cornwall, though, was profoundly unhappy about the 'invasion of his territory' as he described it. He is threatening to declare war."

Easterly stopped just short of pounding his fists on his desk again. "Fang and claw! No major dragon has trespassed into another's territory since—what is wrong with Kellynch?"

"Before you take this too far, you should understand that Cornwall may not be accurate in his accusation. Apparently, Kellynch did not make landfall on Cornwall proper. He remained in the ocean, in the territory that is disputed, so there is a real question as to whether or not he actually entered Cornwall's territory. There is a school of sea dragons there that answer to Cornwall and informed him of Kellynch's arrival."

"I don't suppose you spoke with them?"

"We did, or rather we tried," Laconia said. "But they are a senseless school of bubblepates whose thinking is as murky as the seas they indwell."

Easterly snorted. Pray he did not offer some comparison to tatzelwurms. Laconia did not appreciate aspersions thrown against his species.

"Apparently Kellynch swims far deeper than they can, so they were not able to observe his activities beyond their depth."

"So, I am to expect Cornwall will be on his way to Bath soon, carrying a grudge and a complaint that we may or may not be able to verify? Will the Prince be arriving with him?" Though Easterly's tone was sarcastic, it seemed he did want an answer.

"Cornwall is on his way to Bath without his Keeper."

"Thank heavens for that! And what of Kellynch?"

"We are told by the local wyrms and fairy dragons that he is also, finally, on his way here. In fact, we have had reports that he is not far off. The Elliot family has taken a house in Camden Place, one attached to the dragon tunnels, with a lair sufficient to accommodate a dragon of his size."

"That is good news. With so many dragons visiting the Sage right now, making sure all the major dragons have some small lair to call their own is critical. As it is, Cornwall is fortunate that Matlock made known he was willing to relinquish the property at Royal Crescent in case emergency accommodations were necessary. We still need to sort out temporary Keepers, as it were, for Cornwall."

"I could ask my brother Croft to join us in Bath—he could have a convenient episode of gout to explain his travels—and attend to the needs of the Dug. I doubt a mere captain would suffice for Cornwall—besides I think he is displeased with my audacity in challenging his territorial claims." Wentworth stroked his chin. "I think White could be very helpful as well. Cornwall seems intrigued by him."

"There are so few options—just do it. Write to him, and I will see to arrangements. You will probably need to stay at the house until your brother arrives. I will send a cockatrice and fairy dragons to intercept Cornwall with the location of his temporary lair." Easterly clutched his temples. "Two major dragons with a grudge in a single city is a most dangerous situation."

"There is one more detail we have recently become aware of that you need to know."

"Pendragon's bones—what is it now?"

"I suspect there is a history between Kellynch and Cornwall."

"What sort of history exactly?" Throbbing blue veins stood out on the sides of Easterly's forehead.

"I have not seen it for myself, but I suspect that Cornwall was the one to grant Kellynch his estate in payment of some kind of debt."

"And you know this how?"

"His Keeper, Miss Elliot, was unaware of his being a marine wyrm, and in that discussion mentioned that the charter, though highly illegible, contained a line that could have read that the territory was assigned in payment for a debt, and the dragon assigning it could have been Cornwall."

"Dear God—I do not even know what to make of that. Is Miss Elliot aware of the situation with Cornwall? Where is she?"

"Miss Elliot is in Bath already, I believe, but as to what she knows—" Wentworth sighed. "She is unaware of any of the current issues with Cornwall. She only knows of the concerns with Kellynch's hoard and his unexpected awakening."

"She needs to be informed of the complexities of the situation."

"Just as I told you," Laconia muttered.

"To what ends? The Order cannot hold her responsible for the current troubles. She has only just become Keeper and has no responsibility for what transpired before her time nor is even aware of it. Her father has all but bankrupted the estate and cannot replenish the hoard—she has no control over that. The dragon has been sleeping and awakened without her. Again, she has no power in that matter."

"What are you not telling me?"

"Her father has been apt to make her responsible for a very great deal that is not of her doing. I do not want to see her on trial for crimes in which she had no complicity."

"Are you involved with this woman?" Easterly crossed his arms over his chest and glared at him.

"She is a very fine female. I approve of her a great deal." Laconia licked his thumbed paw and ran it over his head. "She is, her family is, staying in Camden Place. You should go there and see her."

"My feelings are of no concern in this matter. This

is a Blue Order matter—enough said." Wentworth turned aside from both Laconia's and Easterly's gazes.

"See that it remains so. This entire situation is irregular even in the Blue Order annals. There is no way to predict how this is going to turn out, and frankly, when major dragons are involved, expecting complexity and undesirable outcomes seems to be the wisest course of action. Adding complications to an already difficult situation will not be looked upon favorably."

But Anne was not a complication—she was a victim in the affair, one who needed protection. One who needed his protection. Somehow, he would find a way to ensure she had it.

18
Chapter

October 5, 1814

ANNE DISMISSED THE BUTLER and took refuge in the parlor, clutching the letter that confirmed her plans. The black and white marble tiles felt busy and tense beneath the trompe l'oeil walls painted to mimic swags of burgundy taffeta draped from ceiling to floor. The overwrought sensation was only compounded by the furniture: deeply carved dark stained woods with black and burgundy striped upholstery. The bombe chests and sideboards were all topped with marble and crowned with fussy candlesticks and hard to describe decorative pieces. Whomever designed the room never spent hours of agitation within—if they had, they would have had to turn to laudanum to cope.

Was it odd to be relieved that Mrs. Smith was happy to hear she was come to Bath and looked forward to seeing her at Anne's earliest convenience? Probably.

The Elliots had taken a very good house in Camden Place, a lofty dignified situation, appropriate to a man of consequence. Their house was undoubtedly the best in Camden Place; their drawing rooms had many decided advantages over all the others which they had either seen or heard of. Both he and Elizabeth were eager to maintain the respectability of the place. Father would hardly consider Mrs. Smith a suitable acquaintance. Certainly not one who would ever be welcome at Camden Place.

When Anne had first arrived, she had been greeted with a degree of unexpected cordiality. Her family were glad to see her, for the sake of showing her the house and furniture, and boasting how their society was so well appreciated in Bath. Her making a fourth when they sat down to dinner was also noticed as an advantage.

Such distinction to be placed on her shoulders. How could she possibly bear it?

They were in excellent spirits, and had little inclination to listen to any news she might bring. Uppercross excited no interest, Kellynch very little: all that interested them was Bath. Their acquaintance was exceedingly sought after. Everybody was wanting to visit them. They had drawn back from many introductions, and still were perpetually having cards left by people of whom they knew nothing.

Was it wrong to feel that perhaps it would have been just a little bit better should they feel some degradation in this change? Probably. It would require a very liberal mind on their part to admit to such a thing.

But their situation was not all which they had to make them happy. No, there was more! Anne squeezed her eyes shut and pressed her temples hard. Biting her tongue was positively headache-inducing. In Bath, Father and Elizabeth had Mr. Elliot, too. Anne wrapped her arms around her waist—perhaps that would settle her stomach.

Who would have thought he would win not only Lady Russell's approbation but her family's as well? He was not only pardoned for his past transgressions; they were delighted with him. How? How could such a thing have happened?

Apparently with very intentional acts on his part. The question: was it genuine or conniving? Lady Russell, of course, thought the former; Anne's instincts insisted the latter.

Mr. Elliot's first object on arriving in Bath had been to leave his card in Camden Place, following it up by such assiduous endeavors to meet his esteemed uncle and fair cousin that he could not be gainsaid. Upon finally meeting, he demonstrated such great openness of conduct, such readiness to apologize for the past, such solicitude to be received as a relation again, that good understanding was completely reestablished.

Additional intelligence on the extenuating circumstances of his marriage, too, were found. According to Mr. Elliot's great friend, Colonel Wallis—now admitted to Father's acquaintance as well—who knew Mr. Elliot's wife well, she was certainly not a woman of family, but well educated, accomplished, rich, and, most significantly, excessively in love with Mr. Elliot.

There had been the charm. A very fine woman with a large fortune, in love with him!

How was it Father could admit such a thing as a complete apology? A reason, perhaps, even an acceptable reason, if she had been in love, which would never be proven one way or another; but it was not an apology for the things Mr. Elliot had done. Elizabeth could not see the circumstance in quite so favorable a light, she allowed it could be seen as an extenuating circumstance.

The question though was why. Why would he seek reconciliation now? What would he gain by it? In truth, with his late wife's fortune, he was probably the richer man, and Kellynch would surely be his in time. So, he had nothing to gain by being on good terms with the head of the family.

Some might think it was for Elizabeth's sake, marrying her would be socially acceptable. But society did not understand the issue of dragons. Was it possible, as Lady Russell suggested, he wanted to do right by the Blue Order and marry Anne as they had desired she do years ago?

Anne sighed. Could she do that? After the horrid offer he had made her? After having reunited with Wentworth? Could she submit to the Order's preferences, be persuaded against her wishes, her instincts, a second time?

"Oh, there you are Anne. We were wondering where you were hiding today." Father, clad in a newly made green tailcoat, sauntered into the parlor with Mrs. Clay simpering on his heels.

"I had no idea you were looking for me." Actually, she had been hoping he had not been. Anne rose and curtsied, setting her letter aside.

"Reading again? I would have thought there was nothing left for you to read any more with all the hours you devote to the activity. It is a wonder you are not yet in need of glasses." Father raised his eyebrows and glanced at Mrs. Clay who tittered obligingly.

Insipid. Intolerable. Insufferable.

"Thankfully I have friends who are quite ready to write to me to supply me with new reading material," Anne asked–it was the right things to do under the circumstances. "Where is Elizabeth?"

"She has an appointment with her favorite modiste." Mrs. Clay sat on the settee too close to Father.

Improper.

"I am surprised you did not attend with her. I know she values your opinion." Anne looked directly at Mrs. Clay.

"Mr. Shephard is expected to call today. There is some sort of droll business he needs my input on." Father rolled his eyes and shrugged.

"He asked specifically to see me as well, so I could not go with Miss Elliot today." Was Mrs. Clay batting her eyes?

"I see." Anne chewed her lip. It was a good way to prevent a hundred untoward thoughts from tumbling unrestrained from her mouth. Remarks about Father and Mrs. Clay.

Unfortunately, it was hardly a subject she could be direct about, regardless of how direct Lady Russell had been. She had been right though, in her concerns. If Father should become involved with the woman, things could only go from bad to worse. Ironic that the very propriety that Father evidenced in nearly all his behavior was the very thing preventing Anne from gathering a sure sense of the situation.

Mrs. Clay leaned forward a little. Was her hand pressed against her belly? It might be, but then again it might not.

Indecent.

"So, what think you of Bath, Miss Anne, now you are seen it for yourself?"

Anne winced, but correcting her father's guest's grammar publicly would be considered rude. "I can see that Father and Elizabeth are very happy here, and in that I am content. And you, Mrs. Clay? I understood this was your first time in Bath."

"I can hardly imagine a more pleasant place. I am ever so appreciative that I have been afforded the opportunity to come. I am sure now you are come Miss Anne, that I cannot suppose myself at all wanted anymore. I am sure my Father is calling today to make arrangements for my return."

Was it possible? Such good fortune?

Father sat up very straight and looked offended. "Certainly not! I will not hear of it. My dear madam, this must not be. As yet, you have seen nothing of Bath. You have been here only to be useful. Anne is here now for that. You must not run away from us now. You must stay to be acquainted with Mrs. Wallis, the beautiful Mrs. Wallis. To your fine mind, I well know the sight of beauty is a real gratification."

How generous of him! She, not Mrs. Clay, was here to be useful. No, no, she dare not dwell upon that now.

"Miss Elliot and I had accepted an invitation to an afternoon tea with her next week." Mrs. Clay peeked through her eyelashes at him.

Insupportable coquette.

"Clearly you must stay, then. It would be abominably rude for you to break off your engagement with her. As far as I am concerned the matter is now settled." Father ended the declaration with a flourish of his hands that always pointed to the end of a discussion.

Anne pressed her hand into a fist under the edge of her skirts. With so many dragon problems to deal with, the last thing she needed were warm-blooded problems as well.

"Far be it from me to argue with you Sir Walter, it will be as you say." Mrs. Clay giggled. Giggled! "It will be so pleasant to continue to enjoy Bath with you and your family. This is the second trip this year for you, Miss Anne, is it not? I recall you were lately in Lyme as well?"

"Lyme, indeed." Father sniffed. "The party at Uppercross went as I understand. What really, what is a seaport to Bath? What sort of company might you find in a place like that?"

"You might be surprised. We actually saw Mr. William Elliot there." That was probably the wrong thing to say, but truly, who could blame her?

"I had no idea!" Mrs. Clay pressed a hand to her chest. "I did not think he had any acquaintance there."

What would Mrs. Clay know of his acquaintance and why would she be concerned with his whereabouts? If she were with child, then whose—

"He has called at Camden Place regularly you know." Father seemed desperate to return the conversation to Bath. "You shall see him soon, no doubt. When you do, I am sure you will agree, he has a very

gentlemanlike appearance; his air is one of elegance
and fashion, his face good shaped, his eye sensible;
but, at the same time, I must lament his being very
much underhung, a defect which time seems to have
increased, I am quite sure that these five years have
altered almost every feature for the worse."

"He declared to me that he thinks you appear exactly as you did when you last parted." Mrs. Clay said.

"How I would like to be able to return the compliment entirely; I am embarrassed I cannot. I do not
mean to complain, however. Mr. Elliot is better to
look at than most men, especially in Bath. I have no
objection to being seen with him anywhere." He
leaned back and propped his feet on a low footstool.
"It is a great problem in Bath you see, the many very
plain faces I am continually passing in the streets. The
number of its plain women! Mind you, I do not mean
to say that there are no pretty women, but the number of the plain is out of all proportion. On walking, I
have observed that one handsome face is followed by
thirty, or five-and-thirty frights. Once as I stood in a
shop on Bond Street, I counted eighty-seven women
go by, one after another—"

Just how long had he stood in that shop to count
eighty-seven women walk past?

"—without there being a tolerable face among
them. It had been a frosty morning, to be sure, a
sharp frost, which hardly one woman in a thousand
could stand the test of. But still, there certainly are a
dreadful multitude of ugly women in Bath; and as for
the men! They are infinitely worse. Such scarecrows
as the streets are full of! It is evident how little the
women are used to the sight of anything tolerable, by
the effect which a man of decent appearance produc-

es. I never walk anywhere arm-in-arm with Colonel Wallis—"

"Without all the ladies' eyes upon you, much to his chagrin?" Mrs. Clay fluttered her eyelashes. "You certainly have every bit as pleasing a figure as him, and you are not at all sandy-haired."

Ingratiating. Invidious.

Father looked decidedly smug. "How is Mary looking these days? The last time I saw her she had a red nose, but I hope that may not happen every day."

"Oh! no, that must have been quite accidental. In general, she has been in very good health and very good looks."

"If I thought it would not tempt her to go out in sharp winds and grow coarse, I would send her a new hat and pelisse."

"You are such a considerate father!" Mrs. Clay applauded softly. Applauded!

She must not roll her eyes, not in company. Not in this company. Was it worth arguing that such a gift would not be liable to any such misuse?

A knock at the door! Such a conversation Mr. Shephard would interrupt.

The butler appeared in the doorway. "Mr. Elliot."

"Good day, sir." Mr. Elliot removed his hat and bowed.

Anne drew a little back. Contrary to what Father said, Mr. Elliot had hardly changed.

"You of course remember my daughter, Miss Anne." Father gestured toward her.

Mr. Elliot's eyebrows rose and he blinked. "Miss Anne? I hardly recognized you—and I mean that in the most complimentary way possible."

"Thank you, I am sure." What did one say to such a remark? Anne curtsied.

He was quite as good looking as he had been at their last meeting. His manners were so exactly what they ought to be, so polished, so easy, so particularly agreeable. He sat down with them, and improved their conversation very much. His tone, his expressions, his choice of subject, his knowing where to stop; it was all the operation of a sensible, discerning mind. Perhaps the improvements Lady Russell spoke of were real indeed.

The butler appeared again and whispered something to Father.

"You must forgive us. Mr. Shephard has arrived and Mrs. Clay and I must attend him."

Appropriate pleasantries were exchanged, and they departed. Mr. Elliot turned his full attention on Anne. "Are you enjoying Bath?"

"I have only just arrived, so I hardly feel qualified to offer an answer." Surely, he did not want a true answer.

He laughed softly. "Such a direct answer."

Hardly. If only he knew. "I think you will find me to be very direct now."

"I had been given that warning." He winked.

"From whom?" Anne's cheeks prickled and the hair on the back of her neck stood up.

"Our mutual acquaintance, Lady Russell, mentioned something of the sort."

"You have become acquainted with Lady Russell?"

"We were introduced by a mutual acquaintance. I am very glad to come to know her. She is a very interesting—woman." What did he mean by that tone?

"She mentioned she had heard of you in her travels."

"Indeed, it was a most memorable visit—we saw one another in London you see."

Odd that she had not mentioned they had actually become acquainted. Lady Russell was so careful about revealing herself to dragon hearers. Very odd. "Lyme, London, now Bath. You do move about quite a bit."

"One of the few advantages to being a widower I suppose—I am free to move about as I choose." He shrugged, so cavalier.

"Lady Russell suggested that you were quite reformed since last we met."

"Reformed? Goodness that is a very strong word. It makes me sound as though I were quite the rake."

Yes, it did, not inaccurately. "Perhaps that is a strong term, but you certainly won no friends in the eyes of the Order."

He hung his head. "That I cannot deny. I am most heartily ashamed with so many of the things I said and did, or rather failed to do."

"Indeed?" She chewed the inside of her cheek. "Our mutual friend seems convinced of the sincerity of your repentance."

"You seem less inclined to believe me."

No, she was not going to play that game. She lifted her eyebrow and cocked her head.

"I suppose you are wise in that. I should not be surprised as you are known as a font of good sense. So then, I shall prove it to you in my actions."

"Actions? What have you done?"

"I hope it does not offend you, but after what happened in Lyme—"

She gasped and pressed a hand to her chest. "What do you know of Lyme?"

"With the local fairy dragons and cockatrice working to persuade half the population that nothing happened on the Cobb, it was not difficult to put it all together."

"How many in the Order are aware of what happened that day?"

"Given the look on your face, I imagine you would like it to be less known than it is."

Her cheeks burned.

"Having completed a significant course of study of Blue Order materials, I thought, perhaps rather foolheartedly, that there might be something I could do."

"What did you do?"

"With the help of a few local winged dragons, I found the sea cave where Kellynch was lurking and I approached him."

"You approached Kellynch, alone, without his Keeper to introduce you?" She trembled. Was that fear—no, something different, a little unfamiliar. Indignation. Yes, that was it. "Did he not threaten you?"

"Blue Order Law says he cannot harm a human unless his life is at stake. I had no weapon; thus, he could only make threats." Was he brave, or simply foolhardy? "I asked him why he had awakened so suddenly and left Kellynch. Do you know what he told me?"

"I have no idea."

Mr. Elliot's voice dropped to a whisper. "Apparently his hoard has been stolen, and he means to make things right."

Anne's heart raced. She had not forgotten that conversation with Kellynch. Something about Mr. Elliot's calm … "And he just told you—a complete stranger, unknown to him, with no one to speak for you—he told you such a personal tragedy; one that makes him look rather feckless as dragons go. What would have compelled him to such candor with you?"

He cocked his head and flashed his brows. "People frequently tell me far more than they would ordinarily tell a stranger. I have no idea why. I suppose I have a kind face. In any case, regarding Kellynch—"

"I am aware of the issues. You need not involve yourself in the matter. I am now full Keeper to Kellynch and the matter is mine to resolve."

"Pray do not take offense, I mean only to help."

"What kind of help can you be in such a situation?" It was a rhetorical question.

"I can think of two ways most immediately. First, I can do what I should have done years ago and marry you as the Blue Order desires. Then you will not have to manage this situation on your own. We can share the Keeper's duties—"

"And the other?" She folded her arms across her chest and leaned away from him.

"I suppose I cannot blame you. After the way we parted, it is only natural that you are not pleased by the notion. I do owe you a profound apology—"

"The other way you wish to be of assistance, sir? We can talk about the rest at a later time."

"Of course, as you wish. The other," he reached into his coat pocket and withdrew a gold coin. "Do you know how I came by this?"

Anne's stomach clenched. "I have no idea."

"I saw it fall from Kellynch's jaw in the sea cave."

"Where would he have come by such a thing? And even if he did, I am certain that no dragon would lose track of a single one of his coins."

"Apparently he was angry enough that he did." He flipped the coin, caught it and pressed it into Anne's hand. "It is illegal for a dragon to possess gold against their charter and only royal dragons are afforded that privilege. The dragon is in some very serious trouble. I think it took to stealing gold—from where I have no idea—because of the missing hoard. I think this needs to be presented to the Order and we—that is you—need to ask them for leniency in dealing with him because of his clearly deranged state of mind— hoarding madness it is called in some texts."

"You have not said, but it seems you are implying that I am somehow to blame for this."

"I have said no such thing. It is just that you are his Keeper and usually, according to Blue Order records, the Keeper is held responsible for such things. That is why I want to help you. I do not wish to see you punished for what I do not believe is your fault. And the best way for me to protect you is—"

No, she did not want to deal with that question now! She jumped to her feet. "I see. Thank you very much for your concern and for the information you have brought me. Clearly, I have a great deal to think about. A very great deal. Pray excuse me, I very much need to be alone right now."

"Of course." He blinked as if in surprise, rose, and bowed. "I will show myself out."

Anne stared at the door as it swung shut behind him. Her feet began moving even before it thumped closed. Movement—it was the only thing that would keep her from jumping out of her skin. Maybe. Hopefully.

Now he was ready to do his duty, to marry her and be a good Dragon Keeper. Was it possible that he would make such a dramatic change in just five years? Lady Russell was convinced, that should be enough, should it not? But no, something was not right.

When had his wife died? She stopped, squeezed her eyes shut and turned her face toward the ceiling. Mrs. Smith had written to her of it—the end of last winter! He had been a widower less than a year.

With his wife and her fortune to entertain him, why would he have concerned himself with dragons during her lifetime? So, it could only have been in the past twelve-month that he would have been pursuing anything draconic. How had he learned so much as Lady Russell said he had in so short a time when Anne had been studying diligently for the last five years? Something was not right.

How could a man change so much—change genuinely, not just on the surface, in such a short span of time? No, it was not possible. He could not be what he appeared to be on the surface. He just could not.

But what if it was her old resentment speaking? Could she afford to make that mistake?

She drew several deep breaths. Who was it who had told her: We have all a better guide in ourselves, if we would attend to it, than any other person can be? Mama perhaps? It was good advice though, if she had the strength to follow it.

But did she?

Could she?

But who else was there to trust anymore? Wentworth? Yes, he was trustworthy but, where was he? No, she could not wait on finding him.

A laugh welled up within, bubbling over to echo off the parlor walls. Though it was not he who had given her that advice, it was the sort of thing he would have most heartily agreed with. And that was her answer.

Mr. Elliot was not to be trusted.

19
Chapter

October 7, 1814

ANNE TRIED TO make herself small in the corner of the fussily decorated parlor, nearest the window with the brightest light. The ornate Trafalgar chair she occupied, polished and new, was a mite too tall for her and had so little padding in the seat that comfortable was the least accurate way to describe it. She stabbed her needle in and out of a piece of fancy whitework— ostensibly her excuse for sitting in the uncomfortable chair, far away from Father and Mrs. Clay. Thankfully, they were content to have her too far away for polite conversation—she could hardly have defended the importance of her project to them if they wanted her participation in their discourse.

Elizabeth rushed in, skirts swooshing, chest heaving, a creased sheet of paper—a letter of some sort perhaps?—fluttering in her hand. "Papa! I have just received a communication," she waved the missive like a flag of triumph, "from Laura Place!"

Father sprang from his burgundy and black striped bergère and all but ran across the black and white tile to her, nearly slipping and falling in his haste. "The Dalrymples! They have written to us?"

"Indeed, we have been invited. Lady Dalrymple is being kept at home by a bad cold and is in sore need of company this evening."

"How excellent! We shall be there of course." He turned over his shoulder and glanced at Mrs. Clay who nodded vigorously.

So much excitement to keep company with a stuffy old woman likely with a red nose and a disagreeable cough!

"You do not seem to appreciate the value of the invitation." Elizabeth peered down her nose toward Anne.

Anne fixed her needle in her project. No further sewing would happen this morning. "I will not be able to attend. I am engaged to spend the evening with an old schoolfellow."

"Schoolfellow? What sort of person is this schoolfellow of yours?" Father eyed her narrowly as he returned to his chair. No doubt what he really wanted to know was whether there were some member of Anne's acquaintance that might be a suitable or useful acquaintance for the Elliots to improve their standing in society.

"We attended school together in Bath. Her name is Mrs. Smith, formerly Miss Hamilton, though now a widow, and she lives in Westgate Buildings."

Mrs. Clay glanced at Elizabeth who sneered and

rolled her eyes. Was she so unable to determine her own reactions for herself? Mrs. Clay stared at her hands. Apparently, she was.

"Westgate Buildings! Who is Miss Anne Elliot to be visiting Westgate Buildings? A Mrs. Smith." Father flicked his hand in a powerful dismissal. "A widow Mrs. Smith. Who was her husband? One of five thousand Mr. Smiths whose names are to be met with everywhere. What is her attraction? That she is old and sickly? Upon my word, Miss Anne Elliot—"

Did he know how much she hated it when he called her by that name?

"You have the most extraordinary taste! Everything that revolts other people, low company, paltry rooms, foul air, disgusting associations are inviting to you. But surely you may put off this old lady till tomorrow. She is not so near her end, I presume, but that she may hope to see another day. What is her age? Forty?"

"No, sir, she is not one-and-thirty; but I do not think I can put off my engagement, because it is the only evening for some time which will at once suit her and myself. She goes into the warm bath tomorrow, and for the rest of the week, you have informed me, we are engaged."

"A widow Mrs. Smith lodging in Westgate Buildings! A poor widow barely able to live, between thirty and forty; a mere Mrs. Smith, an everyday Mrs. Smith, of all people and all names in the world, to be the chosen friend of Miss Anne Elliot, and to be preferred by her to her own family connections among the nobility of England and Ireland! Mrs. Smith! Such a name!" Father's voice rose with each sentence until he nearly shouted.

Mrs. Clay pressed her hands to her cheeks and turned her face away. Could this be the first time she had actually heard Father's opinions on those of less rarified breeding than his own? She rose shakily and hurried from the room with only the barest of curtsies.

"See what you have done Anne!" Elizabeth hissed like an angry goose.

"Perhaps it would be wise to recall that Mrs. Smith is not the only widow in Bath between thirty and forty, with little to live on, and no surname of dignity." Anne stood and strode for the door. "How interesting that it appears not all of such company are entirely dreadful to the family of Elliot."

That last bit was probably unnecessary and possibly even unwise. Provoking those she lived with was probably not a good idea. But if it got Father to put a little more thought upon the widow he was spending far too much time with, then it would be worth the cost.

Anne still trembled a bit as she fastened her bonnet and pelisse. Just because she forced herself to practice boldness now did not mean it was comfortable or pleasant. A brisk walk in the cool afternoon air would do her a world of good.

The walk to Westgate Buildings—downhill, which was notable as nearly everything in Bath was uphill—took nearly half an hour. Plenty of time to ponder how things had changed since she was last there.

Mrs. Smith was a widow now, and poor. Her husband had been extravagant. His death had left his affairs dreadfully involved. She had had difficulties of every sort to contend with, and in some stroke of malicious luck had been afflicted with a severe rheumatic fever, which settled in her legs making her, at least for the present, an invalid. No longer able to afford the terrace house she and her husband once let, she was now in lodgings near the hot baths, living in a very humble way, unable even to afford herself the comfort of a servant, and of course almost excluded from society.

Even so, at least from her letters, Mrs. Smith offered good sense, agreeable manners and a disposition to converse and be cheerful beyond her expectation. Neither the dissipations of the past—and she had lived very much in the world—nor the restrictions of the present, neither sickness nor sorrow seemed to have closed her heart or ruined her spirits. Hopefully those impressions would hold true when they met face to face once again.

Westgate Buildings, made of Bath stone like most everything else, rose up, plain and sturdy, before her. Four stories tall, with narrow windows that left it with a rather severe expression, like a sour school mistress. The front door hung slightly askew, like a crooked front tooth, which lessened the severity.

The landlady, stout, stooped and good-humored, showed her upstairs to Mrs. Smith's rooms—a noisy haphazard parlor shared by other lodgers and a dark narrow bedroom behind. Father would be appalled by the conditions she endured and declare it proof of Mrs. Smith's coarseness and crudity that she could live so much like a rat in its den. Nothing would ever convince him of her elasticity of mind, that disposition to be comforted, that power of turning readily from evil to good, and of finding employment which carried her out of herself. It was the choicest gift of Heaven.

"Miss Anne!" Mrs. Smith in her white lace cap, frayed woolen bed jacket and fingerless knitted gloves reached for her from the bed. "At last you have come!" Her features were weathered to be sure, but her eyes held the same gentle smile and caring Anne had known from years ago, and her Blue Order signet hung on a cord around her neck.

"It is so good to see you! I am sorry I could not get away sooner. Father and Elizabeth have so filled my schedule—"

"You need say nothing more, I understand. No point dwelling upon such things. You must tell me all the latest news! I am sure you have been quite busy. Your letters have been so few and far between!"

Anne pulled a battered wooden chair near the narrow bed covered in a patched drab counterpane, opposite the open window, and sat down. "I know you do not mean to chasten, but you are right. I have been a shameful correspondent recently. I pray you will forgive me."

"You know I shall," Mrs. Smith winked and dropped her voice to nearly a whisper. "All the more because I have heard so many interesting things about you."

"About me? How? I was given to understand you do not get out very much." Anne leaned close in a conspiratorial whisper.

"Only to the warm baths these days."

"Then how would you know anything of me?"

"We have far more mutual acquaintances than you know." Mrs. Smith cocked her head and lifted an eyebrow. "Members of the Blue Order are hardly ever really separated. You look puzzled. Really? You well know that news travels by fairy dragon more quickly than by royal post!"

Anne's cheeks prickled and cooled. She swallowed hard. "What have you heard?"

"I can only guess by your presence here that you have not managed to reconcile with Kellynch?"

Anne dropped her face into her hands. "I had no idea the news would spread so far. The whole of England must know by now and think me a failure at Dragon Keeping."

"It is hardly that bad I am sure." Mrs. Smith beckoned toward a shadow just outside the window. A large black bird with a straight pale bill hopped onto the windowsill—wait, that was no bird! Its back half was long and serpentine, covered with black feather-scales. "May I introduce my Friend Rooke?"

"I am pleased to meet you, Rooke." Anne stood and curtsied.

Rooke squawked and flapped, bobbing her—yes it did seem to be a female—head. "Good to finally meet you—I've heard so much about ya, Miss Anne."

Was it possible? The dragon spoke with the same sort of accent the landlady had? She forced herself not to smile. Of course, it made sense, but it felt rather homey and quaint.

"Forgive me for staring, I have never met one of your kind before. I did not even know you had a Friend."

"The Blue Order has been very good to me. After my husband died with his affairs—well, as they were you know—they sent Rooke, a most lovely cockatrix, to look after me."

"I do not look as other cockatrix you have known, Miss?" Rooke jumped to the end of the bed and cocked her head almost sideways, the tip of her tail flicking.

"I pray I do not offend, but no. The others in my acquaintance are rather showy creatures." And proud—Lady Russell would never serve anyone in such a capacity even if she were their Friend.

"Well not all of us can be beauties, can we be?" She bobbed her head up and down. "Some of us are rather more useful than that."

"I am sure you are. I am very grateful to know my friend is not all alone."

Mrs. Smith reached forward to scratch Rooke under the chin. "Besides nursing me most admirably, she has really proved an invaluable Friend. As soon as I could use my hands again, she taught me to knit, which has been a great amusement." Just how did a cockatrix know how to knit, much less teach it? "She is a shrewd, intelligent, sensible Friend with a fund of good sense and observation, worth attending to. Call it gossip, if you will, but Rooke is always sure to have something to relate that is entertaining and profitable; something that makes one know one's species better. One likes to hear what is going on, to be *au fait* as to the newest modes of being trifling and silly. To me, who lives so much alone, her conversation, I assure you, is a treat."

Rooke hopped from one foot to the other, wings fluttering just a mite. "What she means to say is that it all puts me in a way of being able to tell you with great certainty that the news is not as widespread as you fear. It is mostly fairy dragons bearing tales. One tells another you know, who gets confused and changes things around a mite. By the time the third or the fourth flutterbit repeats it, there is precious little of the true tale remaining. No one takes them very seriously."

"Well then I suppose that is a good thing." Anne sighed.

"I would not rest too easy, Miss, though. Things are not well in the Order. What with Cornwall up in arms and coming here as well."

"Cornwall? The Prince's dragon?" Please, please let it be a coincidence; let it have nothing to do with Kellynch!

"'ave you not heard?"

"Our local fairy dragons are apparently rather un-informed."

Rooke hopped close, bobbing her head forward and back. "Well then, as I 'ave 'eard it, there is a brouhaha brewing that could rock all of the Blue Order. Cornwall, he says that someone has been pinching the gold from his hoard."

Anne gasped. "No, that is not possible!"

"It is difficult to imagine who would have the au-dacity—or the cleverness—to try and steal from a firedrake—and apparently succeed." Mrs. Smith shared a knowing look with Rooke.

"There is a great deal of speculation, but not a sin-gle strong leading. Some be sayin' Cornwall be a bit dicked in the nob like the king himself." Rooke snig-gered. "So, the Blue Order has bigger issues at hand than your'n with cranky ol' Kellynch."

"I suppose so," Anne forced the words out, but her tongue felt thick and numb. "But it is difficult to be glad about such a thing. An angry firedrake cannot be good for the kingdom."

"Hardly. That's why the Dragon Sage is come to deal with the matter herself no less. She got a way about her, ya' see. They say she knows dragons, un-

derstands them better than we understands ourselves." A shudder ran down Rooke's back all the way
to her tail feathers. "It be a bit hard to fathom."

"I have been corresponding with her regarding
Kellynch for many months now and she always has
such practical, useful advice."

"Of course, it is coming from a woman! If you
want to know how to tend a feeling, sensible creature,
the best advice is always going to come from a woman." Mrs. Smith soothed Rooke's ruffled feathers.

"Forgive me. Got me so distracted, I nearly forgot
ta' tell you." Rooke hopped near Mrs. Smith's knee.
"Your Kellynch, he been seen—no, no, not by any
warmbloods mind you so you ken relax—by some
water wyrms in the Avon, north of here. He should
be here soon."

"Merciful heavens! Where will he go?" Anne
clutched her skirt in her fists.

"That you needn't worry 'bout none. Your family
is at Camden Place, no? There is a temporary lair
connected to the dragon tunnels under the big house
there. Surely that is why your father took it."

"A temporary lair? I had no idea there were such
things. I am certain my Father would not have known
either, but I am not averse to take advantage of a
happy coincidence when it happens. I have heard of
the tunnels, but never seen them myself."

"I could show you the tunnels and how to get to
Camden Place by them. If we leave now, you could
prolly be there before Kellynch arrives—be there to
greet him as it were."

"You should let her take you, Miss Anne. You can
call again when matters are more settled. But you
must promise to tell me everything!" Mrs. Smith

laughed softly, but her eyes spoke to the seriousness of the matter.

"You have my word. Thank you both very much." Anne curtsied and followed Rooke as she took to her wings and led the way outside.

"Have you ever been in dragon tunnels?" Rooke asked as she flew down the narrow alley leading into the mews behind Westgate Buildings.

"Only on Kellynch estate. I did not even know they ran beneath Camden Place." Anne ran to keep up.

Rooke landed beside a nondescript sort of storage shed in the mews. Slightly dilapidated, splashed with mud and half covered in vines that probably bloomed prettily in the summer, it was the sort of place one never really noticed. "Wait there, I will get the key." She took off and disappeared before Anne could ask any one of a dozen very good questions.

What would she say to Kellynch when she saw him? What could she say? Wentworth was the one who had ordered him to Bath, not her. The Blue Order had not sent for her yet, so she had no news to share with him. Surely his anger toward her could not have changed. There was no reason to believe this meeting could go well.

Rooke swooped in and back-winged as she landed, stirring up dust and dry leaves on the ground, a large key in her talons. "Take this and unlock that door. And be quick. No need to draw attention to a lady like yourself using such a door."

The cold iron key, rough and heavy in her hand, bore a dragon's head at the top. No mistaking that key for anything else. She pushed it into the lock and turned hard. The door squealed and creaked as though opening were an arduous, unfamiliar exercise.

"The basket to your right has torches and a tinder box. Light one."

Anne fumbled with the flint and steel, but eventually the torch lit. Was it possible that Rooke was snickering behind her? Definitely. She was being laughed at by a dragon.

Anne pulled the door closed behind her and locked it, allowing her eyes to adjust to the dim glow of the torch as she returned the key to Rooke.

"Kin ya' see well enough to walk now?" Rooke asked hopping from one foot to the other.

"I think so."

"Come along then." Rooke took to the air, flying near the ceiling as the roughhewn tunnel sloped steeply down.

Cool smells of dank limestone and traces of dragon musk filled the surprisingly large space. A film of moisture covered the stone beneath her feet. Major dragons used these for travel, that was why they were so big—at least fifteen feet tall and maybe a little more side to side.

"Slow down, I cannot see you!" Anne called, peering into the dark tunnel trying to make out Rooke's black form.

"I am just ahead of you. Can you not go faster?"

"The floor is too slick. I will fall if I run."

Did dragons sigh? "Just keep going straight, I will wait for you at the next turn."

Lovely, that was just barely not being left alone to find her way through these tunnels herself. To be fair, Rooke's short legs made walking with Anne impractical and flying slowly did not seem possible. But even with the torch, the way was dark, uneven, damp and cold. She had not really known what to expect, but it was not this.

"Come along now, come along," Rooke called, her disembodied voice echoing off the walls. "We are going to take the right-hand passage now."

The fork in the tunnels just came into view, along with Rooke's inky black form, clinging to a small rocky outcrop along the wall.

"Do many dragons use the tunnels?" Anne asked as she caught up with Rooke. She held out her arm and Rooke perched on it.

"It depends really. With the Dragon Sage's arrival, there is an unusual amount of traffic these days. Look there—" She pointed ahead with her wing.

The back of Anne's neck went prickly and cold.

"You there up ahead, we are approaching from behind you, do not be startled by us. Remember these are common grounds 'eld by the Blue Order and not part of any 'eld territory." Rooke looked over her shoulder and whispered. "It be always best to remind a bigger dragon of such things before they notice ya'."

"Are you speaking to me?" The familiar voice echoed off the tunnel walls as the tall bird-like cockatrix looked over her shoulder. "Anne?"

"Lady Russell?"

"Lady Russell? I never heared no dragon called by such a human name before!" Rooke flapped with an expression of disapproval.

Lady Russell crossed the distance between them in three long, flapping steps, hissing and growling the entire distance. "You will hold your tongue and not speak of this to anyone. You will not speak of what you do not understand!"

"You need not threaten her!" Anne pulled Rooke

close and sheltered her with her free arm. "She is my friend!"

"She is a nosy busybody, and I will not have her presenting a danger to me and mine." Lady Russell clapped her beak very near Rooke.

"I said stop that! Rooke will say nothing of this encounter if I ask. Is that not right, Rooke?"

"Of course it is, Miss Anne." She shivered against Anne's chest. Whether she would hold her tongue or not remained to be seen, but at least she was smart enough to acquiesce in the moment.

"Why exactly should I trust her?"

"Because her Friend is my friend and has been for a very long time. I trust Mrs. Smith and that should be enough for you." Anne stomped a step toward Lady Russell.

Lady Russell growled, but backed away half a step.

"Where are you going?" Anne asked.

"To find you at Camden Place, of course. You insisted that I come, so I am here. Why do you seem so surprised?"

"Then you can show me the way there?"

Lady Russell snorted angrily.

"Thank you for your assistance Rooke. Lady Russell will guide me the rest of the way. You need not be bothered on my account any longer."

"Thank ye kindly." Rooke bobbed her head and flew off without another glance at Lady Russell.

"Where ever did you come across that hideously low creature?" Lady Russell chewed at something caught between her long toes.

"Why did you have to be so rude to her?"

"I do not like seeing you in the company of another dragon."

"Then perhaps you should have come with me in the carriage."

Lady Russell muttered and grumbled something indistinguishable. "Come, Camden Place is this way."

"I have heard Kellynch is to be here soon."

"As have I, which is precisely why I am here now. I expect you will need help managing the brute. Step lively—he has not arrived yet, but soon."

"There is something I must talk to you about."

"Then talk as we walk. Trust me, you do not want him to arrive with no one there to greet him. He will be expecting your Father and it will be difficult enough—"

"It is not about Kellynch, it is about you." Anne stood rooted in place.

Lady Russell stopped three steps from her. "About me? Whatever could you mean by that?"

"I have become aware of some serious problems regarding—"

"Regarding me? I would thank you to mind your own business and leave me to mine. I am perfectly capable of managing—"

"I beg to differ. The Crofts have made me aware—"

"What do they know?" Lady Russell clapped her beak rapidly as if that made her point true. "I do not care what the man thinks he is. He is nothing but a nosy busybody who intrudes where he is not wanted. And his woman...."

"She saw you that day at Kellynch."

Lady Russell flapped and tossed her head. "I do not acknowledge their acquaintance. They are not known to me, what does their opinion matter?"

"A very great deal when it seems you are in violation of a great number of Blue Order laws."

"I am no member of the Blue Order. I do not consider myself under their rule of law. Or have you forgotten I am from Australia."

"It does not matter where you are from. Whilst you are here, you are under their law."

"I am a minor dragon, they do not bother with—"

"They do when there are violations of the law as great as yours."

"Exactly what law have I violated?" Lady Russell stomped and stared straight at Anne.

"You have been presenting yourself as human for decades now. That is an illegal persuasion—highly illegal."

"If it were so bad, why should I have been allowed to go on with it so long? Clearly it is of no matter to anyone."

"You were in hiding the whole time and carefully managed to avoid detection."

"Uppercross assisted me. Do you think a major dragon would assist me in wrongdoing?" Lady Russell fanned her tail and spread her wings. Did she think making herself big made her right as well?

"He is a delightful and easy going creature. I think he thought it the lesser of two evils, aiding you so that you would manage Kellynch."

"What is that supposed to mean?"

"That you are in a great deal of trouble. I have been advised that your only hope is to throw yourself upon the mercy of the Order and plead whatever you must to receive their leniency."

"Or what?" Lady Russell stretched out her neck and hissed.

"Truly I do not know. But I know dragon justice is

swift and merciless. At the very least I imagine that they could have you sent back to Australia—at worst, I cannot even think about it."

"Nonsense. Utter nonsense. They would do no such thing and even if they tried, they would have to catch me first. I have evaded them for many years now. Why should that change now?"

"It is my responsibility to turn you in to the Order."

Lady Russell opened her wings and growled, larger and more menacing than she ever had been. "You would do no such thing."

"I do not want to. I want you to go with me, and we will together approach the Order, the Dragon Sage in particular, and ask for their help rectifying matters. I am certain they would rather help us make it all right again than engage in reprisals."

"That is fine and well for you to say. It is not your life that hangs in the balance."

"I am trying to protect you. And I fear that my life may be in as much peril as yours. I am the closest thing you have to a Friend. I am sure you are aware that Friends are held accountable for the actions of their minor dragon Friends."

Lady Russell snorted. "Friend? We have no such arrangement. I am a fully independent creature. What are you to me? I rely on you for nothing."

Her words landed with the force of an open hand. "Why are you making this so difficult? I am trying to help you."

"You help me? Where did you come by that sort of conceited independence? I have always helped you."

"Deceived me and manipulated me you mean."

"Excuse me?" Lady Russell's eyes grew wider and wilder than ever before.

"Wentworth. You persuaded me against him, not for my own protection, but for yours. I loved him and he loved me—my one chance at happiness. You stole it from me for your own convenience. You knew he heard dragons, and you could not chance being revealed by him. So, you persuaded me. You were no sort of friend to me at all. I do not think you ever have been."

"I did what was necessary to protect myself. Even your precious Order allows me that."

No remorse! She had absolutely no remorse! "Not in that way. I still cannot believe that you would have used me so ill. What sort of friend does that?"

"You need me—do you think you can manage Kellynch without me?"

"Can I trust that you will not throw me to him in order to protect your own interests?"

"How dare you! If that is how you feel, you can deal with him on your own. Go! The lair is straight down that path. The stairs within lead to the mews behind the town house." Lady Russell hissed and trotted away, her long steps bobbing her tailfeathers in time with her steps.

"Wait! I will not see Mr. Elliot if he comes. That was so important you—you must be there to chaperone."

"You have already seen him without me. You are a liar." Lady Russell called from beyond the torch's dull glow.

Anne leaned back against the stone wall, the cold penetrating her spine as she tried not to slide down to the floor. What would happened if she could not convince Lady Russell to seek out the Order herself and they came looking for her?

Strange sounds echoed from the path leading to the lair. Splashing and snorting? That had to be Kellynch. Anne ran toward it, though any sensible person would have run the other way. There was hardly anything sensible about Dragon Keepers.

20
Chapter

WENTWORTH HELD ADMIRAL Easterly's door open for Sophy, in her navy-blue military-inspired walking dress, who smiled as she passed him. Why did women seek to look like officers? The appeal escaped him.

Easterly, looking especially well put together, rose and bowed to her. She curtsied in return and sat on the plain wooden chair nearest Easterly's desk in the narrow, confined room. Had the pile of books on his shelves grown since the last time he was here? Surely, they had—the piles on his desk as well. There was barely enough room for the dragon pillow today.

Mina, her sleek silver form rather rounder in the middle than normal, slithered from her pillow on the other side of the desk, met by Laconia in the middle of the desk. Much rubbing of cheeks and purring and circling and tail twining ensued. Did they really have to be so open about their regard for one another? Had it not been enough that Mina regularly visited their lodgings, playing out their little ritual each time?

Laconia had dismissed his objections as jealousy. What utter nonsense.

"Good day, Mina." Sophy extended her hand, fingers curled toward herself.

Side by side, Mina and Laconia approached to enjoy the expert scratches Sophy offered. Odd how quickly both tatzelwurms had taken to her.

Granted, jealousy was not the sort of thing to which a man admitted, but sometimes it was a bit off putting to watch how the pair threw themselves at Sophy's feet.

"You have quite the touch there, Mrs. Croft." Easterly laughed as he edged around the desk to return to his seat. "Mina usually is rather reserved around people."

"So is Laconia," Wentworth muttered.

"Since you are staying with us, Frederick, I think it is a very good thing they feel so at home. I think White might have a great deal to do with it, too, you know. He does so enjoy his conversations with them." Sophy offered him what could only be called a big-sisterly admonishing glance.

Did she really have to do that here, in this company?

"I do wonder if that might be because their types seem so similar." Easterly rubbed his chin.

"In some ways they do, I suppose. But then again, not. I really do not know if that is the reality of it, or just the appearance." Sophy shrugged. "Perhaps the Sage has some insights into that. White—and my husband and I by association—have been invited to visit her in a few days. She is very interested in knowing more about our marine dragon Friend. It seems there is not a great deal about them in dragon lore and both she and the Historian are eager to learn more from him."

"You have been honored! I hear her schedule is very full. Rumor has it that she will be extending her stay at least a fortnight to accommodate all those who are trying to meet with her! Would you believe there is even an entire afternoon devoted to a salon only for fairy dragons?" Easterly chuckled. "Fairy dragons! I cannot begin to imagine how any person of sense could want to spend that much time in such twittering, flittering company, much less derive anything sensible from the encounter."

Mina looked over her shoulder at him, great blue eyes blinking slowly. "Then you are a rather short-sighted creature, I think. There is a great deal more to we small dragons than you seem to believe."

"Pray forgive me my Friend, I mean no insult to you and your kind." Easterly soothed her ruffled hackles. She was more upset than her tone let on.

"I know we are thought to be spring-hopping addlepates." Her long fangs showed in her draconic smile.

"Only by fools who do not know your kind well."

"And the same is true of fairy dragons." She licked her shoulder and pressed into Laconia's side.

"Then I will take your word on it and adjust my opinion accordingly." Easterly offered to scratch under her chin, which she accepted.

Did Easterly really mean that or was he simply placating her? Laconia's expression remained just a mite wary, so it was difficult to know what to make of it all. But he clearly cared for his Friend's sensibilities, and that was pleasing.

"I imagine you have other issues on your mind, Admiral, than simply the Dragon Sage's schedule." Sophy was always adept at turning a conversation.

"Indeed, you are correct. I have word that Cornwall should be arriving late today, perhaps early tomorrow. Envoys have been sent to direct him to the accommodations beneath the Royal Crescent house…"

"Rest assured, we are as prepared for his arrival as is possible. His list of requirements has been fulfilled to the letter, though some of them are rather odd."

"I can well imagine. One has to wonder whether that is the Prince Regent's effect on him or the other way around."

"Or perhaps they influence one another? Has there been any word if the Prince will be coming to Bath as well?" Wentworth chewed the inside of his cheek.

"I believe he is currently in Brighton overseeing plans with the architect Nash for the pavilion there." Easterly's tone suggested disapproval, but his eyes suggested relief at not having to deal with both the Prince and Cornwall at the same time.

"Is that not unusual, that the Keeper would not be present for his dragon's complaint? I was given to understand that was part of the nature of managing a Keep." Sophy glanced at Wentworth as though looking for confirmation.

"The nature of the duchy's ownership makes the relationship between dragon and Keeper different to that in most Keeps. Typically, a Keepership is a lifetime appointment, but since the Duchy of Cornwall goes to the Prince of Wales, heir to the throne, Cornwall's Keeper becomes Londinium's Keeper upon ascension to the throne and the heir becomes Keeper to Cornwall, and perhaps another dragon depending on the titles he holds. Not to mention that our royalty do not easily embrace anything which would make them appear to be subservient to the royal dragons. It is all rather messy, I fear."

Sophy pressed her temples. "Londinium? I thought the reigning dragon brenin was Buckingham. Is that not what is listed in the Blue Order records?"

Easterly clutched his forehead with his broad hand. "Dragons are dragons, I am afraid. As I understand it, the dragon's true name is Londinium, but somewhere along the line, he became fond of a young prince who in his infancy called the dragon Buckingham for the house the prince was raised in. The dragon decided to adopt that name as well. Why should not the reigning dragon be able to have as many names as he wishes? The King after all had many names upon his christening."

Wentworth snickered. That did sound very like draconian logic.

"The point is, though, that Cornwall and several other of the most powerful firedrakes do not have very close relationships with their Keepers. So, when there are matters of the Keep to be handled, they prefer to handle them themselves. Which, in this particular instance, may or may not be to our advantage." Easterly wrinkled his lips into something between a frown and a scowl.

"White is an excellent diplomat. I am sure he will be invaluable in assisting with whatever Cornwall needs or desires. And I am sure having the only hippocampus in the kingdom attending to him will not be disagreeable." Sophy stroked Mina until she purred. Such a subtle implication that the cranky dragon would be in good hands. She was a master at such things, really both she and Croft were. Cornwall could not be better managed.

"I will convey that message. There are quite a number who will be relieved to know it. The intention is that these matters be dealt with here in Bath. Lord and Cownt Matlock do not wish to see these matters pushed to the entire Conclave."

That felt seriously out of order, especially coming from a military man like Easterly. "I should have thought the matter serious enough—"

"Indeed it is, but Conclaves can be messy and dangerous. This one in particular has even greater potential for that, considering who is involved. Cownt Matlock is particularly insistent that this be handled at as low a level as possible."

That could only mean the Matlocks feared this could devolve into a dragon war, with dragons taking sides for or against Cornwall. Wentworth shuddered along with both tatzelwurms. Absolutely nothing about that could end well. Nothing at all.

"Be assured everything that can be done to assuage Dug Cornwall's sensibilities will be done, even to the point of having barrels of his favorite pickled herrings available to him," Sophy said softly.

"Bloody royals with their ridiculous demands," Easterly muttered.

"If we can contribute to maintaining Pendragon's Peace, that is reward enough. And you might not want to allow any fairy dragons to overhear that particular sentiment." Sophy's eyebrow rose, her way of issuing a warning.

Dragon's blood! This was serious!

"Very good, very good. You will forgive me if I cannot stay for an exchange of niceties. I must pass along this information directly." Easterly pushed up from his chair.

"Of course, no offense taken." Sophy leaned close to Mina. "Would you like to accompany us back to the house? Cook is preparing a special fish stew in honor of our guest, and I am sure she would appreciate your opinion on the seasoning before it leaves her hands."

Mina licked her lips as Laconia licked her cheek. "We would be most pleased to be of service."

Mina joined them as they left the Blue Order, winding through Wentworth's feet down the streets of Bath, much like Laconia did. A few stopped to watch, but most attended to their persuasion that there was nothing interesting to see. Somehow the nimble creatures did not make it any more difficult to walk with two tatzelwurms than it was with one. Who would have expected that?

"Pray, Frederick, might we stop at Molland's on the way back? I should like to place an order there."

"For you or for your guest?" Wentworth chuckled. "I did not know dragons preferred sweets."

"Both to be precise. It seems that they employ a cook who specializes in draconic pastries—yes, I know, I was surprised too in finding out such a thing existed. And, if our guest has a sweet tooth, it can only be to the benefit of all that it is attended to."

"You are a wonder, truly a wonder." And he meant that, too. Who would have thought of such a thing?

He held the door open for her as they entered Molland's, the tatzelwurms with them whispering to one and all how lovely it was to have such beautiful cats guarding the place against rodent intrusion. Considering the smiles that followed them, their persuasions were very successful.

Racks and racks of baked goods and sweets lined the walls behind the counters. So many scents assailed them: warm and yeasty, sweet, spicy, fruity. Both tatzelwurms rose up high on their tails and sniffed the air, forked tongues darting out to taste it, too. Who could blame them? Wentworth's mouth watered in spite of himself.

A low hum filled the shop, almost like a fog hanging over the patrons, more women than men. Most of the men were among those sitting at the four, no it was six tiny white ironwork tables near the bright storefront window waiting to be served, to be admired through the glass by the passers-by. The sort of place Sir Walter Elliot would surely seek out, to lend the influence of his superior patronage to the humble pastry shop. The group at the counter waiting for their orders was almost exclusively ladies, chattering—probably gossiping—among themselves. How soon could he get out of the cacophony into the open air again?

"Look!" Laconia pointed with his thumbed paw. "That is Anne! You must go and speak to her! I will introduce her to Mina!"

At a small table, near the window, Miss Elliot, Miss Anne, and a man and woman he was not familiar with sampled a tray of sweets and a pot of tea. Probably choosing what to order for their next party at Camden Place. That was the sort of thing Miss Elliot would be doing.

The man, bearing the distinct features of an Elliot himself, sat beside Anne and seemed to be trying to attract her attention. Not only did she seem disinterested, she looked decidedly miserable. His jaw clenched and he scowled.

"Excuse me, Sophy." He tipped his head toward her and followed Laconia across the shop toward Anne. What was he going to say to her? They had parted ways under such strange circumstances. It had not been so long ago, but it felt… heavens! Was that what the aching in his chest had been?

Laconia sprang up into Anne's lap. Miss Elliot and the other woman jumped and cried out.

"Gracious! What a surprise!" Anne welcomed Laconia and scratched under his chin.

He purred and leaned into her, so loud the teacups on the table nearly rattled.

"What is that creature doing?" Miss Elliot gasped, pushing back from the table. "Get it away from here."

"Do you know it?" The other woman asked, a hint of disgust in her voice as her lip curled back.

"What a unique specimen." The man reached toward Laconia.

Specimen?

Anne blocked his hand with her arm around Laconia. Laconia's ears flattened, and he revealed his fangs. "I do indeed know him, and he is a shy creature. It would not do to impose your acquaintance upon him uninvited."

"Acquaintance, with a cat?" Miss Elliot sneered.

"Indeed." Laconia rumbled, his persuasive voice in fine form. "She is all things gracious and thoughtful and kind and wise. She knows best in this matter."

"I think it is rather sweet." The other woman said, though her expression was puzzled.

The Elliot-looking man's eyebrows rose. "Perhaps your little friend is right, he seems a good judge of character." He withdrew his hand.

The way Laconia and Mina stared at him—he heard dragons. The hair on the back of Wentworth's neck stood and his skin prickled. When Laconia took an immediate dislike to a dragon hearer—

"You have brought a friend with you? She is very elegant." Anne glanced first at Mina, then caught Wentworth's eyes.

Laconia purred loudly, then spoke in his normal voice, the one the others could not hear. "She is Mina. I would like her to know you."

Anne reached down with fingers curled toward herself.

Mina sniffed her fingers and hand thoroughly then bumped her head under Anne's hand. "You are as he says. You smell right." She rubbed against Anne's ankles.

"I did not know you had such an affinity for cats." Miss Elliot reached for her teacup, frowning.

"I met this one—his name is Laconia—whilst in Uppercross with Mary. Captain Wentworth—" She gestured toward him, "is brother to Mrs. Croft and called whilst he visited them. Elizabeth, Mrs. Clay, Mr. Elliot, may I present Captain Wentworth?"

They murmured sounds of assent, not enthusiastic to be sure.

He stepped forward and bowed. "I am pleased to meet any friends of Miss Anne."

"What brings you here?" Mr. Elliot asked, his

voice tinged with the wary note of a predator who spied competition for his prey.

The fur on Laconia's neck stood on end and he pouffed subtly. Mina followed suit. Anne stroked both tatzelwurms, the look in her eye sorely like cornered prey.

"To Bath or to Molland's?" Wentworth asked, stepping a little closer to Anne.

Mr. Elliot laughed as he edged toward Anne. "I like a sense of humor!"

"Is that Mrs. Croft?" Anne inclined her head toward Sophy standing at a counter on the far side of the shop.

"Indeed, you have ferreted out my mission—accompanying my sister and protecting her from the dangerous denizens of Bath."

All color drained from Anne's face, and she wavered just a bit.

Pendragon's bones! She had not looked like that when she faced down Kellynch! But she was right, Cornwall was a different creature entirely.

"Are you well, Miss Anne?" Mrs. Clay glanced from Miss Elliot to Mr. Elliot as though to see if they had noticed.

Laconia raised up and put his paws on Anne's shoulders, rubbing his cheek to hers. "She needs to leave this place."

"No, no, I am fine." Anne looked at Mrs. Clay as she ran her hand down his long back.

"No, she is not." Mina trot-hopped to Wentworth and bumped the back of his leg as though to push him toward Anne.

"Might I see you home, Miss Anne? It would be no trouble at all." Wentworth offered his hand.

"We are awaiting the Dalrymple's carriage to convey the ladies home." Mr. Elliot stood quickly, chest puffed.

Was he resorting to draconic means of vying for dominance? Wentworth pulled his shoulders back and looked down at him. Height had its natural advantages.

"Their carriage only has room for three of us." Miss Elliot tried to sidle between Mr. Elliot and Anne.

"Then I shall walk." Mr. Elliot lifted his chin and drew a deep breath.

"Were you not just complaining that you had hurt your ankle, and that you appreciated the opportunity to sit and rest here?" Miss Elliot batted her eyes at Mr. Elliot.

"A gentleman," Mr. Elliot emphasized the word just a bit too much, "would never take a lady's place."

"I am much obliged to you, but I am not going with the carriage. I prefer walking." Anne shifted Laconia from her lap to her arms.

"It is raining." Mr. Elliot tried to step between her and Wentworth but Laconia intervened. "If you are unwell, you should not walk in the rain."

"Oh! Very little, nothing that I regard."

"Though I came only yesterday, I have equipped myself properly for Bath already, you see …." Wentworth held up his umbrella a little too close to Mr. Elliot's face.

Anne jumped to her feet, Laconia's front legs over her shoulder and his serpentine back half wrapped around her waist. Gracious, she was stronger than she looked, he was a substantial creature. "Being confined in a carriage—I believe I need air right now, even rainy air. I thank you for your offer, Captain, I would very much like to walk home with you." She strode quickly past him, ignoring the swell of protests from her erstwhile companions.

Wentworth followed; Mina close at his side. They paused at the door. "Pray forgive me just a moment, I need to let Sophy know of my change in plans."

"You need not inconvenience—"

"Change in plans you say?" Sophy appeared just behind Anne's shoulder.

"Mrs. Croft!" Anne jumped and nearly dislodged Laconia.

"Miss Anne is not feeling well, and I will be escorting her home." He warned Sophy not to argue or question him with narrowed eyes.

"We will be escorting her home." Laconia's tail swished quickly along Anne's skirts.

Mina chirruped agreement.

Sophy nodded, though her expression suggested there would be many questions when he returned to Royal Crescent. "Go on, I do not mind. I can now linger at a few other shops on the way home without the guilt of forcing you to accompany me."

"Gracious as always, my dear sister." Wentworth bowed and held the door open for them both.

Laconia wriggled and Anne set him down as Wentworth opened his umbrella. He offered Anne his arm, and they set off. "You are at Camden Place?"

"You have heard correctly." She looked at the ground in front of her. "Does Laconia always weave between your feet when you walk?"

Her warm, soft hand in his arm—words were hard to find. "Since he was a wyrmling. He is quite nimble."

"As is his silver friend."

"My Friend is Admiral Easterly." Mina chirruped without missing a beat weaving with Laconia.

"The Naval Liaison to the Blue Order?" She clutched his arm tighter.

"He is called that." Mina replied, not bothering to look at them.

The rain fell a little harder and they paused under the porch of the haberdasher's shop, a colorful assortment of silk handkerchiefs and cravats in the window.

"Have you any further news of our friends at Lyme?" Anne's voice trembled. Did she feel guilt for what had happened?

"I am afraid you must have suffered from the shock, and all the more from its not overpowering you at the time."

She turned her face aside. "I suppose you do me an honor, believing my sensibilities are so refined, but perhaps associating with dragons has left me rather more robust than other young ladies."

"Louisa and Benwick continue to improve. As I understand, the outlook is very good. It all seems to be working out quite well." He chuckled under his breath. "That day has produced some consequences which must be considered as the very reverse of frightful. According to a certain fairy dragon, I am told that there seems to be a growing warmth between them as they convalesce together."

"The twitterpate and the stupid one. They deserve each other." Laconia, blunt as ever.

"Forgive me if this is a very personal question, but that does not bother you?" Anne peeked at him. Oh, the warmth, and was that dread in her eyes?

"Me? Far from it, I am pleased for them both." And a little relieved, but she did not need to hear that, at least not now.

"I should hope it would be a very happy match." Her voice seemed lighter, even pleased. "There are on both sides good principles and good temper."

"With all my soul I wish them happy, and rejoice over every circumstance in favor of it. They have no difficulties to contend with at home, no opposition, no caprice, no delays. The Musgroves are behaving like themselves, most honorably and kindly, only anxious with true parental hearts to promote their daughter's comfort. All this is much, very much in favor of their happiness." Dear Lord what was he saying! Stop, he had to stop, rein in his tongue! "I regard Louisa Musgrove as a very amiable, sweet-tempered girl, and not deficient in understanding, but Benwick is something more. He is a clever man, a reading man; and I confess, that I consider his attaching himself to her with some surprise. A man like him, in his situation, with a heart pierced, wounded, almost broken! Fanny Harville was a very superior creature, and his attachment to her was indeed attachment. A man does not recover from such a devotion of the heart to such a woman. He ought not; he does not."

Her eyes brightened just a bit—should that make him so happy?

"I should very much like to see Lyme again." Anne glanced up shyly, cheeks flushed. What was she not saying?

"I should like to show it to you some day, properly."

"I have travelled so little, that every fresh place is interesting to me; but there is real beauty at Lyme."

Focus—future musings were not the thing for the moment! Damn! "Will you permit me a rather personal question?"

She nodded and Laconia pressed against his ankle.

"You seemed quite uncomfortable at Molland's. Perhaps in the presence of Mr. Elliot—your cousin? Or do I assume too much?"

"On all counts, that is correct."

Laconia and Mina muttered growls under their breath.

"Would it be too forward of me to ask why?" He must not take her hands in his, though he resented every rule of propriety declaring it so.

"Considering I was trying to locate you to appeal to you for assistance, no, not too forward at all."

"My help? Pray tell me what has happened?"

She glanced about, pausing until a fat man trundled past, out of earshot. "Regarding Kellynch. I fear something is very wrong."

"You will need to be more specific than that. The affair at Lyme made it very clear that something is quite wrong."

"Yes, yes, it is just that I do not know what to make of it. Oh, there is so much I have not told you. Kellynch holds me to blame, personally—which he made clear in our last conversation, yesterday when he arrived at Camden Place. Or rather the conversation that took place via a cockatrice sent by the Sage to facilitate conversations between us. I have not actually seen his face. Which, all things considered right now, is probably for the best."

"He is here, now?" Wentworth gulped. Easterly and the Crofts needed to know immediately. "Do not fear. Clearly you are not to blame for it. The Blue Order is quite aware of your father's shortcomings. They will surely not hold you accountable."

"I hope for that, but things are far more complicated. Kellynch is already saying that he will not submit to the Blue Order as they have not seen the laws upheld for all these years."

"While he has a point, Kellynch too is at fault and will be made to see that—dragons have a way—"

"There is more. Mr. Elliot—"

"Elliot? What of him. Has he done anything untoward—" He probably should have worked harder to conceal the growl in his voice.

"He has decided to renew his attentions toward me. At least his intentions are … more conventional … than they were when he offered for me five years ago."

Wait! What? "Attentions … intentions … conventional? You refused him?"

"And intend to do so now as well. He has no sympathy for dragons at all, though he claims to be fully reformed, I do not believe it. In fact, I fear he is trying to frame Kellynch for high crimes against the Blue Order."

"How?"

She reached into her reticule and pressed something hard and heavy into his hand. "He said he confronted Kellynch in Lyme and this dropped from his jaw in the sea cave."

Wentworth glanced into his hand. A gold coin! His heart clenched and his face grew cold.

"It is just like the one we found earlier in the tunnels near his lair. I am certain Mr. Elliot is hoping to have Kellynch convicted of crimes and removed from the estate."

"Why would he want to do such a thing?"

"He hates major dragons and, assuming he has not changed from his stance five years ago, he would like nothing more than to inherit the land unencumbered by the Blue Order."

Dragon's Blood! Could the coins have come from Elliot? Not likely, but if Anne thought they did, then that was proof she had no knowledge of what Kellynch might have been doing! She might be spared any suspicion of responsibility in Kellynch's most serious transgression! It was possible. A bead of sweat trickled down the side of his face, or was it a stray raindrop? "Will you permit me to keep this? I believe I know who to go to with this information."

"What are you considering? You look like you think there is something more." Her eyes narrowed and she all but peered into the privacy of his own thoughts.

"Perhaps, but—"

"But what? I am his Keeper and if there is something important, I need to know."

"You are his Keeper and surely the best one Kellynch has had in generations. That is true without a doubt. But, will you trust me when I tell you this is far more complex than you can imagine?"

"Then tell me. Or do you think a woman is not capable of understanding such things?" A spark of anger flared in her eyes. Damn, it was beautiful!

"The Dragon Sage is a woman and I have no doubt she will be consulted in this matter. As to what you are really asking, of course, I know you are capable, that is not the question."

"Then what is it? I do not want to shirk my duties as Keeper."

"No one can accuse you of that. There is none so capable, so responsible, so competent as you."

"Then why are you keeping things from me?"

Where was the malleable, indecisive, dare he say, weak woman he had known? Was it knowing dragons that had made her so magnificent? He took her hands in his and held them close to his chest. Damn propriety. "I promise you shall know everything when the time is right. I will keep nothing from you then. But, pray, trust me. For your protection, there are things you should not know. Not yet."

"My protection? And who will protect me? My Father? Surely not."

"No, not him. But if you will permit me, I will."

Chapter 21

October 10, 1814

ANNE'S BEDROOM IN Camden Place was in all ways finer, and rather larger, than that at Uppercross. The bed linens were soft and smooth and smelling of lavender. Even though the window faced the mews, her preternatural hearing could still pick out the sounds of the city long past the time that the good denizens of Bath had gone to bed. She had never really realized just how quiet the countryside was before now. The walls sported a pleasing soft pink paint, reminiscent of the roses on the paper hangings in her room at home, with three still-life bouquets painted in oil to enhance the reminder. The chamber lacked an ample writing desk—this one was far too dainty and dare she say it, feminine, to meet her needs, but the rest of the furnishings were sufficient and elegant in their simplicity. All in all, it should have been an excellent chamber for sleeping. It should have been.

Nevertheless, Anne tossed and turned until dawn. *But if you permit me, I will.* Those words rang over and over in her ears, her mind, her heart. He wanted to protect her, something truly no one had ever done. Not really. Lady Russell claimed that was what she was doing, but she was only protecting herself.

What a cold knot that reality left between her ribs. It felt almost like betrayal to think that of her friend—but what sort of friend had she been?

None, really.

Now she was friendless. Such a sharp, aching word. Anne sat up and wrapped her arms around her knees.

It felt right, but was it true?

Was it?

Mrs. Smith was her friend, there would be no doubt in that, even if she could only offer her support, that was something. And the Crofts, they had already been so kind in helping her understand the complexities of Lady Russell's situation. There was White, and Laconia, and Uppercross. She had friends, human and dragon.

And Wentworth.

She was not alone.

But still none of that answered the most significant question: what would come of this situation with Kellynch? Would she even be deemed fit as a Keeper once all was said and done? And if she was not, what then?

If Father was turned out of Kellynch, where would they go? Would they have any means of support? Was there anyone who would take in the disgraced house of Elliot?

Her eyes burned and her throat tightened until she could hardly breathe. She must get her thoughts under control. None of this was helpful, even if it was all true.

Focus on those things she could impact today. Perhaps she should call upon the Crofts today.

Something scratched at her window. On the third floor, it could not be an intruder. A bird perhaps? More scratching, more insistent.

"Mrrrow!"

Laconia? She threw the counterpane and sheets aside and dashed to the window. Tangling in the curtains, she yanked open the window. Rosy rays of first light filtered lazily through the glass. Laconia and Mina tumbled in like moonlight and shadow, landing with a soft thud on the carpet, feet first like huge cats.

"Are you well? Is something wrong?" She offered her hands for them to smell, and once accepted, stroked their long backs. Neither seemed injured, though Mina's belly was full and tight and just barely lumpy.

Eggs? Surely that was why they traveled together. Laconia was so much like his Friend.

What sort of reason was that for her eyes to be burning now?

"Cornwall has arrived in Royal Crescent." Laconia rubbed his cheek against her leg.

"He is grumpy and cross and smells bad." Mina wrinkled up her nose—such an indignant expression for such a dignified creature. "I do not want to be near him at all."

"Cornwall? Why is he here?" Could that have been the name on Kellynch's charter? Did Cornwall's arrival have anything to with Kellynch at all?

Perhaps he was just here to meet the Dragon Sage. Surely that was the reason. So many dragons were here for just that reason. Her constricted chest eased.

"That is the Blue Order's business." Laconia's tone dropped to something deeply displeased.

"Are you looking for refuge from Cornwall?"

"Thank you no, Mina needs her nesting box, and we are on the way there."

"We want you to befriend one of our wyrmlings." Mina rose on her tail and pressed her paws on Anne's thigh.

"Gracious! I am honored, truly honored." Anne dropped to her knees beside them. "Are you certain, you know my father is no friend of dragons—"

"But you are, and that is sufficient." Laconia rose up and looked into her eyes. "You smell right, and you will be a good Friend."

"How could I refuse? I am certain your wyrmlings will be extraordinary."

They both purred, the tips of their tails flicking. Mina leaned over to Laconia and seemed to whisper something into his ear.

"A letter has been left for you with the manservant. It would be best that no one else has the opportunity to see it."

"We will leave you to it. I must get to my nest." Mina hopped to the window and slither-crept out, urgency in her voice.

"Go, go with her. I will do as you ask." She urged him out the window.

A letter? From whom? She slipped on her dressing gown and dashed downstairs. Hopefully the rest of the family were still in bed, as was their habit—but one never knew if they would change when there was opportunity to be inconvenient.

The butler confirmed there was a letter for her, just delivered and waiting for her to awaken. She took the letter and ran back to her room, heart thundering, half from the exertion, half from intrigue.

She locked the door and pressed her back against it, slowly sliding to the floor. A position of no dignity for a lady, to be sure, but dignity must give way to urgency. Surely it did.

The letter's direction was hardly legible, to "Miss A. E."; the uneven creases spoke to hasty folding. This must be the work of some disquiet of mind, some perturbation of soul. The hand was familiar, achingly familiar. Her hands trembled until the words almost blurred beyond reading.

I can wait no longer in silence. I must speak to you by such means as are within my reach. You pierce my soul. I am half agony, half hope. Tell me not that I am too late, that such precious feelings are gone forever.

Yesterday I saw you as I never had before. I am most heartily ashamed that in my own pride and resentment, I lost view of your true character, your nature, your strength.

Owning my bitterness and, yes, my stubbornness, may I offer myself to you again with a heart even more your own than when you almost broke it, eight years and a half ago. Dare not think that man forgets sooner than woman, that his love has an earlier death. I have loved none but you.

Unjust I may have been, weak and resentful I have been, but never inconstant. For you alone, I think and plan. Have you not seen this? I think you must have penetrated my feelings, though I wish I could say the same of yours.

I can hardly write in anticipation of your reply. I fear you may not believe that there is true attachment and constancy possible among men; Laconia is sure of it; I am sure of it. Believe mine to be most fervent, most undeviating,

F. W.

P.S. I await you, uncertain of my fate. A word, a look, will be enough to decide whether I will be yours this evening or never.

Three times she reread the words, committing them to mind and heart. Each reading only heightened the effect, leaving her dizzy and breathless, unable to stand. Such a letter was not to be soon recovered from. Truly who would want to recover from such a message?

But a response was required. A response, she must gather herself enough to find words—those would be required to reply. Yes, they would be utterly necessary.

The answer was clear—to her at least. But how to make it clear to him as well? A letter would be easy, but impossible—she had no Friend to carry the message directly to him. She hardly knew Rooke well enough for such a favor. And she was a gossip, a kind and well-meaning one to be sure, but such news should not spread via cockatrice and fairy dragon. She had to see him, face to face.

But how? A lady did not call upon a gentleman. Wait! The Crofts, he was staying with them! She could call upon Mrs. Croft. Surely, she would take pity upon Anne and allow her an interview with Wentworth. Yes, that would do very well.

She dressed with care: a sprigged white muslin gown with van Dyke trim at the sleeves and hem. Wentworth was unlikely to notice—he had little eye for such fripperies—but it made her feel almost pretty with all the attending confidence and happiness that came with such a feeling.

Still too early to pay a polite call, breakfast would be an appropriate way to pass the time until it was. Anne strolled to the breakfast room, her feet barely touching the floor.

So, this was what it was like to be sublimely happy.

The blue-green morning room walls still felt odd. Mornings were bright and light and yellow, not green. At least the peach brocade curtains were drawn back to allow plenty of light in—at least as much light as could find its way into the first-floor room, shadowed by other terrace houses nearby. The oblong table, set with a crisp white cloth, had a decided advantage over a round one—it was possible to be farther away from the head of the table, if one wanted. And today she wanted.

Father barely looked up at her when she sidled between the back of his chair and the oversized mahogany sideboard, laden with fragrant Bath buns, cold meats, preserves, and a rack of toast. He probably would not like to hear she had the same sort of problem making it through the breakfast room at Uppercross Cottage. His breakfast room comparable to that of a cottage? Unthinkable!

Elizabeth and Mrs. Clay sat slightly away from the table, in a pair of carved chairs tucked into the bay window. Speaking softly, they seemed not to want to be overheard. They would not like knowing their discussion of the coming concert was easy for Anne to hear. She would allow them to believe in their privacy, for she neither needed nor desired conversation today.

She took a Bath bun, some berry preserves and a cup of tea to the table, situating herself to put as much distance between herself, Father and Elizabeth as possible.

"You look quite self-satisfied this morning." Elizabeth murmured, clearly disapproving.

"I think you look very pretty. Elizabeth's old dress looks very well on you." How kind of Mrs. Clay to notice.

"I slept very well last night." It was not good to lie, but there were times it was expedient for ending a conversation.

"Very good for you." Elizabeth's smile could not have been more insincere. "You should have more consideration for those who have not been so fortunate."

"Are you unwell? I had no idea." Nor did she actually want to. Tending to an invalid sister would most seriously interfere with her plans.

"Perhaps you should think of someone other than yourself. We are all most unwell."

Mrs. Clay sipped her tea. Odd, it smelled like ginger tea. Why would she be drinking that?

"What is wrong?" Pray they did not deign to answer.

Father sneezed three times in rapid succession and made a show of producing his handkerchief—of the finest silk of course. Lesser fabrics disagreed with his skin. "I fear I may have a cold."

Probably courtesy of the evening spent with the bored Lady Dalrymple. How generous. It should be quite the mark of distinction that his cold came from such a noble source. Did Father realize that the cousins he so esteemed heard dragons?

"We have tickets to the concert tonight." Elizabeth dabbed her eyes. "If Mr. Elliot will not accompany us, I fear we will not be able to attend."

Mrs. Clay sipped her tea and pressed her hand to her belly. "It would be such a shame to miss the event."

"Perhaps Lady Dalrymple might attend with us? There could be nothing improper about going in a dowager's company." Anne bit her tongue. Why had she dared offer a suggestion?

"Do be serious Anne! How would she not be offended to be invited as an afterthought, only because Father could not go? The idea is preposterous. I cannot believe you could be so insensitive—"

"The suggestion was well meant." Anne stood and left the morning room with Elizabeth chattering something that she did not care to attend to as she closed the door behind her.

What point was there giving Elizabeth's inanities any mind at all? She was who she was and it would never change. Ever. The best one could do was learn to ignore most of what she said, much like one did with fairy dragons. It would require practice though. Choosing to ignore anyone felt somehow unkind.

Until she could achieve that, she needed air, fresh air. Thankfully the morning air in the garden did not agree with Elizabeth. What more could she ask for?

The garden in the mews behind the house, hemmed in by a stone fence high enough to prevent seeing out or seeing in, was still green, but flowerless. The peculiar smells of the Avon, and—what was that? Dragons? Yes, that was definitely it—many dragons—hung over the garden. Hardly comforting or homey, but still better than the house. She sat on the small white wooden bench tucked between two large, leafy bushes. A modicum of privacy and quiet, exactly what she—

"Anne?"

No! Pray no!

Lady Russell, feathers fluffed and regal, sauntered toward her with long, sure steps. "Good morning, Anne."

"I did not expect to see you. What do you want?"

"What sort of greeting is that? What has become of your manners?"

"And what sort of greeting is that?"

"My, you are not yourself this morning at all." Lady Russell perched on the bench beside Anne, folding her very long legs beneath her until they were utterly hidden underneath her fine blue plumage.

Close. Far too close.

Anne stood and took two large steps back. "When we last parted, you seemed very displeased with my company. What has changed that you suddenly find me worth seeking out?"

Lady Russell blinked several times, long eyelashes nearly touching her cheeks. She would probably be hunching into her thinking posture if she were still standing. "Perhaps, yes I was hasty and impatient with you. Clearly you were overwrought with all that has been going on. Upon reflection, I realized it was my duty to overlook your high tempers and hasty words."

"My hasty words?" Tension crept up the back of her scalp and her head began to ache.

"There is no need to apologize. Consider it all forgotten."

Clearly Lady Russell was the one doing the forgetting—a very great deal of it. Surely, she could not really believe she was without fault. But what profit would it be to mention that now? "What brings you here this morning?"

"I am worried about you, my dear, very worried. This business with Kellynch is very troubling."

"I am quite aware of that."

"Of course, you are. I am sure you are most anxious about it all. That is why I am here."

"I have not requested your assistance." Nor did she actually desire it, but perhaps she should avoid that detail.

"No, you have not. I understand how hard it is when you must have so much on your mind. You have never much liked to ask for help."

"I do not want—"

"Of course, you do not want to trouble me. But I am here for you. Never fear, I have everything figured out for you." She bobbed her head vigorously as though trying to persuade Anne to agree through her gestures rather than her voice.

The hair on the back of Anne's neck prickled. "Do not presume to know what I need."

"It is no trouble."

"I did not ask if it was trouble, I said do not impose your solutions on me."

Lady Russell clapped her beak rapidly. "Why should I impose anything on you? You are a rational creature, indeed, and once you have heard me out, I am sure you will agree."

"And if I do not wish to listen to your notions?"

"Anne, do be reasonable." Lady Russell somehow slipped her legs out from under her and stood in a single graceful motion. "You and I want the same things."

"What precisely do you want? Me to do as you tell me?"

"I want to protect you from what is coming."

"What precisely do you think that is?"

"You and your family are in a great deal of jeopardy from this matter with Kellynch. Far more than you understand." Lady Russell's head crest rose as if to emphasize her point.

"I think I understand a great deal more than you give me credit for."

"What do you think you understand?"

"I am Keeper to Kellynch. The dragon and the estate have been mismanaged for generations, and we are reaping the fruit of those bad decisions. But now Kellynch has awakened we can begin to rectify it all, with the help of the Dragon Sage and the Blue Order."

"You really think that slip of a girl who thinks she knows dragons can help you with such a matter? I have known Kellynch for all this time—"

"He has been asleep almost the entire time you have been here. As near as I can figure, you have really only spoken to him once before the current affair began, and that was to see yourself installed as Watcher—which I still do not understand how that could have happened when the dragon was supposedly hibernating." Anne's voice turned hard and sharp. No, it was not ladylike, nor was it polite, but there was no reining it in.

"I told you—"

"You have told me a great many things, many of which have been lies and manipulation to get me to do your bidding. I do not know what I can believe from you anymore, if anything at all." Lovely, now she was stamping like a child.

Lady Russell fluttered her wings, clapped her beak as though smacking her lips, and twitched her head. Was she actually striving to hold her tongue? That was unusual. "I will ignore your most untoward outburst and accusations. You are upset and afraid. But none of that supersedes the need to see reason. Yes, you are a Dragon Keeper, and yes there has been mismanagement which has led to the current problem. What you seem to be ignoring is that you will be held responsible for it. I do not want to see you punished—"

"For something I had no hand in? No, I refuse to believe the Order would hold me accountable for the sins of my ancestors."

"Anne, you are a woman."

"So, I have been told."

"You realize that puts you at great disadvantage. Your father cannot and will not defend you in any Blue Order action."

Precisely what she most wanted to be reminded of in this moment. "I do not need him to. I can stand for myself."

"All this nonsense with the appointment of the Dragon Sage has surely gone to your head. Have you forgotten the fate of your friend Mrs. Smith? Penniless and alone, without husband or family. You seem to think you can stand before the Blue Order Court as an equal. I assure you, you cannot. You will be eaten alive, if not literally, certainly figuratively."

"I am willing to take my chances."

"You are being foolish! There is a far better way for you. I assure you."

"What do you think that is?"

"You need a man, a husband to protect you, to cover you, to stand up for you in court and bear the brunt of the indictments against you. You should be glad there is such a one who will take on such a burden for your sake."

"Someone willing to take goods so inferior and damaged as myself and Kellynch? Oh, that is very gracious. Who exactly is this paragon of virtue to whom I should be eternally grateful?"

"Mr. William Elliot."

Anne swallowed back bile, though spitting it at Lady Russell's feet would be a very draconic expression of her distaste—or so she had recently read. She would refrain now, but if Lady Russell continued to vex her …

"Not only is he willing to marry you, he wants to. He has finally recognized the duty he has to his family name and legacy. He relishes the opportunity to be so useful to those with whom he is connected by blood."

"He despises dragons! I am sure of it. He is only looking for a means by which to remove Kellynch so he can have—"

"How can you denigrate him so!"

"Very easily!" Anne threw her hands in the air. "No one, absolutely no one makes such significant changes to their character in so short a time."

"You have become very cynical and it is most unbecoming."

"Perhaps it is not cynicism but wisdom, and you do not like the possibility that you will not have your own way!"

"Anne Elliot! How dare you say such things to me! I do not deserve such infamous treatment. Especially when I am here trying to save you. Do you really think there is another man who will step in to protect you from what could be your undoing?"

Anne drew a deep breath and held it, blood roaring in her ears. Yes, yes there was, and he had already made her an offer. "I will stand for myself before the Blue Order, but if more is required, then yes, there is such a man."

"Who? I demand to know!"

"You may demand all you like, but I do not choose to answer."

"This is a mistake, a terrible, tragic mistake. Do not think I will easily allow you to make it."

Anne put her hands on her hips, flaring her elbows wide. "I do not believe you have a choice."

Lady Russell hissed and growled and flew away, just barely skimming over the top of the fence.

22
Chapter

ANNE TREMBLED AS she stood. *This is a mistake, a terrible, tragic mistake. Do not think I will easily allow you to make it.* Was that as much of a threat as it sounded? She swallowed hard. It might be, it just might. But what would she do? Lady Russell was not the violent sort, but a very great deal of mischief could be worked without ever having to resort to force.

Nonetheless, this was truly out of her depth. Bless it all, how she hated to feel that way! But Lady Elizabeth had warned her that it was a common feeling among Dragon Keepers and Friends alike. That should make her feel better.

Should, but no.

Wentworth had promised to help her. She needed to talk to him.

Looking over her shoulder, she slipped through the garden gate into the mews. No one was likely to notice she was gone, but even if they would, she was in no humor to give consequence to their questions.

The scents of the Avon mingled with the dragon musk carried on the cool morning air, stronger now that she had left the garden walls. The streets bustled with the usual business of the morning; loud voices and hurried traffic pressing on every side. So many dragon-hearers among the crowd. Were they here with their dragons to call upon the Dragon Sage?

If they were, did that also mean they would be witness to whatever proceeding would be necessary to sort out matters with Kellynch? Her cheeks burned and eyes prickled. More witnesses to the Elliot failures of dragon management. And surely that reputation would rest upon her as well.

Was it pride—a form of Elliot pride—that the notion set her stomach turning arsey-varsey? Probably. She laughed aloud, though it was a grim little sound. All this time she had thought herself free of the defining Elliot trait. But no, she had only managed to modify it to wear a slightly different face.

The grandeur of the Royal Crescent rose before her as she rounded the Circus. An impressive row of Bath stone townhomes four stories tall, definitely above any to be found in Camden Place. Father would not be pleased to know his tenant, a lowly admiral of the Navy, was housed in such a place. Several fine coaches waited for their passengers to embark in front of their respective houses. Three elegantly dressed ladies walked together toward the far end of the crescent. What were they speaking of? From the distance, she could not tell if they were Blue Order folk or not.

She paused at the beginning of the street and swallowed hard. These were just houses and nothing more. Oh, but her errand was by far the most important one—

Stop, just stop. She strode to the correct door and knocked firmly. What point in getting lost in thought? Just get on with it.

A somber, dragon-hearing butler answered the door and inquired after her name. Tall and imposing, as butlers should be, he wore a suit, not livery, and a Blue Order signet on his left little finger set in a dark metal—probably brass. Why was that comforting?

He disappeared inside only to reappear a moment later. "Mrs. Croft thought you might call today, miss. She and the rest of the family are not in right now, but she left you this." He handed her a neatly folded note, sealed with a drop of blue wax.

Anne took the note and turned away, heart thundering too loud to hear. She hurried into the green that faced the Royal Crescent, and ducked into the shadow of a large tree along the far side. Cool, green scents surrounded her as the shade drew her in. The low hanging hardwood branches felt like the woods near Uppercross' lair. Her chest released, and she gulped in air that tasted vaguely like that far away, safe place.

Leaning against the tree trunk, she cracked the wax seal. Mrs. Croft's hand was strong and steady, more legible than pretty, one could almost hear her steady, sweet voice in it.

Dear Miss Elliot,

I hope it is not presumptuous, but I had hoped to enjoy your company this afternoon. Unfortunately matters with which we are both familiar have called all of us away to the Office.

I anticipate we will be able to conclude our business by evening, and we all still intend on attending the concert at the Upper Rooms this evening. We do so hope to see you there.
~SC

How little she said, and yet how much. Did she know of Wentworth's letter? Such matters were not the sort of thing he was likely to talk to his sister about. But Mrs. Croft was well-traveled and wise. Surely, she suspected something—and Laconia probably had a hand in that as well.

Her tone was welcoming and encouraging—what could that mean but that she approved! Not that her approval was needed, but still, somehow it felt so very important.

If she was to be disappointed in her errand, this was the very best way to be so. There was nothing to be done for it. Despite the likelihood that she would have to deal with Mr. Elliot, she had to go to the concert tonight.

Anne spent the better part of the afternoon trying to convince Father that he was indeed well enough to escort them that evening. To his credit, he did spend more than a quarter of an hour staring at the looking glass, trying to determine the exact state of his nose. But in the end, he deemed it a shade too red to be exposed in public and retreated to his room, where he might be allowed to recuperate in peace.

Not surprising, but at least she had tried.

After dinner, she, Elizabeth and Mrs. Clay dressed for the concert and gathered in the drawing room to await their escort. Odd how she enjoyed her toilette in a way she never had before. Truly she had not expected to see much use for the pink striped opera gown—another cast-off from Elizabeth—but having tailored it to fit her properly, and refreshing the ribbons a bit, it felt as though it had been made for her, and exactly right for the occasion of accepting an offer from a man she—yes, she loved him!

How was she to face the drawing room and restrain herself from effusions of joy? Somehow, she would have to find a way.

Stuffy and as over ornamented as the parlor, the drawing room felt stifling, especially when, as now, the windows were not open. Stubborn blue brocade drapes blocked all fresh air, leaving the room smelling stale and vaguely smoky. The peach upholstered furniture tried to be light and bright and pleasing, but only achieved a pudgy stodginess and reminded one of an old dowager aunt. Rather like she imagined Lady Dalrymple.

Anne sat as far as she could from her sister, as Elizabeth was in a particular mood and displeased by everything she saw—at least everything about Anne. Thankfully the ample room offered her plenty of appropriate seats to choose from.

"Why do you insist on sitting so far away? I do not like having to talk so loudly to you." Elizabeth glowered.

Mrs. Clay edged her chair a little closer to Elizabeth. Had the two conspired on their dress tonight? Mrs. Clay's modest grey ensemble—perhaps a remnant of her half-mourning wardrobe—was quite the foil to the plum silk Elizabeth wore. "My gown is a cast-off from you. I should not think you would want me near."

Elizabeth's eyes grew wide, then narrowed. So, she did not appreciate sarcasm after all. Odd for one so proficient in it. "What has left you so disagreeable? It is a shame Lady Russell is not here in Bath. Her presence always seems to keep you under better regulation."

If only she could simply beg off going tonight. But, with the promise that he would be there, tolerating Elizabeth's disagreeable conversation was worthwhile.

The butler appeared in the doorway. "Mr. Elliot."

The man himself, in a smartly tailored suit that appeared quite new, held his hat under his arm and bowed. "I am most delighted to escort you all to the concert tonight. I am all in anticipation of its joys."

Why did he look at her that way when he spoke that last word? The skin on the back of her neck prickled.

"You are most gallant to come to our rescue." Elizabeth rose and glided toward him with Mrs. Clay not far behind.

The way he looked at Mrs. Clay. Father often looked at her that way, too. That could not be a good sign. But that was not her business tonight—and perhaps it would never be. Hopefully not.

"I am always pleased to be of service to my family." He tipped his head toward Elizabeth, but looked at Anne. "Shall we to the coach?" He ushered Elizabeth and Mrs. Clay toward the servants who were waiting with their wraps against the chill night air.

He helped Anne on with her pelisse and saw her out the door as well. Polite to be sure, but just a mite disturbing as well.

Elizabeth monopolized the conversation for the full quarter of an hour ride in the almost-but-not-quite cold carriage to the Upper Rooms, clearly seeking Mr. Elliot's undivided attention. He replied as necessary, but the creases at the corners of his eyes suggested he might be just a bit tired of her. Who could blame him?

He rapped on the ceiling with his walking stick and the coach rolled to a stop. "Look, is that not Lady Dalrymple and her daughter?" He pointed out the side glass into the crowded street, lit by several lamp posts, several streets up from the Upper Rooms.

Mrs. Clay slid open the glass and peered out. "Indeed, it is! I am certain of it."

"Surely you and Miss Elliot should make haste to meet her." He pushed the door open before Elizabeth could agree and stepped out to hand them down.

Anne tried to follow, but he stepped back into the well-appointed carriage. "You look tired, Miss Anne. I should like to drive you the rest of the way to the Upper Rooms." He pulled the door shut and rapped on the ceiling.

The coach lurched into motion. The air filled with the earthy-herbal scent of his cologne, much more noticeable now without Elizabeth and Mrs. Clay's perfume masking it. No wonder Laconia hated such scents so much.

"It is not proper that I should be in a carriage alone with you. Pray allow me out." She slid to the corner farthest away from him, her skirt catching on a small crack in the leather seat. Perhaps it was not as well-appointed as it seemed at first glance.

"I am your cousin, there is no harm." He made a show of settling himself in the seat opposite her.

At least that was something. She probably should find some conversation, but no, there was nothing she wanted to say.

After several minutes, he sighed. "You clearly do not like this, I am sorry." He rapped on the ceiling again, and the coach stopped. "We can easily walk the rest of the way from here."

He handed her out on to the cobblestone street and sent the driver on his way. "Is this more suitable, Miss Anne?"

"Much." She scanned the milling crowd near the Upper Room's entrance only two buildings away. Only a sliver of moon lit the sky, never her favorite time to be out and about in the evenings. No sign of the Crofts or Wentworth. Perhaps they were inside already.

"You seem very distracted." His tone asked a question she had no intention of answering.

"No, I am quite focused." She quickened her pace.

"Pray wait, Miss Anne. I would like it very much if you would allow me to speak to you for a moment before the concert." He reached for her arm, but she pulled away.

"I do not want to be late. This is not a good time at all."

He caught her arm again, this time very firmly. "It will not take very long, I am certain."

"I have no desire for such a conversation."

He pulled her, tripping slightly over the cobblestones, toward a small alley beside the Upper Rooms, dark and narrow, like a dragon's lair.

"Let go of me."

A dark shadow swooped down, blocking her way to the street. Mr. Elliot released her arm.

"Jet? What are you doing here?"

The black cockatrice extended his wings and squawked. His wingtips nearly touched both buildings hemming in the alley.

"Did you not know, Miss Anne, he is my Friend." Mr. Elliot nodded at Jet who folded his wings and hopped a little closer.

Her heart threatened to escape her chest. She pressed her hand to her ribs. "Your Friend? He has been spending a great deal of time on Kellynch."

"I know, I asked him to do so."

"You asked him? And you did not tell me—I am the one managing dragon affairs on the estate. You should have let me know." Her heart settled back into place, pounding to strengthen her limbs and voice.

"I am well aware that you are the Dragon Keeper, but I have been worried about you. I wanted to—"

"To spy on me and the affairs at Kellynch. You have no faith in me."

"To know what was going on and how I might help."

"You had no right. As far as I am concerned, that is trespass—"

"I have every right to be concerned for the estate that is entailed upon me. You never made me aware of the problems. You should have." Now he sounded offended. Offended!

"Why would I tell you? The estate is not yet yours. And you have made your attitude about Dragon Keeping quite clear."

"Because you needed help, and I could have assisted you."

"I am not in need of assistance. Certainly not yours. I would thank you to let me go on my way now. I have the matter very much in hand." She balled her fists and pulled back her shoulders.

"I think not." Lady Russell stepped out of the shadows behind Mr. Elliot, blocking her only other possible route of escape. "You are very much in need of help."

Anne's knees wavered just a mite. "What are you doing here? Mr. Elliot—"

"We are well acquainted, Miss Anne. She has made me quite familiar with the very dangerous situation you are in." He glanced back at Lady Russell.

Anne edged back. "The danger of being in this alley with you?"

"With the Blue Order, Kellynch and his estate." Mr. Elliot closed the distance between them. "Laws have been broken, the estate is in debt, Keeper's obligations have been neglected, and you, Miss Anne will be held accountable for it all. The Order will not be understanding."

That is not what Wentworth suggested, nor was it what the Sage assured her. "I am not afraid. I am ready to stand before them."

"But you should be. Dragon justice is swift and fierce." Jet spread his wings and hissed, herding her closer to Mr. Elliot.

"You should not have to pay the price for the sins of your father and his father before him, not when the means of salvation are so close." Mr. Elliot licked his lips.

"You need to listen to him Anne." Lady Russell's voice took on that sandpaper sound that hurt her head.

"You will not attempt to persuade me." Anne stomped and shouted. "I will not have it."

"Let me protect you. As your husband, the responsibility will be on my shoulders and you will not have to bear it yourself." His voice flowed like honey, sickly sweet and sticky.

"Why would you want that? You are heir to the estate and your position is assured."

"If the estate is taken from your father, then no, my position is not assured. They could decide to end the Elliot holding on Kellynch entirely. But if you marry me, I will assure the Blue Order of better Dragon Keeping in the future. Together we can preserve the family legacy."

"I can do that myself. I do not need to marry you." She spat the words like an angry forest wyrm spitting at a trespasser.

"They will not listen to a woman. You need my protection."

"You need his protection." Lady Russell echoed, her voice grating Anne's skull.

"Stop it! No, I do not, and I will not have it. Leave me be." She darted for the street but Jet cut her off, snapping and growling.

"Do not make this more difficult than it needs to be. You will marry me." He closed the distance between them.

"No, I will not." She shoved him back.

"Do not force my hand."

She dodged aside and ran toward Lady Russell, but she hissed and snapped and forced her back.

Mr. Elliot lunged for her, grabbing her pelisse. She shrieked. Something above her answered back. Who else did Mr. Elliot have guarding this place?

"You must marry me." He ripped her pelisse away from her chest, tearing the front away. Part of her bodice ripped away with it, revealing her chemise.

She screeched and pulled away, tearing her gown further.

"You cannot go out in public like that. You must accept my protection now." He closed on her.

"Leave me alone!" She kicked and struck out with her fists, several blows hard. Dragon's blood, no one ever told her how much that could hurt her hands and feet.

He slapped her hard, knocking her into the Bath stone wall behind her. Her head smacked the stone with a dull thud that brought stars to her eyes as she slid down the wall to the cold stony ground.

Something growled, low and menacing from the street side and a black form hurtled toward her. The air above exploded with a flurry of shrieking wings and talons.

"Get away from her!" The voice sounded like Laconia.

"Stop him! Stop that cockatrix!" Was that a dragon? No, a man.

"Cut off the other end of the alley."

"Subdue that black one." That was a dragon, probably a cockatrice.

"He's going to run! Stop him."

So many voices and nearly all unfamiliar. A raspy tongue licked her face. She forced her eyes open, but in the dim light of the alley it was difficult to see. Dark eyes stared into her face.

"Are you well?" Wentworth asked, taking her arm.

"Mrrow?" Laconia bumped her cheek with the top of his head.

"How did you find me?"

"With so many dragons in Bath, do you think such

a thing could remain a secret for long?" Laconia whispered. "I will go help the others now." He bounded off into the noise.

"What happened?" Wentworth supported her as she stood, held her as the world spun around her.

"He demanded I marry him. Lady Russell was trying to persuade me—"

"Lady Russell? That is Lady Russell? The same Lady Russell—" His hand tightened on her shoulder.

"Yes, the same."

"She has been persuading you and your family—everyone on Kellynch—that she was a lady?"

Admiral Croft appeared behind Wentworth, grim creases lining his face. "The cockatrix has been subdued, as are Elliot and his Friend."

"You mean Lady Russell? She has not been injured, has she?"

"No, she is well. The other two I fear are a bit worse for the wear." Admiral Croft glanced over his shoulder, probably toward the two in question.

"What will you do with her?"

"Not I, Miss Anne, the Blue Order. Her crimes have become known to the Order and a warrant for her arrest issued." She would not ask how it had become known. It really did not matter. "I will accompany her to the offices, though. I know she has been a friend to you and will try to see her treated accordingly." With a small nod, he turned and left.

Wentworth stepped a little closer, his voice low, for her only. "Why did you not tell me?"

"What was I to tell you?" Anne pulled her arm from his grasp.

"Perhaps the truth of what happened those years ago! It would have been good to know. I would have liked to have known."

"The power of communication goes both ways. You could have tried if it was so important to you. Besides, what would you have done with that information? Would it have made you resent me, hate me, any less?"

"I have never hated you." His voice dropped lower, almost impossible to hear.

"But resented, yes. That sentiment you do not deny. Would it have changed that? Or would you, do you, think me weak that I succumbed to her persuasion? Is that why you are so insistent about keeping from me the truth of those coins and what you suspect is going on with Kellynch?" She pulled the torn bits of her gown and pelisse to cover her chemise.

"It is an impressive dragon who can persuade hearers so effectively. I hardly know what to say." He peeked over his shoulder toward the Blue Order representatives leading Lady Russell away.

"But what you do not say is telling. You do not say you understand; you do not ask how I felt about what happened then; you do not ask me what I want or need."

"What you need is clear. I want to protect you—"

"So did he, and I want nothing of it. I am Keeper of Kellynch. I will stand before the Blue Order on my own merit, and if that is not enough, then so be it. I will not have you or any other man acting as though I am so insufficient that I need his protection in a matter that he has nothing to do with himself."

"Do be reasonable, Anne. I only want—"

"I thought I knew what you wanted, but now I am uncertain. Perhaps that is not at all what I want."

"Are you rejecting—"

"Pray excuse me, Miss Elliot—" an unfamiliar man in Blue Order livery approached. "I have been asked to escort you to the Order offices. You are requested to remain there until this matter has been sorted out."

"Am I under arrest?" She gasped, shuddering.

"No, Miss. The Sage has invited you to stay as her invited guest." He removed his overcoat and wrapped it over her shoulders, hiding the damage Mr. Elliot had wrought. "It is not an invitation you should refuse, though."

"I suppose not." She turned her back on Wentworth and followed the man to the street.

23
Chapter

WENTWORTH WATCHED HER, standing in a narrow moonbeam, turn her back to him, spine straight, shoulders back, utterly and completely resolved and committed to her course of action. That was what he said he wanted in a woman: resolve, commitment, strength of purpose.

It was not supposed to look like this, with her turning her back on his help, his protection, his support. He always thought she would want it, need it, even relish it. But she was just walking away, ignoring the loud crying and commotion behind her.

"You need to go with her." Laconia rose up on his tail and pressed his paws on Wentworth's hip. Where had he come from? "Go now." His claws prickled through Wentworth's trousers.

"I cannot. She does not want me, and I do not think the Order will accept my presence either. Not now." He could barely force the words past the lump in his throat.

"What did you do? How could she possibly turn you away at a time like now?"

"I do not know."

"I can smell it when you lie. You need to try." Laconia spring-hopped away, growling under his breath. Wentworth would probably not see him the rest of the night. Laconia would probably spend it with Mina, or Anne.

Lucky sot to be able to get to her with such ease— or at least he imagined it would be so.

Wentworth turned into the dark alley, making his way toward angry voices and hissing. Six, possibly seven men in Blue Order livery as well as Croft circled the protesting voices that echoed off the nearby stone walls.

"Release me!" The tall cockatrix cried, plaintive and perhaps even afraid. "I have done nothing!" Her long plumage, vaguely blue in the dim moonlight, drooped and her head hung low.

"So, you are Lady Russell." Wentworth approached her, the circle of men opening to admit him.

She hissed at him, but the effort seemed more for show than anything else. Her legs were bound with an iron chain and a heavy leather blanket was buckled across her chest to contain her wings. Still it would be wise to stand out of the striking range of her sharp beak should her demeanor suddenly change.

"It would be wise of you to go quietly through the tunnels with your escort to the Order," Croft said softly.

"I am not bound by that precious treaty of yours. Release me, and I will go directly back to Australia and never set foot on these grounds again." She lifted her head, feathers fluffing, her tail spreading behind her.

"When you became Friends with Sir Henry, you became bound to the same laws that bound him." Croft pointed at two liveried guards and a pair of cockatrice.

"What is to become of me?" She started to shriek, but one of the cockatrice guards flapped his wings to silence her. The last thing they needed was a cockatrice shrieking to send the crowd in the Upper Rooms into a panic.

"You will be dealt with according to the Blue Order laws. You should consider yourself fortunate that the Dragon Sage is here. I expect she will be the first to look into this affair."

"That ignorant slip of a—"

Three guards stomped toward her. Heavens they were protective of the Sage!

"Watch what you say about the woman who could very well keep you from being eaten in a judicial action. If there is any in the kingdom apt to be sympathetic to your side of the matter, it is her. Take her to the offices. Go quietly—they will not hesitate to use whatever force necessary and will not be held responsible for injuries you may sustain." Croft waved them toward the tunnel entrance, at the far end of the alley.

The large black cockatrice beside Elliot screamed and worked his wings free of their bindings. Despite his chains, he leapt into the air, screaming. A cold shudder coursed down Wentworth's back.

Three cockatrice guards converged on him, two at his wings and one actually landing on his back. The guards wrestled with him, pelting him with their tails. If their claws did not draw blood, it would be a wonder. They dragged him back to the ground where a pair of men forced a leather hood over his eyes and bound his wings in two layers of leather blankets.

"As for you, the Blue Order Court will convene shortly to deal with you. One more attempt like that and my guard is authorized to use deadly force—and I think they just might like that," Croft all but growled.

Wentworth strode to Elliot. "You best hope that she is not seriously injured, or I will deal with you when the court is finished."

"She is my betrothed. You have no right." The arrogant look really needed to be removed from Elliot's face.

"There has been no announcement, no acknowledgement of such a contract. It does not exist."

"Perhaps you have not been listening to the right fairy dragons. By tomorrow, all in Bath will know of our engagement and the wedding will be all but planned." Elliot smirked.

An unfamiliar squawk sounded overhead and wings fluttered.

"I doubt it!" A black cockatrix, looking more like a crow with a pale beak than the fancy sort of bird cockatrix normally resembled, landed near Wentworth's feet. "I heard it all, I saw it all! Anne is my friend. I will see the truth is shared! You 'ave done my Friend Mrs. Smith enough harm. I will not allow you to bring her more grief through Anne."

"How much did you see?" Wentworth asked.

"Enough to alert the guards and your tatzelwurm friend."

"This was your doing? I owe you—"

"What has he done to your Friend?" Croft crouched down near the cockatrix, glancing a cease-and-desist at Wentworth. "What is your name?"

"I am Rooke, an assignee of the Order." She bobbed her head in a sort of bow. "I were assigned by the Order to 'elp care for Mrs. Smith. He—" she pointed her wing toward Elliot, "'as forced her into poverty and privation."

"Once you have contradicted news of the betrothal, return to me at the Order. I believe the Court will want to hear from you."

"I will return directly." She squawked and launched into the dark sky.

"Get them back to the Order, there are cells waiting in the caverns below the courtroom." Croft waved them off, standing silently with Wentworth as they disappeared into the tunnels, leaving an echoing stillness in their wake. "What a bit of ugly business. He is the sort of fellow who ought to have his ears put out and never hear dragons—or much of anything else—again."

Wentworth shuddered. Barbaric, simply barbaric, but definitely draconic.

"He is the one Miss Anne thought to be framing Kellynch?" Croft wrinkled his lips into a distinct expression of displeasure. "He is right lucky we found him before Kellynch did."

"Kellynch has little regard for any of the Elliots—would he really have been offended on his Keeper's behalf?"

"A dragon's pride is one of the strongest forces on earth. You would be surprised." Croft crossed his arms and tapped his thumbs on his shoulders.

"Frederick!"

Wentworth jumped.

Sophy dashed through the darkness, in and out of the few moonbeams. "Laconia told me—well actually it was rather unclear, just that I needed to find you both, here."

"Find me? I should have thought he would have sent you to Miss Anne," Wentworth said.

"Miss Anne? What has happened to her?" Wide-eyed, Sophy turned to Croft.

"A local cockatrix alerted one of the patrolling cockatrice guards. Mr. Elliot was imposing himself upon her. A score of Blue Order guards came in to deal with it. Have never seen the like of it before—it is incredibly difficult to catch such a thing before the damage is done." Croft patted Sophy's hand. "Miss Anne has been escorted to a guest room, courtesy of the Sage, and the rest, including Lady Russell, are in custody." He lifted his bushy brows as he spoke the name.

"Oh, I see. You have met her now?" Sophy looked at Wentworth, her dark eyes demanding an answer."

"I have."

"Then we should go directly back to Royal Cres-cent." Sophy looped her arm in his.

"No, I should go to the offices directly. I imag-ine—"

"I will manage that for the time being and send for you if you are needed. Go with her." Croft marched toward the tunnels without a backward glance.

"We need to talk." Sophy pulled him toward the street.

"I do not have anything to talk about. I insist—"

"Do not force my hand, little brother. You know I

will have my way."

He rolled his eyes, which thankfully she probably could not see in the darkness. At least she did not acknowledge the expression, which was good enough.

The brisk, silent walk back to Royal Crescent, in the nearly cold gloom of insufficient moonlight, offered none of the solace it should have, not even permitting him to gather his thoughts for fear Sophy might pick them apart even as he did so. She had an uncanny knack of knowing what one was thinking even before he did.

She led him upstairs to a sitting room she had immediately claimed as her territory when they settled into the house. It had probably been originally purposed as a dressing room sometime in the house's past with doors on either side leading into adjacent rooms. But furnished with several chairs, a small sofa and low table, it suited Sophy's use well enough.

"Talk to me. I have no doubt there is a great deal on your mind." She sat on the largest chair in the room, a duchess holding court.

How many times had they acted out this same scene in the years since their mother had died? Yes, Sophy could be bossy, overbearing, and opinionated when she chose, but there was no one who cared for her family better, or whose advice he more wanted, when he actually wanted advice. Which was definitely not the case now. "Since you obviously know that so well, perhaps you would be so good as to tell me what I am thinking."

Sophy laughed. "I think you are on the cusp of doing something entirely stupid, and I would very much like to give you the chance to think it through very well before you commit to that course of action."

"What did Laconia tell you?"

"I would rather hear it from you."

Wentworth fell into the bergère farthest from Sophy and threw his head back. "There is nothing I wish to talk about."

"Not even Lady Russell?"

Uh! She had that tone that would just not be gainsaid. "How long have you known about her?"

"I discovered her just after Miss Anne returned from Lyme. It was quite a shock, coming upon her on the footpath on my way to call upon Miss Anne. By the way, you need to know, she had no idea of the magnitude of Lady Russell's crime."

"What is that to me?"

"I should think it would be everything to you. When Anne refused you eight years ago, I think it was, she could not hear dragons, so had no idea of what she was experiencing. Moreover, she was persuaded by a dragon who is probably the most persuasive creature in the kingdom."

Wentworth huffed. Some might consider dragon persuasion a suitable excuse, but one could hardly be persuaded against something one was utterly set upon.

"Have you ever considered what it means that it took such a creature to turn her away from you? I am convinced that no lesser effort could have managed the feat."

"It makes no difference."

"She has refused two eligible offers since then. I think it should make a great deal of difference."

"Musgrove is a weak-livered Dragon Keeper who is persuaded by the same cockatrix and Elliot the rake upon whom the estate is entailed? Yes, that puts me in very good company. Frankly, I am tired of all these dragon-muddled matters, thank you very much." Wentworth threw a hand in the air, nearly knocking over a truly ugly vase. "I would just as soon walk away from them and the ridiculous Order before it wreaks any more havoc upon my life."

A lesser woman would have gasped at such an outburst. Sophy only sighed. "You are frustrated, angry, and lacking the kind of command and control you are accustomed to at sea. But you must remember, dragons are like storms, you cannot control them, you can only learn how to live with them. How much different is that to what you have known?"

Wentworth growled under his breath. "I am tired of the price one has to pay for consorting with them."

"Do not let Laconia hear you saying such things. He will be deeply offended." Sophy clucked her tongue. "I think your pride has been injured."

"You know nothing."

"No, no, I am beginning to see, very clearly now. Your pride is wounded, and you would rather take the easy route of preserving it. I expect you made her another offer, did you not?"

"That is none of your business." He clenched his jaw and gritted his teeth. Blasted, nosy, intrusive—

"I expect she was supposed to respond to you tonight. You anticipated she would accept you—"

"And once again the damn dragons have interfered with my happiness." He clutched the arms of the chair lest he send the dreadful vase to the floor.

"You think attaching yourself to a woman who cannot hear would set you free of such complications?"

"Hardly. Laconia has made it clear he will not live

in a household with a woman who cannot hear."

"I do not blame him."

"Frankly I am not sure I do either." Wentworth leapt to his feet and paced the length of the too-short room. If he did not move, he would surely burst. Five paces down, five back. He needed the deck of a proper ship and the wind in his face—

"So, what are you going to do about this?"

"What is there for me to do?"

"What did she say to you?"

He stopped and leaned against the wall, back to Sophy and head cradled in his elbow. "She called me resentful. She said she had no need for my protection. She said she would stand before the Blue Order on her own merit, neither wanting nor needing me to stand with her."

"Good on her! Did you not always complain you thought her weak-willed, even spineless at times? Her greatest fault in your eyes has been that she seemed easily persuaded. Clearly that is no longer the case. I am surprised you are not delighted."

"Delighted by a woman who rejects me—"

"Rejects you or rejects your attempts to take away her agency in the most important matter that she has been charged with."

"I am taking nothing from her. Merely trying to protect her—"

"You have decided that she is incapable, perhaps even incompetent." Her smug tone would drive him from the room if she did not rein it in!

"I never said such a thing."

"You did not have to. If Croft did to me what you are trying to do to her—"

He whirled to face her. "What do you know of it?"

"You think there are secrets when there are dragons involved?" She snorted a knowing sort of laugh. "I know that you have refused to tell her about Cornwall and the gold. I only imagine that you think keeping her ignorant of the matter will ensure the Order does not hold her responsible for what you think Kellynch has done."

"What is wrong with that?"

"You are not even the dragon's Keeper and you are making decisions regarding both him and his Keeper. You have no right, Frederick. It is not your place."

"No right? Her father has abdicated his authority. I am ... I am ..."

"He gave that authority to her, not to you. You are, honestly, nothing to her, certainly no one with a right to decide what she should and should not know. I am appalled. I would have thought you would know better."

"Know what?"

She rose in a single smooth moment and strode to his side. "We ladies are rational creatures. We none of us expect to be in smooth water all our days. Not all of us want a man to shield us from the inevitable storms of life. Especially those of us connected to dragons. If I may be so bold as to speak for a class so broad and diverse, we want someone with whom we can share the task, as a partner and a friend, as I have shared the Admiral's travels and adventures with him. Unless I am very sorely mistaken, and I do not think I am, your Anne is such a woman. And if that is the sort of way you are determined to treat her, then she should not have you."

Wentworth's jaw dropped.

Sophy held up her hand—she would not be interrupted. "You have these eight years proclaimed you wanted a woman of sense and intelligence, who would be firm of purpose and not easily swayed by anyone. Now you have met her, perhaps you have changed your mind?"

He bowed his head, clasping his hands behind his neck. "You should have seen the look in her eye."

"I can readily imagine. Such a woman is not easy to live with—or so my dear husband has informed me. But then neither are dragons. I am quite certain that you have no regrets about befriending Laconia. In fact, I think he delivered you from yourself during some very dark times."

"He did. I cannot imagine being without him."

"He is very fond of Miss Anne. Perhaps that should tell you something. Perhaps inform your course."

"Perhaps." Perhaps it did.

Or perhaps it told him nothing at all.

24
Chapter

October 11, 1814

THERE MUST HAVE been a touch of poppy in her tea as she fell asleep far more quickly than she would have expected, and awoke with her head muzzy from odd dreams and fragments of memory.

She peeked her eyes open and stretched aching joints. Early morning light filtered in through the hazy windows that blocked the view from outside. A sensible precaution in such an establishment, but it did create the sense of a thick overcast sky just before a storm. Maybe that was fitting, all told. The ivory and green print drapes fluttered in the slightly damp breeze from the open transom above the window. The air smelt like rain.

The room was relatively small, nicer than her chamber at Uppercross Cottage, but not so well-appointed as Camden Place. The bed linens matched the curtain's print—stylized bird type dragons. Did all the guest rooms use the same fabric? Street noises from outside filtered in and echoed just enough to be noticeable—the floor had no carpet to dampen the sounds like Camden Place had. The furniture—the bed, a press with three drawers, dressing table and chair—were simple oak and small in scale, leaving the room rather more open than seemed typical.

Was that to leave room for dragons? A small servants' door covered in green baize blended into the shadows near the far side of the room. Was that for servants, or for dragon use? Or even for both.

"Mrrrow." A long, heavy form beside her moved.

Laconia? That was the comforting weight pressed against her all night! Had he used that door?

He reached his broad thumbed paws up to her shoulders and leaned into her. "I licked your face while you slept. I did not think you would mind."

She touched her cheek, several scrapes rough and sore under her fingertips. "Thank you, that was very kind. I did not realize you were here."

"I do not mind, the tea made you sleepy. You needed sleep." He rolled over and exposed his belly. "Now you need to get up and visit our eggs. After you scratch."

She sat up slowly, knees, shoulders, back all stiff and protesting. Was it the firm bed or the events of last night? Probably both.

Laconia purred as she petted and scratched his belly. Some of the tension eased from her shoulders. Fairy dragon song was known to be soothing. Did tatzelwurm purrs have the same effect?

Perhaps it was just her.

He rolled and sat back on his coiled serpentine tail. "Mrrow. Mina is waiting for us. She is anxious for you to meet the eggs."

How did one meet an egg? "Are you certain it is appropriate for me to just wander about the Order? It seems as though I should be waiting for a summons of some sort." She stood and scanned the room. Where had the nightdress she was wearing come from? And where were her clothes? A proper gown would be necessary to leave the room no matter what the circumstance.

"A trunk was brought for you and unpacked—what you want should be there." Laconia leapt off the bed and spring-hopped to the press three steps away.

He was right, fresh body linen and her drab walking dress were there, neatly folded, and her nankeen half-boots stood on the floor nearby. "I cannot imagine how I slept through that."

"I think the tea was quite strong. The Order was in quite a frenzy last night. Just as dragons are not supposed to turn on one another, I do not think the warm-bloods of the Order are supposed to."

"I am very grateful for all your help last night." She found a hairbrush on the dressing table and pinned up her hair. "May I ask why you slept here?"

"Wentworth needed to think. Come, I will take you to the eggs." He spring-hopped to the door, just two hops from the press.

There was little to be done for the bruises on her face, especially the prominent black mark under her eye. But then, as quickly as gossip carried, the whole of dragon-hearing Bath probably had heard what had gone on and would not be surprised to see her in that condition. The thought was hardly comforting. She followed Laconia out.

The plain limestones tiling the hall were scuffed and scratched. More than the marks of heavy boots, it seemed talons and claws had left their traces. No wonder Admiral Croft would have had the heavy sail-cloth with him to protect Kellynch's floors from White's front hooves.

Clearly this building had been fitted especially for dragon use. How very different from Camden Place, and really all other houses she had known. It made sense though, but Father would see it all as very improper and inconvenient.

The wide staircase, its wrought iron banister scrolls bearing iron dragons, led her two stories down to another wide corridor where Laconia guided her to a door bearing the placard: *Admiral R. Easterly, Chief Liaison to His Majesty's Navy*. He chirruped and pushed the half-open door wide and ushered Anne through.

The room was small with white walls bearing a few framed maps on the wall and a cluttered desk near the middle of the room. Behind the desk stood a book-case with bowing shelves overflowing with books and paraphernalia. On the bottom-most shelf, Mina peeked over the edge of a large wooden box. A woman, a gentlewoman given the fine blue muslin gown she wore, sat on the floor, holding an egg roughly the size of a large goose egg, maybe a bit larger, examining it in the filtered light from the window.

"A very fine, egg, to be sure. Thank you for allowing me to visit." The woman said, replacing the egg in the box next to Mina.

"You brought her!" Mina rose up on her silvery serpentine tail, almost knocking her head on the shelf above, and chirruped.

"Pray excuse me, I did not know you already had a caller." Anne stepped back.

The woman rose and faced Anne, so serene, so composed, as though everything about this situation was completely normal and natural. She was pretty, in a comfortable sort of way, not an intimidating one, and had the bearing of the mistress of a grand manor. Bright, warm eyes lent sincerity to her gentle smile and nod at Laconia. "Would you be so kind as to introduce us?"

Laconia rose on his tail and chirruped. "Lady Elizabeth, Dragon Sage, this is Miss Anne Elliot."

"The Dragon Sage?" Anne gasped and curtsied. What was the proper etiquette for such a meeting?

"I am pleased to make your acquaintance, Miss Elliot. Laconia and Mina have told me a great deal about you. Pray come closer, I believe Mina wishes to introduce her eggs to you." She beckoned Anne toward the large box.

Laconia led the way to Mina's side and slithered into the box with her, twining around her and licking her face a bit possessively.

Anne knelt beside Lady Elizabeth and peered into the box. Nestled in the fresh smelling hay were three substantial eggs. The shells were mottled brown and grey, like bird's eggs, but the shells seemed more leathery than hard.

"That one." Mina rolled the largest of the eggs toward her with her large thumbed paw. "He will be a very fine wyrmling."

"Go on, pick up the egg. I assure you; you will not harm it." Lady Elizabeth scratched behind Laconia's ears.

The eggshell gave just a bit under her fingers as

she lifted the unexpectedly heavy egg. Something inside moved, just slightly, and Anne jumped.

"Do not be startled, they do that at times. Put it to your ear and you might even hear him, too."

How could one tell an egg was a he or a she?

Anne held the egg to her ear. It purred.

"It is as I said," Laconia rumbled along with the egg. "You will be good friends."

"How do you know?" Anne cradled the egg close to her chest, feeling its soothing hums more than hearing them.

"You smell right."

"It is not unusual for minor dragons to select Friends for their hatchlings, or at least try to. Sometimes the hatchling has other ideas in mind, but often enough, the hatchling decides to stay with the Friend that has been selected for them. You can talk to him you know, the eggs are too newly laid for him to understand you yet, but it will be good for him to become accustomed to your voice. I talked to my Friend April that way, and she recognized me immediately."

What did one say to a purring egg? "You will be a very fine tatzelwurm I am certain. Your mother and father are quite remarkable. Your sire is a sailor with quite the reputation you know."

Mina licked Laconia's face.

"The eggs should hatch in four or five weeks, I think. Spend time with them as much as you can. It will make their hatching much easier for all of you." Lady Elizabeth chuckled under her breath. "I should tell you the story of my Friend fairy dragon's hatching. She was quite the stubborn little soul from the moment she cracked shell. And she has not changed since. Would you like to meet her?"

On the one hand, it was a simple and very friendly invitation, but on the other one did not refuse an invitation from a person like the Sage, if she should even want to, and the Sage surely knew that. "I would be honored to meet her."

"If you will excuse us then, Laconia, Mina. I think Miss Elliot and I have a great deal to discuss." She said it so gently, so kindly.

That probably was not a good sign. Anne stood, a sailor's knot tying itself in her stomach.

"April is upstairs in my dressing room, enjoying a bit of quiet before the day begins. She is such a social creature, one would not have thought she would relish a bit of solitude, but our schedule has been so full—"

"Pray I do not wish to intrude."

"You are the first call on my agenda, Miss Elliot. She will be expecting you." Lady Elizabeth led the way up the stairs to the same floor Anne's room was on, but on the opposite side of the grand stairway. She stopped at the third door on the right, the mews side of the building. "Do come in."

The dressing room was larger than Anne's room, lined with light wooden paneling and soft brown on brown striped carpeting underfoot. Two substantial desks anchored the two short ends of the narrow room, with several chairs, a smallish sofa, a mahogany cradle, and no furniture that resembled a dressing room at all.

A blue-green drake who stood on two legs, probably a bit taller than herself, rocked the cradle, crooning something melodic in the back of her throat, her hood flaring and relaxing in a hypnotic pattern. A turquoise fairy dragon sat on the drake's shoulder, twittering a soporific song. A tall regal-looking man, of whom Father would have greatly approved, looked over the drake's shoulder, nodding.

"Mr. Darcy!" Lady Elizabeth glided to his side, so much warmth in her voice it was almost indecent.

"Never fear, I am not interfering with Nanny's routine. Little Anne is just now asleep. I would not dare wake her." He reached out and took Lady Elizabeth's outstretched hands.

Anne—the Sage's daughter was named Anne! Surely it was a family name, but still, it somehow eased her trepidation.

"Mr. Darcy, I suppose Sir Fitzwilliam would be proper in this case, may I introduce you to Miss Anne Elliot, daughter of Sir Walter and Keeper of Kellynch."

Anne curtsied.

A strange scratching, tumbling sound resounded from behind a green baize door on the far side of the room which suddenly burst open. "Me too, me too! I want introduced!" A little red firedrake, smaller than Nanny, tumbled in, stumbling over wings and feet too large for her body.

"Hush!" Nanny hissed, leaning protectively over the cradle, hood fully flared. "If you wake little Anne, I will see you banished to the dragon's lair in the tunnels."

Sir Fitzwilliam turned aside as though hiding a chuckle.

"Pemberley, you may have your introduction, but it is not right to burst in uninvited. I promised you would meet all our guests. You need to respect our plans." Lady Elizabeth's brows knit as she cast a severe look at the drakling.

"I sorry. Please. Can I has introduction? I want meet angry wyrm's Keeper."

Anne's jaw dropped. It was not polite to gape, but what else could one do upon seeing a dragon scolded by a woman? "Is Kellynch very angry? I am sorry—"

"Vicontes Pemberley, may I present Miss Elliot, Keeper of Kellynch."

Anne curtsied, and Pemberley bobbed in something like a bow.

"I am afraid Kellynch is rather discomposed, but in truth, that is a matter for the Blue Order Court to deal with. We will talk about that soon enough. First though, I would like to present my Friend April." Lady Elizabeth gestured to the fairy dragon who buzzed toward them and hovered in front of Anne's face, so close her eyes crossed.

"I do not know if I wish to be acquainted with one associated with that cockatrix." April circled Anne and landed on Lady Elizabeth's shoulder.

"She has met Lady Russell?"

"I am afraid we all have." Lady Elizabeth gestured toward a pair of chairs near the desk farthest from the cradle. "Or should we go elsewhere, Nanny?"

The drake peered into the cradle. "She is sleeping. It will be good for her to get used to sleeping when there are other sounds about. April will help if she gets too restless."

April trilled softly and nestled into the side of Lady Elizabeth's neck. They sat at the long edge of the desk.

"Pray forgive us. Even with a dragon nursemaid and a fairy dragon to help, traveling with an infant is difficult for all of us."

Sir Fitzwilliam chuckled from the other side of the room. "But you would not pass up the chance for her to be exposed to so many dragons as she could meet in Bath."

"Is it true that the baby hears already?" Anne asked.

"As far as we can tell."

"She is very fortunate then. My sister and I began hearing very late it seems."

"So did my aunt. It was a startling transition for her. Although I have heard for as long as I can remember, I do have some understanding of what it is like to come into one's hearing late."

"Pray excuse me, it is time to present Pemberley to Cornwall. I will take her." Sir Fitzwilliam beckoned the drakling toward the door.

"Surely you must need to attend—" Anne half stood.

"Cornwall takes great pleasure in being inconvenient to man and dragon alike. He was made aware of my very full schedule and that I would not be available this morning." Lady Elizabeth and Sir Fitzwilliam shared a knowing glance.

"But he is the Prince's—"

"We are well aware of his rank. But every dragon must respect the Order and its needs even above their own demands. A reminder is clearly in order. Pemberley, do you recall the proper shows of dominance in this case."

"Yes, Keeper. I 'member." Pemberley flapped her wings just a little. "I practice. I good."

"And Cownt Matlock will be there as well to intervene should Cornwall prove intractable." Sir Fitzwilliam tugged his shirt cuffs straight under his jacket sleeves.

"If they begin quarreling—"

"I will remove Pemberley immediately. She does not need any example of poor manners." He tipped his head and followed Pemberley out.

They discussed the whole affair so matter-of-factly, so easily, as though conferring on how to handle quibbling relations, not creatures who could bring down the entire kingdom! What manner of Dragon Keepers were they?

"Pray forgive the interruption. You were telling me about your introduction to dragon society?"

Anne blinked several times. "Yes, yes … you have met Lady Russell. She has been my guide in nearly all dragon matters. I have of course studied everything the Blue Order has provided, but …"

"May I ask, how did you come to know she was a dragon?"

Anne related the story as quickly and factually as she could.

Lady Elizabeth chewed her lower lip, brows knotted. "I cannot imagine the shock you must have experienced to discover such a thing about your friend. Every dragon I have ever spoken to I have known was a dragon."

Anne turned away from her piercing gaze. "I do not think she has ever really been my friend. At least not in the sense that you and I might consider friendship. She used Kellynch—the estate and the dragon—for her own purposes and everyone else there as well. Convinced us to do and say and believe what she wanted so that she could live life as she pleased."

"I will not pry, but it seems that it cost you a great deal."

Anne nodded as she struggled to swallow back the knot that inhibited all speech.

"And you were not aware of the crimes she was committing in so doing?"

Anne shook her head and forced out whispery words. "Not until the Crofts told me. I should have known. I am sure it was somewhere in the material the Blue Order sent me. I am sure of it. I should have known. I could have. But it all seemed so normal to me that it did not really occur that it was a problem."

"Little about the entire circumstance at Kellynch is normal."

"My Dragon Keeping—"

Lady Elizabeth rapped the desk sharply with her knuckles. "What Dragon Keeping? Your Father is entirely responsible for what has happened, not you."

"But he made me Keeper—"

"Indeed, and we—the Blue Order—are all thankful for that. But that does not and will not transfer responsibility away from him for his failings. Nor does it make you responsible for the criminal actions of Lady Russell."

Criminal actions. Even with everything that had happened it was difficult to think of her thus. "What is to become of her?"

"Pray do not tell me you think she should be excused for what she has done?"

Well, yes, in some ways … at least she had thought so at one time, but no. "She said that her deception began as a lark with her Friend Sir Henry and soon they were in so far they could not get back out again."

"That is what she told me. Do you think it is true?" Lady Elizabeth's lips pursed in a thoughtful sort of way.

"It is consistent with what I have heard from the servants, the Uppercross family and my Father, so I believe so."

"I will keep that in mind, then. Did you ever discuss the matter with Laird Uppercross?"

Anne clenched her hands tightly, trying to shake off the feelings of a schoolgirl interrogated by the head mistress. "No, not directly, though I did get the impression he was displeased with her."

"He was the one who brought the matter to my attention—or were you unaware of that?" Lady Elizabeth cocked her head and lifted her eyebrow. "With the situation only getting more complicated, he was concerned for her if her secret came to light in the midst of sorting out matters with Kellynch. He was most solicitous for her wellbeing."

"He is a good friend, though I doubt Lady Russell will see it that way."

"I expect you are correct. She does not seem well disposed toward anything that is not the way she would have it be." Lady Elizabeth tipped her head toward April. "But then, you are often impatient with things that displease you, too."

April cocked her head and cheeped. "Of course, I am. Who does not want things to their own liking?"

"Who indeed?" Lady Elizabeth scratched under April's chin, and she trilled happily. Such an easy relationship the two seemed to share.

No wonder Lady Elizabeth was Sage, she made everything about dragons look simple and easy and normal. "What will the Order do with Lady Russell?"

"That is a very good question for which I do not yet have a good answer. Her offense is serious and long standing. Her mischief has not been without harm to you, to Kellynch, and probably others. But I am not of the opinion that the suggested consequences fit her crimes."

"I do not wish to see her eaten if that is what you mean. Can she not be taught to do better somehow? Forgive me for being so bold, but you corrected Vicontes Pemberley to teach her what is expected of her rank, cannot the same be done for her?"

Lady Elizabeth smiled and nodded, a pleased, knowing look. "Dragons are not generally malleable creatures. Do you think she is capable of learning?"

"Certainly not from me. She considers herself my mentor and is far too proud to learn anything from me. But perhaps, if there were someone she respected, it might be possible."

"I will keep that in mind. I spoke with her last night, but she was under considerable agitation at the time, so it was not an entirely profitable conversation. I am hoping more might be achieved today."

"Perhaps I could—"

Lady Elizabeth shook her head with a definitiveness that could not be opposed. "I would rather see you sheltered from her temper at the moment. Moreover, you have far more important things to deal with, and I do not want to see you distracted. The Order has reviewed Kellynch's complaints against his Keeper and found them sound. Your Father must appear before the court in three days when the case is to be tried."

Anne gasped.

"Although Kellynch has tried to include you in those charges—mainly in a fit of draconic temper, I think—I am satisfied on the testimony of Uppercross, Shelby and even Lady Russell that he has no grounds for those complaints and have petitioned the court to have them stricken from the case. However, as Keeper to Kellynch, it is your duty to serve your dragon's complaint, even if it is against your Father."

"Surely not!"

"I am afraid it is your duty, and there is no one else who can do it for you. The complaint by the Order against Mr. Elliot assaulting your person will also be heard at that same court session as will a complaint by Cornwall against Kellynch."

"Dug Cornwall has a complaint against Kellynch?"

"Unfortunately so. Since it is alleged to have happened prior to your taking the Keepership, you will not be held accountable for your Dragon's actions should he be found guilty. The Order has been investigating the matter—it is rather complex."

Her heart froze into a solid knot in her chest. Royalty had a complaint against Kellynch. What could it be and what would it mean for them all? Considering all things draconic, probably nothing good.

"Exactly. I am afraid I do not have time to explain it all now, but I will send someone to Camden Place to familiarize you with all the necessary details before the trial."

Chapter 25

October 12, 1814

SHE SAT UP in bed, pulling the lavender scented soft wool blanket around her. The soft pink room was not so much cold. No, the cold was internal. Even if she were to have a fire lit in the little marble faced fireplace in the corner, it would not help. Nor would drawing the heavy ivory brocade bed curtains around the bed. She might as well get up.

A quick glance in the mirror revealed exactly what she expected. Dark circles stood out under her eyes, a fitting accessory for the even more colorful bruises on her cheek. Father was going to love that.

She stared into her closet and reached for a morning dress. But no, why not prepare for the inevitable? Donning a walking dress now would save her the trouble after the inevitably contentious conversation with her father resulted in the need for a great deal of air.

Another of Elizabeth's cast-offs seemed appropriate for the day. A green and plum striped gown with a matching plumb pelisse that would hopefully keep the October chill at bay. A deep poke bonnet would help disguise the marks on her face whilst she was out, but nothing would help here in the house. Lovely, just lovely.

Fastening her hair in a simple knot, she took a final glance in the cheval mirror. Tired, sad and old—that was how Father would describe her, and he would be right.

She made her way down the marble tiled grand stairs to the morning room on the ground floor. The appetizing scents of fresh rolls hung in the air, leaving her stomach churning even harder. Perhaps a little tea would help.

She peeked into the blue-green morning room. Today it seemed even more green than usual, casting an unflattering pallor on all the occupants. Father would be appalled to know. He might never eat in that room again.

The usual fragrant Bath buns, cold meats, preserves, and a rack of toast decorated the sideboards, along with a plate of queen cakes that were a favorite of Mrs. Clay's. Ordered from Molland's by the look of them. Despite the faint green cast, everything looked quite pleasing and would have been tempting had her stomach been in any state for food.

Father sat at the far side of the table, near the window. Elizabeth and Mrs. Clay, both dressed to go out for the day, sat near. Odd for him to change his habit so.

"Good God Anne!" Elizabeth exclaimed, nearly dropping her teacup. "What happened to you? Were these friends you were staying with not respectable people?"

"Are you in pain? Do you require anything?" Mrs. Clay's words were kind, but with a sickly solicitude that left a foul taste in Anne's mouth.

"You are an utter fright today, Anne. Absolutely disgraceful. Pray tell me you do not intend to go out and be seen in such a state." Father glowered over his newspaper.

He was in a lovely mood after so late an evening. "Good morning to all of you." She picked her way toward the tea service.

"I asked you if you were going out? You are dressed for going out. Where do you think you are fit to be seen?" Father demanded.

"I do not know right now." She shrugged and took her teacup to the table, sitting as far from Father and Elizabeth as she could.

"Thank goodness for that. You will go back upstairs after breakfast and not show yourself in public again until you are fit to be seen."

"I will do what I need to do, sir. There is business I must accomplish far sooner than these marks will heal."

"Well do not expect to be seen with me looking so ghastly and common." The way he said that—he was certain that would be a punishment to her.

"That is a hardship I am certain I can bear." From the corner of her eye she could just make out Elizabeth's cold stare.

"You missed a most agreeable evening last night. I am sorry you were called away to tend your sick friend." Mrs. Clay glanced from Father on her left to Elizabeth on her right as if she hoped she could somehow restore equanimity at the table.

So that was the persuasions the dragons had used to explain her disappearance.

"You really ought to make more effort to engage in the hospitality the Dalrymples offer us. They took us home you know, since Mr. Elliot's horse turned up lame and he could not convey us back home. They asked after you and expressed a wish to see more of you." Elizabeth dabbed her lips with a crisply folded white napkin.

"Not looking like that," Father muttered to his newspaper.

"I had other very pressing matters to attend to."

"What sort of matters could be more important than maintaining family connections? It was bad enough that you left the concert early the other night—really, I do not understand what you are about. If you are so intent on being unsociable, why do you not just go back to Uppercross. We do not wish to risk offending our cousins." Elizabeth returned her teacup to its saucer, unaware that her memory of Anne at the concert was a draconic persuasion.

She glanced at Father who rolled his eyes. "Your sister has a good point. Perhaps it is time for you—"

Anne set down her still empty teacup and turned to fully face him. "Pray, Father might I speak to you in your office. Alone?"

"I do not see why that is necessary! What can you not say in front of me?" Elizabeth folded her arms and tried to don an authoritative expression. She would be disappointed to know it was only haughty.

"Pray Father, alone." Anne stood and strode out toward the room Father had claimed as his study at Camden Place.

Heavy footfalls rang on the tile behind her. Thankfully only one set, Father's.

She stormed into the room and stopped dead center, facing the large desk, not turning to look when father stomped in and slammed the door shut behind him.

"What is the meaning of this Anne? I will not be spoken to in my own house in such a manner!" He stationed himself behind the desk.

"You may take that up with the Blue Order, then, not with me. What I have to tell you is from them, not of my own making." She folded her arms over her chest.

"I do not care for anything they have to say. You may keep it all to yourself. You are Dragon Keeper now; it is your job to manage all that nonsense."

"Kellynch has filed a complaint against you for violations of the Charter and of the Accords themselves."

"That is your problem now, not mine, Dragon Keeper." He snarled the final words.

"That does not change anything that has happened in the past. You are responsible for your choices and actions, or failures to act in these matters. The Order is very clear, I do not take on the blame for those things with which I was not involved."

"I have washed my hands of them. They cannot compel me—"

"Yes, in fact they can. You are to appear at the Blue Order court two days hence to answer for the charges against you."

"And if I do not?"

"I imagine they will send their guard here and take you in by force."

He edged back half a step, losing color in his face. "They cannot do such a thing."

"Actually, they can. And they will if you do not cooperate. I have seen their guard myself. I know you do not care for my opinions, but you are in a very precarious situation. It will not help your case if you are uncooperative." Would they send cockatrice after Father along with the men?

"What do you think they can do to me? They have no real authority."

"You stand to lose the estate. The dragon is the true landowner—"

"Stuff and nonsense." He slammed his fist on the desk. "A beast cannot own land. They can do nothing of the sort." He dropped into the chair behind his desk and leaned back, chest puffed and proud. "And now, not even young Mr. Elliot will take my estate."

Bile rose in her throat. Good thing she had not eaten. "What do you mean by that?"

"My son will inherit from me."

"You do not have a son."

"I will soon enough."

"Without a wife you cannot have a son."

"I am off today to purchase a license. Elizabeth will plan the wedding breakfast. She will require your assistance, I am sure."

"Mrs. Clay?"

Smug. That was the only way to describe his look. Utterly and completely smug, as though he had just won the day.

"There is no way to know it will be a boy."

"She has born two sons already. There is every reason to expect this one is as well. She tells me all the signs are there."

She drew three long, slow breaths, just enough to clear the bitterness from her mouth. "The Order will not care if there is an heir or not. You stand to be stripped of Kellynch estate—"

He slammed his hands on the desk and sprang to his feet. "Enough! I have heard enough! Do not speak of this or anything of that dreadful Order ever again. I will not hesitate to see you removed from Bath—"

"I cannot leave Bath, not before the court proceedings. Then I will be happy to go far away. Now, I have discharged my responsibility. I will see you at the court proceedings." She yanked the door open, stormed through, and slammed it behind her.

Yes, the walking dress had been the right choice. She needed air, and she needed it now.

Crisp, somewhat damp, dragon musk-filled air swept around her as she stomped down the mews to the street. Overcast skies spoke more of late autumn than they did of rain. Just as well, she had left her umbrella in the house, and it was not worth going back for that.

The shadows cast by her deep bonnet did indeed keep most passersby from staring at the colorful marks on her face. But it did block much of her peripheral vision. She had never noticed it before, but after what had transpired near the Upper Rooms, the sensation of not knowing all that was around her proved almost too much to bear.

Should she return to the Order? Surely, she could find welcome there, Lady Elizabeth had intimated as much. Perhaps later, but she could not face so many people, so many dragons right now. But she needed a friendly face, the comfort of knowing she was not entirely alone. Only one place in Bath could she find that.

By the time she reached Westgate Buildings with its severe windows and crooked front door, her heart pounded in her ears, leaving her head aching and her lungs clamoring for air. She all but tore off the foul bonnet as soon as the landlady admitted her and pointed her in Mrs. Smith's direction. Technically that was rude, but not having to deal with potential questions about her injuries was such a boon she would be grateful for it.

Dark narrow stairs would have been foreboding had a friend not awaited at the end of them. The noise of the other lodgers who shared the haphazard parlor barely changed as she reached the top of the stairs. Mrs. Smith's door stood ajar, but she paused and knocked at the door frame.

Rooke hopped into view and squawked. "Miss Anne! Come in! Come in!"

Anne slipped into the dark, narrow bedroom and Rooke pulled the door shut with a rope tied to the doorknob.

"Your face … so, it is all as Rooke told me." Mrs. Smith propped herself up in bed, face drawn and tight. She drew her tattered bed jacket close around her. "I am so sorry, Miss Anne, so very sorry."

Anne pulled the single chair in the room close to the bed and sat down. Even for a good friend, this seemed excessive concern. "There is no lasting harm, I think. You need not worry."

"It is all I have thought about since Rooke brought me the news last night."

Rooke hopped up on the bed and stared at Anne's face, cocking her glossy black head this way and that. "Wish I 'ad been there sooner." She clacked her beak, a softer version of Lady Russell's expression.

"I am very grateful to you, Rooke, for sending the guard to my rescue. I shudder to think what might have happened without their timely arrival. Your Friend was very brave last night, you know."

"But I have not been." Mrs. Smith sunk back against the headboard, miserable and small. "I cannot tell you how sorry I am. I should have spoken sooner."

"Spoken about what?" Anne's stomach flipped, and settled, cold and hard in her belly.

"Mr. Elliot is not unknown to me. I should have warned you of him earlier. I should have told you as soon as I knew he was paying attentions to you that he was not to be trusted."

"You know Mr. Elliot?"

"Yes, I am sure I wrote to you of it, but it was a long time ago. He and my husband were in business together."

Anne pressed her pounding temples. "I do not recall …"

"He was the wine merchant that my husband transported merchandise for. But the business went badly, and he left us, left me, in the straits you have seen. My husband was easily persuaded you see, and I have long been suspicious of Mr. Elliot's ways. He may have had a dragon, that cockatrice Rooke told me about, involved in the affair. I should have told you immediately."

A wine merchant? Elliot a wine merchant? Anne blinked hard, willing the world to stop spinning.

"Pray will you forgive me for not speaking up sooner? When I heard he was interested in you, I hoped he had changed, become worthy of you. I have often been told I am too hopeful in the good nature of people. But when he had that falling out with Mr. Shepherd not very long ago—"

Anne lifted open hands. If only she could make it all stop! "What has Mr. Elliot to do with my father's solicitor?"

"Rooke overheard them arguing about a shipment of wine that Mr. Elliot was to have delivered to Mr. Shepherd, but never made good on. That made me certain he had not altered his ways. I should have told you immediately. But I was afraid that you might be fond of him and would be angry at my speaking out against one of your relations, so I held my peace."

"My cousin, Mr. Elliot, was a wine merchant doing business with my father's solicitor?"

"Had you known the sort of cad he was, perhaps you might not have been with him last night—"

"That is why I saw the goings-on last night. I watch him for anything that might be used to force him to make things right with my Friend." Rooke squawked and flapped.

"I suppose you have good reason to keep watch on someone who had done your Friend such harm." Anne breathed slowly, deeply, but it did not help.

"I am supposed to help her any way I can, and knowing what is going on is very helpful." Rooke flicked her tail.

"Pray forgive me, I have been so rude in having all of the conversation myself. You seem very pale, are you well?" Mrs. Smith asked.

"No, no, worry not. I appreciate what you have

told me very much. The entire matter is in the hands of the Blue Order now, and they will handle it appropriately I am sure."

"How is your family after all that has transpired."

"My father is difficult, my sister indifferent. Mrs. Clay is pleased to be pleasing—"

"Mrs. Clay?" Rooke hopped and flapped violently.

Heavens above, no! "You have news of her as well?"

"I have regularly seen her coming and going from the house Mr. Elliot let. I do not expect they were merely discussing matters of business." Rooke looked down and dragged her taloned foot along the dingy counterpane.

Anne dragged her hand down her face.

"There is more to the tale?" Rooke hopped a little closer, though Mrs. Smith reached to restrain her.

"Pray forgive me, but I do not wish to speak of it. I must respect the privacy of those involved, at least for now. I am certain that matters will become well known soon enough."

Rooke cawed something that sounded like she was trying to be sympathetic despite her frustration at being denied a fresh bit of gossip.

Mrs. Smith looked as though she had already guessed at the truth. "Is there anything that can be done?"

"It is all very complex. I am not sure." Anne clutched her hands in her lap. "Would you both be willing to speak to the Blue Order about these matters should they ask?"

"Of course, we will." They both nodded vigorously.

"Thank you for that. Pray excuse me, I must go,

now." Anne curtsied and left, her feet heavy and head spinning.

26
Chapter

WENTWORTH STORMED OUT of the Blue Order offices, forceful enough to set the cockatrice guards on the rooftop squawking. The nip in the air, despite the bright sun, helped cool his temper just a mite. Only a mite. And the heavy dragon musk in the air did just the opposite.

His heels clomped loud against the stone walk and echoed against the nearby buildings. Dragons—bloody nuisance dragons!

Naturally Laconia would have told the Sage he was the perfect person to explain the situation with Cornwall to Kellynch's Keeper. Meddlesome, overbearing creature. Just because he was happily settled with a mate, and now eggs, did not mean Laconia needed to try to manage his life as well.

Croft would have been entirely qualified to explain the situation to Anne and leave Wentworth to manage the demanding, petulant Cornwall. That creature made Kellynch look like a tractable, pleasant lizard. But no, Laconia had to purr and rub his head under the Sage's hand, offering his helpful suggestions that Wentworth was the man for the job.

Bother these dragons!

They only made things more complicated and difficult. There were moments that leaving them and everything they meant behind was tempting. Sorely tempting.

A crowd milled near the yellow-orange Bath Stone walls of the Pump Room and the warm baths, like they always did. Sheep unaware of what was really going on around them. Contented little sheep.

Could he go back to being such a creature, blissfully ignoring the Blue Order world? The intrigue, the danger that ran just below the surface of the mundane?

Damn it all, no he could not. Every sense that he had refined at sea—knowing where he was and what was about and what might be lurking nearby, everything which kept him alive would have to be set aside if he wanted to divorce himself from dragons.

No, that would not do. Even if it were possible, he would not.

Somehow, he would master this; he would make a way. He always had. He always would, and Laconia would be there to help him as he always was.

Assuming Wentworth did not do something colossally stupid.

Damn! Damn! Damn! Damn! He muttered in time with his pounding steps.

Therein lay the challenge.

He stalked up Westgate Street—was everything in

Bath uphill? No, this was not the way to Camden Place. Eventually he would get there. Yes, he was taking the long way about. But it was better this way. Much better. A long brisk walk always improved his chances of not saying something untoward.

Blast it all!

Blast and botheration!

Blast Sophy and her meddling. He was no schoolboy in need of his sister's unsolicited advice.

Blast Anne for her sudden backbone and choice to exercise it. But dear God she was beautiful when she did. Fiery, passionate, incomparable. Yes, he wanted her to be determined, to be strong and sure—but perhaps not at the expense of his pride.

Pride.

Yes, it was his pride.

Damn it all. He kicked a clod of dirt hard enough to make it explode in a shower of dust covering the legs of his trousers.

Pride. The defining Elliot trait. The one he despised only slightly less than a weak will. The trait he assiduously avoided … but perhaps not assiduously enough. At least according to Sophy, it was not.

She declared him to be nursing a wounded ego. Did he really wish to allow his pride to stand in the way of what he truly wanted in life, of his happiness—and perhaps Anne's as well.

How would Sophy know anything about Anne's happiness—or what would make him happy?

What did he want? Everyone seemed so certain that he wanted a wife, but was that true?

A squawk, somewhat familiar, echoed overhead. He stopped and peered into the sky. A small black speck circled overhead. Too small to be one of the

Blue Order guard—who was it? He should remember. Perhaps it would come to him later. A cool breeze tinged with dragon musk raised gooseflesh on the back of his neck, and he returned to his brisk pace.

Dragons, he was more or less stuck with. But a wife? Did he really want, really need a wife?

A bachelor was free, master of his own destiny. He was unencumbered by the responsibilities and the burdens of a married man. He could move and do as he liked without answering to anyone. Much like the captain of a ship. It was an admirable life.

Admirable if one enjoyed being seen by society as something less than a true man.

Damn it. Damn it. Damn it. He clenched his fist and tried not to punch the air.

There it was, the harsh truth. Though he might have the rank and respect of an officer, as long as he remained unmarried, society would deem him more than a boy but less than a man: incomplete and immature and not ready to take his place in the community at large.

And lonely.

The rest he could argue and deny, manage to make his way around, but lonely, that he could not escape. Laconia was right. He was lonely for a companion, a warm-blooded one, one who—

"Oh, pray excuse me!"

He jumped back. "Anne? Good God, Anne! What happened?" Her face! Her eyes, so worn, so drawn. He caught her elbow. For a moment she looked like she would pull away, but then she leaned into him hard. He tucked her hand into the crook of his elbow. "Where are you going? Pray, allow me to escort you."

"I do not wish to delay your business." The protest seemed half-hearted.

"You are my business."

She gasped and stared.

"The Blue Order has sent me to explain to you the case of Cornwall against Kellynch."

She wavered and leaned into him heavily, as though her knees might fail, eyes very bright. This was not the woman from the Cobb at Lyme, ready to face down a dragon, not the woman from the alley by the Assembly Rooms, who stood up to that human predator, Elliot.

"What is wrong? What happened?"

She shook her head slowly, forlorn as a lost lamb. "I do not know what to do."

When had Anne ever not known what to do? Except, of course, when she was being illegally persuaded by a certain cockatrix. It was her defining trait, the core of who she was. Seven different things tumbled through his mind, but he bit all of them back.

"I do not know what to do. I do not even know where to begin."

"You will sort it out. I have watched you do just that, amazingly well. I have confidence in you."

"But I do not." She bowed her head, a suspicious shining trail on her cheek.

"Do you want help?" He held his breath, counting heartbeats to keep from saying more.

She squeezed his arm and swallowed hard, a faraway look in her eyes as though calculating the cost. What had taught her to think in such terms?

He pressed his hand against hers, firm, but not so firm she could not easily slip away.

"Yes." The breeze nearly carried away her whisper. "I need help."

"Allow me to escort you home—"

She pulled back. "No, that is not the sort of help I need."

"I know, but we should not talk of those things here."

A little look of relief in her eyes! "I do not wish to go back."

Heavens above, what happened? No, that was not for right now. "I am sure there is a room available at the Order if you wish. Or—" Pray let her agree! "—I am certain Sophy would delight in you coming to Royal Crescent."

She would not meet his eyes, her face so pale she just might faint. "I … I would like that very much, if you do not object."

He pressed her hand again and set off, slowly, far too slowly, for Royal Crescent.

The walk which should have taken half an hour took up the better part of an hour, with her leaning on him heavily. Not speaking, just one slow step after another, agonizingly long. What could have happened to leave so strong a woman as her in such a state? If only he could know.

At Royal Crescent at last, he ordered tea from the housekeeper and steered Anne into the red and yellow parlor facing the mews. It was not his favorite room, but asking her to climb the stairs now might be too much. The little garden that filled the window was autumn-sparse, but vaguely reminiscent of the gardens of Kellynch. Perhaps that would help. She sat on the plush red fainting couch near the window, collapsing into the high scrolled side. He pulled up a

Trafalgar chair very close.

Silent tears trickled down her injured cheek. He pressed his handkerchief into her palm, lingering a moment as he touched her hand. She managed a weak smile.

"What help do you need? Is there something I can do? Pray tell me what I can do."

"Everything, everything is wrong and worse than I ever expected. I do not even know where to begin."

"Begin anywhere, and we can piece together what tack to take."

She drew several shuddering breaths and dabbed her eyes with the handkerchief. "Father thinks his son will inherit Kellynch, but he refuses to appear at the Blue Order court and the estate may very well be taken from him entirely. He is to get a license and marry Mrs. Clay because she promises him it will be another boy as she has two already. A son is the only reason he would marry her, I am sure. She is the daughter of a solicitor who has been buying wine that I think was stolen from Kellynch's hoard by the man who wanted to marry me to protect me but I think was just trying to protect himself because he knows a wife would not testify against her husband, and he thought I knew what he was about and why he was trying to frame Kellynch with his earnings from the wine so he could get rid of the dragon, but Lady Russell did not think so and now she is in a very great deal of trouble with the Order, and I do not know what will become of her and it is all my fault and I do not know what to do to resolve any of this!" Gasping for breath, she dropped her face in her hands, quivering.

He bit his tongue against the many questions fighting to be answered. No wonder she was overwhelmed. So very, very much. It was a wonder she could still stand.

One thing at a time. Sir Walter and Mrs. Clay's affair did not need to be dealt with immediately. The Blue Order guard would see he appeared in court when summoned, so that could be left in their hands. But the rest?

"Who stole the hoard?" he whispered. Pray she would slow down and breathe as she spoke this time.

"Mrs. Smith told me Mr. Elliot was known as a seller of fine wines. He contracted with her husband to ship them. Mr. Shepherd recently inherited a large sum of money and bought wines from him. He brought wine to Kellynch once and its label matched the crates Lady Russell and I found in the empty hoard room. Jet, Mr. Elliot's cockatrice Friend, has been on Kellynch since the year nine—I did not know then that they were Friends. I would not have permitted him to stay had I known."

"Of course." A shudder ran down his spine. A spy keeping watch over her all this time!

"We have been troubled by trespassers on the estate. Shelby would chase them off, but never actually caught any of them. I had thought it was Cook selling scraps from the kitchen at night. But now, now I believe that Jet somehow helped Mr. Elliot to sneak on to the estate and steal from us for these five years."

"That would make sense. It would have been difficult to steal the hoard in its entirety all at once. But it still surprises me that Kellynch might have hibernated through such a violation."

"I do not understand it either. But, not long ago, after such a trespass, I found the estate charter trod in the mud. He must have had it and dropped it whilst there. He asked me about it in the year nine when he visited. I could not find it then, nor since. But perhaps he found it for himself while he was at Kellynch—gracious! Perhaps he found it even before I looked for it and asked me for it as some sort of cruel tease. It is very much in his character."

Wentworth muttered something a lady should not hear. Damn! A woman who heard dragons could probably hear that, too!

"When I wrote condolences to him on the death of his wife, I also told him I had found it. It is possible he did not even realize he had lost it until I pointed it out. I think it quite possible he believed I had worked out what he was doing, even though I had not." She clutched her hands together and stared at them.

"So, you think his quest to marry you was to protect himself from your testimony against him?"

She nodded, meek and unsure. "He has always wanted the estate without the dragon. I am sure that is why he has tried to use the gold coins to frame Kellynch for possessing illegal gold."

"No, I do not think that is what has been going on."

She looked up at him, eyes wide and a little afraid. "What do you mean? How do you know?"

"On behalf of the Order, I have been investigating a matter with Cornwall for some time. I had been asked to seek Kellynch's help, as a marine wyrm, to investigate a contested shipwreck near Cornwall's territory. The coins you gave me, according to the cargo manifests, they match what would have been on that ship. They are not common coins. There is little chance Elliot could have come by them himself."

She pressed a trembling hand to her lips. "You think Kellynch might have stolen them himself? From Cornwall, the Prince's dragon?" The question ended in a plaintive little squeak.

"I do not like it, but it does appear so."

"It does not make sense. Why would he have stolen from the dragon who granted him the estate? Unless I have misread the document, which is possible with all the stains—I thought Cornwall granted Kellynch the estate in payment of some debt. It does not make sense. Even for a hoarding dragon in the throes of hoarding hunger, stealing from one so much more powerful seems irrational. Besides, Kellynch's hoard is wine, why would he steal gold?"

"Why indeed? Why indeed? Have you the original charter here in Bath?"

"In my books at Camden Place."

"We must—" he sighed and bit his tongue. "Would you be willing to send for those to be brought here? Perhaps further study of the document in light of some of the histories in the archives here might give further insight into the nature of Kellynch's motives."

"What will that tell us?"

"I do not know, but it certainly seems worth knowing."

"But against Cornwall?" She lifted empty open hands. "Can anything make a difference? He is royalty! What hope does Kellynch have?"

"That does tend to move things in Cornwall's favor." He raked his hair with his hand. "But dragons are a bit different to men in that regard. The Accords tightly control the ways in which dragons can interact with one another. Theft, lying and deceptions are dealt with stringently among them, especially the major dragons, who might use those offenses to start a dragon-on-dragon war. Those must be avoided at all costs, so the Accords can actually restrain even a royal dragon's behavior."

"Even if that is true, if Kellynch is guilty of stealing gold, will not the punishment be very severe?"

"It could be."

She drew several long, slow breaths. "If Kellynch is executed," her voice wavered, "what becomes of the estate?"

"It becomes property of the Blue Order, to assign to another dragon as necessary."

"And my family will be left without a home. Whether Kellynch is guilty or not, either way, Father is going to lose the estate."

"I am afraid so. I hardly see another way." Damn it all. If only he could offer some comfort, some assurance. She had been a Dragon Keeper after all. The Order should offer her at least some sort of assistance. But there was no guarantee that they would.

She wiped her cheeks with the back of her hands. "What is to become of a disgraced, unseated, Dragon Keeper then? Do Dragon Keepers need governesses?" She pulled her shoulders back. Already looking for solutions, for ways to manage. That was the Anne he knew.

He looked deep into her eyes and spoke slowly, intentionally. "You could become my wife."

"I cannot bring such disgrace upon you. You have a career among the Blue Order ahead of you. Association with me—"

He took her hand and held it firm. Finally! "Should you not permit me to decide that? My prize money permits me to decide if I wish to work for the Order or not. And if I have a wife, I just may not want that."

"You would give that up—"

"I am not so certain I want to spend my days chasing down so many intrigues." Her eyes were so lovely and so sad. He stroked her still damp cheek with the back of his fingers. "But I am certain I want to spend them with you. And Laconia agrees—he insists actually."

She chuckled softly and pressed her cheek into his hand. "I have regretted nothing more than being persuaded by Lady Russell."

"And I have regretted nothing more than allowing my resentment to fester and my pride to keep me from seeking you out again. Pray, will you permit me another chance?" He held his breath.

"I will."

27
Chapter

October 13, 1814

THE NEXT MORNING, Mrs. Croft poured tea for Anne in the morning room, a restful, generously large room painted in sunshine yellow and adorned with land-scapes featuring the seaside, lakes, and several rivers. The large windows facing the street brought in the morning light and fresh breezes—tinged with dragon musk. A round table and pair of side-boards against the wall, all in ebony with inlaid mother of pearl chinoiserie elements, fitted in the room properly, adding to the light and airy feeling throughout. The fragrant, jasmine tea, tasting like mother's garden, felt right in the space, sweet and tranquil. Would that things would stay that way.

But there were dragons involved.

The Admiral and Wentworth had left for the Blue Order offices early that morning—a very great deal of business to attend to, they said, and departed before she could inquire about any further details. Had they told Mrs. Croft their business? Was she politely refusing to bring up difficult topics of conversation, or did she really not know? It was difficult to tell and entirely improper to ask.

Probably just as well—Anne did not really want to talk about it.

Mrs. Croft, notable for her lack of the mobcap that most married women wore, passed her a platter of warm, sweet-scented Bath buns. They would go very well with the tea. "Keep in mind that Frederick has said nothing to me. But, knowing him as I do, am I right to guess that congratulations might be in order?"

Anne nearly dropped the platter. "What would give you that idea?"

"When a man, who has been brooding as long as he has, suddenly stops, it attracts no little notice. Heavens, even the Admiral noted it, and he is not exactly one who might be considered observant of such things." She chuckled and lifted an eyebrow, a little too knowing.

Anne stared into her teacup. "We have … an understanding … but what exactly is to become of it depends on the outcome of tomorrow's … events."

"Pray forgive me if I seem like a meddling older sister—which I do not believe I am—but I do not understand how that has any effect upon any understanding between you. It is your father who is under scrutiny, not you."

"Be that as it may, it is difficult to know how one might feel when considering becoming connected to a family in disgrace. Right now, it is only a very likely possibility. When it happens, I do not want him trapped with no way out." Even if Wentworth had insisted it was unnecessary, it was.

"I think you underestimate him."

"I know, which is why I must allow him a way out, just in case." Anne pulled off small pieces of her Bath bun and lined them up on her plate. The sultanas were distributed very evenly throughout the bun. She must ask where Mrs. Croft ordered them.

"Have you given any thought to the wedding breakfast?"

Wedding breakfast? No, that had truly been the farthest thing from her mind. Who would even host such a thing?

The butler, in Blue Order livery, appeared in the doorway, a silver salver in hand. "A message just arrived for Miss Elliot. It is from the Order. A chair is waiting outside to convey her there."

Heart thundering, Anne took the folded note from the tray. The handwriting—it was from the Sage. "Pray forgive me. I must leave immediately. Lady Elizabeth—" She glanced over her shoulder. The butler had disappeared. "It is in regards to Lady Russell. I thought that was to be dealt with tomorrow. I am hardly prepared."

"If the summons were from anyone else, I would be concerned, but from Lady Elizabeth, I am sure it will be well. It will be." Mrs. Croft took Anne's hands and squeezed them firmly.

"I hope you are right. I truly do." But she hardly expected it.

Anne hurried upstairs for her bonnet and pelisse. It would probably be easier if she knew what she hoped for from the Order, or even what she dreaded. But she did not.

Even with everything she had done, Lady Russell had been her friend for a very long time, and her mother's friend before that. Did not that count for something? It seemed like it should, but how exactly it might felt entirely unclear.

Half an hour later, another Blue Order butler ushered her through the ground floor of the Offices, down a wide limestone staircase lined with scrolled iron railings, to a room on the first level of the basement—just how many underground levels were there? Anne had not dared ask, but it did make one wonder.

Torches and mirrors lit the stairs and the wide hall that came off the broad landing and led them to the right. An open door, light spilling out into the hall, invited them.

"Miss Anne Elliot," the butler announced at the arched doorway, beside a heavy oaken door, banded with iron straps.

Anne took a hesitant step through.

Lady Elizabeth sat behind a large oak desk in the middle of a large red room with a polished limestone floor. Every sound seemed to echo off the walls and floor making it seem much bigger and colder than it was.

Frosted windows lined the far wall behind her, just below the ceiling. Those must have been near the street level, given the shadows that passed by. Light from the narrow windows reflected off cleverly placed mirrors, brightening the room considerably. Candelabras lit the dark corners opposite the windows. More mirrors behind them multiplied the light. The faint smell of honey—beeswax candles—hung in the air along with the stronger scent of dragon musk.

A long plain wooden table stood to the right of the desk. A vaguely familiar bald man with well-defined scars on the left side of his head and a red and black drake bearing a pronounced spinal ridge sat behind it. Regional Undersecretary Peter Wynn and his friend, Jasper.

She had not seen him since her last trip to Bath five years ago, but they had corresponded a number of times in the years immediately following that visit. Two, maybe three years had passed since a letter had come from him.

Baby firedrake Pemberley, her red hide freshly brushed and oiled, sat on the floor next to Lady Elizabeth's desk, a little like a dog at attention. Oh, that comparison would probably be insulting! Her eyes were bright and attentive, the tip of her tail twitching in anticipation, or was it excitement? Or maybe it was simply with the effort to be quiet and still. A plain wooden chair stood perhaps a yard away from Pemberley, facing Lady Elizabeth's desk.

"Pray come in Miss Elliot." Lady Elizabeth stood and gestured toward the empty chair. Her gown was Order-blue, cut in a military style, reminiscent of an officer's coat. "Pray forgive the very short notice. Cownt Matlock only just gave his approval for us to meet, and I did not want to chance him changing his mind before we could do so."

Anne drew in deep measured breaths with each step toward that chair. If she could just continue to breathe, all would be well. "May I ask what this is about?"

Mr. Wynn muttered something she could not quite make out under his breath, and Jasper picked up a pencil and opened a large book.

"That comment does not need to be part of the record, Jasper. I will tell you when to begin keeping notes." Lady Elizabeth glowered at Mr. Wynn.

A sensible person would have run for cover upon finding themselves on the receiving end of that look. Mr. Wynn grumbled further. A bright blue blur streaked from Lady Elizabeth's shoulder to hover in front of Mr. Wynn, scolding and chittering very high and fast, then dove for his ear.

He jumped and covered his ear with his hand. "Pray forgive me, Lady."

"Miss Elliot, I believe you are already acquainted with Regional Undersecretary Wynn and Jasper?"

Anne nodded.

"Jasper will be taking the official records of this meeting—you may begin now. Mr. Wynn will represent the local jurisdiction. However, by decree of Cownt Matlock, the Blue Order council maintains authority in this case, and as its representative, I will be the presiding officer."

Mr. Wynn tried to school his features into something acceptable, but with only minimal success.

Lady Elizabeth, raised her eyebrow, but said nothing more. "April, please ask them to bring in the prisoner."

Prisoner.

The cold word cast icy tendrils, sliding down her spine and reaching for her heart. So, the fine lady cockatrix was now 'the prisoner.'

"I petitioned Lord and Cownt Matlock to permit Lady Russell's case to be tried by special council, away from the main court. The cases to be considered tomorrow are particularly difficult and contentious. I believe that those would unfairly influence judgements against Lady Russell. However, as the most gravely injured party, I am willing to hear you if you object to this plan."

The case was to be heard privately with no further audience to hear how she had been persuaded and manipulated by Lady Russell? What had she done to deserve such favor? "Thank you for your concern, Lady Elizabeth. I think it best to proceed as you suggest."

Lady Elizabeth turned to Pemberley, "Remember you are here to observe only. It is a great privilege you are being afforded. If you have questions, we will discuss them afterwards. Do you understand?"

"Understand." Pemberley's baby voice seemed so sincere.

Lady Elizabeth scratched under Pemberley's chin. How easy she was with the dragons and they with her.

Jealousy was not an attractive emotion.

The sound of chains and shuffling steps came from the darkest corner of the room, just beyond a large candelabra. Gracious, there seemed to be a doorway there. How had she missed it?

A white cockatrice with a crooked leg and a scar along the length of his serpentine tail flew in. A somber, but not harsh looking, woman in a deep brown riding habit followed slowly, holding the clanking chains fastened to irons on Lady Russell's legs. A glossy black and silver cockatrice with a crooked tail that looked like it might have been broken flew in behind them. Sir Fitzwilliam Darcy, regal in his Order-blue coat with bright brass buttons, guarded the end of the procession, a Blue Order sword like the one Wentworth had carried strapped at his side.

Lady Russell's eyes widened as she gazed at Anne. Her head feathers drooped and tail feathers seemed oily, even dirty. She stomped and shook her feet, rattling the irons against the stone floor. "I demand you remove these. I am not a common criminal! You have no right."

"You are hardly common, but you are a criminal." Lady Elizabeth folded her arms across her chest. "You have not shown yourself compliant with the Order's requests the past several days. The restraints will remain."

Lady Russell hissed and snapped toward Lady Elizabeth.

"That is not the way to plead your case," the unfamiliar woman said, her tone soft and level, and somehow authoritative in a way Anne had never heard before.

"I did not ask your opinion." Lady Russell snapped near her face.

"I do not need your permission to give it. If you do that again, you will be hooded and have to stand trial unable to see what is happening around you."

Lady Russell gasped and pulled back.

Gracious, the unfamiliar woman was truly formidable!

"Approach the court." Mr. Wynn stood and gestured that Anne should do the same.

Lady Elizabeth remained seated, opening a folio of papers on the desk before her. "Mrs. Fortin, present the prisoner."

"The cockatrix who presents herself as Lady Russell stands before the special Blue Order court."

"I do not need you to speak for me." Lady Russell sneered and tossed her head, her head feathers flopping. "Tell them Anne, I am entirely able to speak for myself."

Lady Elizabeth removed a small gavel from a desk drawer and rapped it on a wooden pad on the desk. "Able, yes, but not allowed. You will limit yourself to answering the questions of the court. You will not address Miss Elliot directly."

"I have known her all her life. Of course, I shall address her."

Lady Elizabeth slowly rose and pulled up the hood of her cloak. How did she make it stand up so crisply?

Mrs. Fortin and Sir Fitzwilliam stepped back. Something about his eyes. Did he know what she was about to do, and if he did, why were there hints of amusement in his expression? April landed on his shoulder and twittered something in his ear. He tried not to smile.

Lady Elizabeth stepped, firm and purposeful, around her desk, grasping the edges of her cloak. "No more!" She leapt the distance from the desk to Lady Russell in a single bound, arms held open, flaring the cloak wide.

Lady Russell squawked and jumped back. Lady Elizabeth jumped forward again, flapping her cloak and—was the Dragon Sage growling?

Angry and perhaps disoriented too, Lady Russell snapped and tried to peck at Lady Elizabeth who deftly dodged. She caught Lady Russell's head in the folds of her cloak and wrapped it tight. Lady Russell danced back, but could not free her head.

She tripped over her chains, landing hard on the stone floor. Lady Elizabeth freed her cloak, swooped in, and plucked a single feather from the back of her neck. Lady Russell screeched and dropped her beak to the floor.

Lady Elizabeth stood over her, making an odd warbling deep in her throat. "You may release her chains, Mrs. Fortin." She folded her hood back and pulled her cloak away from her shoulders. "Jasper, let the court record include Lady Russell's recognition of dominance and Mrs. Fortin's title as Headmistress of Briarwood Sanctuary, assistant to the Lord Physician of Dragons."

Lady Russell shook each foot as Sir Fitzwilliam removed the shackles, and he helped her stand. She flexed her long toes, showing off her talons. Lady Elizabeth turned her back and returned to her desk, Lady Russell following her with her gaze. Why did she not take advantage of her new freedom? Sir Fitzwilliam and both the black and white cockatrice edged a little closer to her.

Lady Elizabeth laid the bright blue feather on the center of the desk, making a show of running it through her fingers. Lady Russell dropped her gaze and hunched.

"Mr. Wynn, please read the charges against the cockatrix who presents herself as Lady Russell." Lady Elizabeth sat at her desk.

Mr. Wynn cleared his throat. "The cockatrix is charged on a total of seven counts: three counts of assuming an illegal identity by the illegal persuasion of both dragon hearers and the dragon-deaf. The fourth count: persuasion of dragon hearers not in the service of self-preservation, continuing over the course of years. The fifth count: utilizing persuasion in the course of an assault on a dragon hearer, Miss Anne Elliot. And the sixth count: engaging in unnecessary persuasions of the dragon-deaf, including the same Miss Anne Elliot, prior to her coming into her hearing."

Yes, it had been very wrong what Lady Russell had done, but somehow it felt very odd, even freeing, to hear someone, someone authoritative and in authority, declare it so. Anne clasped her hands very tightly.

"Finally, the seventh count. She is charged with failure in her duties as Watcher to Kellynch including but not limited to the loss of Kellynch's hoard." Mr. Wynn's voice was shrill as a cockatrice shriek.

Lady Russell shifted her weight from one foot to the other, settling and resettling her wings across her back.

"And how do you plead on these counts? Keep in mind, if you contest these charges, the matter will be tried before the full court tomorrow." Lady Elizabeth folded her arms on the desk and leaned forward. "It is my own opinion that you will find less sympathy there than you will here. But it is your choice. How do you plead?"

Mrs. Fortin leaned close to Lady Russell and whispered something Anne could not make out. Lady Russell hunched into her thinking posture, drawing her head low into her shoulders, chittering softly as though talking to herself.

"How do you plead?"

Lady Russell raised her head slightly, her voice very soft. "I may have done some of the things you have said."

"That is not a plea. How do you plead?"

"I suppose I occasionally persuaded—"

Lady Elizabeth rapped the gavel hard. "I will only ask you once more. If you do not offer a proper plea, I will turn you over to the bondsmen and the mercies of the court. Mrs. Fortin will no longer advocate for you—"

With a brief glance at Lady Elizabeth, Mrs. Fortin edged in front of Lady Russell and looked her directly in the eyes.

Anne held her breath, until her lungs screamed, but what would happen if she disturbed that confrontation?

Mrs. Fortin stepped aside. Anne sucked in a quiet, desperate breath.

"I have done as you said. I am ... am ... guilty." Lady Russell muttered the final words into her chest feathers.

"Let the records show a guilty plea on all counts."

Jasper wrote furiously, her tongue sticking out slightly between her fangs.

Lady Russell had pleaded guilty, to everything. Guilty. How was that possible? Was it simply a matter of Lady Elizabeth showing dominance over her? Could it be that simple? That hardly seemed right. Perhaps the threat of facing the full court had something to do with it, too.

"The prescribed penalty for your crimes is the harshest one established for minor dragons." A chill hush fell over the room as Lady Elizabeth glanced at each one of them in turn. "However, the complexities of this case have afforded me some latitude in judgement."

Anne gripped the hard seat of her chair.

"It is arguable that Kellynch bears much of the blame in these matters. Had his hibernation been handled according to protocols—"

There were protocols to hibernation? She probably should not have skipped those sections in the books on hibernation.

"—the cockatrix presenting herself as Lady Russell would have had proper supervision and guidance to follow Blue Order laws. Thus, Kellynch is in no position to exact punishment upon her and a certain leniency may be applied to her transgressions."

Sweat trickled down the side of Anne's face. Thank heavens! For all she had done, death was not a fitting punishment for Lady Russell. But how did one punish a dragon?

"Thus, a custodial sentence will be applied."

A cage? She would be kept in a cage like an animal in a circus? No, that was too cruel. Anne bit her lip.

"You will immediately cease identifying yourself as Lady Russell and will now take the name Viola, for the Australian flower that matches your coloration."

Lady Russell looked offended, as though she might argue. A sharp look from Mrs. Fortin quashed her response.

"All material possessions acquired by you under that name will now fall under the management of Mrs. Fortin in compensation for her work in taking custody over you and seeing to your proper rehabilitation. You will immediately give up Kellynch cottage and take residence at Briarwood Sanctuary and remain there until such time as Mrs. Fortin deems you a fit member of Blue Order society."

"Why her? Cannot I stay with Anne?" Lady Russell turned an entreating stare upon Anne.

No, absolutely not! Anne drew breath to speak, but Lady Elizabeth held up an open hand.

"One of your victims should not be the one who must also reform you. Mrs. Fortin is the Blue Order's leading expert on bird-type dragons. It is my official opinion that Viola's best chance for rehabilitation is with Mrs. Fortin. If Mrs. Fortin deems her intractable and irredeemable, then the court will have no alternative but to turn her over to Kellynch."

Lady Russell gasped and chittered.

"The court is affording you every possible opportunity and leniency, Viola. It will be in your talons to determine what is to become of you. Since it has already been determined that you will attempt escape, and long-term restraint in shackles results in serious injury, your wings shall be clipped to prevent flight and your talons filed to prevent running, and they are to remain so until Mrs. Fortin and I agree otherwise."

Lady—Viola—trumpeted an ear-splitting shriek, half-terror, half-protest.

"If you resist in any way now, or in the future, your sentence at this special court will be overturned and you will be remanded to the regular court—"

"No, no. I … I will … comply." Viola's head and wings drooped; her tail feathers hung limp against the floor.

Mrs. Fortin smoothed the feathers along her back. "You are very fortunate to be offered such mercy. I have every faith in you that you can make good of this. It will not be easy, I am sure, but Briar and Ebony will assist you as well." The black cockatrice chirruped something that sounded encouraging, at least in a draconic sort of way. The white one echoed the sentiment. "You should thank the Dragon Sage for convincing Cownt Matlock to allow her jurisdiction over your case."

"Thank you, Lady Elizabeth," she muttered, head still very low.

That was the first time Lady—no, it was Viola now—had ever thanked anyone in Anne's hearing.

"You are dismissed to the custody of Mrs. Fortin. Do not make me regret this, Viola." Lady Elizabeth stood. "I have been your advocate. Do not make me regret that choice."

"May we have a word with Miss Elliot?" Mrs. Fortin asked.

Lady Elizabeth nodded.

She and Viola approached Anne. Even in the way she walked, Viola seemed an entirely different creature.

"May I write to you and tell you of her progress?" Mrs. Fortin's large, dark eyes radiated quiet strength and understanding.

Lady Russell—no she was not Lady Russell any more—snapped her beak. "No, she does not need to know. I would not have you write such things about me."

"If not her, then I will write to the Sage herself. Part of what you must learn is humility, Viola, and considering what you have done to Miss Elliot, it would seem appropriate that she should be made aware of your development."

"I only wanted the best for you, Anne. You know that."

"I once thought that." Anne looked directly into her huge glittering eyes. Would there be any trace of understanding there?

"It is true."

"I do not think so." Anne swallowed hard, her throat tight. "You have always wanted the best, but for yourself, not anyone else."

"That is cruel!"

"You have treated me exactly as my family has, a means by which to accomplish their own comforts with no consideration—"

"How can you say I have no consideration for you."

"Because it is true. Why else would you have tried to persuade me to marry Mr. Elliot several nights ago."

Lady Russell scratched the stone floor with her talons and let her head hang low. "He had caught me trying to learn the truth about him. He learnt my secrets and threatened to expose me if I did not! It was in self-defense."

"And that simply proves my point. You considered no other solution than to see me tied to such a man the rest of my life."

"That is not fair! I know you. You would have managed him like you manage everyone else."

"And that is to be some sort of comfort to me?" Anne clenched her fists, shaking at her side. "Pray go now. I will no longer pretend that you have ever been concerned for my good or that you have ever really been my friend. I will read your letters, Mrs. Fortin, if you write to me. I can make no promises to return the correspondence, though."

"I will not ask you to. Briar, Ebony, come, we will do what must be done to follow the court's orders and leave immediately for Briarwood."

"I will escort you." That was not an offer, it was a command. Sir Fitzwilliam, hand on his sword, followed them through the opening to the dragon passages where they were swallowed by the darkness. No doubt he would assist if necessary, as well.

She was gone now. Anne might never see her again. Surely, she should feel some grief, some mourning, some emptiness at that. But no, just a cold sense of resolution. It would have to do for now.

"This court is now adjourned. Mr. Wynn and Jasper, give me some time alone with Miss Elliot."

"Yes, of course. When you have finished with the Dragon Sage, pray Miss Elliot, come to my office. There are a few matters I need to go over with you before the proceedings tomorrow." He and Jasper scurried out of the room.

Lady Elizabeth pulled her chair close to Anne's and invited Anne to sit. Pemberley crept close. Anne sank into the chair.

Pemberley laid her head in Anne's lap. "I sorry. She not nice. Not all dragons mean like her."

Lady Elizabeth smiled. "She likes to be scratched behind the ears."

Anne scratched behind Pemberley's ears, and she thumped her tail happily. How astonishing.

"Pray, would you permit me to share a story with you? You might find it rather … relatable."

What had the Dragon Sage in common with her?

"The dragon I served as junior Keeper tried to force me into a most unsuitable marriage. I have some little sense of what you must be feeling."

"I had no idea."

Lady Elizabeth offered a surprisingly candid tale of her experiences with a proud, pushy and petulant dragon—one who had also been wronged by his Keeper— that led her to run away from home and become betrothed to Sir Fitzwilliam before the entire Dragon Conclave.

Pemberley looked up at Lady Elizabeth, adoration in her eyes and voice. "It good. I asked Cownt and he sayed yes. I has two Keepers now."

"Yes, and you have a little junior Keeper now to help us watch over and teach all the ways of dragon-kind."

"I be good to little Keeper. Her name Anne like you." Pemberley nudged Anne's hand for more scratches. "It nice name."

"Dragons are not universally cranky and nasty and awful, though sometimes it seems that some go out of their way to make us believe it. But they are apt to feel wrongs against them most powerfully."

"You are not cross, are you, Vicontes Pemberley? And of course, Uppercross is a very good-natured soul."

"He is exceptional." Lady Elizabeth smiled the way Uppercross often inspired Anne to smile. "He was concerned for Lady Russell's safety and made me aware of her situation in the hopes that some better solution might be reached than simply turning her over to Kellynch."

"I will thank him for it when—if—I next see him."

Lady Elizabeth patted Anne's hand. "If Kellynch does not lose his territory tomorrow, you will be his Keeper."

"How can that be? I am certain that my father will be found in dereliction of his duties and removed from the estate. How can I be his Keeper if I do not even live on the estate?"

"I do not know, to be honest with you. Something will be sorted out. But the question I have for you: are you willing to continue on as his Keeper? Even in cases such as yours, dragons, who are very long-lived, like the continuity of being served by a single family. They often tolerate the bad generations because they loathe change and do not wish to invite any more of it than necessary. Our much shorter lives are quite the bother to them, making them change Keepers far more often than they would like."

"The only time I have spoken to him, Kellynch said that the treaty had been violated, making all agreements null and void. Since the beginning, nothing he had been promised had been honored. He only wanted what was due him. I promised he would have his wine, but then he said something about his lair, food, the personal attentions due him, and a proper territory—so many things he was dissatisfied with. I do not think he will accept me. I believe he would rather eat me." Anne tried to suppress a shudder. "And then there is the other matter—"

"He said that, about wine?" Lady Elizabeth's brows furrowed.

That was her concern? "I thought it odd at the time, but the wrongs have been ongoing for so long—"

"That is very interesting. And it just might prove a suspicion that I have had. Pray forgive me, I must go investigate this further."

28
Chapter

October 14, 1814

THE NEXT MORNING, on Wentworth's arm, with
Admiral and Mrs. Croft on her other side, the walk to
the Blue Order offices on the cobblestone streets
seemed shorter than it had ever been. At least it was
still uphill. What relief that some things would always
remain the same.

Dragon musk hung on the crisp morning air, so
familiar now it seemed normal. Would Bath ever
smell right without it? Did non-hearers like Elizabeth
or Mrs. Clay even notice it, or was it just lost among
the other scents of the city?

She had not bothered to send a note to Father or
Elizabeth to tell them where she was staying. The
servant Mrs. Croft had sent to pack and bring her
things to Royal Crescent said that only Mrs. Clay

made any inquiry after her. At least someone at Camden Place would know where she was in case she was needed. That was a good thing.

Or was it? What would she do if they suddenly sent for her, in need of something? She shook her head sharply. No point pondering that now.

"Are you well, Anne? Do you need to stop and rest a moment?" Mrs. Croft looked at her across the admiral's broad chest.

Though neither of the Crofts were required to be at the trial, Cornwall was. As a courtesy to him, they would also attend and stand in the stead of his thankfully absent Keeper. A dragon of his stature could hardly manage without proper attendants, could he?

He would not have to know that they were there to support Anne as well. He probably would not like the notion of sharing.

"Thank you, no. I am well, just a bit distracted." Anne quickened her pace just a bit.

Wentworth pressed his hand on hers. That was what she needed to focus on. He had not changed his mind and had promised her he would not.

Hopefully, at the end of the day it would still be true.

The offices, with the cockatrice guard stationed on the roof—were there more guards there than usual this morning? It certainly seemed so—rose up before them. Admiral Croft rapped the drake's head doorknocker sharply.

The blue liveried butler ushered them to a sitting room to wait for the bondsmen who would escort them to court. They barely had sat down when the bondsmen arrived; four of them, tall, broad men, wearing Order-blue robes with deep hoods that obscured their faces, frightening in their anonymity. It was not as if any of them had been accused of wrongdoing. Why would they be placed under such sentries?

Laconia spring-hopped in right behind the bondsmen. They stopped him.

"The Dragon Sage has given me permission to attend court with Miss Elliot." He glanced over his shoulder.

Through the bustle of the corridor, Anne could just make out a blue gowned form that could only be Lady Elizabeth, nodding somberly.

The nearest bondsman stepped aside to allow Laconia to pass.

He wove around Anne's ankles, purring loudly. "She thought you might find the formalities of court as unsettling as she did the first time she attended and that a Friend nearby might help."

Anne's eyes suddenly burned, and she blinked furiously.

Wentworth crouched to stroke Laconia's head. "So now you have two Friends, do you? When did this happen?"

"When you stopped being stupid." He rose up on his tail to put his paws on Wentworth's shoulder and bump his head against Wentworth's cheek.

The Dragon Sage was right, not all dragons were grumpy and disagreeable. Some could be very good friends.

The bondsmen led them down the wide grand stairs; three full flights, bordered by iron railings and lit by torches along both sides that ended in a large, nearly circular room. Across from the stairs were three rough, wide archways—entrances from the dragon tunnels. A peculiar damp cold filled the room, reminiscent of the dragon tunnels. Like a basement, but somehow more, the kind of cold that no cloak or blanket would remedy. Laconia pressed against her ankles. He liked it no better than she.

Columns throughout the room seemed to hold up the vaulted ceiling that was perhaps thirty feet high at its apex. Torches stationed on every column and at regular intervals along the walls lit the room. With the aid of many mirrors, the room was bright enough to not feel ominous, but only barely.

To their right stood a high podium with several tables on either side: the Minister of the Court's bench and seats for the rest of the special council according to Mr. Wynn descriptions of the intended proceedings. Anne's heart beat a little faster. This really was a courtroom. There really would be a trial. She had not been so foolhardy as to doubt the reality of Blue Order justice, but now felt undeniably real.

The Crofts were led off toward the left-most tunnel—where Cornwall was waiting no doubt. As cranky as major dragons were in one another's presence, he would be kept away from Kellynch until their case was tried.

"You are Kellynch's Keeper?" a bondsman asked, pointing at Anne.

She tried not to roll her eyes. No, she was just here in a fit of whimsy.

"Come with me, please. The tatzelwurm should remain here. It would not do to surprise Kellynch."

Laconia spring-hopped to Wentworth who released her arm and nodded encouragingly. Yes, focus on that.

Where would he be? There, the witness box to the

far right. How many of those chairs would yet be filled?

The court felt large and empty, at least at the bottom-most level, as she strode through. An upper gallery ringed three quarters of the room, about ten, maybe twelve feet above the floor. An audience was gathering—did they have to pay for this privilege?

No! Pray no! Why did it have to be? Those were the Dalrymples, the Viscountess and her honorable daughter. No doubt the Elliots would be cut by their cousins after this. Father would be—

No, that was not her concern now. He had made his choices and he would have to—

"Why do I need to go there? To the bottom of the room and certainly not to a place that looks like an animals' pen!" The shouting voice was Father's.

She turned toward the voice. Three bondsmen surrounded him, their posture ominous, threatening.

"Anne? Anne? Is that you? Tell these brutes—"

"Do not interfere, Miss. Kellynch needs his Keeper." The bondsman stood to block her view of her father, though she could still hear his angry cries as they moved toward the tunnels.

He blamed her. He always would. Sir Walter Elliot make a mistake? No, that was not possible. Someone else would always be to blame.

Today it would not be her.

They entered the right-most of the dark tunnels.

"You will wait in the first of the waiting rooms with him until you are brought into the court."

Would it make any difference to the bondsman that Kellynch probably wanted nothing to do with her? Probably not. He did not seem the sort to be dissuaded from fulfilling his orders.

"Laird Kellynch, I bring your Keeper." The bondsman pointed to an opening in the tunnel wall, lit by torches on either side.

She drew a deep breath and squared her shoulders. The last time she had tried to talk to Kellynch, through the cockatrice intermediary the Blue Order had sent, he was angry and unwilling to listen. What point in expecting anything different now?

Kellynch rested in the alcove, his long body curled up beneath him, his head perhaps eight feet up, high enough to tower over her. A show of dominance as Lady Elizabeth had warned her. With dragons, everything was about dominance. At least none expected her to dominate Kellynch as Lady Elizabeth had Viola. A mere person could not dominate a major dragon.

"I do not want you here." Kellynch growled, his tall spinal ridge quivering with his heaving breath. He bared his long, pointed fangs and snarled.

Anne bowed her head and curtsied. She stepped just inside the alcove's entrance. "I expected as much. But it is out of my hands. The Order requires me to be here, so I shall stand as your Keeper until I am officially removed from the position."

"I do not like you." A bit of spittle dripped from his fang, landing with a slimy plop on the rough stone floor.

"I understand why. But pray do not judge me by my forefathers. I have had little chance to prove myself to you. I would still like to be able to do that." Could he detect the quiver she felt in her voice?

"Why would I care what you want?"

"In truth, I do not know. My father never has, so why would you?"

He leaned down and peered at her, sea green eyes narrow. "I want only what is due me by law."

"I suppose we are much alike. I want the same thing."

"What is due to you?"

"My dowry—a sum promised to me in the marriage articles between my parents. But there is nothing left to pay it—my father has spent everything. I understand broken promises."

Kellynch snorted. Oh, his breath—acrid, rotting fish! "It makes no difference if you understand or not. Promises have been broken. And worse, what you say now suggests that there is no hope of them ever being fulfilled."

"You are right. I am sorry. I know it makes little difference nor does it do anything to make things right, but—"

A bondsman appeared in the alcove. "It is time, follow me."

Kellynch slithered beside her as though she were not even there. Father gasped as they passed. Kellynch turned his head back to hiss at him. Father nearly screamed. Was it possible that the bondsman chuckled? That certainly could not be proper.

The bondsman led them to a lone chair, in a space large enough for Kellynch to—what did wyrm types do, sit, stand, recline?—surrounded by rails that suggested they should not move from their assigned space. She sat and pulled her shoulders back. Just because she felt small did not mean she needed to act that way too. Father might be an embarrassment to the Elliot name, but she would not be.

Laconia approached, stopping a respectful distance away.

"May I present the tatzelwurm Laconia to you? He … he has been my friend." She looked up at Kellynch.

Laconia stretched out his front paws and pressed his chin to the floor.

Kellynch wove back and forth as though thinking, his spinal fin swaying softly as though in a breeze. "Approach half-wyrm."

That was a new term. Was it as insulting as it sounded?

"What do you want?" Kellynch grumbled deep in his throat.

"May I sit with your Keeper? The Dragon Sage wishes me to keep company with her during the trial." Laconia flattened himself even more against the ground.

"You respect my territory. You may approach." Kellynch settled back into his coils, looking a little pleased.

Laconia slithered to her side and pressed against her legs, purring. Was there a more soothing sound — or was it a feeling?—than a tatzelwurm's purr?

"He is there, with the other witnesses." Laconia pointed a thumbed paw toward three rows of chairs to the right of the judge's bench—witnesses to be called during the trial.

Wentworth sat front and center, straight and proud, just barely glancing in her direction. Why did that make her feel better?

Heaven's above—Mrs. Smith was among the witnesses! White too?

A high, ear-shattering gong sounded from near the stairs. "All rise for the processional."

Anne rose on shaking legs as somber, blue robed

forms filed down the stairs. At the bottom, they proceeded to the left toward the tunnels. Oh, she could just barely see, but yes, there were dragons waiting just at the tunnel entrance.

The first man, who must be Lord Matlock, Chancellor of the Order, tall and proud in his blue robes, paused at the tunnel opening. An enormous blue-green fire drake emerged from the darkness, orange eyes glittering in the torchlight: Cownt Matlock. His stride, his bearing, everything about him announced him as the dominant dragon in the room and all knew it.

A very broad man in a judicial wig followed. That had to be Baron Dunbrook, Minister of the Court. A large, stone-grey drake, standing at least seven feet at the shoulders and that much again at the top of his head joined him from the tunnel entrance. Barwin Dunbrook.

Next in line was Lady Elizabeth, a tiny, stately figure among the men and dragons. It was all she could do not to laugh when little Pemberley—Vicontes Pemberley—waddled up to her as serious and proud as a baby dragon could be. Was it normal for such a young dragon to attend Blue Order events, or had Lady Elizabeth made that happen?

A smaller man, with a shock of white hair and a bit of a limp followed: Sir Carew Arnold, Minister of Keeps. He seemed a very mild, meek sort of man with his slow step and hunched shoulders, but Admiral Croft had warned her his temper was otherwise. A dark wyvern with light streaks met him. That had to be Langham. She was larger than Uppercross and certainly less portly. She walked with the bearing of a proper lady, proud, but not inappropriately so.

The parade continued the circumference of the room until they reached the council seats. Mr. Wynn and Jasper, a journal and pencil held under her arm, joined them there—apparently Regional Undersecretaries did not have the rank to join in the procession.

"The Blue Order Court is now in session," Baron Dunbrook boomed from behind the judge's bench. How was he able to make his voice so clearly heard throughout the whole room? "Earl and Cownt Matlock presiding officers."

The awful sounding gong chimed three times—where was that horrid thing and who was striking it? Several cockatrice—guards stationed on the rails of the nearly full upper gallery—screeched, and Laconia shuddered against her. If he rang that thing again, Anne might very well join them.

Lord Matlock and the rest of the council took their places and sat down, followed by the rest of the room, except for Mr. Wynn who stood before the judge's bench.

"If it pleases the court, I present before you the case of the Blue Order, on behalf of Miss Anne Elliot, versus Mr. William Elliot and his Friend Jet."

"Bring in the prisoners." Had Baron Dunbrook practiced that gunfire-sounding voice?

All attention turned toward the center tunnel where four bondsmen led Mr. Elliot and Jet out in shackles that rattled and jangled ominously with each step.

Anne's heart pounded so loud she could barely hear Kellynch ask, "What did he do to my Keeper?"

"You have much bigger complaints. It is no concern of yours." She did not look at him.

"Present the charges."

"On October 10, 1814 the defendant, Mr. William Elliot and his Friend Jet, did perpetrate an assault on the person of Miss Anne Elliot, striking her and rending her garments in an attempt to compromise her into marriage after she had refused his offer of marriage."

"How do you plead, Mr. Elliot?"

"Not guilty. Miss Elliot's injuries were sustained because she had over indulged in wine and were no fault of mine or Jet's."

"Is that true?" Kellynch whispered.

"No, it is not." Laconia hissed, his tail lashing.

"Has the prosecution any witnesses?"

"I call Rooke, Friend of Mrs. Smith. Approach the bench."

A bondsman rushed in with a plain, sturdy iron dragon perch and set it beside Mr. Wynn. Rooke flew across the court and landed on it.

"State your name for the court."

"I am Rooke, Friend of Mrs. Smith, assigned by the Blue Order to see to her care."

"I object!" Mr. Elliot cried. "She is an operative of the Order. She will say whatever the Order wants."

"Silence! You have not been given leave to speak. One more outburst, and you will be gagged for the remainder of the proceeding." Baron Dunbrook snarled.

Two burly bondsmen beside him edged closer, ready—and perhaps eager—to act on such an order.

"I resent that remark." Rooke flapped her glossy wings, her long black serpentine tail lashing. "I 'ave a reputation for truth in all I say, tho' many don't like it. I be loyal to my kind. Why would I turn against another cockatrice if it weren't true?"

"What did you see that night, and how did you come by seeing it?" Mr. Wynn asked, a hint of frustration in his tone. The torchlight glinted off his bald head, interrupted by the long scar on the side of his face.

"I go out every night to stretch me wings and keep an eye for opportunities for my Friend. She sews, you know, and I watch what the fancy ladies are wearing so that she might make such things to sell to them, providing for herself as it were. So, I were out near the Upper Rooms to see what were being worn to the concert. With all the fine folk here for the Sage's salons and whatnot, I thought to see many new things, ya see. I saw much more than I wanted."

"What did you see?" Mr. Wynn pinched the bridge of his nose.

"Miss Anne there were with that Mr. Elliot," she pointed with her wing. "And he looked like 'e pulled her into the alley and I sayed to myself that could not be a good thing, no, not at all. He were trying to convince her to marry him, and she were refusing. Then Jet appeared all fierce like, and I knew there were going to be trouble, so I flew straight to the Order and called for the guard."

"And are you certain of what you heard him say? It would have been at a great distance."

"As certain as I am that the fine lady in the feathers right above us, she just sayed to her daughter that—" her voice shifted into a very formal, human tone, "—it was shocking, simply shocking that the heir to a great estate could behave in such a way. It is no doubt a reflection on ill-breeding and on the state of the family that its head has not taken him properly under his management." She pointed to Lady Dalrymple in the gallery.

From the other side of the room, Father gasped and choked back something probably quite offensive.

Mr. Wynn peered up toward her. "Is that what you said, Lady?"

Far from being embarrassed, Lady Dalrymple seemed quite pleased to be so noticed. "It is indeed."

"Let the court record show that the cockatrix's ability to hear at such distances has been confirmed."

"Pray, may I be permitted a question in my own defense?" Mr. Elliot asked, so polite and proper. He probably took the threat of a gag very seriously.

"Speak, warm-blood," Barwin Dunbrook boomed, his voice uncannily like his Keeper's.

"What possible reason would Miss Anne Elliot have for refusing an offer of marriage from me? I am heir to the Kellynch estate; she is Keeper to the dragon there. What more natural match is there for her to enter into? While it is clear that her dowry was frittered away in years of bad management, I was willing to overlook the matter in the hopes of being able to protect her from the consequences of the deplorable dragon keeping there. What woman would turn away such a magnanimous gesture?"

Anne clenched her fists and gritted her teeth.

The Dragon Sage stood and went to confer with Cownt Matlock and Barwin Dunbrook. Not their Keepers; that was interesting.

"The court would hear Miss Elliot speak to the matter." Cownt Matlock stood very tall, demonstrating himself the largest dragon in the room. "Approach the court."

The blood drained away from Anne's face. She stood, knees trembling. Laconia pressed in close. He wove between her steps as she walked just like he did with Wentworth. It should have made it more difficult to move, but somehow, it was very supportive. That made little sense, but it was.

"Do explain, Miss Elliot, why an unmarried woman and member of the Order would refuse an offer of marriage that would so neatly resolve the dragon keeping issues of the estate." The question was bad enough, but coming from a huge firedrake like Cownt Matlock made it far worse.

She sucked in a deep breath and pulled her shoulder's back, allowing the faces in the gallery to fuzz into the dim flickers of the torches. "He is a known hater of major dragons. He once called them parasites upon men. I could not attach myself to such a man."

Gasps and muttering filled the gallery and overflowed to the courtroom below.

"I confess, in my youth and arrogance, I did not appreciate the Blue Order as I should have. But I have reformed—spent hours in study at the Blue Order offices, here, in London, all over England. You will find witnesses—"

Anne whirled to face Mr. Elliot. "Study does not mean reform! Your goal has always been to remove Kellynch from the estate. What is more, I believe you responsible for the theft of Kellynch's hoard."

Kellynch bellowed and the court erupted into chaos.

29
Chapter

NO! DRAGON'S BLOOD and damnation!

Wentworth jumped to his feet. That was not how they were going to present that issue. What was she thinking? When Sir Walter was accused of wrongdoing regarding the hoard, then they would pursue the issue!

Baron Dunbrook pounded his gavel. "Order! I will have order in my court!"

Finally, Barwin Dunbrook stood upright on his rear feet and bellowed. The room stilled, a tense pregnant sort of stillness that might erupt at any moment. The hair on the back of Wentworth's neck stood.

"You make a very serious accusation, Miss Elliot. You are aware that the theft of a major dragon's hoard is a capital offense? It would seem your accusation might be motivated to save your Father. Why was this not submitted to the court properly?" Dunbrook's gunfire voice did nothing to calm the stillness.

"I have only just discovered the evidence that made it all make sense." Anne squared her shoulders and stared straight ahead as Kellynch's head hovered above her, staring down at her, perplexed and anticipatory.

"Are you prepared to make your case? The court does not tolerate spectacle nor misdirection."

"Yes ... yes sir, I am." She glanced back at Wentworth, just briefly. Just long enough.

Did she have any idea of the torture it was to remain in the witness box and allow her to face the court on her own?

Yes, she was Keeper to Kellynch. Yes, she was capable, but damn it all, he should be permitted to protect her!

"State your case. Briefly." To say Baron Dunbrook did not look pleased was an understatement. But what did he expect when holding court with dragons?

"Five years ago, Mr. Elliot visited Kellynch estate. During that time, he asked, as heir presumptive, to meet Kellynch. I took him to the lair, but not within. At that time and in his company, I first encountered Jet, his Friend. They made no acknowledgment of their relationship to me and Jet asked permission to stay on the estate, which I gave him. Since that time, Jet has come and gone freely from Kellynch lands."

"There is no crime in going where I am permitted!" Jet cried.

Dunbrook slammed his gavel. "You will speak when you have been given permission and not until. If you cannot comply, you will be hooded."

"Why would Jet have sought permission to be on the estate without revealing his relationship to Mr. Elliot, except to carry on some sort of secret business?"

"That is speculation, Miss Elliot." Dunbrook seemed interested despite his tone.

"On that same visit, Mr. Elliot asked me for the estate charter which was not in my possession. I have been looking for it ever since that time and was unable to find it until this June, in a most unlikely place. It had been trod in the mud on Kellynch grounds during a time that the shepherding drake reported trespassers on the estate. Shortly thereafter, we discovered the hoard cavern empty. I believe that Mr. Elliot stole the charter from the manor, perhaps with Jet's help and used the map on the back to find the hoard room and steal from it."

"Suspicion is not the same as proof." Dunbrook and Lord Matlock exchanged hard to interpret glances, but they were listening and that was key.

"There is more. Mrs. Smith," she looked over her shoulder toward the witness box, "her husband was in business with Mr. Elliot for several years, during which time he was known as a wine merchant."

Noise and angry calls rose throughout the room, to be silenced again by Dunbrook's gavel. "Mrs. Smith, approach the bench."

Wentworth helped her up, weak and frail as a grandmother, and assisted her to the front of the room to stand beside Anne. He stationed himself slightly behind and between them. Laconia wove between them purring.

"Tell the court what you know, Mrs. Smith."

"My husband, Charles Smith, was in the business

of transport. He transported a variety of goods for Mr. Elliot who eventually became known as a wine merchant. The business began failing, though—not enough supply I was told at one point, and Charles died, unpaid and his affairs in shambles, shortly after."

"So, you were a wine merchant, Mr. Elliot?" Lord Matlock crossed his arms over his chest and scowled.

Behind them, Kellynch growled deep in his throat.

"There is no crime in an honest business. A man must make his living." Elliot tried to look confident, but the shackles and chains blunted the effect.

"You do not deny it?"

"No, I do not."

"When did he begin shipping wine?"

"In 1809." Who would have thought Mrs. Smith could sound so sure and strong?

"Does that correspond with his visit to Kellynch estate?"

"Yes, sir it does." Anne stared straight ahead, a tiny tremor in her hand the only testament to her tension.

"That proves nothing!"

Barwin Dunbrook stomped two steps toward Elliot and hissed.

"This is your final warning Mr. Elliot. You will speak when spoken to and not otherwise. When did you stop selling wine?" Baron Dunbrook ordered.

"Earlier this year."

"Which corresponds to the discovery of the depleted hoard. What have you to say to that?"

Elliot's face turned red, then puce. "It still proves nothing. Coincidence alone, nothing more."

"Pray, Baron Dunbrook, there is more. Mr. Elliot

sold wine that matched exactly the empty crates left in the hoard room," Anne said.

Kellynch thumped his tail hard enough to be felt.

"What is your evidence?"

"He did business with Mr. Shepherd, Sir Walter's solicitor. Rooke saw them make the transactions," Mrs. Smith said.

"Mr. Shepherd recently came into an inheritance and began indulging in fine wines. He brought wines, that I believe to have been bought from Mr. Elliot, to my father, wines that matched the crates in the hoard. And sir …"

No, pray do not go there!

"I have proof that places Mr. Elliot in the hoard caverns."

Damn!

Kellynch bellowed and rose up very high, waving his head to and fro. Could Anne not see how much this was agitating him? That could serve no good purpose.

Dunbrook's gavel banged. "Present your evidence."

Trembling so hard she could hardly manage, Anne removed two coins from her reticule. "Mr. Elliot presented me with this coin, which matches one that was found in Kellynch's hoard room. I am told these are of a peculiar nature and had to have come from the same place." She glanced at Wentworth.

"She is correct about the nature of the coins." He nodded slowly. Perhaps he need not have said that, but he had to do something lest he run mad.

"Bring those to me."

"The gold is mine!" Kellynch lunged toward the bench. "It was stolen from me."

Barwin Dunbrook trumpeted and Cownt Matlock growled. Kellynch flinched back.

Baron Dunbrook took the coins and beckoned Lord Matlock, Sir Arnold and the Dragon Sage to examine them.

"How did you come by this coin, Mr. Elliot?"

"I ... I found it in the sea cave in Lyme where Kellynch exposed himself before the dragon-deaf!" He pointed at Kellynch, as though to take the attention off himself.

"That case will yet be heard." Barwin Dunbrook bellowed. "Answer my question."

"It was in the sea cave. I have never been to this hoard you are speaking of."

The Blue Order officers conferred among themselves and the Sage stepped forward, seeming so diminutive among the large men and huge dragons. Even the firedrake who stood beside her was tiny. Yet she radiated a sense of calm and authority Wentworth had never seen before. "There is one more definitive test, that of smell. Kellynch, did you detect human scent in your hoard room?"

"Yes, faint but it was there."

"Allow the bondsmen to blindfold you." The Sage waved toward several bondsmen waiting near the stairs. "We will present you with cloths to smell to see if any match the scent in your hoard room."

Kellynch grumbled and muttered.

"It is not a request." Cownt Matlock snarled.

Kellynch lowered his head and several bondsmen hurried up with a hood-like affair of leather and buckled straps. He snorted and grumbled as it was fitted into place.

Anne dashed to his side and placed her hand on

his scaly green-brown hide. "I am here. Your Keeper is here, and I will not permit advantage to be taken of you like this."

That seemed to calm him.

Remarkable.

Plain linen cloths, each marked with a different number of inked dots, were presented to Elliot, Sir Walter, and Wentworth with instructions to wipe their faces and hands and the back of their necks with them. Sir Walter tried to refuse, until a bondsman threatened to perform the task for him. They handed the cloths to Lord Matlock.

"Lord Matlock approaches from your left," Anne said in a clear strong voice.

Kellynch swung his head in that direction, lowering it slightly.

Lord Matlock handed Anne two of the cloths. "Lower your head toward my voice. Your Keeper and I are holding three articles for you to smell."

Kellynch moved from one to the next, smelling each one twice. Finally, he took the middle cloth in his teeth and shook it violently. "This was the scent in my hoard room. Trespasser! Thief!" He hissed and snapped.

"Lower your head so the blindfold may be removed." Matlock waved the bondsmen into motion and they quickly freed Kellynch. He strode toward the judge's bench. "Let the record show, Kellynch selected the scent of Mr. William Elliot."

"I demand justice! He stole my hoard. I am owed—"

Gasps filled the gallery as Dunbrook banged this gavel. "Order! The special council will deliberate."

The dragons and the council crowded together

around one of the tables while Langham and Cownt Matlock extended their wings to shield them from prying eyes. Even the baby Pemberley edged in close. Surely, she would not be part of the decision making—would she?

Wentworth chanced a glance at Mr. Elliot. He stared, pale and glassy-eyed, at the council—perhaps the reality of the situation had finally sunken in.

The deliberations ended and Dunbrook called the court to order. "It is the decision of the court that Mr. William Elliot and his Friend Jet are guilty of the theft of Kellynch's hoard, and there is only one punishment for the crime. You will be turned over to Kellynch to be eaten."

Mr. Elliot began babbling and stammering as the bondsmen dragged him toward Kellynch.

Kellynch trumpeted in triumph, tossing his head, but poor Anne stood beside him, white and trembling. Who could blame her? The sight would be grisly.

"If it please the court," the Dragon Sage stepped forward facing Kellynch, "there is one small mitigating circumstance. Kellynch, you are not a hoarding dragon."

Kellynch stopped mid-bellow and Anne stared agog.

Not a hoarding dragon? What? How?

"The wine was mine! The charter, it belonged to me!"

"Indeed, it did, but that does not make you a hoarding dragon." She signaled a bondsman who brought her a large demijohn filled with a burgundy liquid.

With long confident steps she approached

Kellynch. "Would you like to have this?"

"Of course, I would. I like wine." Kellynch leaned toward her.

She wrenched out the cork and held it up to him. "Can you smell it? What do you think?"

He breathed deeply and sighed, spinal ridge rippling down his back. "An excellent vintage. I would like it very much."

She offered it to him and he took it in his jaws, upending it into his mouth.

"I submit to the court that this is not the behavior of a hoarding dragon, especially one that has been hoard-starved."

Kellynch dropped the demijohn and it shattered on the stone floor. "What do you mean? I like wine, it is mine by charter. How can you say—"

"Enough lies, Kellynch. You are not a hoarder. Your cache of wine was stolen, but not your hoard, and you are not entitled to eat Mr. Elliot for it."

"But I have been wronged, and I deserve—"

"How you have been wronged, and what you are entitled to will be addressed shortly." The Dragon Sage held her ground and Kellynch loomed over her, breathing heavily into her face. "I insist you permit us to punish Mr. Elliot properly. Your cooperation will be credited to your favor shortly."

"Why should I trust you?" Kellynch hissed.

"Because I understand the wrongs you have suffered and I will see that they are made right."

"What do you think you know."

"Come closer and I will tell you." She whispered into Kellynch's ear.

Anne leaned a little closer, but it seemed as though she could hear nothing.

He became very still and very quiet, frighteningly so.

How could a room so large as the court room be so very, very quiet?

Kellynch bobbed his head slowly. "The court may have Elliot to do with as they will."

Dunbrook banged his gavel—again. He certainly seemed fond of the sound. "The mandatory sentence for theft from a major dragon is confinement in a Blue Order workhouse until such time as the debt to the dragon may be paid off. An additional ten percent will be added to the amount in reparations for the assault on the dragon's Keeper. Take Elliot and Jet away."

Elliot's knees buckled and he nearly swooned. Jet cawed and attempted to flap his wings. Shackles and chains clanked as they were dragged from the court.

"Release me! Release me now! You have no further reason to hold me. That scoundrel stole from the beast, not me. You have no further cause to hold me." Sir Walter banged the rail before him with his fist.

"Need I have you gagged? Your case will be dealt with in turn." Baron Dunbrook shot back. "The court will now hear the case of the Blue Order versus Laird Kellynch."

"What of the complaint I have against the Order?" Kellynch screeched.

"What complaint have you against the Order?" Cownt Matlock sat on his haunches and stared at Kellynch as though entirely surprised.

One did not often surprise a firedrake.

"The Blue Order has betrayed me since the very first moment of my introduction. I have been deceived at every turn, promised things I have never been given, then held to ridiculous rules even in the face of my privations."

"I already said the case against Sir Walter Elliot—"

"His offenses are bad enough, but they are hardly the sum of the damages against me."

The Dragon Sage stepped forward, hands held high and open. "There has not been time to make the rest of the special council aware of your complaints. Pray, Lord Matlock, Cownt Matlock, allow us to hear his complaints now."

Both Matlocks looked confused and even a little offended.

The little red firedrake, Pemberley waddled between the two. "Listen her, she right. She understand things. Many things."

Cownt Matlock snorted—but perhaps he was trying not to laugh at the baby dragon. "It is irregular, but we will hear."

The Dragon Sage extended her hand toward Kellynch. "Pray then, Kellynch, present your offenses to the court."

She was not what he had expected. Ladylike in every sense of the word but with a presence that every dragon in the room respected—every one of them. How had she known Kellynch's secret?

"I have been lied to since I petitioned to join the Blue Order. Cornwall—"

A loud bugle came from the tunnels and thundering steps pounded toward the courtroom. Was the room shaking? Dust fell from the ceiling.

"How dare you accuse me of lying! Do you know who I am?" Dug Cornwall thundered into the courtroom, the Crofts and Sir Fitzwilliam Darcy running after. Bigger that all the other dragons in the room, his dull gold hide seemed to absorb the torchlight. Everything about him screamed privilege and royalty. "I am second only to the Brenin! I will not hear such slander against me."

Cownt Matlock leapt, wings flapping and landed only yards from Cornwall. Barwin Dunbrook and Langham followed, hemming Cornwall between them. Cornwall snapped and snarled. Though the largest of the dragons, the three standing against Cornwall would overcome him quickly, if it came to that. Pray that it did not.

The Dragon Sage gently restrained Pemberley from joining the action. The little firedrake stomped and snorted, wisps of smoke rising from her snout. If the whole scene had not been so dangerous, it would have been humorous.

"You will stand down!" Cownt Matlock boomed. "You are subject to the Blue Order court along with every dragon in England."

Cornwall carried on for several long minutes in a truly royal show of temper. Had he done that before the Prince Regent became his Keeper or had he learnt it recently?

Cownt Matlock belched a jet of flame, singeing Cornwall's snout.

So that was what actual dragon fire looked like! And smelt like—rotten eggs! Wentworth's nose wrinkled, and he coughed.

Cornwall screeched one last protest, then allowed himself to be led to a place that had already been set aside for him, knocking aside the rails serving as a symbolic boundary. Lovely, just lovely.

Wentworth glanced around the room. The only

possible escape might be the right-most tunnel. The dragons blocked all other routes.

Damn.

The Crofts stood to one side of Cornwall, standing in the place of Keepers, though clearly impotent in the situation, and Sir Fitzwilliam—Dragon's blood! He carried a Dragon Slayer in his right hand. Pray let blood not be shed!

Wentworth eased back toward Anne.

"Present your complaint, Laird Kellynch." Barwin Dunbrook continued to stare at Cornwall as if his gaze alone would elicit compliance. Optimistic creature.

"Cornwall deceived me from the beginning. I learned of the Pendragon Accords that created peace between the men and dragons of England from a passing cockatrice at the seaside, near Land's End. Tired of the constant harassment by whaling ships and fishing vessels, I asked Cornwall how I might become a part of this Blue Order. He said I could buy myself entry if I had something that he deemed of sufficient value."

"Membership into the Order has never been a commodity to be bought and sold, even by royalty. It is the decision of the Conclave to admit or deny membership to immigrants. Let the records show Cornwall's offer was an illegal one." Cownt Matlock growled as he shifted his weight from one foot to the other.

Laconia did that when he tensed to spring. Bloody hell!

"In exchange for the location of a shipwreck bearing gold, he promised me all the privileges of a major dragon under the Order. I would have a proper estate and a title would be created for my Keeper that I might have a fitting rank as well. I gave him what he wanted, the location of the Merchant Royal."

The audience in the gallery drew in a collective breath. The Merchant Royal. Everyone knew treasure on that lost ship was legendary.

"But I was deceived. I thought I would have a proper estate in exchange but instead, I was assigned a worthless land-locked estate with Keepers who failed to provide what was due me in every way. Forced to eat mutton, horrid gamy mutton, not fish. Unable to access the sea—torture, simply torture."

"Just as I was unable to access my gold!" Cornwall bellowed. "The information you gave me was worthless. You got as good as you gave."

"You wanted the location of the wreck. You never asked me if it was accessible."

"It should have been clear to you! Why would I want to know the location if I could not possess it?"

"How would I know? Sea dragons do not hoard!"

"But you accepted a hoard as part of the contract." Cornwall half rose on his back legs and flapped his wings, the wing-wind blowing hard against Wentworth's face.

"I am not stupid. Why would I refuse the offer of something valuable? And even that, like everything else, was eventually denied me."

"And that is why you hibernated?" The Sage approached Kellynch slowly, carefully, hands held open in front of her. "The Blue Order—"

"Do not tell me I should have gone to the Blue Order after they permitted me to be cheated in such a fashion. They had already failed me. I thought perhaps that if I slept long enough, the next Keeper would be better."

"But he was not?"

"Worse, as was the one after that who did not even attend when I last woke." Kellynch glanced at Anne, wild-eyed.

Anne mouthed words that looked like 'I am sorry.'

The Sage stopped ten feet in front of Kellynch, craning her neck to look up at him. "Did you return to hibernation when Sir Walter took over as Keeper?"

Kellynch roared, rocking back and forth.

"I suspect you only pretended to hibernate and spent a great deal of time away from the estate, allowing others to manage your responsibilities under the pretext that you were hibernating."

"The Order had done nothing for me, why should I do anything for them?"

Anne gaped at the Sage, then at Kellynch. "I had no idea!"

"The signs you told me of did not add up to waking from a true hibernation, but I was not certain until just now." The Sage glanced briefly at Anne.

"I returned to the sea, yes, and I thought to give up the Blue Order. But Cornwall had gotten his prize, and I still had nothing of value to me. That would not do." Kellynch turned to Cornwall, his mouth open in something that looked very much like a mocking smile.

"You stole my gold! You were seen in my waters! It was you!"

"You are jumping to conclusions," Lord Matlock shouted. "You have no proof—"

Kellynch threw his head back, in something that sounded very much like a laugh which became a cough, then he regurgitated a pile of slimy gold coins on the court room floor. "You took from me; it is only fitting I did back to you in kind!"

Good God! How much gold had he been carting about in his stomach! That was surely more than all Wentworth's prize money—

Cornwall tried to leap on Kellynch only to be stopped by Cownt Matlock and Barwin Dunbrook. Sir Fitzwilliam brandished the sword with eerie expertise. Bondsmen flooded the floor, all bearing swords, and surrounded Cornwall.

Cornwall salivated and writhed, screaming and slashing the air with his wings.

"That is hoarding hunger!" the Sage screamed. "Swallow the gold again, quickly! He must not see it!"

Kellynch pounced on the pile of gold and began gulping it down like a sea bird gulping a large fish.

"You!" Cornwall snorted wisps of flame at Anne. "You are his Keeper. You allowed this theft from me. You are responsible!"

"No, she is not!" Wentworth jumped in front of her, hot smoke nearly singeing his face. "Kellynch has been taking the gold for far longer than she has been Keeper. And she knew nothing of it."

Kellynch swallowed the last of the gold and slithered near Wentworth, between Anne and Cornwall.

"How could she not know? She had my coins in her possession."

"She showed them to me and thought them proof that Mr. William Elliot had planted them when he stole Kellynch's hoard. She believed he was trying to frame Kellynch as a gold thief in order to have him removed from the estate."

Kellynch lowered his head to shoulder height. "You thought Elliot was trying to harm me, and you sought to protect me?"

"He has confessed! Kellynch has stolen from my hoard. The penalty is death. He is mine!" Cornwall roared and leapt toward the judge's bench.

The Dragon Sage ran back to the front of the court room and climbed from a chair to a table to stand on the judge's bench, the highest place on the courtroom floor. Her head now above Cornwall's she flared her robes wide and shouted. "Stop. You will stop now. You have violated the Accords as much as he. The law is clear. You made a contract with Kellynch and dishonored it. Your rank does not make you immune to the law."

"Of course it does. I am the most powerful dragon here! I am law." He spurted flames toward the ceiling as his powerful voice echoed painfully off the chamber walls.

Matlock and Dunbrook launched at him while Langham spread her wings and gestured for all who could to get behind her as she slowly stepped backward toward a wall. Little Pemberley mimicked her actions to one side, not big enough to accomplish much, but it was most admirable nonetheless. Feet and tails pounded the floor, reverberating through the soles of his feet. Bellows and trumpets and growls filled the air as another blast of flame flared, scorching the ceiling. Kellynch fell in alongside Langham, near where Anne stood, flattening his body to be as wide as possible with Laconia at his side, fur and tail pouffed, fangs bared.

"Thank you, Kellynch." Anne reached out to lay her hand on his nearest coil.

He glanced over his shoulder. "You are my Keeper."

Dragon thunder! Was this the same dragon from the sea cave at Lyme?

Wentworth peeked around Kellynch's thick brown-green coils, taking care not to cut himself on the sharp spinal ridge along his back. Cornwall lay on his back in the center of the courtroom, throat exposed, his tail pinned by Dunbrook, and Matlock sitting on his belly. Sir Fitzwilliam Darcy held a Dragon Slayer sword to his throat. Pray this would go no further. Dragon blood had not been shed in over a century.

Sophy and the admiral had somehow made it back to the right-most tunnel. The admiral flashed a brief hand signal. The way was clear to the tunnel now should escape be necessary.

"You will submit to the Order or the Dragon Slayer will taste blood." Sir Fitzwilliam shouted loud enough for the entire room to hear.

"You cannot wound me warm-blood!" Cornwall's throat swelled, another belch of fire imminent.

Matlock swiped Cornwall with his front talons, tearing away a sizeable chunk of bloody skin. "First blood is shed. You must submit or die." Though bleeding profusely, it was only a flesh wound.

Cornwall roared and pawed at Matlock, not quite able to lay talons on him. "I will never submit."

Sir Fitzwilliam slashed the Dragon Slayer across his throat. Blood poured out.

No! If the Dug died this way, what would it do to the Order—

Wait, it was not arterial blood. It was only skin deep—a warning and another chance, the kind only men offered. "The Order has drawn blood. You must submit!"

Cornwall flailed and thrashed, flinging blood on dragons and bondsmen alike for several long minutes, but Matlock and Dunbrook did not relinquish their hold. His head dropped back hard on the stone floor, and he panted. "I submit."

Cownt Matlock grabbed scales from the base of Cornwall's neck in his teeth and tore them away as Cornwall screamed with humiliation. Matlock handed them to Sir Fitzwilliam—a binding signature on a treaty of surrender.

The dragons and Sir Fitzwilliam, sword still ready, slowly backed away from Cornwall, eyes on the bleeding Dug. Cornwall righted himself and shook his wings into place, showering all in range with droplets of blood.

"How do you plead to the charges against you?" Lord Matlock stood before Cornwall, unflinching.

Of course, with others to do the fighting for him, why would he flinch? Perhaps that was not a charitable thought, but if battle ensued, Wentworth would follow Sir Fitzwilliam Darcy, not Matlock.

"Kellynch got territory and a Keeper with a title." Cornwall sneered.

"Was that what was promised him?"

"How should I know? The issue at hand is he stole my gold."

"Is there a copy of the charter?" Matlock looked over his shoulder toward Anne who was just peeking out from behind Kellynch.

"I have brought my copy, though it is difficult to read." Anne barely managed to open her reticule and remove the folded, dirty pages.

The Sage approached and took the document, nodding encouragingly.

Sir Arnold, Minister of Keeps, took it from her and spread it out on the table near the judge's bench. He produced a quizzing glass from his robes and peered at the document.

Wentworth moved to Anne's side and took her hand. She clutched it tightly. Was Kellynch staring at them?

Sir Arnold waved the other officers in close and pointed at several spots in the document. Matlock waved the dragons over and the group conferred.

Baron Dunbrook took to his bench and banged his bloody gavel. "The Charter is irregular and was never properly filed with the Order. However, Kellynch's reliance on the document was entirely reasonable under the circumstances. The document validates the complaints made by Kellynch. The court finds in favor of Kellynch."

Cornwall crouched, hissing and growling. Sir Fitzwilliam twitched his sword—just barely—in Cornwall's direction.

Kellynch gasped. "What does that mean for me?"

"Since your Charter was never opposed in the Conclave in all this time, it will be considered accepted as written. As such, you are due reparations in line with what you were promised in the Charter." Lord Matlock stepped forward.

"More trickery and deception." Kellynch hissed.

"No," the Dragon Sage picked up the charter and stood beside Lord Matlock. "For the consideration given Cornwall, you were promised membership in the Blue Order, a proper territory, a titled Keeper, a suitable hoard, food, and attentions to your person."

"The Order has a property near Lyme with access to the coast which can be assigned to you." Sir Arnold joined the Sage and Matlock.

"I will no longer be landlocked?" Kellynch's eyes grew wide.

"And there is a fishing ground suitable to your needs nearby as well. As to your hoard—"

Wentworth stepped forward. "If it pleases the court, may I suggest that rather than assign a hoard to a non-hoarding dragon you permit him to keep the gold already in his possession, as long as he promises never to venture near the Merchant Royal wreck again."

"It is mine! Only royal dragons may have gold!" Cornwall bellowed, slimy saliva dripping from his jaws.

Matlock and Dunbrook exchanged glances with one another, then with their dragons.

"It seems a fitting consequence for Cornwall, paying the price of his deception as it were. The court is in agreement with you." Did Lord Matlock look just a little relieved? Perhaps he was pleased they did not have to come up with some other way to punish Cornwall.

The tip of Kellynch's tail flicked like Laconia's did when he was happy.

"Have you forgotten Kellynch's crimes? He revealed himself to the dragon-deaf!" Cornwall snarled and snapped.

Wentworth lifted an open hand. "A shameful act, to be sure—but he was under great provocation. That must be a mitigating factor." Hopefully he had not just overstepped himself.

"He is correct, in light of the wrongs suffered by Kellynch, I beg the court for leniency," Anne strode to Wentworth's side. "The damage was contained and the injured parties, I have heard, consider their injuries good fortune as they are now betrothed."

Dunbrook joined them at the bench again and the officers whispered among themselves a moment. He stepped out. "On the advice of the Sage, the court issues Kellynch a warning that he is not to permit himself to be seen again and as a precaution, for the next five years, you will be required to have your Keeper with you anytime you go down to the sea."

"Keeper?" Kellynch slithered forward and wrapped his tail behind both Anne and Wentworth. "Yes. I will have her and her mate, just as Pemberley does."

Why did the Sage not seem surprised? "Miss Elliot, Captain Wentworth, are you willing to assume the Keepership of this new dragon estate?"

"Are you sure you want such a responsibility?" Anne whispered, eyes locked on his.

He gripped her hand a little tighter. "With you? Absolutely." The temptation to kiss her was almost too strong.

"But I still require a title for them." Kellynch definitely looked self-satisfied.

"Given Captain Wentworth's service to the crown and his military record, I believe a Baronetcy can be easily arranged." Lord Matlock smiled, probably glad to be getting out of this tangled mess so easily. Hopefully he would give the Dragon Sage the credit she deserved for sorting out this matter.

"Then I am satisfied." Kellynch leaned back into his coils, like a man in his favorite chair.

"Does that mean I am free of that beast? That my land is no longer blighted?" Sir Walter cried with no little glee, slipping out from behind Langham.

Sir Arnold's face turned a shade of red that could hardly have been healthy. He glanced at Baron Dunbrook, who gestured for him to continue.

"Sir Walter Elliot, the Blue Order finds you in contempt of the Pendragon Accords section CXXXVIII, subsection XLVIII by willfully failing to perform any and all necessary duties of a Dragon Keeper over the entire course of your tenure as Keeper. As such you will be stripped of all the privileges of that position."

"Excellent. I never asked to be a beast keeper in the first place."

"Effective immediately, you shall relinquish your lands to the Blue Order."

"That is my family's land—"

"No, it has never been. In light of the very minimal service your family has done for the Order, a small living will be granted you, enough for you and your daughter to live a very modest and quiet life."

"A baronet must be seen to live as a baronet!"

"Then you should have performed your duties as a baronet. Have him taken to my office where the full arrangements will be explained." Sir Arnold waved at the bondsmen who converged on a sputtering and fuming Sir Walter.

Anne glanced up to the gallery. Wentworth followed her gaze to the Dalrymples who were whispering between themselves. Considering the narrowed eyes and creased foreheads, Sir Walter could expect a cut from them the next time he encountered them in society.

Baron Dunbrook mounted the judge's bench yet again. "Let the judgement for Kellynch and those against Cornwall and Sir Walter Elliot be entered into the record. The court is now adjourned."

30
Chapter

CORNWALL, IN A FIT of royal pique, vacated Royal Crescent immediately after the court dismissed. The entire event was both fearsome and embarrassing at the same time. Cornwall acted more like a child throwing a temper tantrum than a royal creature of dignity and worth. Wentworth, who had far more experience in mingling amongst those of quality than Anne, said it was not the first such demonstration of temper he had seen. Unfortunately.

Perhaps that was why Father felt entitled to his conniptions. He might not be a royal, but title did come with its privileges.

In a private meeting, held in the Sage's large-enough-to-include-a-dragon office, with Kellynch and his Keepers, Lady Elizabeth counseled Kellynch to never pass near Cornwall's territory again and for Anne and Wentworth to be most attentive to

Kellynch's comings and goings. The blow to Cornwall's pride, in a public arena no less, was extreme, and even the protections afforded by the Pendragon Treaty might not be enough to stay Cornwall's wrath.

Thankfully, and a bit surprisingly, Kellynch agreed. What was more, he had agreed with no argument, and with deference to his Keepers, both Anne and Wentworth.

That wonder had resulted in quite the pounding headache. How could such a rapid turnabout in character be explained, much less trusted? Lady Elizabeth suggested that perhaps, just perhaps, now that Kellynch's fury at the wrongs done him had subsided, he was eager to put the past behind him and make a fresh start in proving himself an asset to the Order at Kellynch-by-the-Sea—the new name for the Timber Hills estate.

Kellynch insisted it would be a degradation for a dragon such as himself to live in a territory not named for him. While he maintained he needed all the honors of English landed dragons, he did not mind having a few more. Like having two Keepers like little Pemberley. Moreover, he had the distinction of having the patent for Wentworth's creation as baronet written with a remainder that ensured the eldest dragon-hearing child—male or female—of the baronet would inherit both the title and the estate.

How the Blue Order would manage that—Anne was glad it would not be her purview to sort out. But the Order had agreed, so it would be their problem to work it out.

October 20, 1814

Several evenings later, Anne sat with Kellynch in the dragon lair below Royal Crescent, brushing and oiling his scales as Uppercross had taught her. The tall underground chamber, accessible by tunnels that led to the Avon and the Blue Order offices, was dimly lit by torches hung at strategic points along the rough-hewn stone walls. The warm orangey light flickered along the ceiling and walls, casting shadows that seemed to have a life of their own throughout. The place smelt of limestone, damp, and dragon musk, tempered by hide oil. Cold and dank, but oddly not unwelcoming.

A heap of straw in one corner offered him a bed of sorts. Though not what he would have preferred, it was clean and insulated him from the cold stone. When they got to Kellynch-by-the-Sea, his lair would be fitted with a fresh water pool for him to lounge in. The Order said it could be accomplished, so she would let them work their wonders and not ask too many questions.

"Yes, yes, just there. That is exactly right!" He stretched out on the cool stone floor a mite longer to present another itchy patch.

Upon close inspection, his grey-green-brown hide was in deplorable condition, dry, flakey and patchy, even cracked in a few places. Likewise, his teeth were in rough shape as well. Lady Elizabeth had arranged for a specialist in dragon teeth to visit soon. He likely had several rotten teeth which could not have been improving his disposition.

"Do you think very ill of me?" he murmured.

Anne stopped brushing and stared at him. "Why do you ask?"

"I know I have been quite put out for some time and angry with your family." He craned his neck to stare back at her. "I understand that would make some warm-bloods resentful."

"It is a bit difficult to forget that you threatened to eat me." Prickles ran down the back of her neck. She might never stop reliving that moment in her nightmares.

"Well, yes, about that. It does seem that perhaps I overreacted a mite to the whole situation." The way the corners of his mouth turned down made him look regretful. Could a dragon look sheepish?

"That would not be the word I would have chosen to describe the situation." He really did not want to know how she would have described it.

"All told, considering what I had endured for so many years, I think I was rather patient and restrained."

Of course he did.

"On that matter, I am afraid we will have to agree to disagree." Anne picked up the long-handled brush and returned to oiling his scales.

"I would not have you unhappy you know. Have I not insisted you and your mate have ample rank among the Order, with a title and a proper home with none who have any claim on it but you? What is more, you have the distinction of Keeping the only marine wyrm in all of England. Is that not pleasing?" He settled his head into a small divot on the stone floor and sighed.

No point in mentioning those were all marks of superiority he claimed for himself. "I suppose it is.

But not so pleasing as Keeping a content dragon."

"Then I think you are well on your way to being pleased." He edged a little closer to her. "As am I."

Interesting how Kellynch was definitely not without a touch of the Elliot pride himself. Not that Anne would ever tell him so, of course. Hopefully, just a touch could be lived with.

Hopefully.

Friday, November 4, 1814

Two weeks later, an ordinary license in hand, Anne and Wentworth stood before a Blue Order Bishop in Bath Abbey—another honor Kellynch insisted upon. His Keepers would be married in that fine place, since it was a parish church after all—and perhaps even more significantly, he could watch the proceedings from a well-placed dragon tunnel, making certain all went according to the promises given him.

All being well, in the future that need would likely fade with time. Or so the Sage suggested. But for now, it was a mite irritating.

Still, though Anne hardly needed a church so fine for her nuptials, it pleased Father and Elizabeth that she would be wed there, under the fine vaulted, fan ceilings and lit by the stained-glass windows that took up the overwhelming majority of the walls.

Nor did she need a new silk gown, done up in Order-blue with fitted sleeves and swags of lace trimming the skirt hem. But it was lovely having a gown fitted and made to her preferences.

Wentworth, handsome in his navy-blue jacket and

breeches, seemed pleased with the arrangements. Not for their grandeur, certainly not that, but for the fitting way they came together to suggest everything in their lives was beginning anew. With so much difficulty and regret behind them, a clear marker of the remaking of their lives was a good thing. His reasoning was very difficult to deny.

"Forasmuch as Sir Frederick Wentworth and Miss Anne Elliot have consented together in holy wedlock, and have witnessed the same before God and this company, and thereto have given and pledged their troth either to the other, and have declared the same by giving and receiving of a ring, and by joining of hands; I pronounce that they be man and wife together. In the Name of the Father, and of the Son, and of the Holy Ghost. Amen." Though his voice was very solemn as befit the occasion, the bishop's eyes creased with just a bit of merriment as he glanced toward the dragon tunnel entrance where Kellynch lurked.

The soaring ceiling and enormous open space within the abbey meant that Kellynch could have joined the other witnesses to the ceremony. The bishop had invited him to do so. But Kellynch declined. Whether it was sudden shyness or a touch of embarrassment after all his faults had come out in court along with Cornwall's, it was difficult to say. He insisted it was enough for him to observe from the shadows.

Apparently, not very many dragons bothered watching such warm-blooded ceremonies and the bishop felt it an honor to have Kellynch present at all. Luckily, he felt the same about the rest of the dragons that attended as well. That limited those few in attendance to dragon hearing members of their families, leaving only one who could not attend. With the help of a persuasive harem of fairy dragons who lived in the Abbey bell tower, Elizabeth had been struck by a sick headache that morning—or rather the strong suggestion of one—and begged off attending. Though some would surely say it was an excuse to cover her jealousy, that was not, and would not be Anne's problem.

Laconia wove his way between Anne and Wentworth, leaving a swath of black fur on her silk skirt and his white stockings under his breeches, purring a loud, happy rumble, quickly lost in the cavernous room. Behind them, White nickered his approval. Such a striking creature, with his silvery white coat, he looked like nothing so much as a carving in the abbey's marble ornaments come to life, somehow entirely fitting the setting.

White had never seen a warm-blooded wedding and applied directly to the bishop himself for permission to do so. Thus, he stood with the Crofts, witnessing their marriage. Mrs. Smith stood, with Rooke perched on the pew back nearby, and Admiral Easterly stood up with Anne and Wentworth, both rather more mature than the typical attendants, but only Father attempted to complain about that. Father, who had given her away without speaking a word at all, stood with Mary and Charles, on the other side of the church, away from the attending dragons. Charles seemed happy enough, but Mary—oh, the things which she must be thinking.

Things which were certainly not Anne's problems either.

Oh, so many things that were no longer her problems! The lightness and freedom of it!

Her feet nearly floated above the floor as they signed the marriage lines and retreated to the pretty little landaulet bedecked with greenery and a few autumn flowers—white and yellow Michaelmas daisies, golden marigolds and fluffy white baby's breath—waiting for them outside the abbey. Wentworth had bought it for her as a wedding gift.

After today, it would be hers to drive, but as they paraded through Bath after their wedding, it would be most proper for him to drive, particularly since White insisted he be one of the pair to pull it for them. Another concession to the hippocampus' sense of whimsy.

A whimsical dragon? After the scenes at court, who would have thought such a thing possible? But then who would have thought Kellynch's change in—well nearly everything about him—possible? Apparently, where dragons were concerned, rules of normal convention rarely applied.

"What are you thinking, Lady Wentworth?" Wentworth, smelling of shaving oil and evergreen, pressed his shoulder to hers as he held the reins that were really only just for show.

White led the staid old grey dappled horse beside him in a clever harness White himself had designed. Many horses disliked dragons, but this one had been especially trained to their presence.

"I think it shall take me some time to become accustomed to that name, Sir Frederick." She flicked some of Laconia's fur off his stocking.

"Well, you can take comfort that your sister Mary thinks little of these new creations."

"But your creation was unique and special, it

brought with it a lovely estate near Lyme—"

"Which she thinks is wholly undeserved and neither of us have yet to see." He rolled his eyes, a hint of skepticism in his tone.

White glanced over his shoulder at them, his hooves clopping softly on the cobblestone. Oh, how he was restraining himself from butting into their conversation!

"We have been assured it is being prepared and made suitable for our occupancy. And considering the trouble that came from leaving Kellynch dissatisfied before, I do not think the Order would dare risk his ire now." Anne leaned her head on his shoulder.

"I quite agree." Laconia leaned forward from the back floor to put his paws on the seat beside Anne.

"Ever the optimist, my dearest, sweet, Anne. And you too my Friend. On your recommendations, I shall withhold my judgment until we can determine for ourselves if the fireplaces are smoky, the rooms drafty, and the furniture faded and shabby."

"You are a clever man. As long as you and Kellynch have access to the sea, I am sure we can make do."

A little of the tension in his shoulders eased and he smiled in a way that meant he felt understood. "Are you ready for the breakfast my sister has declared so necessary to mark this occasion?"

"I think it very kind of her to do this for us. And she is right, a new baronet should be afforded all the amenities of a society wedding—for Kellynch's sake far more than our own."

"I was afraid you would say he should be seen to be living as a baronet." He snorted as White turned his gaze back to the street ahead.

"I assure you. I will never say that."

Wentworth laughed his full-bodied laugh that made White join in as well.

"You are doing that much more often now. I told you she smelled right." Laconia slithered up to join them on the narrow seat, purring in such a way that declared his new favorite spot was to be wedged right between them where both might scratch behind his ears.

"And you were correct as usual." Wentworth scratched behind Laconia's ears. "Will you join us for the breakfast?"

"I think not. I do not like crowds."

"No, you never have."

"I will go to see Mina. The eggs have begun to purr quite loudly now. I want to talk to them, and to tell Anne's new Friend about all that has transpired."

"Heavens! Do not fill his mind with expectations I cannot fulfil!" Anne scratched under Laconia's chin.

"I hardly think that possible. After witnessing you stand up to Kellynch, I cannot imagine an expectation you could not meet." Wentworth winked at her and turned to Laconia. "You will join us at Royal Crescent later, then?"

"Of course, where else would I be?"

White stopped at the front door of the Royal Crescent House the Blue Order had allowed the Crofts to occupy even after Cornwall's withdrawal. Laconia spring-hopped down and slithered toward the Blue Order offices. Wentworth helped Anne down, his hands lingering on her waist a mite longer than necessary.

White tossed his head and headed toward the mews, whispering to any who might see that there was an old and unremarkable driver guiding the little carriage there.

"Do you know how many my sister has invited to the breakfast?" Wentworth tucked her hand into the crook of his arm. How handsome he was in his navy-blue coat and breeches.

"As many as are appropriate to attend a newly created baronet and his wife." Anne laughed. "And no, I do not know exactly how many that is either."

He looked down on her with such an expression! Gracious, that was the way Sir Fitzwilliam looked at Lady Elizabeth when he thought none were watching. Her cheeks burned.

The butler admitted them and took them directly to Mrs. Croft in the very full drawing room. Marigolds and Michaelmas daisies filled vases and bowls on every free surface of the gold and white room, perfuming the air and covering the hints of dragon musk that seemed almost part of the everyday scent of Bath. So many gentlemen and ladies mingled throughout that one could hardly see the very fine furniture or hear whichever lady was taking her turn playing on the pianoforte in the corner near the street side windows. Good thing the seat at the pianoforte was already taken, lest Anne hurry to occupy it by habit alone.

"Anne, Frederick! Did White take you on a tour of the entire city? I was getting worried something untoward—"

"Under White's and Laconia's watch? Hardly." Wentworth leaned close to kiss his sister's cheek. Her navy-blue gown with military-inspired trims next to Wentworth's similarly colored suit seemed to bring out the family resemblance between the two.

"There you are, Frederick!" Admiral Croft sauntered up. "Do be a good fellow and come with me. Lord Matlock wants to speak with you. Order business, I imagine."

"Is there ever anything else with him? May as well hear him out. You will excuse me." Wentworth bowed to Anne and Mrs. Croft, and followed the admiral away.

"I do hope nothing is wrong." Anne bit her lower lip.

"There is no reason to expect that, rather the opposite I imagine. I suspect the earl wants to inform Frederick of the improvements to the manor at Timber—rather at Kellynch-by-the-Sea in anticipation of that information getting to Kellynch himself. The Order is anxious to make right the wrongs suffered by Kellynch. They are rather anxious that the major dragons do not come to believe that the Order does not keep its promises. So, I think they would rather do too much than too little to make Kellynch happy."

"And we must bear the burden of our dragon's pleasure. Not what either of us would have imagined that day you discovered Lady Russell—"

"So, you have arrived at last." Mary approached, managing to look frumpy, dowdy even, in her best pale green sprigged muslin gown. "You know, up close and not in that drafty old church, you seem less thin in your person. Your cheeks, your skin, your complexion are all greatly improved. Clearer, fresher, I think. Have you been using anything in particular? Gowland lotion perhaps? Father is always on and on about using it. He says it has carried away Mrs. Clay's freckles."

Apparently, the dragon scale lotion Uppercross

recommended did have a pleasing effect. Probably best not to try and explain that to Mary. "No, nothing really."

"And now you are Lady Wentworth. I suppose I would rather have you take precedence over me than Henrietta or Louisa. And it is good that you bring more agreeable connections to the family than Charles Hayter or even Captain Benwick will. That must be counted a good thing for us all. I do not suppose Elizabeth is happy at all, though, for you ruined her chances to get Mr. William Elliot."

"Have you forgotten? He was tried and found a criminal?" An angry red flush crept up Mrs. Croft's neck to her cheeks.

"He is heir to Kellynch, and that is the sort of thing Elizabeth had always hoped for." Mary sniffed and pressed a handkerchief to her nose.

Anne drew a deep breath, held it, and released it slowly. "Have you forgotten Kellynch—"

"I cannot say I understand this business about Kellynch no longer belonging to Father—"

"Mary! This is hardly a fitting topic of conversation for a wedding breakfast." Charles hurried up to join them, directing a very sharp look at Mary.

"I do not see what the bother is whether it is talked about here or elsewhere. It is a very real concern of mine, why should I not speak it? It does not look well upon the family at all that Father should lose everything."

"But perhaps it is not the sort of thing Anne should wish to concern herself with now," Mrs. Croft said.

Now or ever again, to be more accurate, but that need not be said just now.

"Why ever not? It is the most pressing issue to the family."

Mrs. Croft took Mary's arm. "Pray excuse us, Lady Wentworth." She ushered Mary away. Considering the look in her eye, the conversation to follow would probably not be pleasant. She did not suffer fools, or Mary Musgrove, gladly.

"Pray forgive your sister," Charles shrugged, a little sheepish. His brown wool coat and breeches were a little out of style and in need of a good pressing. "She is quite at sixes and sevens trying to sort all this business out. You must admit, for one who avoids dragon matters, the whole affair is rather confusing."

"No doubt." Anne sighed. Charles, good natured, optimistic Charles. He was what he was and that would never change.

"I understand the Crofts will be continuing on with their lease at Kellynch." Charles rocked forward on his toes.

"Yes, they and White are very pleased with the countryside and the house. Moreover, it gives the Order a little time to spread an acceptable story to explain—"

"Anne! Anne!" Father, face red and decidedly inelegant trundled up, the milling crowd parting to make way for him. What joy was to be hers.

Charles bowed and excused himself. Probably best that way.

Anne backed up until she reached the wall. The conversation to come was not one to be had in the middle of a crowded room. Granted, the portrait of a strange couple staring down over her shoulder did little to create a sense of privacy, but it was the best the room offered.

Father stood directly before her, as angry as she had ever seen him. "You must remedy this intolerable situation immediately. I demand——"

"Father, I do not know what you think I am able to do in this circumstance. But I assure you——"

"Talk to that abominable dragon. Require him to return my lands, my properties——" He would never understand that the land was never his in the first place.

"I am sorry, but I cannot do that."

"Willful, stubborn girl! Of course, you can."

"No, Kellynch turned over the property to the Blue Order in consideration for the estate now called Kellynch-by-the-Sea. Neither he, nor I, nor Wentworth, have any interest in the former Kellynch estate."

"Talk to them! Do something! Have you seen the ridiculous stipend we have been given to live on?" Of course, she had, she had even negotiated to make it a modicum greater than had first been proposed.

"It is sufficient to keep a roof over your heads and food on the table, is it not?"

"But such a roof, such food! It is intolerable! Hardly any servants, no horses, no trips to London! How can we be expected to live this way? It is not to be borne."

"I have done all I can on your behalf. There is no one left to be worked on."

"Then, you must take us in at Lyme. It is the only way."

"I assure you, sir, it is not." Wentworth appeared behind Father's shoulder, in tone and bearing, an officer not willing to be crossed.

Father turned to face him. "You are a baronet

now. Surely you understand the extreme privations—"

"Kellynch will not have you on his lands. Ever again. That was made clear to you by Sir Arnold, was it not? When you signed the official resignation of Keepership, he made it clear that Kellynch had also washed his hands, as it were, of you. He has final say of who is allowed in his territory."

"Clearly the beast can be worked on. You must," he looked over his shoulder. "Anne. I insist."

Wentworth stepped forward, but Anne laid a hand on his arm. "No, Father, I cannot, and I will not. Surely you have other friends whose dragons—"

"The Dalrymples have already cut us, in public no less!" A purple tinge crept over his face, the shade of true mortification.

"I am very sorry for that." It certainly would not do to mention that the Dalrymples had invited her and Wentworth to a dinner in their honor next week.

"You will excuse us, Sir Walter, I was sent to fetch my lovely bride—her company is much in demand." Wentworth tucked her hand in the crook of his arm and whisked her toward the opposite side of the drawing room, leaving Father sputtering at the portrait in the corner.

"Whether that was true or not, thank you. He was in no mood to permit me to say no."

"While the Dragon Sage and Sir Fitzwilliam have asked to see you, I was happy to remove you from his company. I cannot complain that Kellynch will not have him or Elizabeth on his territory ever again."

"It will be rather difficult to explain to Elizabeth, but there is little to be done for it I suppose."

"Lady Wentworth!" Lady Elizabeth, resplendent in

an Order-blue muslin gown sprigged with tiny flowers hurried toward them on the arm of Sir Fitzwilliam Darcy, her tiny blue fairy dragon buzzing along behind them. "Pray tell me, how is Kellynch this fine day?"

Anne curtsied. "He watched the ceremony from the dragon tunnels and seemed very well pleased. He has been very happy with the dragon accommodations at Royal Crescent and thinks you very decent for permitting him the use of them until we all retreat to Lyme."

"It is rather spoiling him a bit, I admit." Lady Elizabeth smiled as her fairy dragon Friend landed on her shoulder. "But I have found that when mollifying an offended dragon, one should rather do too much than too little."

"He has become quite tractable in recent days." Wentworth laughed. "The change is quite remarkable. He is almost as pleasant as Uppercross himself!"

"Uppercross is a most unique fellow to be sure," Sir Fitzwilliam had the oddest look on his face. "I was certain all wyverns were cross and crochety before I met him."

"Will it go badly for Uppercross for having kept Lady Russell's secret for so long?" Anne bit her lip. This was not the best time to ask such a question, but better now than wait any longer for the news.

"He has been issued a stern reprimand and been assigned a tutor for remedial instruction on the Accords and all its laws. His Keeper and junior Keeper have also been required to attend those tutorials. Any further violations after this will be punished far more strictly." Lady Elizabeth tried to look severe, but her eyes sparkled a little too much.

Cool relief suffused Anne's chest. "He will probably relish the tutor's company and treat it as though he is hosting a tea in his lair."

"I suspect you are right." Lady Elizabeth chuckled. "He is such an agreeable soul. Thankfully, with no history of any sort of trouble before, we all expect he will return to his regular law-abiding behavior quickly and easily."

"Young Pemberley was quite remarkable in court," Wentworth said. "She is a credit to you both."

"Indeed, she is," Sir Fitzwilliam winked at Lady Elizabeth. "Elizabeth is currently writing a book on Dragon Keeping for the very young dragon. We hope it will become the foundation for a new generation of Blue Order Dragons. By the way, congratulations, Sir Frederick. Having seen record of your naval service, there is no doubt that your title is well deserved."

"Well, I would much rather have that be known than the rest of the Order believing it solely the result of a demanding dragon. A man does have his pride you know."

Anne snickered under her breath.

"Do you intend to take a bridal tour?" Lady Elizabeth asked.

"We do not have a great deal of family to visit—I think we will go directly to Lyme when the house is ready. Shropshire is a very great distance from Lyme, and my brother is a bit of a curmudgeon."

"I think it best not to leave Kellynch alone at this time. I am afraid he might take it as a sign that things have not changed the way we all hope they have," Anne added.

"That is very wise. You will both make excellent Dragon Keepers. I have no doubt. I look forward to your correspondence."

"Oh, but I do not want to bother—"

"I know so little of marine wyrms. It is no bother."

"What my wife is trying not to say is that she hopes very much for an invitation so that she might spend some time getting to know Kellynch under favorable circumstances."

"You are very welcome, as are Pemberley and all your dragon Friends." Wentworth bowed from his shoulders.

"With Nanny and little Anne, Walker, Pemberley and April, we do travel with a rather extensive entourage these days." Sir Fitzwilliam ticked them off on his fingers.

"I fear the winter is a disagreeable time to travel with a young child. Perhaps the spring? You will not mind if we bring our Anne, will you? I do so want her to grow up surrounded by every possible sort of dragon." Lady Elizabeth said that like it was the most ordinary wish of every mother.

"I think Kellynch would consider a visit from our Dragon Sage an honor," Anne said.

"Have you considered Matlock and Easterly's proposal?" Sir Fitzwilliam locked eyes with Wentworth.

"What proposal?" Anne turned to Wentworth, eyes narrow, lips pressed hard.

"The one he made just a few minutes ago. Fear not I have kept nothing from you." He held her eyes in a steady gaze as he said that.

She nodded slowly.

"The Chancellor and the admiral have both requested that I keep on as an agent of the Order, a liaison to the sea dragons if you will, with Kellynch working with me, of course."

"Are there concerns with the sea dragons?"

"Not currently, but counting a marine wyrm in their numbers seems too valuable a resource to otherwise waste." Wentworth rolled his eyes.

"It is not the sort of life for the faint of heart, for certain. But your naval record suggests you are anything but," Sir Fitzwilliam gazed directly at Anne, "and your own management of Kellynch recommends you for the endeavor as well. Though Matlock may not have expressed it well, it is the sort of thing requiring commitment from both of you."

"It seems the sort of thing that might be good for Kellynch," Anne said. "He has a lively mind and boredom does not suit him. He has been quite bored for so very long."

"I—we—will give it all due consideration. Let us move into our new home and settle in. We shall make a decision within a month after that. Would that suit?" Wentworth asked Anne as much as Sir Fitzwilliam.

"Very well, thank you."

"My dear friend!" Mrs. Smith approached, frail and thin, but her cheeks glowing and her eyes sparkling, leaning on Admiral Easterly's arm. "We have the most delightful news."

Anne hurried to take her hands and squeeze them warmly.

"I know the day should be entirely yours, but I know you will not begrudge me the chance to share something that I am certain will bring you joy as my friend."

"Then do not keep me waiting. I insist you share this joy with me now."

Mrs. Smith leaned closer, her voice just above a

whisper. "The Order has been looking very closely into Mr. Elliot's affairs and has agreed that I am due a considerable sum he owed to my Charles before his death. Lord Matlock has decreed that the sum will be added to the debts owed by Mr. Elliot, to be paid back by his labors for the Order. In their generosity, they have set aside a trust for me in that amount to be administered by the Order on my behalf. The percents from that trust that will allow Rooke and me some very modest independence, suitable to a widow of my station. In return, the Order may ask us to do some writing and carrying of letters on their behalf and from time to time to house guests, but as I love company, I am quite content with the arrangement."

"That is excellent news!" Wentworth clapped Admiral Easterly's arm—what did he have to do with the matter?

Anne would have to thank him later. "Indeed, it is. I am so pleased for you and Rooke. You will be diligent in writing to me when we are off to Lyme, will you not?"

"Of course, I will. Rooke has even offered to carry the letters herself."

"Hungry for fresh gossip I am sure." Anne laughed.

"If you choose to work with the Order, it will be invaluable to have a direct means of communication to you and Kellynch." Admiral Easterly cocked his head and lifted his eyebrow.

"Kellynch and I will discuss the matter after we have settled into the new estate, as I told Darcy, rather Sir Fitzwilliam."

"And you will not be moved before—stubborn old sailor. Come, Mrs. Smith, I believe our hostess is about to call us all to the dining room. We should allow the bride to take her place of honor." He led Mrs. Smith away.

Anne pulled Wentworth aside on a little balcony that overlooked the mews garden. "I will have my share of conversation with respect to this matter."

"Of course, you will. I had nothing else in mind. I simply did not want to debate that with Easterly."

"Good." She exhaled heavily.

He put his hands on her waist and drew her scandalously close. "Tell me, Lady Wentworth, what do you wish for? A quiet life, that for all appearances looks normal and mundane to the outside world."

"You make that sound so appealing."

"It would be. You would be mistress of a very well-run estate, able to manage everything as you please, entertain, be the pillar of the local community. What is to repine in that?"

"Or—"

"Or, we could take the Order up on the offer to serve as their agents, forever knowing that our ordinary lives could be upended at a moment's notice by business that could become messy, dangerous, or even deadly."

"Surely you are exaggerating."

"Cornwall's outburst at court could have taken a very different tack very easily. Imagine what that could have looked like. If the draconic officers of the Order had been forced to kill Cornwall, do you think the rest of the English dragons, much less the Brenin, would have taken that well?"

"I have no idea."

"Neither does anyone else, even the Sage herself. Is that the sort of life you want?"

"I would not have thought I had the spleen for it. But perhaps, I do. And Kellynch, we must ask him of course, but I think it may just appeal to him as well."

"Are you certain?"

"You want to do this. I can see it in your eyes."

"Not at the cost of you." He gazed at her, looking so serious, as if life and limb were at risk.

Anne stared into his eyes for several long breaths. "If we can do this together, like the Sage and her knight, I think, yes, it is the right thing for us."

"Then, my dearest Anne, I am entirely and completely persuaded." Whatever else she might have said, he silenced with a kiss.

Epilogue

November 15, 1814

ANNE AND WENTWORTH sat on a worn carpet in the middle of Lady Elizabeth's dressing room, their backs to the frosted windows. Much of the furniture that had been there when Anne had last visited had been pushed up against the walls to accommodate the hatching.

Afternoon sun filtered in, bathing the room in a homey glow and the faint scent of lavender as it hit the bowl of dried flowers on the table. Mina's hatching box had been moved there when the number attending the hatching grew too large for Admiral Easterly's cramped office to hold. A warm fire blazed in the fireplace on their right. Something about not wanting the hatchlings to take a chill. Mina and Laconia perched inside the hatching box, slowly circling the eggs, chirruping encouragements to the hatchlings inside.

The Crofts sat opposite them; Mina had developed a great fondness for Mrs. Croft and decided she would be a good Friend for one of the wyrmlings. White, of course, fascinated by everything, requested an invitation to observe the event, which was readily granted—Laconia and White had become good friends, after all. Admiral Easterly sat a little distance behind the Crofts, in a chair, tending the saucers of fish broth and dried cod that Lady Elizabeth said would be necessary to sate the wyrmlings' initial hunger.

Nanny, Pemberley, and baby Anne in her carved wooden cradle with April perched atop it, waited attentively behind Anne and Wentworth. Lady Elizabeth thought it good that Pemberley watch the hatching and that little Anne be present near dragons whenever possible. If the infant could hear as Lady Elizabeth believed, it made sense, in an odd sort of way. Walker, Sir Fitzwilliam's magnificent cockatrice, sat on an iron dragon perch, near the frosted windows, standing guard against any intruder. It seemed odd since the windows were closed and intruders were unlikely, but Sir Fitzwilliam had mentioned it was Walker's preferred station at a hatching, so who was she to question that?

Kellynch peered in through the opening to the dragon passages in the corner opposite the fireplace. He might have been able to squeeze into the room, if he wrapped his coils very tightly, but he did not insist on the privilege, content to have been invited at all. Major dragons rarely attended minor dragon hatchings. According to Lady Elizabeth, minor dragons suffered from an instinctive fear that the hatchlings might be eaten. So, she vouched for Kellynch's promise of good behavior, and Laconia convinced Mina to allow him admittance.

Lady Elizabeth and Sir Fitzwilliam sat on low stools on opposite sides of the hay filled wooden hatching box, ready to attend to any party needing help. Their air of calm helped mitigate the growing anxious anticipation in the room.

The grey and brown mottled eggs purred and mewled and quivered. One of them, far larger than the others, Mina pushed toward Anne and Wentworth. "Your Friend."

Why was that egg so large and so loud? And where was a Friend for the third egg? Laconia had said nothing about it—

"Look!" Mrs. Croft exclaimed, pointing at one of the smaller eggs.

A small tear in the dappled eggshell ripped down the shell, splitting it in two.

A slimy grey-striped wyrmling tumbled out, looking very surprised indeed. She pushed herself up on her legs and screamed, "Mrrrooww!"

How did a sound that size come from a creature that small?

"There is no need to scream, little dear. Come closer, and we will see you cleaned up and fed." Mrs. Croft held up a flannel scrap that she and the Admiral had already rubbed along their necks to give it their scent.

The grey wyrmling sniffed the air, enormous tufted ears pricked. She slithered toward them, immediately bumping her head against Mrs. Croft's hand.

"Food or clean first?"

"Hungry!" The wyrmling chewed at the flannel.

Admiral Easterly passed broth and fish to Admiral Croft who pressed in close to his wife and plied the baby with as much food as she could swallow. She wrapped her tail around his wrist, forcing him to use the other hand to feed her.

White edged in, and leaned close to the wyrmling. She reached up and licked his nose quickly, then returned to her meal. White's eyes grew very large, and if it were possible, he smiled, a little dumbfounded.

"Rrrrow!" Another baby shrieked. A tiny black wyrmling cried from the center of the box, his head casting about as though lost. He pawed at the hay with his broad thumbed paws, crying as though the world were coming to an end.

Mina spring-hopped to his side, licked his face, and picked him up by the scruff of his slimy neck. What was she doing? Nothing in Anne's readings on hatchings had ever described such a thing.

Laconia joined Mina at the side of the box and together they slithered toward Nanny and the cradle with the wyrmling mewling and fussing loudly all the way.

Sir Fitzwilliam followed them, eyebrow raised, but Lady Elizabeth just nodded as though this were entirely expected.

Mina dropped the wyrmling into the cradle. The baby giggled and cooed. The wyrmling stopped crying and began to purr. Pemberley leaned over the cradle and licked the top of the wyrmling's head and April trilled something happy sounding.

Looking a mite resigned, Sir Fitzwilliam retrieved a flannel and food for the hatchling.

Did Lady Elizabeth know Laconia and Mina were going to do that? What sort of question was that? Of course, she did.

"Look!" Wentworth nudged her with his elbow and pointed to the huge egg now alone in the nesting box.

The egg fell over and rolled, meowling and growling, with bumps and bulges appearing through the shell.

Lady Elizabeth held up an open hand. "Do not interfere, it will not help. Patience…"

Anne grasped Wentworth's hand and squeezed hard. Not being able to help the little thing felt like punishment, even if it was the right course.

The egg tumbled and growled, snarled and hissed. Was that what it should sound like? The others broke so easily. How long could this continue before the little creature inside became too exhausted to continue?

A tear trickled down her cheek, to lose a little Friend before even having met—it was too cruel. Anne scooped up the leathery egg in her hands and brought it close to her face. It stopped moving. "You can do this. I know you can. Do not panic. You can feel my hands through the egg, focus your efforts on the other side. Use your claws, your fangs if you must. You can do this."

Wentworth leaned over her shoulder. "Yes, she is right, you can. Do as she says. She always knows what to do."

Heart racing, panting just a mite, she pressed her cheek to his, the stubble of his beard scuffing her cheek. He leaned back against her, a promise that somehow it would all be well.

A huge bulge formed along the side of the egg facing them.

"That is right. Just a little more—push hard now!" Anne's hands trembled as the egg shook with the force of the wyrmling's exertions.

A tiny tear and a single claw appeared at the top of the egg. Anne squealed, leaning into Wentworth's shoulder not to jostle the hatchling.

"Yes, yes, that is it, just a little more." Wentworth's voice was slow and steady, an officer cajoling the best out of his men.

A thumbed paw shoved its way out, and another. Wait, what? Another, a third paw? That was not possible. What was wrong with the wyrmling?

"Mrrrow!" A tiny black and white head appeared, forked tongue flicking, wrestling against the shell.

A fourth paw appeared, just under its chin. That could not be—

The egg split open and fell away, exposing two black and white wyrmlings, minute compared to the others, wriggling and wet with egg slime, in Anne's shaking hands.

"Hungry! Hungry!" The one with the black nose cried.

"Cold!" The one with white tipped ears screeched.

Lady Elizabeth appeared next to Wentworth, handing him flannels and food for the hatchlings.

Two? There had been two? Nothing she read said that was possible.

Wentworth took little Black Nose into his lap and handed him slivers of dried cod as fast as he could gobble them. Anne scrubbed White Ears clean and held him close until he stopped shivering. She offered him a dish of warm fish broth that he slurped noisily.

"Hold still," Wentworth scrubbed Black Nose in between bites. "I would not have you taking a chill. Slow down a bit!"

"Hungry." The wyrmling's tail lashed about until it wrapped around Wentworth's wrist. "Not cold."

"And I am trying to keep it that way." Wentworth gave the little wet head another scrub.

"More?" White Ears pleaded, looking up at Anne with his mother's blue eyes. "Like he?" He pointed a thumbed paw at his littermate.

"Of course, little one, as much as you would like." Anne cuddled him a mite closer as she reached for some dried cod. "What do you think of this?"

He gobbled it, a little like a seabird gulping a fish. "Mrrrow!"

"Be careful or you will choke!"

"More! Not choke! More!" White Ears bumped Anne's hand with the top of his head, purring.

She tore the cod into smaller pieces so he could eat faster. "Better now?"

He purred more loudly. "You understand. Stay together?" He paused in his eating and stared at her with the most plaintive expression.

"Of course, you and your egg-mate as well."

White Ears chirruped at Black Nose who turned his sparkling green eyes on Anne.

"It seems the little fellow wants to stay as well," Wentworth scratched under Black Nose's chin.

"I think we shall be a very merry little party then. Perhaps we ought to hold off traveling to Lyme until the hatching hunger has faded?" Anne glanced at Lady Elizabeth who nodded vigorously. "Assuming Kellynch agrees of course."

Pray he was agreeable! If not, they might have a very challenging time of it.

"Kellynch," Lady Elizabeth called over her shoulder. "Another distinction to add to your territory. Twin tatzelwurms are very rare indeed."

"Bring them, I want to see." Kellynch called from his corner.

Surely, he was jesting. Had he forgotten major dragons ate hatchlings?

"He is their laird. It is appropriate. Go on, you can carry them to Kellynch. Just keep their mouths full, and they will not complain." Lady Elizabeth rose and helped Anne to her feet as Wentworth clambered to his.

The twins objected until Lady Elizabeth popped another sliver of dried cod in each mouth. Mina and Laconia were suddenly beside them, Mina's fur pouffed and her ears erect.

Kellynch stretched his grey-green scaly head and first three spinal ridges into the room, his whiskers twitching.

The hatchlings stopped eating and peered over Anne and Wentworth's hands at Kellynch.

"Who?" Black Nose squeaked, trembling against Wentworth's chest.

"I am your Laird." Kellynch whispered. "Come closer."

"Set them on his snout." Lady Elizabeth stroked Kellynch's long snout and pointed to a spot just between and in front of his huge sparkling eyes.

Anne swallowed. That hardly looked safe or comfortable. But a woman who faced down an angry firedrake in court was not to be argued with. She placed White Ears on Kellynch's snout. Wentworth followed suit with little Black Nose. Mina and Laconia crowded close, their front paws on Kellynch's snout as well.

Were they being friendly, curious, or ready to effect a rescue if necessary?

The wyrmlings purred and licked the ridges on Kellynch's nose. He squinted and crossed his eyes to watch them, something like a smile lifting the corners of his long mouth. They slithered up his face and curled up behind his eye ridges, the tips of their tails flicking serenely.

Kellynch snorted a contented little sound. "I shall have them in my Keep. They will be Corn and Wall."

Anne gasped. She and Wentworth both looked to Lady Elizabeth.

She sighed and blinked thoughtfully. "As long as you do as you have been asked and never go near Cornwall or Land's End again, I suppose it will do no harm."

"Good. You may now complete your cleaning of their majesties as it would not do to permit them to remain all slimy and cold. I will return to Royal Crescent and make a place in my lair for them. We will go to Kellynch-by-the-Sea when they are ready."

Kellynch was going to share his lair with the hatchlings? With minor dragons? Anne snuck a glance at Lady Elizabeth.

"They will require a great deal of attention. Hatchlings are very hungry." Lady Elizabeth pinched the bridge of her nose.

Kellynch coughed and brought up a half-digested fish on the stone floor at her feet, just missing the edge of the carpet. Corn, with white ears, and Wall with the black nose, pounced on it, purring and mewling. "Not as hungry as baby sea wyrms."

Lady Elizabeth covered her face with her hands and laughed until tears streaked her face. "I have never seen a major dragon feed a minor dragon—I do not think such a thing has ever been recorded."

"Somehow, I think it bodes very well for us and Kellynch-by-the-Sea." Anne scratched behind Kellynch's ear.

Wentworth slipped his arm over her shoulder. "Yes, my dear. I think it does."

**Enjoy other books in the
series:**

**Pemberley: Mr. Darcy's Dragon
Longbourn: Dragon Entail
Netherfield: Rogue Dragon
A Proper Introduction to Dragons
The Dragons of Kellynch
Kellynch: Dragon Persuasion**

For more dragon lore check out:
Elizabeth's Commonplace
Book of Dragons
and
Dragon Myths of England
At RandomBitofFascination.com

Acknowledgments

So many people have helped me along the journey
taking this from an idea to a reality.
My friend Peggy, who died just two weeks before this
book was finished. Her encouragement and enthusiasm have meant so much.
Debbie, Diana, Julie, Ruth, and Anji thank you so
much for cold reading and being honest!
My dear friend Cathy, my biggest cheerleader, you
have kept me from chickening out more than once!
And my sweet sister Gerri who believed in even those
first attempts that now live in the file drawer!
Thank you!

❧Other Books by Maria Grace

Available in e-book, audiobook and paperback

Available in paperback, e-book, and audiobook format at all online bookstores.

On Line Exclusives at:

www.http//RandomBitsofFascination.com

Bonus and deleted scenes
Regency Life Series

Free e-books:
Rising Waters: Hurricane Harvey Memoirs
Lady Catherine's Cat
A Gift from Rosings Park
Bits of Bobbin Lace
Half Agony, Half Hope: New Reflections on Persuasion
Four Days in April

About the Author

Six-time BRAG Medallion Honoree, #1 Best-selling Historical Fantasy author Maria Grace has her PhD in Educational Psychology and is a 16-year veteran of the university classroom where she taught courses in human growth and development, learning, test development and counseling. None of which have anything to do with her undergraduate studies in economics/sociology/managerial studies/behavior sciences.

She pretends to be a mild-mannered writer/cat-lady, but most of her vacations require helmets and waivers or historical costumes, usually not at the same time.

She writes Gaslamp fantasy, historical romance and non-fiction to help justify her research addiction.

She can be contacted at:

author.MariaGrace@gmail.com

Facebook:
http://facebook.com/AuthorMariaGrace

On Amazon.com:
http://amazon.com/author/mariagrace

Random Bits of Fascination
(http://RandomBitsofFascination.com)

Austen Variations (http://AustenVariations.com)

White Soup Press (http://whitesouppress.com/)

On Twitter @WriteMariaGrace

On Pinterest: http://pinterest.com/mariagrace423/